Rave reviews for *Libri*

"Nonstop action and laughter power Hines's riveting second journey into the 'peculiar life' of Isaac Vainio.... Like a good pinball game, Isaac's adventures are frantic, fascinating, and more than a little noisy. Hines supplies everything a reader needs—werewolves, ghosts, robot insects, a fire spider that eats candy, and homages to classic SF—for a very good time."
—*Publishers Weekly*

"[A] love letter to science fiction and fantasy, with real emotional weight at the center ... a rollicking adventure story full of ridiculous little touches. It's a seriously fun ride for anyone who's loved geeky books their whole life."   —io9.com

"Butt-kicking librarians, pyrotechnic spiders, and vampires that don't suck—Jim Hines serves up an incendiary and fun new urban fantasy!"   —Charles Stross, Hugo award-winning author

"Isaac Vainio is a hero for the rest of us, the library nerds and bookworms—all of us who read books wishing we could be like our favorite heroes, or that they could be like us."
—*RT Book Reviews*

"When it comes to this series, I'm afraid it's hard for me to process thoughts coherently. There's so much going on, and so much of it is pure awesome, that I end up flailing for words like Kermit the Frog on a three-day bender. The concept itself is pure brilliance, a literary love letter and a bibliophile's wish fulfillment rolled into one. Who hasn't yearned to conjure up his own lightsaber, her own phaser, their own healing potion or time machine or magic sword?"   —Tor.com

"Secret organizations, supernatural threats, and an unknown killer of unimaginable power—*Libriomancer* is one of the best reads I've had in a long time. It's a lightning-fast race against time and magic to prevent the darkest secrets from history from unleashing a supernatural war on the world. I can't wait for the next one."

—Lisa Shearin, national bestselling author
of *All Spell Breaks Loose*

"I can't see how any fan of Libriomancer would be anything less than thrilled with the follow-up, and the promise it brings for the rest of the series."   —GeekDad

"In *Libriomancer*, Jim C. Hines makes a very literal, and completely fantastic, interpretation of the magic of reading."
—*The Livingston Post*

CODEX BORN

JIM C. HINES

Magic ex Libris: Book Two

DAW BOOKS, INC.

DONALD A. WOLLHEIM, FOUNDER

375 Hudson Street, New York, NY 10014

ELIZABETH R. WOLLHEIM
SHEILA E. GILBERT
PUBLISHERS

www.dawbooks.com

First paperback printing, August 2014
1 2 3 4 5 6 7 8 9

To Amy, Skylar, and Jamie.
Thank you for putting up with me through another one.

Acknowledgments

One year ago, I was doing the new-book dance[1] and desperately trying not to freak out over the release of my first hardcover with DAW. I failed, but I was trying. I was so excited about the idea of a magic-wielding librarian, about bringing Smudge back, about getting to write a story about the love of books. I was also terrified, because I had absolutely no idea how this book would do.

Libriomancer went into a second printing within two weeks. Then a third, and a fourth. It made the Locus Bestseller list. It was picked up by the Science Fiction Book Club, released as an audio book from Audible, and just came out overseas from Del Rey UK.

Thank you all so much. I feel like the clichéd TV drunk who keeps hugging everyone and saying, "I love you, man!" but it's true. Thank you for reading, for your emails and your reviews, for telling your friends about the book and for simply sharing the wonder with me.

Thanks to everyone at DAW, too. For seven years Sheila Gilbert has believed in me and helped me improve each of my books, including this one. Thanks also to Joshua Starr, Katie Hoffman, Jodi Rosoff, and everyone else who

1. This involved running to four different book signings in the first week, refreshing the Amazon rank on my phone every ten minutes, and running around to show everyone in the house—even the cats—the shiny new book.

worked behind the scenes to help make *Codex Born* happen, as well as to artist Gene Mollica, who actually managed to track down a cover model with Lena's smile.

Joshua Bilmes at JABberwocky has been the other constant in my career, helping to sell my books here in the U.S. and elsewhere. Joshua has always gone above and beyond to support his clients, and it's very much appreciated.

Margaret Yang gets a special shout-out here, both for her helpful feedback on *Codex Born*'s storyline and for her invaluable linguistic assistance. I will be forever indebted to her for stopping me from calling a group of magic-users "The Stomach of Mister Bi."[2]

Thank you to author Kelly McCullough, who also read a draft of the story and helped me whip it into shape. (Even if he did limit his feedback to just the English words.)

Finally, a big old hug of gratitude to everyone on Twitter, Facebook, and my blog, who helped me with more nitpicky details than I can count, from the plausibility and potential problems of trying to read books underwater to an extensive debate about whether or not sparkling vampires could metabolize marijuana.[3]

As a reward for reading this note, here's a behind-the-scenes tidbit: the T-shirt Isaac wears in chapter 13 originally said simply, "Ook." I changed it because I didn't think everyone would get the joke, but you and I know what Isaac's favorite shirt *really* says.[4]

Thank you, and I hope you enjoy the second volume of *Magic ex Libris*.

2. Darn it, now I kind of want to write a story about a stomach-themed magic guild.
3. I'm not saying whether these particular examples made it into the book or not. You'll have to read and find out for yourselves.
4. If you don't understand why, get back to the bookstore and stock up on Pratchett's *Discworld* series. You'll thank me later.

"Gutenberg's invention, while having given to some national freedom, brought slavery to others. It became the founder and protector of human liberty, and yet it made despotism possible where formerly it was impossible."

—Mark Twain

Chapter 1

People say love changes a person. They have no idea.

Frank Dearing was the first man I ever met. He made me whole. He provided me with purpose and identity. And he gave me a name. "Greenwood" might not be the most original moniker for a dryad, but it was mine.

Nidhi Shah gave me strength and a larger purpose. Through her, my life grew from a single farmhouse to a larger world of people, plants, and magic.

Then there was Isaac Vainio. I thought his greatest gift to me would be a sense of freedom, however limited. But through him, through his curiosity and his often deranged need to poke the universe and ask "What does this button do?" I found something more.

I spent fifty years confined by my nature. Isaac helped me to discover hope.

AS A LIBRIOMANCER AND a researcher, this was one of the moments I lived for. I loved that this brilliant, untrained fourteen-year-old girl had just shattered an entire body of magical theory.

I hated the fact that I couldn't figure out how she had done it.

Jeneta Aboderin slouched in a white plastic lawn chair on the old deck behind my house. Plastic sunglasses with pink-slashed zebra stripe frames hid her eyes as she read from an electronic tablet. "You're not concentrating, Isaac," she said without looking up.

Her words blended the faint Nigerian and British accents she had acquired from her mother and father, with a generous helping of teenaged annoyance at me, the thickheaded librarian who couldn't pull magic from a simple poem.

"Am, too." Not my most brilliant comeback, but I was off my game today. I was concentrating so hard my forehead would be permanently creased. I just wasn't *feeling* the words. I glanced down at my own brand-new e-reader, a thin rectangle the size of a trade paperback, with a gleaming glass screen and a case of rounded black plastic. The buttons were recessed into the edges, and the whole thing looked like it had come straight off the set of *Star Trek*.

I was afraid I was going to drop the damn thing.

"Try again," Jeneta said.

I scrolled up through Walt Whitman's *Leaves of Grass*, back to the beginning of a poem I had read fourteen times so far this afternoon. I had memorized it the second time, but reading the words helped me to touch the book's magic. At least in theory. "Maybe if I started with something simpler, like creating moonlight?"

She snorted. "'Look Down, Fair Moon' isn't about moonlight."

"Are you sure? It's right here in the title." I tilted the screen toward her and pointed. "Maybe I've got a defective reader."

I imagined her eyes rolling behind her glasses. She yanked the reader out of my hands, and her fingers tapped a staccato beat on the screen. "Check out this one. 'Dream Deferred,' by Langston Hughes." Slender brown fingers sank into the poem, emerging moments later with a raisin held between them. "You think Hughes was going on about raisins? It's a metaphor."

She left the "duh" at the end unstated. Shaking her head, she popped the metaphor into her mouth and said, "He packs every syllable with hope and fear and desperation, until the words are ready to explode. How can you not feel that?"

Her exasperation at my obvious thickheadedness didn't bother me. I was more interested in how easily she had produced that raisin from an electronic device. Johannes Gutenberg himself, the man who *invented* libriomancy, had said it couldn't be done.

Gutenberg had built his printing press more than five hundred years ago based on his theories about magical resonance. He had believed that physically identical books would hold the collective belief and imagination of the readers, and that a man with sufficient magical gifts could tap into that belief, using it as a focus for his own power.

Growing up, Gutenberg had been a third-rate practitioner at best. He had mastered only the most basic of spells, and even then needed help to cast them properly. Libriomancy had transformed him overnight into one of the most powerful men in history.

Electronic books lacked the physical resonance of print. The words were nothing but a collection of zeroes and ones translated into a transient image on whatever screen you used to read them. We had always assumed that e-readers would be useless for libriomancy, that the variety of reading devices and the impermanence of the files would prevent anyone from tapping into that collective belief. Porter researchers wrote dire predictions about the dilution of our magic as more readers moved from print to electronic, whittling away at our pool of belief.

And then Jeneta Aboderin had accidentally loosed a three-foot, long-nosed vine snake from her Smartphone in the middle of algebra class. That event had left a hundred Porter researchers fighting for time with Jeneta and the chance to try to figure out exactly how the hell she had done it.

After all, part of the mission of Die Zwelf Portenære, the secret organization Gutenberg had overseen for all these centuries, was to learn as much as we could about magic's potential. More importantly, if I could master this trick, I wouldn't have to lug thirty pounds of books with me every time I went into the field.

The Porters, as they were known to those not comfortable with Middle High German, also worked to hide the existence of magic from the world, and to combat an ever-changing list of potential magical threats.

The other Porter researchers were probably cursing my name and trying to understand how Jeneta had ended up working with me in Copper River, Michigan. I was the newest member of our research branch, having been promoted a mere two months earlier, and none of my work had anything to do with electronics or e-books.

Jeneta plucked another raisin from the e-reader and handed it to the large spider soaking up the sunlight on the deck railing. Smudge and Jeneta had taken to each other at once. Smudge lazily extended his forelegs to take the raisin from her fingers. A droplet of red fire appeared between his legs, and he stuffed the burning snack into his mouth.

"I had another dream last night," Jeneta said quietly, not looking away from the fire-spider.

I reached over and took my reader back. "No more raisins. You know the rules. You're on a twenty-four hour magic ban after the nightmares." I did my best to keep my tone comforting, but to my ears, I came off more like a cross between a school counselor and a babysitter trying too hard to be cool. This was why the Porters had trained therapists on staff. "What were you doing yesterday?"

"I dunno. I just ... after campfire, I needed a break. There's been a lot going on, you know? Three weeks ago I was in summer school, trying to make sense of geometric proofs. Now I'm doing magic."

Her mouth softened into the first unguarded smile I had seen from her all afternoon. "I went down to the docks to think. I got to watching the minnows swimming around. After a while, I tried reading to them."

"You read to the minnows?"

"Shut up. It was amazing. At first I was just sitting there, going through a collection by Sonia Sanchez. I was reading 'Personal Letter Number 3,' and I noticed the minnows were moving to the beat of the words, even though I'd been reading to myself. When I started reciting the poems out loud, they went nuts. Like they were dancing."

I checked to make sure my digital recorder was getting this. Pulling raisins from poetry was one thing. I'd been swiping toys from science fiction and fantasy novels for years. Using the emotion of a poem to influence others, even minnows, was a whole other school of magic. "Could you do it again? Not today, but in a controlled environment where I could observe? I could set you up with some of Smudge's feeder crickets."

"Probably. I didn't do it on purpose, though. It just happened. They felt what I felt. Sanchez makes me want to move."

"How long did it last?"

"An hour. Maybe two. I lost track of time." She tossed her thin braids back over her shoulders. "When are you going to give me a straight answer about these dreams?"

"I told you they're not just dreams."

Jeneta groaned melodramatically. "Please don't give me the boundaries lecture again." Her voice turned deeper, a passable imitation of me, though she mangled my accent. "The more magic you use, the weaker your boundaries become, and the easier it is for the magic of your books to infiltrate your thoughts. Let me tell you about this time at Mackinac Island—"

"I wasn't going to talk about Mackinac Island," I lied. "I was about to say I know what you're going through."

She stopped playing with Smudge. "You've had them, too?"

"A few months back. I was down in Detroit, and I tried to—" I caught myself. Jeneta was as inquisitive as any other libriomancer. If I told her I had been able to reach through a book to spy on another libriomancer, she'd be trying it herself before the week was out, no matter how dangerous the consequences. "It doesn't matter what I did. I charred the crap out of the book, and someone . . . something came after me. Like magic was an ocean, and I had stirred an Old One from the depths. It tried to drag me down, to tear me apart."

"To devour everything that made you *you*."

I pretended not to notice the tremor in her hands. "Exactly. Mindless rage and hunger."

"How did you stop the dreams?"

"By going into a coma." I stared at the garden beyond the deck, walled by rosebushes so colorful they seemed unreal. "I told you, they're not dreams. I was awake when it came after me. Lena brought me to Nicola Pallas' place. She managed to pull me back."

Even the Regional Master of the Porters had been hard-pressed to save my sanity that time.

"They warned me about possession," she said. "How characters and poems could start talking to me, trying to lure me in."

Overuse of a book's magic thinned the metaphorical walls between that book and the real world. Every case of possession varied depending on the books involved, but they all ended with an incurably insane libriomancer. "What we saw isn't possession, either."

"So what is it?" she demanded.

"We don't know." Since before the founding of the Porters, something had lived within magic itself. Something that fought to break through to our world and consume it. None of us knew exactly what it was or where it had come from. Or how to stop it.

This was the other, secret purpose of Die Zwelf Portenære, The Twelve Doorkeepers. A select few among the Porters devoted themselves to understanding our enemy and learning how to keep it from entering the world.

My encounter earlier this year had earned me a place among that group. Gutenberg had assigned me to identify our enemies, to answer questions that had baffled the Porters since their founding. That was why strings had been pulled to get Jeneta a fully-paid trip to summer camp in Michigan's Upper Peninsula, along with an "Advanced Youth Opportunity" internship working with me at the Copper River Public Library.

"You don't know," she repeated flatly. "I mean, I'm glad I'm not hallucinating or going crazy, but you're telling me there are magical monsters trying to eat my mind, and nobody knows what they are?"

"Pretty much, yeah."

"Damn." She thought for a moment. "How would these devourers even evolve?"

Typical libriomancer response. Something weird wants to kill us? Cool! Where did it come from, and how does it work? And, depending on the inclinations of the libriomancer, how can I catch one and take it apart?

"I don't think they did." I had multiple theories, based in part on research done by previous Porters over the years and reports on the aftermath of the handful of recorded encounters. There were many conflicting explanations, all but impossible to test. "I think we created them."

"You mean the Porters?"

"Not necessarily, but people, humans." I sprawled back in my chair. "It's a hunch. They could be three-headed psychic aliens from another dimension or the astral projections of dinosaurs from millions of years ago. But there was . . . not a connection, but a sense of recognition. Like passing a stranger on the street and, just for a second, before your brain catches up, feeling like you knew them when you were younger."

She lowered her sunglasses and raised her eyebrow in a motion so smooth she had to have practiced it in the mirror. "You believe in aliens?"

"I'm dating a dryad, and you pulled a snake out of your phone. You're going to draw the line at aliens?"

"If you try to tell me aliens built the pyramids, I am so out of here."

"Don't be ridiculous." I waited a beat, then added, "The pyramids were built by mummified elves."

I wouldn't have thought it possible, but her eyebrow climbed even higher. "Mummified elves?"

I was a lousy liar, but for once I managed to keep a straight face. "A friend of mine fought one of the things once. Damn thing was like a nightmare straight out of a Keebler commercial."

"I think you're right."

"Of course I am. Elven magic is nasty stuff."

From the look she shot me, the only thing in the world worse than devourers was an adult trying to be funny. "About the devourers. They hated me too much. It was personal."

"What happened when you woke up?"

"I snuck out to the showers. The water's always too cold, but I didn't care."

"Like you'd scrape your own skin off to feel clean again," I said, remembering my own dreams after Detroit.

"Yeah." She plucked a weed growing through the boards at the edge of the deck and poked it at Smudge. Smudge crouched, then jumped forward to set the end on fire. "Try reading the Whitman poem again. 'Pour softly down night's nimbus floods.' Visualize it."

I picked up my e-reader, letting her change the subject. Though she tried to hide it, I could see she was fighting tears. I pulled up the poem, read it yet again, and imagined clouds lit from within as they drifted slowly over the full moon. It was a cool, damp night. The poem stressed the contrast between the sky's beauty and the horror of the Civil War dead strewn over the battlefield.

"'Bathe this scene.'" Jeneta sounded different when

she read. More confident. Powerful. "'Pour down your unstinted nimbus, sacred moon.' Twice he uses images of water, of cleansing and baptism. The washing away of sin. Why?"

She sounded like a teacher. I wondered if she was channeling her mother. I touched my fingers to the screen. "He was pleading."

"Exactly." This was familiar ground for her, much safer than whatever had invaded her mind. "Wash this ugliness from our souls and memories. Wash this horror from our world. Forgive us. Redeem us. 'On the dead, on their backs, with their arms toss'd wide.' Why are they on their backs, Isaac?"

"They're looking to the sky, to God."

"That's the heart of the poem. Grief. Shame. Hope. That's your connection. Touch those feelings, and you can use this poem to bring an entire crowd to tears."

I tried again, imagining the emotions and reaching for their echo within the e-reader, but as before, I felt nothing.

"Maybe Whitman's not your thing." She tapped her own screen, scrolled through a long list of books, and shoved it into my hands.

"Shel Silverstein?"

She tilted her head to glare at me over her sunglasses. "If you diss Silverstein, I will hurt you. I'm talking chainsaws, machetes, and a fire-spider in a very uncomfortable place. Smudge has my back on this. Right?"

Smudge turned toward me and rubbed his forelegs together.

"Traitor." I skimmed the poem. "Whatif?"

"You never get the whatifs? Never worry about your house burning down or Smudge getting eaten by an owl?"

My cell phone buzzed before I could answer. I grinned like an idiot when I saw who it was. Sticking with the theme of the afternoon, I adopted my most somber poetry-reading voice and said, "I think that I shall never see a poem as lovely as a tree."

"Why thank you," said Lena Greenwood. "Spending time with Jeneta has been good for you. And how is the world's sexiest librarian doing today?"

"He spends too much time thinking and not enough time feeling," Jeneta said loudly.

I stuck out my tongue and turned down the volume on the phone.

Lena chuckled, but there was an edge to her usual playfulness. Her laughter cut off too quickly, and she didn't come back with a joke about finding ways of getting me to stop thinking.

"What's wrong?" I asked.

"Nidhi got a call from Chicago. They're sending her to Tamarack. I'm about to head over to pick her up."

"Another feral werewolf?" The Upper Peninsula had three of the largest werewolf packs in the world, but it had been eight years since the last known attack against a human. The pack did a very good job keeping its members in line.

"Wendigo. One of the weres found him dead last night."

I sat up straighter. "How did he die?"

"We're not sure yet, but the weres said whoever dumped the body smelled human."

"Damn." This wouldn't be the first time a mundane had killed a magical creature. It didn't happen often, and it rarely ended well for the human. If this had been an accident or an act of self-defense, that was one thing, but a wendigo was hard to kill even if you knew what you were up against. That suggested either a rogue magic-user or else someone who had stumbled onto the existence of magic and decided to play monster-slayer. Either way, we needed to find whoever had done this. Gossip traveled fast, and every intelligent nonhuman in the U.P. would be on edge by the end of the week. If the Porters didn't resolve this quickly, it would only escalate. "Let me drop Jeneta off, and I'll meet you at the old schoolhouse in Tamarack."

"I'll see you there. Love you."

"Love you, too."

As soon as I hung up, Jeneta said, "I can help."

"No."

"I heard her say it was a wendigo. I've read about them, but I never—"

"Nein. Non. Nyet. Naa. Gaawiin." I gathered Smudge onto the palm of my hand and transferred him to my left shoulder.

Jeneta cocked her head. "What was that last one?"

"Ojibwe." I looked pointedly at her e-reader until she sighed and stuffed it into her worn camouflage backpack. "Nothing in the papers your parents signed gives us permission to drag you into a murder investigation. Especially when there could be more wendigos in the area. Do you know how much paperwork I'll have to do if my intern gets eaten by a cannibalistic monster?"

"My parents didn't sign anything about me teaching magic to old people, either," she shot back.

"I'm only twenty-six, and shut up." I waved her inside. "Give me a minute to grab my books. Besides, it's not like I haven't been teaching you, too."

"Whatever, grandpa." She shouldered her backpack, then hesitated. When she spoke again, she sounded younger. "Be careful."

"I'll do my best."

And then she was her normal self again, head held high as she strode through the house. "Hey, since you won't let me come with you, the least you should do is let me drive the convertible."

I grinned. "Let me dig up my Ojibwe dictionary. I need to look up how to say 'No way in hell.'"

Smudge crouched by the corner of the windshield and watched the pine trees rush past. Walls of jagged rock rose and fell to either side of the road as we cut through the hills.

Old railroad tracks and an abandoned depot marked Tamarack's eastern boundary, roughly thirty miles out from Copper River. Back at the start of the twentieth century, both towns had been booming. Booming for the U.P., at least. When the silver mine here in Tamarack shut down in 1934, the town had been home to more than two thousand people. These days, the place made Copper River look like the big city. The population was closer to two hundred, a sizable minority of whom were members of the local werewolf pack.

This part of the state was pockmarked with mining ghost towns. Tamarack wasn't dead yet, but it had much of the same atmosphere. Old street signs marked overgrown side streets that hadn't seen maintenance in decades. Many of the houses on the edge of town looked ready to collapse in the next strong breeze. An entire block had been overrun by apple trees. I spotted a pair of teenagers smoking cigarettes and watching us from a two-story house, balanced on the roof beside a gaping hole where a maple had smashed through the rafters.

At the heart of town, a gas station with a single pump, a small grocery and hunting supply store, and a Baptist church shared the intersection with the town's lone traffic light. I turned off the main road and drove another half mile to the schoolhouse. A yellow pickup truck was parked in the lot, and I spotted an older-looking man leaning against the tailgate, chewing a toothpick. I relaxed slightly when I spied Lena's black-and-green Honda motorcycle behind the truck. A pair of matching helmets hung from the back.

I held a hand to Smudge so he could climb onto my shoulder, then popped the trunk. I retrieved a copper-riveted satchel of oiled brown leather that looked like something Indiana Jones might carry. Which, if I was honest, was the main reason I had bought it. The strap dug a groove into my shoulder, weighed down by every book I had been able to stuff inside.

"Isaac Vainio. You took your sweet old time getting here."

I slammed the trunk and turned to greet the werewolf. "Jeff DeYoung. Was it you who found the body, then?"

"Nah, that was Helen." He spat the toothpick onto the blacktop. "You're looking pretty good. We heard about that mess in Detroit earlier this summer. They say old man Gutenberg himself had to help chase those vampires back into their holes."

"They don't know the half of it," I said. Jeff had one of the thickest Yooper accents of anyone I knew, transforming every "the" into "da," and "those" into "doze."

"And you can't share the other half, right?" He clapped me on my shoulder—the one without the fire-spider—then pulled me into a quick hug and inhaled sharply. I didn't want to know how much he learned about me in that one sniff. I did the same, breathing in the faint sweat-and-tobacco smell of his hair and jacket.

"I'm afraid not." He looked much as he had the last time I saw him, a year or so back. The same worn-out orange hunting jacket hung loosely over his eye-gougingly bright green-and-gold Hawaiian shirt. Jeff was a stick of a man, all wrinkled skin and age spots. Gold-framed bifocals dug into his bulbous nose. He and his wife Helen were the first werewolves I had ever met. They had left the wild to settle down in Tamarack, and while they still chased the occasional rabbit, most of their meat these days came from a store.

"Helen took Doctor Shah and the dryad back about fifteen minutes ago," said Jeff. "They smell like you. How long have you all been sleeping together?"

"We're not *all* sleeping together," I said quickly. I had to consciously set aside my normal caution in talking about our relationship. Jeff could smell through the lies, and he was one of the few people who wouldn't bat an eye at my romantic situation. "I've been with Lena for about two months. And Lena is also with Doctor Shah."

"But not you and the doctor? Huh. Seems like that would be easier, logistically speaking."

"Logistics aren't everything." I swatted a mosquito on my left index finger. The little bloodsuckers usually stayed away from Smudge, which was another reason I liked to keep him around, but a hot, wet summer had left us with a thicker crop of mosquitoes than usual, and they were hungry. "We haven't got all of the kinks worked out yet."

Jeff smirked. "You never struck me as a man of many kinks. Sounds like this girl's been good for you."

Typical werewolf mindset. In the words of a former friend, "Weres will jump into bed with anything on two legs and a few with four." An exaggeration, but one with plenty of underlying truth.

Nobody knew where the first Lykanthropos naturalis had come from, though the dominant theory involved a magical experiment gone wrong sometime in the fifth or sixth century. Others believed lycanthropy had been a deliberate curse, punishment for some unknown but unforgivable crime.

These days, creatures who had evolved or come into existence "naturally" were outnumbered by those born from books. I doubted even Gutenberg could have foreseen that consequence of his new school of magic. The first book-born creature I ever encountered was a sparkler, a middle-aged woman with thinning hair who had accidentally reached into a popular vampire novel and managed to infect herself with the vampire's venom.

The Porters carefully cataloged each new vampire species, but the werewolves offered more of a challenge. Unlike most vampires, werewolves could interbreed. As a result, instead of a hundred or more distinct species, you got a single race with a broad spectrum of abilities. Some could shapeshift at will; others were slaves to the moon. One werewolf might be severely allergic to silver, while his brother merely suffered from lactose intolerance.

As a general rule, it was safe to assume they were faster and stronger, with sharper senses than any human. And of course, depending on his genetics, Jeff might have anywhere from two to eight nipples under that shirt. Not that I had ever gotten up the nerve to ask. He would have been happy to show me, I'm sure. Werewolves were notoriously open about physical matters.

"Being with Lena has been ... educational," I admitted.

Jeff laughed, but thankfully didn't press me for details. We hiked through the woods behind the school, following an old trail around a marsh until we reached an overgrown road. Knee-high weeds were well on their way to reclaiming the broken gray pavement. From there, we walked uphill for roughly ten minutes, passing old driveways and gutted, too-regular pits in the earth where houses had once stood.

"I thought you were done with fieldwork," Jeff commented. Despite his age, he wasn't even winded.

"Gutenberg and Pallas moved me to research." I wiped my forehead and the back of my neck, then swatted another mosquito that was trying to bite through my jeans. "But we're short-staffed in the Midwest right now, and I did a couple of papers on wendigos during my training."

A chain-link fence at the top of the hill blocked a steep drop-off. Lena Greenwood, Nidhi Shah, and Helen DeYoung stood staring down at something on the other side of the fence. Nidhi was snapping pictures with a digital camera.

"You take the scenic route or something?" Helen asked without looking.

"Why, you miss me?" Jeff joined them at the fence, pausing briefly to give his wife's backside a quick squeeze before peering down.

"It's ugly." Lena broke away from the others to greet me with a kiss. As always, the feel of her body pressing against mine set off a cascade of physical and emotional responses: desire, excitement, amazement that she had chosen me, conflict over the circumstances of that choice, and awkwardness at knowing her other lover was standing six feet away, deliberately not watching.

Short and heavyset, with large eyes and dark lips,

Lena didn't look like someone who could go toe-to-toe with a pissed-off vampire and walk away without a scratch. Her skin was the rich brown of oiled oak. A single black braid hung to the middle of her back. Cutoff jeans emphasized the curves of her hips. She was barefoot, her toes curling into the dirt with each step. A pair of curved wooden swords—Japanese bokken—were thrust through her belt.

If I were to pick a single word for what attracted me to Lena, it would be her passion. Not merely physical, but for everything she did. She threw herself into life with no reservations, never holding back. She possessed a fearlessness few humans ever matched.

Nidhi Shah coughed softly. "We were getting ready to try to retrieve the body."

Judging from her outfit, Nidhi had come straight from her office. She wore a teal shirt with iridescent buttons, black slacks, and Converse high-tops. The sneakers were her formal black pair. When it came to footwear, Nidhi refused to let fashion trump comfort and practicality.

She was in her mid-thirties, older in appearance than Lena by a good five years. Her hair was pinned back, revealing a blue tattoo on her temple. The Gujarati characters for *balance*, a spell placed by the Porters to help her in her duties, were the only magical thing about her.

I stepped toward the fence. "Do we know who it was?"

Helen shook her head. One hand rested on the semi-automatic pistol holstered on her left hip, her only visible sign of nervousness. "I don't recognize the scent of either the victim or the man who dumped him."

"You're sure it was a man?" asked Nidhi.

"You can't smell the body spray?" Jeff snorted. "Lucky you."

"The wendigo was killed about a half mile into the woods," said Helen. "Whoever it was used a four-wheeler to get the body here. He drove east after that, but we lost him once he reached the road."

The upper bar of the fence was dented toward the ground. Dark streaks of blood striped the corroded aluminum. About twenty feet down, hanging from the broken branches of a white spruce growing out of the near-vertical rock, hung the wendigo.

Imagination was part of what made me a good libriomancer: the ability to visualize the story, to make it so real in my mind that I could literally reach out and touch it.

Imagination could be a curse as well. I would be seeing the remains of that poor creature in my dreams for months to come. The broken limbs, the pain and fear frozen on its face, the bits of white fur, matted with blood.

I turned away. Ignoring Jeff and Helen's worried whispers, I crossed the road and rested both hands against a fat birch. I sucked air into my lungs as my mind played out one scenario after another to explain the injuries the wendigo had suffered.

How the hell had a human being done this? The average wendigo could kill and devour a man in minutes.

Which made the man who had deliberately and methodically butchered this creature far more dangerous than any monster.

Chapter 2

I stepped into too-white snow and dead leaves that crunched beneath my bare feet. I covered my face with my hands. The sun was too large. It burned my eyes, making me want to retreat into my tree.

The surface was death. I needed shelter. How had I come here? Where was the closest ice cave?

I backed against the tree, letting the comforting roughness of the bark rub my bare skin. I curled my toes into the frozen earth, gripping the roots and reaching instinctively for the warmth of my grove-sisters.

I felt nothing. There were many trees, more than I had ever imagined, but they were empty shells. How could they survive the cold without their dryads to give them strength?

I had never been alone before. Not like this. I had never been lost.

Tears warmed my cheeks. How long had I slept?

I shivered then, not from cold, but from fear. I remembered Neptune. I remembered my sisters. I remembered fighting in the arena, the excitement of combat as my wooden sword slammed against my opponent's spear. I remembered the pleasure of the bedchamber.

I remembered all these things, but I couldn't remember being there. It was as though my memories had been ripped away, replaced by someone else's dreams.

This place, wherever I was, felt too real, too bright, too much. Too many sensations. Too many thoughts. I dug my fingers into the skin of my thighs and twisted, trying to focus on the pain, using that sensation to drive out the rest. I sagged to the ground and rocked back and forth, losing myself in the movement.

I could return to the oak. I could sleep and be safe. Choose the long death, as the very first dryad was said to have done when her lover was murdered. Her tree had lived on for centuries, guarded by the grove of her children.

If I followed her example, I would be surrounded not by my sisters, but by mindless trees, only half-alive.

After a while, the sunlight began to fade. I blinked and looked around. Every leaf, every stick was so vivid. I picked a half-buried acorn from the ground and turned it in my hand, marveling at the detail. The tiny scales of the cap, the pale line where cap met seed, the hard protrusion at the bottom that made the acorn look like a miniature wooden breast.

I climbed to my feet, off-balance. This world was wrong. Nothing was as it should be. I needed my sisters. I needed my lovers. I needed—

I slammed my head against the tree to break the spiral of my thoughts.

There were trees here. Were there people as well? Tears spilled freely as I stepped away from my tree, from the one thing that felt safe.

If I stayed here, I would die. I would sleep forever. I would lose myself.

I picked up a fallen branch and hugged it to my chest. I could feel it responding to the life within me. Threadlike roots crawled from the broken branch, twining around my fingers. Gleaming buds poked from the other end. I cradled the branch in my arms as I stumbled away from my tree.

Grass whispered as Lena came to stand behind me. She said nothing, but rested her hand on my shoulder.

I needed to focus on the job at hand. I rooted through my book bag until I found a handheld infrared thermometer. I switched it on and pointed it at Smudge. The screen read 109 Fahrenheit, which was only a degree or two higher than normal for him.

In humans, core body temperature fell at about a half a degree per hour. For a wendigo, the calculation went in the opposite direction. Given a standard body temp of twenty-two degrees Fahrenheit, we should be able to get a rough window on the time of death. Although I had no idea how trauma and blood loss might affect things.

Lykanthropos anthropophagos was well-suited to life in the U.P. Wendigo blood worked as a kind of magical supercoolant. Even the marrow was cold as ice. Their fur literally froze the moisture from the air, forming a protective layer of frost and ice.

Like werewolves, wendigos were born human. But once the transformation took hold, they remained in their monstrous form until death. The Ojibwe legends I had studied described them as gluttonous, cannibalistic spirits. In one story, a wendigo's mere presence caused the river to freeze and the trees to split from the cold.

A lone girl had set out to fight the wendigo, using a pair of sumac sticks with the bark peeled away. Until I met Lena, I had always found that a poor choice of weapon. But the girl defeated the wendigo, crushing its skull. The villagers chopped away the ice, eventually freeing the body of a man.

"Are you ready?" Lena asked.

I took a slow breath, then nodded. "I'm all right."

"I know."

We returned to the fence. Lena took the camera from Nidhi and tucked it into her pocket, then gripped the rail in both hands. The muscles in her arms tightened as she bent the fence lower to the ground. Keeping one hand on the rail, she stepped over and studied the drop-off. It wasn't completely vertical, but nothing short of a mountain goat would be able to climb that slope. Moss clung to the dark brown stone. Roots poked through like the coils of sea serpents.

Lena blew Nidhi and me a kiss, took two steps, and dropped out of sight.

"Dammit, Lena!" I pressed closer to the fence and spotted her clinging with one hand to a clump of tree roots, about four feet to the left of the spruce tree holding the body. She pulled herself sideways and began to scale the spruce. Her fingers sank into the trunk of the tree, letting her climb as easily as a spider.

"She used to be more careful." Nidhi's unspoken message was louder than her actual words. *She gets this from you.*

"Where's the fun in that?" I said automatically. I leaned out and aimed the thermometer at the wendigo's remains. Cold air swirled up past my arms, pimpling the skin. The body's temperature read twenty-six degrees Fahrenheit, meaning death had occurred roughly eight hours ago, give or take. A core reading would have been more accurate, but wendigos maintained a fairly uniform temperature throughout their bodies.

There was no shell of ice around our victim. He would have reverted to human form upon death, but the flesh would take time to thaw.

Light flashed as Lena snapped photos. "He's got what might be a bullet hole in his forehead." She climbed higher and took another batch of photos from her new angle, then called out, "Send me the tarp."

Jeff and Helen lowered a blue tarp with nylon rope strung through the corners. While they worked on retrieving the body, I turned away to think. Normal ice shattered when struck by a bullet, but the ice covering a wendigo's body had a significantly greater tensile strength, thanks to the fur mixed through it. A high-caliber bullet might penetrate, but most of the time, trying to shoot a wendigo would only piss it off.

"Watch the fence," Jeff said as he and Helen pulled the ropes up, hand over hand.

"Watch yourself, Chihuahua brain," Helen snapped.

The cold had minimized the stench of decay, as well as keeping most of the flies away. I waited for them to peel back the tarp, then walked over to help Nidhi examine the body. Without a word, Nidhi handed me a pair of latex examination gloves.

In death, the wendigo resembled a pale, gaunt man with wrinkled blue-tinged skin and thin white hair. The limbs were stiff, preserving the doubled-over position in which he had died. Much of the skin had been cut away, and shallow gashes marred what remained. Most of the damage looked like it had been done with a knife, or possibly a sword.

Nidhi pointed to a dark hole in the forehead. "There's the entry wound."

It was smaller than I would have expected. With every muscle frozen, Nidhi had to turn the whole body to examine the back of the head. There was no exit hole.

I swallowed bile. "They skinned and butchered him like an animal."

"No." Nidhi didn't look up. "You butcher an animal cleanly. Carefully. This kind of overkill comes from rage."

"You think the wendigo killed someone he cared about?" asked Jeff. "This might have been about revenge."

"If so, it wasn't recent," said Nidhi. "The stomach isn't distended."

My own stomach tried once again to rebel. I managed to force my lunch back down. "Most of the damage was done while he was alive." I dropped to one knee and pointed to the forehead. "Look at the ring of dry blood around the wound. Wendigos turn human again when they die, but their entire circulatory system freezes solid."

The wendigo had bled profusely. The blood would have frozen on the surface of the skin, sealing the cuts. Those frozen clots had broken away when the wendigo shrank back to human form, but thin outlines remained, showing where the body had tried to heal itself.

"He was tortured." Lena looked at me, her jaw tight. We had seen this kind of viciousness before, from a madman infested with what Jeneta called devourers.

I peeled off the gloves and flung them away. "I need to see where he died."

Jeff stayed with the body, while Helen guided us through the woods. "You have something in that bag to track whoever did this?" she asked.

"It depends on whether or not he left anything behind." Muddy ruts and broken ferns marked the path of the killer's four-wheeler. When we came to the top of the hill where the vehicle had stopped, I searched for footprints, but found nothing. The ground up here wasn't damp enough.

"Down here." Helen climbed over a fallen tree and gestured to a patch of pale mushrooms growing in the indentation at the base of a thick birch.

Black blood spattered the ground and the plants. Broken branches and gouged earth told the story of the wendigo's death. He had fought like an animal. Four parallel claw marks slashed the birch tree at chest height. Crushed ferns showed where he had thrashed back and forth.

"What are you planning to do?" Helen asked warily. She had never been as comfortable with Porters as her husband was. Most magical creatures resented the laws Gutenberg had set to restrict their habitats and activities. To many of the nonhuman residents of Tamarack, I was about as welcome as an FBI agent stopping by a militia compound. Helen wasn't as paranoid as some, and she liked me, but that didn't mean she liked what I was or who I worked for.

"That depends on whether or not I can make this work." I set down my satchel and pulled out *The Best of Isaac Asimov*.

For five years, I had studied libriomancy with a man named Ray Walker down in East Lansing, learning the full range and limits of my magic. Or so I thought, up until I saw Johannes Gutenberg in action, watched him pull weapons from books without reading them, or steal Smudge's flames to use against an enraged Volkswagen Beetle that had been trying to kill us. That encounter showed that I had barely moved beyond Libriomancy 101.

When the amazement passed, anger stepped in. Had Ray known how much more there was to learn? How much had Gutenberg hidden from the rest of us, and why? Was he trying to make sure nobody ever challenged his power? Or, like an overly strict parent, did he simply not trust us?

I had gone back to reread every libriomantic tome I could find, searching not for what the books said, but what they omitted. I looked for the gaps, for the experiments we should have performed, but didn't. For discussions that dismissed certain theories a little too quickly. I pushed myself to move beyond the rules Ray had drilled into me.

As it turned out, some of those rules were there for very good reasons. In early July, I accidentally conjured up a two-day thunderstorm that knocked out power to most of Copper River and flooded most of Depot Street. Then there was the stray disruptor beam that took out Spencer Mussell's truck. But I had confirmed that certain rules were rather fuzzy around the edges, and I had figured out several new tricks.

I flipped to a story called "The Dead Past" and started reading. "A lot of science fiction authors wrote up toys to let them see the past," I said. "Time portals and chronoscopes and temporal lenses, almost none of which are small enough to pull through the pages."

"Why not make a bigger book?" she asked.

"The books need to be physically identical in order to

anchor reader belief." Though Jeneta's magic threw that rule into doubt. If we built an e-reader the size of a parking lot, could she pull a spaceship through? What if we projected an e-book onto an IMAX screen? Maybe I could finally make my own X-wing fighter. I tucked that thought aside for later. "In order for me to use it, you'd need to distribute thousands of copies of those oversized books."

"Be careful," Nidhi said quietly, though I had no doubt Helen heard her warning as clearly as I did.

"Aren't I always?" Nidhi had been my therapist for several years, and she knew better than most the trouble I had gotten myself into when I was younger. I turned the pages and skimmed the story. "You might want to back up a little."

"You do know what you're doing, eh?" asked Helen.

I gnawed my lower lip. "Farther than that."

Unlike the lifeless screen of an e-reader, the pages of Asimov's story welcomed me. From the opening paragraphs, I could hear Arnold Potterley's quiet desperation as he petitioned for permission to use chronoscopy. I felt the resigned bitterness of the man forced to refuse that petition. I flipped ahead, imagining the excitement and anticipation of a working chronoscope—anticipation shared by countless readers over time.

My fingers sank through the page, sending a thrill through my body. I had performed this same act hundreds of times over the years, and there were days I still fought to keep from giggling like a kid on Christmas morning. No matter what happened, no matter what monsters tried to eat my flesh or steal my thoughts, I could do *magic*.

I saw the chronoscope in my mind, a template created by the imagination and belief of the readers. Normally, the next step would be to use that template to transform the magical energy into solid form and pull it free.

The hard part was *not* doing so. All my training urged me to create, to grasp the chronoscope from Asimov's world, even though I could never bring it into our own.

In magical terms, I was manipulating a semi-collapsed matrix of potential energy through an open portal maintained by my own belief and will. Practically speaking, it was like carrying a Labrador retriever over a tightrope and having a squirrel race past.

I pulled my hand free while trying to draw that partially formed energy into our world. My connection to the text wiggled away like a fish diving back into the pages. I rubbed my eyes and concentrated on slowing my breathing before trying again.

"This would be easier if the book wasn't forty years old," I muttered. Belief didn't last forever, though it was impossible to calculate the exact rate of decay.

"Why not use a newer one?" asked Helen.

"Because Gutenberg magically locks pretty much everything to do with time travel or spying on the past. Partly because the amount of magical energy it would take to actually travel in time would probably burn you to a crisp, and even if through some miracle you survived, there's too much risk of accidentally stepping on the wrong butterfly and destroying all of humanity."

"What's the harm in just looking?" asked Lena.

"If I had to guess, I'd say Gutenberg doesn't want anyone prying into his past." I tapped the book. "Asimov's chronoscope has a limited range. If you try to look more than a hundred and twenty years in the past, you get interference, meaning Gutenberg's early days are safely out of reach." I wiped my hand on my shirt and tried again to touch the book's magic.

"Relax," said Lena. "I might not know as much about libriomancy as you do, but I've seen you do magic, and you don't normally look like a constipated librarian trying to pass a hardcover."

I made an obscene gesture in her direction.

"Maybe later," she shot back.

I snorted, but the exchange did help me to relax. I tried again, allowing my eyes to unfocus until the text became a blur of ink on the page. I reread the story in my mind, concentrating not on the specific details, but the emotion, the excitement and wonder, the *possibilities* blossoming from Asimov's story.

With this book, you could watch the truth about the JFK assassination or see what really happened right before the Berlin Wall came down. Or if you preferred, you could just hunker down on your couch beneath the blankets and watch the lost episodes of *Doctor Who* when they first aired.

More than a century of history at your fingertips. The technology could be abused, as the ending demonstrated, but that was true for most technology, magic or not. And there was so much we could learn.

"Isaac," Lena whispered.

When I blinked, static fizzed across my vision. It vanished before I could focus. "Did you see that?"

"Only for a second or two," said Nidhi.

I almost had it. I reached deeper into the book until my arm appeared to end just below the elbow. I could feel the fuzz of static electricity, like I was touching an old glass television screen. I imagined the room beyond, the cobbled-together chronoscope of the story flickering to life. The chronoscope was too big for me to bring through, but the images it displayed were nothing but light. I used my other hand to raise the book, and concentrated on pushing those images out into the world.

Helen jumped back as the air between us flickered gray. A rectangular space the size of a suitcase gradually settled into focus, showing a grainy picture of the trees beyond.

Manic laughter was generally considered undignified, but when I tried to swallow my triumphant glee, the noise that came out was more like a coughing hiccup. So much for dignity.

"This will show us what happened?" asked Helen.

"Exactly! It will—um." Oh, right. I had created the effect, but I hadn't made any of the controls. I tried to will the spell to move backward in time, to show me what had happened roughly eight hours ago. My efforts had absolutely no effect.

Nidhi walked toward me and gently grasped my wrist. "Your respiration and pulse are both too high," she warned. "Don't take too long."

"Got it. Could someone take Smudge?"

Lena gently lifted the spider from my shoulder. I walked toward the vision, half-expecting it to pop like a soap bubble. Instead, images flashed before me. An array of vacuum tubes. A bronze statue of the god Moloch, a furnace glowing in his belly. A child trapped in a house fire.

Grief flowed through the book, so intense it knocked me back a step. Had you asked me in that moment, I would have sworn it was my own child dying in the flames.

"Why is it showing a fire?" Helen asked. "Nothing burned here."

"The magic is 'tuned' to the story. It's showing us the past, but it's the fictional past Asimov created." I needed to refocus the spell to this world, and I needed to do it quickly, before the story moved into my thoughts and made itself at home.

"There are other ways to find whoever did this," Nidhi said.

"Just give me a minute." This was a known problem, one that arose with crystal balls, magic mirrors, and other scrying techniques. Time after time, they worked exactly as they had been written: showing images from the fictional world they had come from. Reorienting those toys to the real world was all but impossible.

Or so I had been taught. In the past months, I had jotted down three theories on how to bypass that particular rule. A strong enough libriomancer could break past the confines set by the book, but someone strong enough to do that shouldn't need books to do magic in the first place.

Locking the book should also sever the connection between the book and the created object, giving me a better chance of refocusing the chronoscope to find our killer. Which would have been perfect, if I had the slightest clue how Gutenberg locked his books.

Time to test theory number three. I handed the book to Nidhi. "There's a lead-lined bag of flower petals in my satchel. Could you please rub the petals over the book and press them between the pages, especially this page?"

Lena looked over Nidhi's shoulder. "When did you take up flower power?"

"I've been experimenting with ways of preserving Moly." The flower came from *Odysseus*, and could be used to nullify magic. I had requested a specially enchanted bag just so I would be able to carry the petals around without canceling out every spell in a five-foot radius. The one time I got careless, Smudge had lost his flame for a day and a half. When he finally recovered, he set my favorite T-shirt on fire. I couldn't prove it, but I was certain he had done it deliberately.

I had soaked this latest batch of flowers in a glycerin solution, removing the moisture while preserving the shape and texture. Tiny lines of brown crisscrossed the petals. They weren't as potent as newly-formed Moly, but they should work.

As Nidhi pressed the petals into the book, the fictional flames faded, until I saw only a grainy image of the clearing. I reached out with one hand, imagining the resistor dials and adjusting them one by one. The minutes flew backward in my mind. A crow swooped down and vanished again. The scene darkened as the sun dipped beneath the eastern horizon. That put us past the eight-hour window. Were we in the wrong place, or had I misjudged the time of death?

And then the wendigo appeared, surrounded by blood and gore. It was twilight from the evening before, putting the time closer to eighteen hours ago. I would need to recheck my figures. Two other people crowded over the wendigo and disappeared, moving far too quickly for me to make out any details. The wendigo vanished a second later.

I adjusted my mental controls again, allowing the scene to play out in normal time. There was no sound. The chronoscope should be capable of reproducing sound as well as light, but I was doing well just to get this aspect working. Lena had taken Nidhi's camera, and was clicking away behind me. I wondered briefly whether a camera would be able to capture these images, but if they could see it, that meant I was manipulating visible light. As long as she didn't use a flash, they should turn out.

The creature who staggered into the clearing looked

nothing like the withered body Lena had retrieved. The blocky pattern of broken ice armoring its body reminded me a little of The Thing from the Fantastic Four. All told, it probably weighed half a ton. It was digging at a wound in its shoulder, black claws the size of my fingers gouging through ice and fur.

The wendigo jerked, then toppled onto its back. It continued to claw at itself for a time, before curling into a ball. Once it stopped moving, two other figures appeared at the edge of the clearing.

"They're blurry," said Lena. "Can you zoom in on their faces?"

"It's not that simple." One of the men moved forward, but his face remained stubbornly out of focus. Other details were horrifyingly clear, like the ice ax he used to hammer away at the wendigo's frozen hide, and the skinning knife he pulled out next.

"Jumalauta," whispered Helen. I heard the meaning in my head, both a curse and a prayer, somewhere between "God dammit" and "God help us." Both were appropriate for what followed.

"Is he wearing metal?" asked Nidhi.

I had noticed the same thing. The gleam of sunlight on polished metal, pebbled like oversized scales. Armor, maybe? Though it looked nothing like any historical mail I had ever seen.

The man's companion held back at the edge of the clearing. I studied him instead, trying to determine if he was in charge of this butchery, or merely the guard.

Darkness flowed over both men, as if someone had moved to block our view. I looked more closely, focusing not on the men, but whatever hid them from us. Static danced over the rest of the scene, but the shadow remained. "Am I crazy, or does that look like a woman?"

"I see it, too," said Lena. "Isaac, look at the man in back. His left hand."

The shadow moved to one side as if it had heard, but not before I spied the book the second man clutched in his hands. It was far larger than the paperback I had used.

"Is that another libriomancer?" Helen breathed.

The shadow continued to grow—no, it was moving toward us. "I think she's reacting to my spell."

"How?" asked Lena. "I thought we were looking at the past."

No, we were looking at a magical recreation of the past. The spell itself existed in the present, which suggested that whoever or whatever this woman was, she was here with us now, working within the spell to block my efforts.

"You need to end this," Nidhi said sharply.

I had come to the same conclusion. How long had I been standing here? Ten minutes? Fifteen? My arm was numb, and my eyes were so dry I could barely see anything beyond the chronoscope's window.

A flicker of red light told me Smudge had reacted to the threat in his usual way. Lena had moved him onto the trunk of a tree, presumably to keep him away from the Moly's effects. Hopefully he wouldn't set anything on fire.

I tried to collapse the spell, but whoever or whatever this was, she was fighting me. The images stretched and distorted, and black fingers reached toward us.

"Move," snapped Lena.

I ducked aside as Lena snatched *The Best of Isaac Asimov* from Nidhi and hurled it directly through the center of the chronoscope's image. A pained scream stabbed my mind, and I stumbled backward. The spell collapsed to a single point of silver light, then disappeared.

Lena caught me by the arms. I forgot sometimes how strong she was. I started to pull away, but the world had gotten much more wobbly, and I thought better of it. "Give me five minutes to rest. I'll be fine." Then I could try to figure out what the hell we were up against, and exactly how much trouble we were in. "Nice throw."

Lena grimaced. "Touching that stuff makes me want to vomit. But I figured whatever was trying to come through wouldn't like it any more than I do."

Nidhi peeled back one of my eyelids, then checked my pulse. She didn't look happy. "I told you to be careful."

"Yeah." I sagged against Lena. "I really need to start listening to you."

Chapter 3

The oak is ever divided. Reaching deeper, to the cool waters of Earth's lifeblood. Reaching skyward, to the warm breath of the sun.

Within this tree waits home.
Within this tree waits solitude.
She is my mother. My twin. My center, cleaved in two.
Yearning to be one. Yearning to be my own.

I was born into winter. Yearning to sleep through the cold. Yearning for one whose warmth would awaken me.
Within his need, I found myself.
Within his desire, I found joy.
His body takes root within mine.
I reach inward to safety. I reach outward to his need.

I bring my Creator to his knees and receive his prayers.

— In memory of Frank Dearing

I AWOKE ON A low cot, gasping for breath. My feet and legs were tangled in an old wool blanket. The pillow was damp from sweat, as was the side of my face. The lights were out, but the safety-glass window in the door provided a hint of fluorescent illumination from the office outside.

"You're safe." Nidhi had a hand on my shoulder, holding me down with more strength than I would have expected. "What do you remember?"

The flickering magic of the chronoscope. A wendigo twisted in agony. An armored man hidden by the shadow of a woman. I remembered resting while Jeff and Helen discussed what to do with the body. They had decided to bury it in an unmarked grave behind the church. I had stood up too quickly. "Did Lena . . . she carried me here, didn't she."

"That's right. We were worried at first, but then you started snoring. Do you know where you are?"

"Tamarack. We're inside the school, right?"

"What's your name?" Nidhi asked in that calm, clinical tone I remembered from our sessions. She kept her hands folded over the black leather purse in her lap.

"Isaac Vainio."

"What's the date?" She was firing questions faster now, and I found myself responding in kind.

"August fourth. Unless I was out longer than I thought?"

She ignored me. "What's my name?"

"Nidhi Shah." I shook my head before she could continue. "It's me. *Just* me." I closed my eyes, listening for the whispers that were the first sign of possession, but my mind was my own. Whatever other damage I might have done, I hadn't ripped Asimov's story open that badly. Not that I could blame Nidhi for her fears. She had seen libriomantic possession close-up, as well as the damage that kind of madness could cause. "Where's Lena?"

"With the werewolves. I wasn't sure what was going on in your head."

"So you sent her away. Smart." I sagged back into the pillow. Lena's personality adjusted to the desires of her lover. Or lovers, as we had discovered earlier this year. The process wasn't supposed to be immediate, but who knew what it would do to her if any fictional characters moved into my brain?

An orange glow pulled my attention to Smudge, who climbed down the wall and stopped on the metal frame of the cot. The tips of the hairs along his back glowed like embers, and from the way he was watching me, I was the one who had spooked him. I reached into my pocket and pulled out a box of Red Hot candies. I shook one into my left hand and held it out.

The allure of hard cinnamon candy was enough to overcome his nerves. The burning glow had dimmed, but his feet were uncomfortably hot as he crept forward onto my fingers. He hesitated, then snatched the candy. His body cooled as he ate.

"That can't be healthy for him," Nidhi said.

"I pulled him out of a sword and sorcery novel. Who knows what fictional spiders are supposed to eat? He seems healthy enough to me." I waited as Smudge climbed up my arm and settled onto my shoulder. "You were using him to keep an eye on me. A warning system?"

"Isn't that what you use him for?"

"That's not fair. I also use him to repel mosquitoes." I

stretched my arms, grimacing at the tension in my back and shoulders. My jaw ached, too. I must have been clenching it in my sleep. "How long?"

"You've been asleep five hours."

The good news was that I had successfully cast a spell I would have thought was impossible only a few months ago. The bad news was that it had kicked my ass. "Gutenberg tosses magic like that around all the time."

"Gutenberg has been practicing for more than five hundred years. You've had what, a decade?"

"Exactly. I'm young and spry and energetic." I winced and rubbed my neck. "Young and energetic, at least."

"You seem to have survived the experience with your mind intact. Which means you should be able to tell me what the *hell* you were thinking out there!"

I could think of a few things more surprising than Nidhi Shah losing her temper and shouting at me. Smudge spontaneously breaking into a tap-dancing routine, for example. Gutenberg giving up magic and devoting himself to competitive macramé.

I couldn't even remember the last time Nidhi had raised her voice, let alone yelled at anyone. "I was trying to find out who killed that wendigo."

"By experimenting with magic you couldn't control?" She started to say more, but caught herself before she could speak. She clasped her hands tightly together, and took three deep breaths. Her body visibly relaxed. "I'm not your therapist anymore, Isaac. I'm your ... I'm trying to be your friend."

"I know that." *Friend* was as good a word as any. The closest term I had come across for "my girlfriend's other lover" was "metamour," but the word suggested an uncomfortable level of intimacy between Nidhi and me.

Her lips pursed. "As your friend, I will call your therapist and have you yanked off this investigation if I think you're endangering yourself or the people around you."

Every Porter was required to see a therapist on a regular basis. It seemed a wise precaution for people who routinely rewrote the laws of existence to suit their whims. "We just saw a man who might be a libriomancer help slaughter a wendigo. I don't think I'm the one we should be worrying about right now."

Nidhi didn't even blink. "The closest Porter therapist would be Doctor Karim. I assume Pallas assigned you to her when I was removed from your case?"

My silence was confirmation enough.

"I've got her on speed dial. I consulted on one of her cases last year, a bakeneko with bipolar disorder who was living as a barn cat in Ohio. In her manic phase, she liked to reanimate dead mice and chase them through the house."

"Wait, how do you treat a shapeshifting cat for bipolar disorder?"

"Stress management techniques, a light box for winter, lithium when she's in her human form, and diet control. Particularly the catnip tea. Don't change the subject. I've lost Porters before because they didn't respect their magic. They didn't understand the risks. I'm not going to lose you." Her gaze slipped away. "I won't let Lena lose you."

I tightened my fist. "I understand the risks."

"You understand the dangers," she said. "You don't believe in the risks. Not to you. You think you're too clever, just like every other Porter who ended up destroying themselves."

"Three vampires tried to kill me in my own library earlier this summer. Then a possessed Porter sent an automaton after me. If that wasn't enough, I ended up ripping open a book that almost consumed Lena and me both." I stared at the wall, remembering the charred pages of that damaged book ripping free like a dam crumbling from the weight of its magic. Unformed power trying to escape, followed by a presence Gutenberg had described as Hell itself, ripping me into nothingness, devouring my very core.

"And every time, you survived. You reinforced your own deluded belief that you're immortal, exempt from the dangers. I've seen it before. The things you can do are amazing, but with great power comes great responsibility."

"You did *not* just quote Spider-Man at me."

She leaned closer, both her words and her demeanor softening. "What's going on, Isaac? Ever since Detroit, you've been on edge. Angry." She looked me up and down. "You've lost what, five pounds? Ten?"

"No." It was twelve, according to my last weigh-in at Doctor Karim's office. Magic burned a lot of calories, and overuse sent the sympathetic nervous system into overdrive, effectively destroying your appetite. In the beginning, magic sounded like the ultimate diet plan, up until you ended up hospitalized for dehydration and malnutrition.

"Lena's noticed it, too," she said gently. "You've spent more and more time locked up with your books. Does this have anything to do with your discomfort about the three of us? Anger and confusion are normal reactions to a kind of relationship you never expected."

"I'm not mad," I said, a little too quickly. "Yeah, it's a little weird, but I'm getting used to it."

Her response simmered with skepticism. "If that's true, then what's driving you, Isaac?"

"Gutenberg."

"Ah." She nodded.

"He chose to hide magic from the world. I can understand that." I understood, but I didn't always agree. How many diseases could we have eliminated through the open use of magic? How many tragedies could have been averted? Not to mention the potential exploration. Magic could create livable habitats in the deepest crevasses of the ocean, in the hearts of active volcanoes, not to mention outer space. So what if NASA had never given us the moon base we wanted. Science fiction had provided all the tools we needed to build one ourselves.

"But," Nidhi prompted.

"We both know he's been hiding things. Lying about the rules and limitations of libriomancy." Not to mention the devourers.

"Would you teach a middle school science class how to mix thermite?" She raised her hands before I could answer. "I'm not suggesting you're a child. But Gutenberg is more than six hundred years old. To him, we're barely out of infancy."

"If those infants already have the ingredients to make thermite, I'd damn well teach them how to make and handle it safely instead of waiting for them to accidentally burn down the school." I stood up and searched the room for my satchel. Nidhi had tucked it beneath the foot of the cot. I yanked out the Asimov collection and opened it to "The Dead Past." Dry petals of Moly fell from the pages. I tried to catch one, and the blackened petal broke apart like ash at my touch.

The pages looked like someone had lit a fire in the center of the book's spine, blackening all but the outer edges. The damage had rendered the book useless for libriomancy, like a cracked lens in a laser. I would need to update our database. Magical resonance treated identical copies of a book as a single point, which was why we could touch the belief of all readers of a given title. But those same principles meant every copy of Asimov's collection now carried the same magical charring, though only libriomancers would see it. Every copy of this book would be useless for years, even decades. Depending on the severity, the damage could even creep into other editions of the same book.

"You're angry at Gutenberg for keeping secrets from you." Nidhi cocked her head to the side. "Yet every time Lena or I ask you about *your* secret research project for the Porters, you change the subject."

I drew a tally mark in the air, acknowledging the point. "You saw what I've been working on," I said softly. "The shadow that tried to claw its way out of my spell."

"The woman?"

"Or something like her. Jeneta called them 'devourers.' They've been trying to break through to our world. Gutenberg assigned me to figure out what they were and how to stop them."

"That would explain the stress. How far have you gotten?"

"I'm not even close." I carefully closed the Asimov book and tucked it back into my bag. I'd need to write up a report for Pallas. She would *not* be happy. "I don't even know if what we saw through my spell is the same thing that tried to kill me in Detroit. The manifestation was similar, but not identical."

"Helen believes a libriomancer was behind this," Nidhi said. "She's scared whoever it is will come after the werewolves next."

"What do you think?"

"I don't know." Tension lined her eyes and forehead. "There are libriomancers who enjoy power more than they should, but if anyone were capable of this kind of violence, it should have been caught and dealt with long before reaching this point. As for your devourers, we screen for symptoms of possession."

"You can't screen for what you don't know about," I countered. The Porters hadn't yet recovered from the last libriomancer to turn against us. I didn't know how the organization would survive a second betrayal. "How much trouble are Jeff and Helen going to give us?"

"None for now. I convinced them to let us look for the killer on our own."

I glanced up. "How did you manage that?"

"I reminded them that the Porters are a pack. If one of us did this, it's our responsibility to stop that person. Just as Jeff and Helen would personally hunt down any of their people who broke pack law."

"Nice." I ran my fingers over the rest of my books. "I'll look up any wendigo encounters from the past decade. Maybe this is a simple revenge thing."

Nidhi said nothing, but I had worked with her long enough to recognize the tilt of her head and the slight compression of her mouth. She didn't buy that any more than I did.

A knock at the door made me jump so hard Smudge had to grab my ear to keep from being dislodged. I held very, very still until he released me.

Lena opened the door and peeked inside.

Nidhi jumped to her feet. "What's wrong?"

Sweat beaded Lena's brow, and her face was pale. The muscles in her neck were taut. She gripped the door-frame so tightly her knuckles were white. "We have to leave."

I started toward her, but Nidhi was faster. She slipped an arm around Lena for support. Lena accepted grate-fully, resting her head against Nidhi's.

I waited in awkward silence until Lena kissed Nidhi and pulled away.

"Are you hurt?" I asked. "Did someone—"

"It's not me." She frowned and shook her head. "It's not this body, I mean. It's my tree. Something's wrong."

"I'll drive," I said. There was no way I was letting her ride a motorcycle on these roads in her condition. I might have burned through a little too much magic today, but I was in far better shape than Lena.

"I'll be right behind you," said Nidhi.

Lena didn't protest. She tossed Nidhi the keys to her bike while I shouldered my bag.

"Isaac." Nidhi directed a pointed look toward my bag. "Be careful."

"Of course," I said, but I was already thinking beyond the weapons in my book bag. If someone was hurting Lena's oak, I intended to bring my entire library down on their head.

A 1973 Triumph convertible wasn't the most practical choice of car for Michigan's Upper Peninsula. Setting aside Michigan's attitude toward foreign-made cars, the little two-seater was simply too small and unreliable for the no-holds-barred assault winter launched on the U.P. each year. Up here, the ideal winter vehicle was anything you could mount a snowplow to. When I first brought the car up, more than one person had offered wagers on how many times I'd put it into a ditch or get myself stuck at the bottom of an icy hill.

I had pocketed close to four hundred bucks from those bets. This thing was far safer than my old pickup truck. The previous owner had installed a number of magical modifications, including traction spells strong enough for me to do a slalom course at full speed across a frozen lake. Or in this case, to swerve around gravel roads at speeds somewhere between insane and suicidal.

Lena's body was rigid, her eyes closed. She kept her hands clamped around her bokken. She gasped occasionally, tight breaths that hissed through her teeth, but otherwise made no sound.

I was fairly certain the loss of her tree wouldn't kill her. Not immediately, at least. She had survived the death of her previous oak earlier in the year by grafting branches from that tree onto the one in my backyard, but it hadn't been an easy transition.

Besides Nidhi and myself, only a handful of people knew the location of Lena's tree. Of those, I couldn't think of anyone with reason to harm her. But the timing couldn't be a coincidence. "Did anyone else see you this afternoon?"

Lena shook her head. "Jeff and Helen would have known if we were followed."

I turned off the headlights when we reached my street, so as not to alert anyone at the house. The porch and garage lights had come on automatically at sundown. I saw nothing unusual, but as I drove past the driveway to park on the side of the road, Smudge dropped into an alert crouch on the dashboard. Heat rippled over his body.

"Stay here." I grabbed Smudge and my books. Smudge climbed onto the leather strap of the book bag and clung there, all eight eyes watching the house. I leaned over and opened the glove box, using its light to skim a copy of H. Allen Conrad's *Time Kings*.

"Like hell." Lena pulled herself out of the car, leaning on her bokken for support.

Thankfully, she waited for me to finish creating a fully charged and loaded shock-gun. I had been practicing with this particular gun since July, though it wasn't always easy to find a secluded enough space for target practice. The shock-gun was a two-stage weapon. Pulling the trigger fired a tiny, electrically charged pellet at supersonic speed. A split-second later, the gun's power source triggered an electrical discharge that followed the path of ionized air particles.

In layman's terms, I had a pistol that shot lightning. The charge could be adjusted from "Low-grade Taser" to "Barbeque a Medium-sized Dinosaur," and had a range of up to one mile. From a distance, it was designed to look like an ordinary revolver. Best of all, unlike so many fictional ray guns, this one had usable sights.

"Just don't point that thing at my oak," Lena said.

I rotated the cylinder to setting two, which should drop anyone we encountered without killing them. Keeping the gun pointed to the ground, I crept around the garage to the back of the house, Lena pressing close behind. Clouds curtained the moon, making it difficult to see anything beyond the silhouette of her tree, but it appeared undisturbed. I crouched by the corner of the house, searching the yard and the trees beyond, but found nobody.

"It feels diseased," Lena whispered. "Like rot spreading through my bones."

"Could someone have poisoned it?"

"It wouldn't work this quickly, or hurt this much."

From inside the house came a sharp thud, followed by the sound of breaking glass. Lena pulled me back.

"Front door," I whispered. The sliding door leading in from the deck was locked from the inside, and smashing through glass doors tended to alert whoever you were trying to sneak up on.

We circled around to the front. The storm door had a hole drilled through the aluminum frame, which was odd, as it hadn't actually been locked. The twenty-year-old wooden door had three holes, as if whoever was trying to break in hadn't been able to figure out how to disable the deadbolt. I readied my weapon, waited for Lena's nod, and turned the knob.

It didn't budge. Whoever was inside must have gotten the door locked again behind them. I slid the key into the lock, turned until it clicked, and opened the door.

The hinges creaked faintly. I held my breath, but heard no movement from inside. The brass plate on the doorframe was scraped and bent, like someone had held an oversized drill against it. What kind of incompetent break-in was this?

Lena grabbed my arm before I could step inside. "Look down."

The drill had left sawdust scattered over the tile floor. I stared for several seconds before I realized what had caught her attention. There were no footprints in the sawdust.

"The hell?" I mouthed silently.

Lena's bokken flattened in her hands, each sword taking on a perfectly honed edge sharp enough to cut through one and a half vampires in a single strike. She slipped past me to check the kitchen. I waited for her signal, then moved into the library.

I had read far too many books about this scenario, not to mention all the monster movies, to be happy poking through a dark house. I gripped the shock-gun in both hands, half expecting a chainsaw-wielding zombie or alien slime-monster to leap out at me as I checked between each of the shelves.

A grinding sound made me whirl. Lena put her back to the counter and gestured toward the hallway. I moved through the kitchen to cover her as she crouched by the hall and stretched her fingers to touch the hardwood floor. She would be able to feel if anyone or anything was crouching around the corner, waiting to pounce. After a moment, she rose and stepped into the hall.

The noise was coming from my office. From my computer, to be specific. It sounded like the hard drive was trying to spin up, but kept stuttering out. The office itself was empty.

"I'll check the bedroom," Lena whispered.

"Be careful." The prospect of catching whoever had attacked her tree appeared to have given her a second wind, but I didn't know how long that would last.

The monitor was blank except for a blinking cursor prompt. I switched on the desk lamp. Books were scattered over the floor. My heart thudded against my ribs when I spotted a two-hundred-year-old Spanish diary with a freshly-cracked spine and pages pulled loose. It took all my willpower to keep from switching the shock-gun to setting six. Busting into my house was one thing, but someone would pay for this.

The framed space shuttle print on my wall had fallen, and triangles of glass littered the floor. Both the commander and the pilot from that mission had autographed the picture for me. That must have been the crash we heard from outside.

"Nobody's been back here, either," Lena called. "The house is empty."

I picked up the diary and carefully placed it on the desk. There was a bookbinder over in Presque Isle who should be able to repair the damage. I found my new e-reader on the floor beneath the chair. Small electronics were some of the most common targets for burglars, but they had destroyed the reader instead of taking it. The screen looked as if it had been shot at close range.

I sat down in front of the computer. Smudge scurried over to perch on a Petoskey stone paperweight I had gotten for my one-year anniversary at the library. He was still antsy, and I moved several books out of reach of his flames.

I wasn't worried about my data. Gutenberg himself would have trouble getting past the safeguards Victor Harrison had installed in our networks, and most of my research was backed up on the Porter network. But why take the time to destroy the computer?

Bits of broken plastic peppered the floor. A hole the width of my index finger was bored through the case. I held down the power key, then cycled the computer back on. I wasn't hoping for much, but the screeching clatter from inside made me jump back.

It wasn't the hard drive this time. A large silver beetle crawled out of the hole. Gleaming wings buzzed, and it zoomed past my ear before vanishing into the hall.

"What was that?" Lena asked from the doorway.

"Some sort of scarab beetle, I think." Except that scarab beetles from Michigan would be darker in color, and were unlikely to be nesting in my computer. I crouched on the floor and peeked into the hole, keeping my eye back in case there were more. When nothing attacked my face, I popped the side off of the case to study the machine's guts. Ordinary beetles wouldn't have chewed through both plastic and metal, either. "Did you see which way it flew?"

Something buzzed within the computer. I dropped it

and jumped back as a second, smaller beetle crawled out from between the hard drives. This one flew straight for the window, striking hard enough to chip the glass. Smudge raced across the desk in hot pursuit.

By the time I reached the window, the thing had chewed its way outside, right through the double-paned glass and the metal screen.

Lena sagged against the wall. "I think I know where it's going."

I swore as I realized what she meant. If these things had bored through glass and plastic, how much damage could they do to an oak, even a magically strengthened one?

Smudge circled the hole in the window, as if searching for the best way to squeeze through. I tapped the window, trying to get his attention before he decided to melt his way through the glass. A piece of candy brought him scurrying back to my shoulder.

By the time I flipped on the lights out back, Lena was heading for the garden she had planted two months ago. Rosebushes walled the garden, all save an archway in the front. The branches and thorns were strong enough to repel deer and other creatures. Two varieties were in bloom, one a deep, smoky purple, the other yellow. Most of the flowers were as large as my hand.

In the very back, protected by climbing rose vines, Lena's oak stood on the boundary between my yard and the woods beyond. The leaves were thicker than any of the surrounding trees, and smaller branches shone with new bark where they had sprouted in the past months. I followed her outside and ducked through the arch of thorns, stepping carefully between the corn and the red peppers.

Lena reached for me with her free hand. Taking mine

in hers, she pressed my palm to the rough bark, avoiding the rose thorns that could have pierced my hand. Lena's fingertips slipped between mine, sinking into the bark as if it were soft clay. "What do you feel?"

Most days, I couldn't distinguish between Lena's tree and any other. My magic simply wasn't strong enough. Few Porters had that kind of power, which was why libriomancy had spread so quickly. Books gave us a crutch, allowing us to draw on the belief and will of others to supplement our own power.

Today was different. I was raw and exposed from my spells in Tamarack. My barriers were down, meaning I was better able to feel and manipulate magic.

I felt her connection to the oak, the sense of stability and timelessness. The roots ran deep, and while the tree might sway with the wind, it was so much stronger than any human. Much like Lena herself.

This wasn't the first time I had felt the magic of Lena's tree, but never before had I wanted so badly to pull away. An itching sensation spread through my skin, as if something were squirming and burrowing through my muscles. I fought the urge to scratch until I bled. If it was this unpleasant for me, what was Lena feeling?

She swore and yanked her hand back. Her fingertips were bleeding. I spotted tiny metal pincers snapping from a small hole in the wood, but the insect retreated before I could get a closer look.

"Whatever they are, they're killing my tree."

Chapter 4

Frank Dearing was not a good man, but my years with him made me happy.

I loved his fields almost as much as I loved him. I was stronger than his other hands, able to work longer without breaks. I gave strength to the plants that needed it, and I rooted out those dying from rot or insects before they contaminated the rest. Frank's family had lived on this farm for three generations, but I knew the crops in a way he never could.

I seduced him for the first time in early March, a month after I had stumbled onto his farm. Snow melted beneath my bare feet as I hauled bales of hay from the barn. The cold didn't bother me, and I enjoyed the crisp wind on my skin. I had taken to wearing shorts and old T-shirts, hand-me-downs from one of the other hands. They were too small, but I liked the way they hugged my flesh.

When I finished spreading the hay, I returned to fetch the ax and hose. The water trough had frozen over again.

I felt Frank watching as I swung the ax through the ice.

I glanced over to see him standing on the porch, sipping his coffee. His desire warmed my body in a way sunlight never could. I pretended not to notice, but adjusted my stance to better display the curves of my legs and ass. When I hauled broken chunks of ice from the trough, I allowed the water to drip down my chest. My nipples tightened, blurring the line between pain and pleasure.

I used the hose to rinse away the hay that clung to my skin, then slicked my blonde hair back. I could feel the hem of my shirt stiffening from the cold, which surprised me. With the heat surging through my blood, I half expected to see steam rising from my body.

I smiled at the sound of his boots as they crunched through the snow. I would have known him by his footsteps alone, strong and solid.

"What the hell are you doing, girl?" he asked gruffly. "Get into the barn and change into some dry clothes before you freeze to death."

"But I haven't drained the hose yet," I said innocently. A delighted giggle escaped my lips when he blushed beneath his beard. I could feel his desire. It had followed me from the very first time he saw me. Instinctively, I pulled that desire into myself, twined it into my own, and sent it back, strong enough to make him gasp.

"I'll take care of that. You get yourself inside." He slapped my ass to send me on my way, and the pleasure of that sharp blow made me gasp and bite my lip. I blew him a kiss and scurried away.

I stripped off the T-shirt and pulled on a too-large red flannel, shivering as the heavy fabric brushed my skin. I had only fastened the third button when I heard Frank enter the barn behind me. I moistened my lips with my tongue and smiled, but didn't turn around until his arms encircled me, his rough hands tugging the shirt away to

grab my breasts. I breathed in the smell of coffee and cig-
arettes as he kissed my neck.

I was home.

W E WERE STILL STANDING in the garden
when I heard Nidhi pull up on the motorcycle.
Lena's leather jacket hung loosely on her
shoulders as she ran into the backyard to join us. I
brought her up to speed while Lena paced circles around
her tree.

"How many of these things are inside of her?" Nidhi
asked.

"Twenty-eight." Lena shuddered. "I've tried to crush
them, to seal the bark around their bodies, but nothing
works. I've hardened the core of the tree the best I can,
and they're not strong enough to get there yet, but they
burrow through the bark and the outer layers of wood
like it's made of balsa. And when I try to enter the tree
myself . . ." She held up her hands. Blood welled from
tiny cuts and gouges on her palm and fingers.

"That shouldn't even be possible." I knew it was a
stupid complaint as soon as the words left my mouth.
Possible or not, it was happening. But Lena wasn't
physically shoving her hands and body into the oak
like a butterfly crawling back into a cocoon; she *became* the tree. Her physical body was something she
doffed and donned again as she entered and left her
oak. How the hell could these things attack her within
her own tree?

Unless it was an attack on the tree itself, one which
somehow translated into wounds of the flesh? I didn't
understand enough about how Lena's bond with her tree

worked. "If they're mostly hiding below the bark, what if we peeled the bark back to get to them?"

"Skin me alive, you mean?" Lena asked, her tone deceptively mild.

I winced. "Sorry. I didn't—"

"It's all right." She moved her hand over the tree. Bits of bark fell away as the insects burrowed through the wood to follow. "They're too quick anyway. They'd just move to another spot."

"What else have you tried?" Nidhi asked.

"We haven't," I admitted. "Without knowing what they're made of, it's hard to know what weapons would work best. They looked metal, which means there's a chance a magnetic blast might affect them. I could also try to strengthen the tree itself."

Lena frowned. "Strengthen it how?"

I waved a hand toward the house. "Tamora Pierce's *Circle of Magic* series has characters who can empower plants and make them grow at ridiculous speeds. If I can tap into that book like I did with the Asimov story—"

"Then you could char another book and knock yourself into a coma," Lena finished.

"Not to mention the question of control." Nidhi moved to stand between me and the tree, her arms folded. "You have no idea what that would do to Lena's oak. To *her*."

"I could call Nicola Pallas and request an automaton." Gutenberg had constructed his magical golems as bodyguards five centuries ago, armoring them in spells and metal keys from his printing press, essentially turning them into living books. Among their various powers, they had the ability to drain magic from others. I was certain they could kill these insects, but I had no idea what such an attack would do to Lena's tree.

"No automatons," Lena said firmly.

"Why attack Lena's tree like this, and why now?" Nidhi asked. "They could have waited in the branches and swarmed down as she approached, or let her enter the tree then burrowed in after her."

"Please don't give the magical dryad-eating bugs any ideas," Lena said.

They hadn't just attacked Lena's tree. After burrowing into my house, they had also attacked my computer, which had layer upon layer of Porter spells protecting it. My e-reader probably had a lingering taste of magic as well, thanks to Jeneta using it to pull raisins from a poem. "They're drawn to magic. Like overgrown, spell-sucking mosquitoes." Which meant magic might lure them out of Lena's oak.

I turned toward the house, but Nidhi was faster, stepping into the garden's archway and blocking my path. "How much magic will it take to draw them to you? What do you intend to do to them once they're out? Lena had to carry you out of the woods earlier today because you burned yourself out with your time-travel spell."

"Time-viewing spell."

She ignored my correction. "If you blow your mental fuses trying to pull those things from Lena's tree, you'll only make things worse for all of us."

"Stop derailing my plans with logic and reason," I snapped. If I could track down a children's book with one of those cartoonishly powerful supermagnets, I might be able to rip the bugs out of Lena's tree, but it would probably tear up the wood in the process. Not to mention I'd need a trip to the library or bookstore. My collection didn't include many books for that age group.

Not many, but there *was* one that might work. And it

had the bonus of being awesome. "When the Porters need to shut down electronics, they use a book to generate an electromagnetic pulse. You don't have to manipulate the energy like I did with the chronoscope, and energy is actually easier to create than matter."

"We don't know that these things are electronic," Nidhi said.

"Different kind of energy." I gave up on trying not to grin. "We think they're metal, right? Ever see what happens when you put silverware in a microwave?"

I ran into the house and grabbed *Why Sh*t Happens: The Science of a Really Bad Day*. We'd still need to get them to poke their heads out of the tree, but once they did, microwave radiation should be as effective as a bug zapper.

As I turned to leave, Smudge raced down my arm, every step like a droplet of boiling water on my skin. He jumped onto the side of the shelves and sprinted toward the ceiling. Once there, he clung to the plaster and crept forward, his attention fixed on a pencil-sized hole.

"Be careful." I opened the book and skimmed the section that explained how a metal-rimmed plate could do very bad things to your microwave pizza. If there were stragglers in the roof, this was the perfect opportunity for a test run.

Smudge crawled back and forth, never stepping directly over the opening as he laid down one gossamer strand after another.

"You were there when those things drilled through metal and glass, right?" Spider silk was strong, and Smudge was laying it on pretty thick, but—

Three insects shot out of the hole, tearing through the web as if it weren't even there. The first was a ladybug the size of an almond nut, with what looked like brass rivets for spots. It cleared the way for the rest, but at a cost. Webbing tangled its wings, causing it to fly erratically back to the ceiling. Delicate legs gripped the edge of the hole as it scraped its wings together, trying to rid itself of web.

The second was built like a dragonfly. The third, more waspish in shape, flew for the back door.

I tracked the dragonfly, touched the book's magic, and pointed the pages at the ceiling.

The magic wasn't as spectacular as I had hoped, but results were what mattered. The insect flashed orange, like a tiny light bulb burning out, then dropped to the floor.

I turned to get the ladybug, but Smudge was too close. He circled the struggling insect, like a predator playing with his meal.

He struck too quickly for me to see. The web clinging to the ladybug went up like gas-soaked rags. The flame didn't hurt the metal, but whatever the wings were made of, they weren't as strong. One broke away and fluttered, smoldering, to the floor.

The ladybug charged Smudge, who left a blackened path along my ceiling as he retreated. The insect darted in again and again. I couldn't see what it was doing, but every missed strike caused a thread of white dust to fall from the plaster.

Smudge raised his front four legs, waving them like tiny flaming swords. The ladybug hesitated, then sealed its shell and ran directly into the fire.

Smudge flared blue and fell. I lunged without thinking, catching him in an outstretched hand before he hit the floor.

Pain travels quickly along the nerves. I had a moment of clarity as I realized what I had just done, and then I was screaming, "Stupid, stupid, stupid!" through my teeth and fighting the urge to fling the burning spider away. I ran to the kitchen and transferred him to the tile floor.

The ladybug was burrowing back into the hole. Keeping my burnt hand curled against my body, I raised the book with my other hand. But the ladybug disappeared before I could get the shot.

An angry buzzing sound warned me as the wasp swooped toward my eyes. I dropped to the floor. Forget guns and books, I needed a laser-powered fly swatter. I searched the shelves, trying to see where it had landed. It hadn't followed its buddy into the ceiling, and the room was silent, which meant it was creeping around, waiting for a better chance to attack.

The back door slid open. Lena gripped one of her bokken with both hands. "Don't move."

She was staring at a spot on my back. I slowly twisted my head until I spotted the wasp perched on the waist of my jeans. "Aw, crap."

Lena's bokken whipped past, close enough to tug my hair in its wake. The insect shattered into fragments, and her weapon embedded itself in the floor. She wrenched it free and leaned against the shelves.

"There's another one," I said. "It burrowed into the ceiling. I want it in one piece."

"Why?"

"So I can take it apart."

I grabbed a metal spatula and used it to carry Smudge to the kitchen sink where I could examine his injuries. Clear fluid that smelled faintly like diesel oozed from cuts on his forelegs. Blue flame danced over the cuts, never actually touching the fluid. Like gasoline, it was probably only flammable when it evaporated. Leaving the book on the counter, I returned to my library.

My classification was loosely based on the system we used at the Copper River Library, but in addition to sorting books by genre and author, mine were also classified by magic. Healing texts were on the end of the middle shelf, where they would be easy to get to in case of emergency. I picked out a copy of *Household Tales* by the Brothers Grimm and flipped pages one-handed until I came to "The Water of Life."

My hand throbbed, the pain growing worse with every beat. My palm was red and blistered, with blood oozing from the edges, but it was the blackened skin in the middle that most worried me. The pain wasn't bad there, which suggested nerve damage.

Shock threatened to make me drop the book. I sat on the floor, resting it in my lap. "It springs from a fountain in the courtyard of an enchanted castle," I read softly, imagining the scene in my mind. The prince hurrying to get to the spring before the clock chimed twelve, grasping the cup in one hand, reaching . . .

Through the yellowed pages, I touched the hammered metal cup in the prince's hand. I eased the cup from his grip and carefully pulled it free. I spilled half the water onto my shirt. Lena caught my hand, guiding the cup to my lips.

A single swallow of the cool water was enough. The blisters dried, and the charred skin sloughed away from my palm. I used my fingernails to scrape away the worst of the dead skin and dried blood.

My arm was trembling, and sweat streamed down my face and neck. I pulled myself up and brought the cup to the kitchen. I spilled several drops into the sink where Smudge was resting. He didn't move.

"Come on, buddy." I reached down, but yanked my hand back when his flames flared higher. I grabbed the spatula and tried to nudge him toward the water. He just twitched and curled into a tighter ball.

Lena slipped a hand into my pants pocket and pulled out my box of Red Hots. She took one of the candies between her thumb and forefinger, dipped it into the cup, and placed it in the sink in front of Smudge. A single droplet clung to the candy's surface.

Smudge slowly uncurled his legs and crept forward. His two front legs hung like snapped twigs ready to break away. The cuts had stopped burning, leaving only a tarry, blackish scab on each leg. His mandibles closed around the end of the candy.

"Thank you," I said, surprised at how difficult it was to get the words out past the knot in my throat.

She kissed my cheek. "You're welcome."

I didn't look away until Smudge began to move his forelegs again. A ripple of red fire spread over his body, vanishing as quickly as it had begun, except for the scabs on his legs. Those continued to burn, smelling like burnt hair and oil, until both legs were clean and whole once more.

I left Smudge in the sink with another piece of candy and picked up *Why Sh*t Happens*. "I'd call that a successful proof of concept. Let's go clean up your tree."

I circled the oak to make sure stray microwaves wouldn't accidentally fry anything behind the tree. "Where are they?"

Lena pointed with one of her bokken. "The lowest is dug in at knee level." She tapped the bark with her weapon, marking each of the twenty-eight insects. The highest was a good twelve feet up.

"This will probably hurt," I warned her.

Nidhi clasped Lena's hand and said, "Think of it as radiation treatment to burn away a tumor."

"The dragonfly in the house cooked fast." I reread the pages I had used before. "I'll need you to lure them to the surface."

Lena nodded and dragged her fingers through the bark. It wasn't long before she jerked her hand away.

I aimed the book at the tiny pincers, which sparked and popped. Lena hissed in pain, but when I pulled the book away, she said, "Don't stop. It's working."

I cooked the insect until Lena confirmed it was dead. I didn't want to linger too long in one spot, as the microwaves could also boil the water in the tree, drying and cracking the wood. Lena touched the tree again, luring a second insect to the surface.

"They're burrowing," Lena said.

I aimed the book skyward while I waited for her to bait the next. "You said they couldn't get to the heart of the tree."

"They're not going deeper. They're trying to get out."

She pointed to where the first insect was emerging, and I cooked it in place, but they were digging free on all sides. I got two more, and then they were flying toward me. I stumbled back, trying not to trip over the pumpkins. For someone who rarely ate vegetables, she grew an awful lot of produce. I moved the book back and forth, trying to blast insects out of the air. A miniature lightning bolt jumped between two of the bugs, and both fell like tiny burning meteorites.

A beetle landed on my arm. Pincers dug through my shirt and the skin beneath. Another attacked the back of my hand.

Lena's bokken hummed through the air. Nidhi tried

to grab the bugs off of my skin, but for every one she ripped free, three more found me. Others landed on the book and began chewing through the cover and paper.

I ended the spell and flung the book to the ground. Lena joined Nidhi, and crushed several of the things in her bare hands, but by the time we tugged the last one off of me, the rest had returned to the tree.

They had bored numerous holes through *Why Sh*t Happens*. The spine had suffered the most damage. When I picked the book from the dirt, half of the pages tore free.

"How many?" I asked.

"I can feel nineteen crawling around."

I picked a metal horsefly from the ground. The microwave had been a little too effective, warping and melting the delicate metal.

I headed back toward the house. "I need something I can dissect."

Once inside, I pulled *The Demon Trapper's Daughter* by Jana Oliver off of the shelves. I had cataloged this book for the Porters several years ago, and I knew exactly which scene I wanted.

My hands tightened around the cover as I recalled the opening pages of the story, in which the protagonist tried to capture a Biblio-Fiend, a small, mischievous demon who liked to urinate on books. No way in hell I was letting *that* into my living room. But later on, when she faced the larger demons . . .

I flipped to the chapter I needed, shoved my hand into the story, and pulled out a glass sphere the size of a softball. "Let's see what happens if we freeze them." Looking at the hole where the ladybug had vanished, I added, "Assuming we can find the damn things."

"They go after magic, right?" Lena jammed her bokken into the ceiling and gripped the hilt with both hands. Her fingers sank into the wood. Tiny spikes split away from the blade, sprouting buds that uncurled into small, waxy leaves.

I hefted the sphere. I didn't have to wait long.

"Get ready." Lena flinched. "That stings," she muttered, then yanked hard. Chunks of plaster ripped free, exposing broken slats and insulation. The end of Lena's wooden blade had grown like a bonsai tree on superfertilizer. The ladybug was burrowing into the wood, but as I drew back to throw, it took flight, swirling erratically toward the back door.

Lena yanked her tree—sword—whatever it was now out of the way, and I hurled the sphere at the fleeing bug. Glass smashed against the doorframe. Magic spread like liquid nitrogen, creating a white cloud. The door frosted over, and a web of cracks spread downward.

Lena stepped back and brushed a shard of curved glass off of her arm. Tiny slivers shone in her hair and clothes.

"Are you—"

"I'm fine," she said. She pulled a piece of glass over her hand to demonstrate. The shard dented her skin, but didn't cut her. "Tough as bark."

The living room felt like a meat locker. I had never used Oliver's books before. Those things were more potent than I had expected. I hurried into the kitchen to check on Smudge, who was huddling protectively over his half-eaten candy, his body burning merrily against the chill. The water pooled in the other dishes was frozen around the edges. Once I knew he was safe, I returned to the library and joined Lena in searching for the ladybug.

Glass crunched underfoot. The ladybug had to have been caught in the cold, but with so much glass and ice scattered across the floor, it was hard to find a little blob of silver metal.

"Isaac." Lena pointed to the door. The ladybug had gotten halfway through the glass when I caught it with the sphere. Before I could figure out the easiest way to work it free, Lena tapped the door with her sword, bringing the whole thing down in a shower of pebbled glass.

"What happened?" asked Nidhi, running onto the deck.

"We're fine." Lena's bokken slipped from her hand. Nidhi started toward her, but Lena waved her back. "I'm all right."

I grabbed a pair of pliers from the junk drawer in the kitchen. Already the ladybug was trying to move, legs and wings clicking erratically. I tightened the pliers around the body until I felt the metal shell begin to bend.

I brought it to the office and switched on my lamp. The shell was grooved silver. Two of the six legs had snapped off from the cold. One of the wings beneath had burned away, leaving little more than a stub. I fetched a Q-tip from the bathroom and tried to clean the soot from the other, but I succeeded only in snapping it. Under the light, the broken wing looked like a tissue-thin strip of nacre peeled from the inside of an oyster shell.

Beneath the shell were gears that would have made a Swiss watchmaker weep with envy. The eyes were like droplets of red wine. Garnets, maybe?

"What is it?" Lena asked.

"Not a clue." Disproportionately large copper mandibles clicked at my fingers. "What steampunk adventure did you sneak out of? Cherie Priest? *Girl Genius*? You're gorgeous, whatever you are."

"And in the meantime, its friends are drilling deeper into Lena's oak," Nidhi said tightly.

I winced. "Sorry. I got—"

"It's all right," said Lena. "We're used to you. 'Look at the shiny magic thing trying to kill us, isn't it awesome?' I'll be happy to admire them with you as soon as we get them out of my tree."

I held the tip of a wooden pencil in front of the ladybug's head. It snapped cleanly through both wood and graphite. "I see several types of metal in there. Copper and silver. Possibly steel."

"Were they created with libriomancy?" Nidhi asked.

"Most likely." Only a few people could manipulate raw magic. Far more could use books to help them shape that power. "I'll check the Porter catalog when I'm done here to see if I can figure out what book they might have come from."

I looked around the office. I didn't know where my magnifying glass had gone, but I spotted something else that should work. Holding the pliers tight, I squeezed past Lena to the 10" telescope tucked into the corner. A built-in rack on the side of the scope held a set of eyepieces. I grabbed one from the middle and returned to the desk.

Holding the two-inch-long metal-and-plastic tube to my right eye, I peered at the insect. I had to look through the wrong end of the eyepiece to bring things into proper focus, but it worked well enough.

"There are no welds. The shell looks like it's riveted to the body." The rivets appeared to be copper, but they were impossibly tiny, as were the hinges and joints below.

The ladybug snapped at me, the mandibles clicking audibly. The sight of those magnified, serrated pincers reaching for my eye made me jerk back so hard I almost dropped the pliers.

I tested a magnet next, but it had no effect. Whatever

metals this was made of, they weren't ferrous. "I need a better way to hold this thing while I study it." Superglue on the joints should effectively paralyze it, though that might obscure the finer details.

Before I could go digging for the glue, Lena reached past me and stabbed a toothpick through the center of the ladybug's body. She gave the toothpick a vicious twist, eased the pliers from my hand, and set them aside. She raised the still-squirming thing into the air. "Hold it by this end."

I swallowed and took the toothpick. With the eye-piece lens, I could see the tiny white threads growing from the toothpick through the interior workings, like parasites devouring the bug from within. I would have felt bad for it, had its cousins not been doing the same thing to Lena.

A coiled spring down the center of the back appeared to provide movement, but I saw no place for a key, no way of winding that spring once it died. I might be able to wind it with a pair of jewelry pliers, but more likely I'd just break something else. I set down the eyepiece and used a straightened paper clip to fold one of the legs back. A gear the size of a snowflake popped out of place as a result of my clumsy efforts.

I pulled the lamp closer. Mechanically, this made no sense at all. Tiny pistons and gears manipulated the legs, but I saw no way to coordinate or control their movement. "Let's see if you have some sort of brain in there."

I grabbed the pliers, tightened them carefully around the insect's head, and twisted it free of the body.

The ladybug went dead. The spring jumped free, fol-lowed by a sprinkling of gears and rods. No way was this Humpty Dumpty getting put back together again. I set the body on the desk and studied the head through the eyepiece. Inside, tiny silver prongs held an oily sphere in place, like a jewelry setting designed for the world's smallest engagement ring.

I used the paper clip to pop the sphere free. It landed on the desk without bouncing or rolling, despite being perfectly round. I touched it with my finger, and it stuck to my skin, allowing me to study it under the lens. I placed the tip of the paper clip to the sphere, and it clicked onto the metal like a magnet. When I tugged it free and set it on a piece of paper, it clung there just as easily.

"What is it?" Normally I would have enjoyed the way Lena's body pressed against mine as she peered over my shoulder, but now I barely noticed.

"It's called a boson chip." From what I remembered, it would stick to just about anything through a kind of subatomic static charge. I felt a sense of magical pressure, like a balloon inflated to the bursting point. "Harvested from the brain of a fictional silicon-based hive mind. This little thing could store every book in the Copper River Library, and it would still have space for Nicola Pallas' music collection."

"You've seen them before?" asked Nidhi.

"I'm the one who pulled them out of a bad space opera." I stared at the chip. "Victor Harrison had requisitioned a batch for one of his pet projects."

Victor was a legend among the Porters. He had the amazing ability to make magic and technology play nicely together, and had built everything from a telepathic coffee maker to a database server that transformed would-be hackers into various reptiles. He had also jinxed my telescope so that every time I looked at Mars, Marvin the Martian popped up and threatened to destroy the Earth with an explosive space-modulator.

Victor was more than capable of putting together a set of pseudoliving metal insects.

Rather, he would have been capable of doing so, if not for the fact that Victor Harrison had been murdered earlier this year.

Chapter 5

For as long as Frank and I were together, I never questioned my actions. I never asked why Marion Dearing wept when she thought nobody could hear. I gave her husband happiness. How could she object to that if she truly loved him?

I saw nothing wrong in fanning the embers of Frank's lust. He wanted to be seduced, pushed over the edge until nothing existed but desire and satisfaction.

For myself, I knew only joy. I lived for those moments when my body entwined with his, the urgent grunts of his exertions blending with my quiet moans, but there were other pleasures as well. The burn of my muscles when I was out working the farm. Devouring the meals Marion prepared for us.

In the beginning, the other farmhands tried to flirt with me. I tolerated their overly familiar comments and "accidental" touches. Frank wanted others to appreciate what he had, but he was unwilling to share. So when one man tried to take things further, I broke his arm in two places.

I knew I was stronger than the others, but that was the first time I had used my strength against another person. Through that confrontation, I discovered that violence could be just another source of pleasure.

Only years later, long after I had buried Frank in the dirt, did I begin to recognize what I had done. What I had become.

Only then did I begin to understand how dangerous I was.

───◆───

I SPENT THE NEXT hour on my laptop, lost in Porter databases and old research reports. I rarely used the laptop, which might have been why the insects spared it. Magic provided an amazing connection with the Porter network, but even magic couldn't force the outdated hardware to process information at a faster rate.

In one window, I scrolled through various weapons we had cataloged over the years, looking for ideas to clear the rest of the bugs from Lena's tree. I found nothing that looked like it would destroy metal while leaving her oak intact. The sonic screwdriver from *Doctor Who* might have worked, having been canonically established as being ineffective on wood, but nobody had ever figured out how to use the controls on the blasted thing.

I was also reading abstracts of every paper and report Victor Harrison had ever filed. I didn't expect to find a description of a secret self-destruct code that would blow up his six-legged creations, but I had hoped to find *something* that might help us.

"You're a librarian. Can't you do some sort of keyword search to speed this up?" Nidhi stood by the window where she could peer out at Lena's tree in the backyard. Lena had returned to the garden, asking to be left alone.

"Sure, and that would help if he'd filed his paperwork correctly." I fought the urge to throw the laptop against the wall. "Even if he had, the real problem is figuring out what he didn't document. Half the things Victor built could have gotten him kicked out of the Porters." He had won twenty grand one year by betting on the outcome of the Super Bowl, a game he had recorded on his illegally modified VCR a week before it aired.

"He was as bad as you are in some ways," Nidhi said. "Rules were never a priority. Once you start playing God, nothing else matters. You're incapable of walking away from an idea, no matter how bad an idea it might be."

I glanced away, thinking of certain reports and experiments I had failed to file with the Porters. "I know, I know. 'If you really want to kill a libriomancer, hook a bomb up to a big red button and tell him not to press it.'"

For the first time that night, Nidhi almost smiled. "That sounds like Doctor Karim."

"She knows her clientele," I admitted. Regular appointments with a Porter-approved shrink were one rule you didn't get to break. Even Gutenberg had his own personal therapist, though rumor had it she was a hundred and thirty years old and preserved on a heavily fortified computer system, courtesy of a brain download performed using a Richard Morgan cyberpunk novel. "Doctor Karim's worried about post-traumatic stress after the mess downstate. I'm pretty sure she's also screening me for signs of bipolar disorder."

"A manic period is normal after magic use." She looked pointedly at my legs, and I forced myself to stop drumming my heels on the floor. "Lena has been worried about you. She says you're not sleeping well, and when you do, you have nightmares."

I shoved the laptop away and rubbed my eyes. "What other things has she shared?"

"That Doctor Karim has prescribed stronger pills to help you sleep, and you've gone through two refills already." She sighed. "Are you surprised that Lena and I talk about you, Isaac?"

I was, a little. My relationship with Lena had brought Nidhi Shah into my life in a new and unexpected way, but I found it easier not to think about that when I was with Lena. "What else does she say?"

"That you've been cutting back on your work at the library, and you spend hours locked away in your office. She says you and Gutenberg haven't had the smoothest time working together. No surprise there. Anyone with his centuries of experience will have trouble making allowances for those of us with mere decades."

"I am but an egg," I said ruefully. She just stared at me. "Don't tell me you've never read *Stranger in a Strange Land*?"

"Heinlein?" She made a sour face. "No thank you."

I had reread several Heinlein titles earlier this summer, trying to get a better framework for our three-way relationship. Unfortunately, the free love fantasies of Heinlein's work hadn't provided much insight into making such a relationship work in the real world. I had tracked down a few nonfiction titles that were more useful, though my boss had given me a very odd look when she saw my interlibrary loan request go through.

"Those computer chips have to be important," Nidhi said. "Could you use an EMP to wipe them clean? Even a strong enough magnet—"

"Magnets won't touch a boson chip." I jumped up and

began to pace. "Those things can survive a nuclear blast at close range. We need to lure the bugs out of the tree and destroy them all at once, and we need to do it quickly. You've known Lena longer than I have. How much time do you think she has before she has to return to her tree?"

"When her oak is healthy, she can stay away for up to a week if she absolutely has to. But with these things weakening her, I'm not sure."

I glared at the laptop "Why the hell would Victor make something like this?"

"The same reason you keep drawing up plans for magic-based space exploration. Victor loved his toys. He loved to create, but he wasn't always good at thinking through the consequences."

I thought back to what we had seen that afternoon. "The man we saw was wearing metal armor of some sort." I picked up the decapitated ladybug. "Imagine a swarm of these things clinging to you."

"They could serve as armor and weapons both," Nidhi said, nodding. "We thought the wendigo's wounds had been made by bullets, but they were roughly the size of the holes these insects drilled through your door and ceiling."

I shivered, remembering the insects landing on my body, biting into my skin. I imagined them burrowing deeper, through flesh and bone. "He's got to be controlling them. When we showed up in Tamarack and began snooping around, he sent his insects to attack Lena's tree."

"How did he know where to find it?" Nidhi asked.

"One question at a time." I steepled my fingers and tapped them against my chin. "Instead of destroying them, what if we overrode their orders?"

"How?"

I grabbed the phone and dialed the line for Jeneta Aboderin's camp. I spent the next five minutes explaining that I was her internship supervisor, and yes, this really was a crisis.

The counselor on the other end sounded about fifteen. "It's eleven o'clock. Curfew was an hour ago. Everyone is supposed to stay in their cabins until reveille."

"Dammit, man, this is an emergency. We've got a burst water pipe here, and more than two thousand books that have to be bagged and frozen immediately!"

"You're . . . you want to freeze the books?"

"I want to *save* them. Freezing minimizes the damage while we get them shipped off to be vacuum dried." I talked over his protests, channeling a particularly obnoxious and arrogant Art History professor from Michigan State University. "That's just the first step. If we don't get this place dried out quickly, we'll end up with mold, fungus, and possibly even . . ." I lowered my voice to a whisper. "*Silverfish.*"

The counselor stammered an apology and went to fetch Jeneta. He must have been running, because she picked up only three minutes later.

"Do you have any poems that could draw insects out of a tree?" I asked the moment I heard her voice.

"Seriously? You dragged me out of bed for a termite problem?"

"I called because I need your help."

"Oh, really?" I could hear her grin through the phone. "Before I agree to anything, does this mean you'll take me with you next time you run off to do something interesting? Because if I'm going to be—"

"It's Lena," I said. "It's her tree being attacked."

Jeneta hesitated. "How serious is this? If you're calling now instead of waiting until morning . . ."

"They're killing her tree. Killing *her*."

"Oh." In that single syllable, I heard fear evict the excitement and bravado of moments before. "I'll try, but I've never done anything like this before, Isaac. I'm not sure it will work."

"I've seen what you can do, Jeneta. You can handle this. I'll be there as soon as I can." When I hung up, I found Nidhi watching me with a flat, expressionless look I remembered from our sessions together. "You disapprove."

"She's fourteen years old. What happens if she can't control these things? What if they attack her like they did you?"

"Do you have a better suggestion?"

She turned away. "If I did, I'd have stopped you."

"I don't like it either," I admitted. "If you see another one of those things, get the hell out of here. I'll leave Smudge in his travel cage. He should give you enough warning if anything goes wrong. Keep him with you, but don't let him get into another scuffle with the bugs."

I looked through the window. Lena sat in the archway of the garden, her back to the house. Even from here, I could see tension and weariness in the set of her shoulders, the slump of her head. "Call me if anything—"

"I will."

Jeneta wore an oversized blue sweatshirt with the moose-and-lake logo of Camp Aazhawigiizhigokwe on the front. She spent the drive reading, and the soft light from her e-reader cast odd shadows over her face.

"How do you stand it up here?" she asked. "There's only one building at camp with a decent Internet connection. The wireless signal doesn't even reach the cafeteria, and the cell reception sucks."

"It's like working with stone knives and bearskins, I know." The Triumph's traction spells kicked in as we rounded a curve. It felt like an invisible lead blanket had settled over my body, stopping me from sliding into the door. "You'd think they were trying to get you to talk to each other instead of spending all your time checking your phones. Total madness, I know. Someone should file a complaint with protective services."

"Your jokes get worse when you're worried." She didn't look up from her screen. "What happened to that rule about no magic for twenty-four hours?"

"Your nightmare was last night. In another ten minutes, it will be midnight, and I'll be able to tell Nicola Pallas that I didn't ask you to do anything magical until the following day."

"Uh-huh." She packed whole paragraphs worth of skepticism into those two syllables, as only a teenager could.

"I'll be right there with you," I said.

"Will you be in my nightmares if the devourers come back?" she demanded.

"You can stay with—" My brain caught up with my mouth at the last second. My house had been attacked once today, and there was no guarantee it wouldn't happen again. Not to mention the creepiness factor of a grown man inviting a fourteen-year-old girl to spend the night. "With Doctor Shah. *If* anything happens, she'll be able to help."

By the time we reached the house, Jeneta had donned a cloak of pure confidence. I all but dragged her through the house to show her the headless ladybug and the other melted insects. "This is what we're dealing with."

"Cool," she said, studying the broken bug. She picked up the head and poked the mandibles with her fingertip. "Nasty, too."

"Can you get them out of Lena's tree?"

She tapped her reader on her palm. "I've got an Emily Dickinson poem I think should do the trick."

I stopped to grab a few more books from the library.

"Whoa, what happened to your back door?"

"I'm remodeling." I stepped carefully through the broken doorframe, then crossed the yard to the garden. The roses muted the light from the back porch. Within the garden, we found Lena and Nidhi resting on a hammock made of interwoven grapevines. Smudge's portable cage hung from a higher loop of vine.

Nidhi's hair was disheveled, and her clothes appeared rumpled. She was sweating, and her shoes and socks had been tossed in among the pumpkins. I stopped in the archway. Nidhi and Lena had been together for years, but I had never walked in on them during or immediately after the act.

I knew Lena's nature. I knew she drew strength from her lovers. It made perfect sense for her to turn to Nidhi for comfort. It was a smart move. But it still felt like I'd been punched in the esophagus.

"When did you plant grapevines?" I asked, stammering slightly.

"Tuesday morning." Lena climbed out of the hammock and grabbed my free hand, pulling me in for a quick kiss. "I'm glad you're back."

"You're really a dryad?" Jeneta asked.

Lena smiled and picked up her bokken. At her touch, a single green bud sprouted from the wood. "The tree behind us is as much my body as this flesh. And right now, something's trying very hard to kill it."

"No problem." Jeneta sat cross-legged on the ground and switched on her e-reader. "Do you have any clover growing around here? The flowers would be perfect, but even if it's not in bloom, it will help."

"Give me a minute." Lena walked from the garden. Nidhi followed, leaving her shoes and socks behind.

Jeneta watched them go. "Were they just . . . ?"

"Focus on your magic," I said.

"But I thought you and Lena were—"

"We are."

I waited for her to digest this, and wondered which reaction it would be. Jeff DeYoung's werewolf-style acceptance of whatever steams your sauna, or the confused condemnation I had received from Pete Malki. Pete lived down the street, and had stopped by a couple of weeks ago to tell me he thought my girlfriend might be making time with that new Indian doctor in town. I guess, "Yeah. Want a drink?" hadn't been the response he was expecting.

Jeneta landed somewhere in the middle. "That sounds really complicated."

"It can be challenging," I admitted.

"Does that mean you and Doctor Shah are together, too?"

"No." How many times was I going to have to answer that question? I was half-tempted to make a brochure I could hand out.

"There's this kid at camp, Terry, who's always talking about sex. He's been hitting on me and the other girls from day one. Like if he's persistent enough, if he cracks enough jokes or gives me enough compliments about my hair, one of us will let him into our pants." She pushed her braids back, then shook her head in annoyance. "If he keeps it up, I'm gonna make him fall in love with a groundhog."

Lena and Nidhi returned before I could come up with a response to that. Nidhi carried a handful of purple clover.

"Perfect," said Jeneta. "Clear a spot by the tree and spread them on the ground."

Lena examined her garden, no doubt studying both the plants on the surface and the roots of her oak below. She finally uprooted four cornstalks and moved them to the side of the garden. The roots immediately began to burrow back into the earth. Nidhi arranged the clover in a small mound.

Jeneta waved us back and began to read.

> "There is a flower that Bees prefer—
> And Butterflies—desire—
> To gain the Purple Democrat
> The Humming Bird—aspire."

It was as if she had transformed into another person. Her voice was slower, more confident, and the cockiness that normally infused her words disappeared. When I looked at the clover, the flowers seemed brighter. The scent was stronger, overpowering the roses until my eyes watered.

> "And Whatsoever Insect pass—
> A Honey bear away
> Proportioned to his several dearth
> And her—capacity."

"Whatever you're doing, they're reacting to it." Lena swallowed, and I could see her skin twitching. Smudge's cage turned into a miniature lantern as a ripple of flame spread across his back.

I double-checked my book, a novel by David Gerrold that featured a liquid nitrogen weapon. The gun itself was too large to pull through the pages, but I should be able to use the same trick I had tried with the microwave. I skimmed a scene which described the weapon in action. I didn't need the gun, just the stream of liquid nitrogen. Hopefully I could do this without freezing my fingers off.

The first insect emerged from the tree in a puff of sawdust, about ten feet up. Lena raised her bokken. I took a deep breath and readied my book. This appeared to be a bee or wasp of some sort. It crawled down the tree, glassy wings twitching, then flew toward the clover.

> "Her face be rounder than the Moon
> And ruddier than the Gown."

Lena's own rounded features were tight with pain. A second bee flew out of the oak, following the first. Lena gripped her weapon by the blade and smashed the pommel down on the closest bee. She gave it a vicious twist, and when she pulled back, only broken scraps of metal remained.

Other insects were making their way out of the tree now. I stepped back, book ready, but they didn't care about us. They were drawn to the clover, entranced by the power of Jeneta's words.

"Thank you," Lena whispered. She stepped closer to the oak and pressed her face against the wood. Her eyes closed, and her fingertips sank into the tree. Her hair wisped forward, clinging to the bark as if static held it in place.

I waited to make sure no more insects would emerge, then aimed the book at the flowers. I dared to hope this might be as simple as it appeared . . . thus proving that even after close to a decade with the Porters, I still hadn't learned from experience.

The instant I touched the book's magic, the bugs went berserk. They rose from the pile of clover as frigid air poured forth, and liquid nitrogen splashed into thick white fog. A brass-and-steel grasshopper leaped out of the cloud, wings a blur as it flew toward Jeneta. Lena spun from her oak and snatched up her bokken. She knocked the grasshopper back like a tiny baseball, but more were emerging from the fog, stunned but not yet dead.

Jeneta screamed. A metal earwig had landed on her e-reader. She flung it away. More insects clung to the screen, digging through glass and plastic as easily as clay. Nidhi grabbed Jeneta's arm and hauled her out of the garden.

"Whatever works," I muttered, aiming the book at Jeneta's reader. Two more metal bugs had joined the earwig on the screen. When the next stream of nitrogen cleared, they looked like tiny frost sculptures. They shattered beneath my shoe, as did the e-reader.

I poured more liquid nitrogen onto the clover, then closed the book while Lena destroyed the rest of the insects. Plants and bugs alike crunched beneath her feet.

"Is that all of them?" I asked.

"Yes. Thank you." Lena stepped back and sagged against her tree. "Do you think whoever did this will send more?"

"Probably."

Jeneta was crying like a child half her age. Nidhi sat with her in the grass, whispering and running her hands through Jeneta's hair while they rocked back and forth. Jeneta buried her head in Nidhi's shoulder.

"What happened?" I asked. "Was she hurt?"

Before Nidhi could answer, Jeneta jumped to her feet and ran at me. "Why in the name of ever-loving God would you do that to me?" Her fists slammed into my chest, hard enough to bruise. "Was this some kind of messed-up test? Is *this* why you were asking about my nightmares?"

I stepped back and did my best to fend off her punches. "Jeneta, I didn't know they'd come after your e-reader."

She wiped her sleeve over her eyes and stared at me. "You think I'm upset about my *reader*?"

I looked past her to Nidhi, but she appeared to be as confused as I was. Nidhi stepped closer, hands out like she was approaching a wild animal, and said, "Can you tell us what happened to you, Jeneta?"

"You said you needed me to help kill magic bugs. You never said they were devourers."

It was like she had turned the liquid nitrogen on me, chilling my body from the inside out. "What do you mean?"

She swallowed. "You didn't hear them?"

"What is it you heard, Jeneta?" Nidhi asked.

"They weren't attacking my reader. They were trying to attack *me*, through the spell." She started to shiver again. "Dragging me under. Climbing through my bones and chewing me up, and all the while she's laughing—"

"She?" I asked sharply.

"I heard a girl laughing." She stared at me. "It might have been me. I was losing my mind, Isaac. I could feel myself going mad, losing my grip and slipping away."

"I didn't know. I'm so sorry. I never would have asked you to fight them like that." Devourers infesting Victor Harrison's experiment. A butchered wendigo and a man who could hide from my magic. What the hell was going on?

Jeneta folded her arms, visibly working to stuff the fear back into its bravado-lined cell. "You owe me a new e-reader. Don't even think about trying to pass off some secondhand clunker from last year. I want the newest model, and I want an orange case to go with it."

"Fair enough."

Jeneta looked at the fog rising off the crushed bugs and flowers. "What are they doing here?"

I didn't have an answer. I didn't even know what they were.

"Why do they hate us?" Jeneta asked. "Not just people in general. You and me. They know us, and they're going to keep coming after us until we're dead."

"If they come after anyone, it should be me. I'm the one who pissed them off earlier this year." With Lena's help, I had destroyed their . . . host, for lack of a better word. If the devourers were capable of remembering, then they had good reason for coming after me or Lena, but why target a teenaged girl who knew next to nothing about magic? "Nidhi, could you take Jeneta to your place?"

"Of course."

Jeneta said nothing, but her body sagged with relief. I doubted any of us would sleep well tonight, but she'd be somewhere safe, with a woman who knew how to deal with magic-induced trauma.

"I'll watch over Lena's tree," I said. "Could you reschedule any appointments you have tomorrow? We need to take a road trip."

Nidhi folded her arms. "Nobody has the energy for dramatic lead-ups tonight, Isaac. Get to the point."

"Sorry. We're going to check out Victor Harrison's old

house in Columbus, Ohio. I'll need to call Deb De-George down in Detroit first."

Jeneta perked up slightly. "The vampire?"

"How did you know that?" Deb had been a libriomancer, and until recently, a good friend. Three months ago, the vampires in Detroit had turned her, hoping to use her as a spy within the Porters. When Gutenberg caught up with her, I had fully expected him to burn her to ash on the spot. Instead, he had begun using Deb as a liaison between Porters and vampires.

"The right poem can make people babble about all sorts of things," Jeneta said sheepishly. "It was after the Porters found me. They sent a field agent to give me the Orientation to Magic lecture. I wanted the advanced course, and it's possible I might have 'encouraged' her to talk about more than she was supposed to."

I waved a hand. "Deb's not technically a vampire, but yes. The important thing is that she's scared of Gutenberg. Hopefully scared enough to cooperate with just about anything we ask for."

"And you're planning to ask for . . . ?" Nidhi said impatiently.

"I'm hoping they'll be able to help us talk to Victor."

Chapter 6

The glares began the day Frank brought me home. The whispered insults followed soon after. Tramp. Bitch. Slut. Freak. Over time, the whispers grew louder. Marion Dearing followed me into the woods one night, but I was faster. I vanished into my oak, laughing at our game as I left her wandering lost among the trees in the cold and the dark.

She tried to kill me two days after I made love to her husband for the first time. I was working in the chicken coop, an oversized jar of Vaseline in one hand. There was supposed to be a snowstorm that night, and I was coating the combs, feet, and wattles of each bird to help prevent frostbite.

I had heard Marion and Frank yelling after dinner. I had never understood why she hated me. I don't think I even realized she hated me, any more than I realized how much Frank and I had hurt her. We belonged to Frank, and we each worked to make him happy. I smiled, remembering the weight of his body atop mine.

"What are you?"

I jumped, dropping the Vaseline. I broke the jar's fall with my foot before it hit the floor. "Hello, Marion. I didn't hear you."

Marion might have been pretty once, a long time ago. She was heavier than I was, with thin gray-brown hair and a perpetual frown. Wrinkles spread like cracks from her eyes and the corners of her mouth. Her skin was spotted from age, and she dressed in a way that hid her body, making her look like a misshapen sack. She was strong, though. Those thick hands could kill and dress a chicken or birth a calf.

Her eyes were red. She clutched a thick book in one hand, a Bible with a gold cross embossed on the cover. "You're not human. Where the hell did you come from?"

"I don't remember," I said automatically.

She snorted and stepped closer. "Wandering naked and lost in the woods, with no memory where you'd been. Did the devil send you to us?"

I shook my head. "Why would you ask—"

"I know what you are. Sent to prey on the weakness of men. To seduce and corrupt them. I won't let you have him."

"But he wants me." I was simply being honest. I didn't mean to hurt her, but the truth of my words struck her harder than any physical blow.

She lunged forward, and her balled fist crashed into my jaw. I staggered against the cages. "Get out of my home, you whore!"

The blows didn't hurt as much as I had expected. I raised my arms to protect my face. The next time she swung, I caught her by the wrist and tossed her away as easily as I flung bales of hay for the cows.

Marion bounced to her feet, the Bible forgotten on the

wooden floor. Blood welled from scrapes on her face. She wiped her nose on the sleeve of her jacket. Fear flickered past her anger: a quickening of her breath, a widening of her eyes.

I shivered with anticipation. I was enjoying this, almost as much as I had enjoyed making love to Frank. Her fist cracked against my jaw, and my heart pounded harder. I laughed and slapped her arm aside.

She stepped back. "What are you?"

I was too far gone to answer. I buried the ball of my foot in her stomach, kicking her so hard she retched. She crawled away and seized the hoe we used to clean the bottom of the coop. She thrust the end at my face, then swung the blade down. I twitched my foot out of the way, and the hoe gouged the floor.

She attacked again, more confident now. I allowed her to drive me back, then sidestepped, snatching the hoe with one hand. As my fingers curled around the old wood, I felt . . . a memory was the closest word I could find to describe it. An ash tree standing in the sun, roots gripping a grassy hillside. The ash that had been cut down and shaped into this tool.

The handle of the hoe reacted to my touch. Roots sprouted from the end, twining around Marion's hand. She screamed and pulled away, but the roots bound her fingers.

I imagined Frank standing over us, watching us battle for his affection. Seeing proof of how much we loved him. Joy suffused my blood. My delighted laughter filled the barn, and I twisted the handle until the bones of Marion's hand snapped like old sticks in winter.

ONCE NIDHI AND JENETA had left, I returned to the house long enough to change into warmer clothes and fetch my sleeping bag from the closet. Even in August, the U.P. could get chilly at night. I stopped in the kitchen and searched the refrigerator, but nothing looked appetizing. I settled for grabbing a handful of vitamins, which I washed down with a Sprite. Even that was enough to make me queasy, but I clenched my stomach until the surges of nausea passed.

I tacked a makeshift curtain over the broken door, then picked a handful of books from the library and a small reading light, slung my laptop case over my shoulder, and returned to the garden. Attempting more magic so soon would be madness—literally, if I wasn't careful—but I couldn't stop thinking. Our enemy knew Lena's tree, and that meant she was vulnerable. She had survived the loss of her tree before, but while she had never spoken much about the experience, I got the sense it had come closer to killing her than she wanted to admit.

She had transferred herself into this oak. Perhaps it would be wise to do so again, to find a tree deep in the woods that nobody knew about. But would that be enough? The insects had found her here. If they could sniff out the magic of her tree, what was to stop them from tracking her down no matter where she went?

Better to defend her tree, strengthen it against attack. There were plenty of books that described magical fertilizers and spells to empower plants. With the right combination, I could grow Lena's oak as tall and strong as Jack's beanstalk. Though given the end of Jack's tale, perhaps that wasn't the best plan.

Or I could grow Lena a new tree. Did she have to live within an oak? I could grow a whomping willow from Harry Potter, giving her tree the ability to defend itself.

No, Gutenberg had locked Rowling's work. Perhaps one of the ent knockoffs from various fantasy tales, a tree with the ability to uproot itself and move about.

What would happen if I planted Yggdrasil, the world tree from Norse mythology? I doubted such a seed would fit through the pages of a book, but if I could break off even the smallest twig for Lena to graft to her oak . . .

"Right," I muttered to myself. "Because nobody would notice an enormous tree growing miles into the sky." The roots would probably devour most of Copper River. I tried to imagine how much water a tree like that would consume. It could drain half of the Great Lakes, killing off most of the surrounding vegetation in the process.

I set the book aside, jumped up, and paced the length of the garden, doing my best to avoid stepping on the plants. At the rate the pumpkins were growing, we were going to have some amazing jack o'lanterns for Halloween.

What if Lena grafted branches from her oak onto multiple trees? Would spreading herself in such a way help to protect her from attack, or would it splinter her mind?

My thoughts were scampering about with all the frantic energy of Smudge in a rainstorm. I hadn't even begun to consider what Jeneta had done tonight. Why had my magic set things off like a rock to a wasp nest when hers merely lulled them to the flowers? I had watched her work with e-books and print alike, and as far as I could see, there was nothing unusual about her process.

I stopped in mid-step. I had been assuming it was something she was doing, a technique others could learn and master to take advantage of electronic books. What if, instead, it was something inherent in her? What if she was simply more powerful? True sorcerers could shape magic with their minds alone, and if she did possess that kind of power, it might explain why the devourers were drawn to her.

I forced myself to sit down, but couldn't stop my legs from bouncing to an unheard beat. A bad case of post-magic twitchiness was essentially Restless Leg Syndrome for the whole body. Perhaps pleasure reading wasn't the safest idea tonight. After ripping into so many books to-day, the barriers between myself and these books was dangerously thin.

Deb DeGeorge liked to describe spellcasting as shoot-ing holes in a beer keg filled with magic. Shoot a single bullet through the keg, and you can fill your cup from a steady stream. Fire a few more, and the magic starts flow-ing faster than you can keep up with it. Blast the whole thing with a shotgun, and you end up soaked in the stuff.

It was an elegant trap, one which had claimed the san-ity of many libriomancers over the years. As you ex-hausted yourself physically and mentally, your judgment eroded as well, leading you to make mistakes when you could least afford them.

Sleep was the best cure. Naturally, insomnia was a common side effect of magic use. As much as I loved be-ing a libriomancer, sometimes magic was a pain in the ass.

I set my books aside, powered up the laptop, and be-gan filling out a requisition form for my shock-gun. Por-ters were supposed to avoid carrying magical artifacts around long-term, but I thought the circumstances justi-fied keeping the gun until this was over.

My cell phone went off before I could finish. I glanced at the screen and swore. A call from Jeff DeYoung at this time of night couldn't mean anything good.

He wasted no time on niceties, and his terseness confirmed my sick sense of foreboding. "We've got another dead wendigo. Right around the same area. I think this might have been the first one's mate, come to see what happened. Two weres heard the noise and interrupted the son of a bitch, but it was too late to save the wendigo."

I straightened. "Did they see him? Were they able to track where he went?"

"Laci didn't see shit," Jeff snapped. "And Hunter died before we could get him to the hospital."

"I'm—" I bit back the word "sorry." A werewolf wouldn't appreciate empty words. "I can drive out with a healing potion."

"Laci's got a thick head. She'll be okay. She and Hunter had snuck off for a late-night romp, and weren't expecting anyone to try to kill them. They found the body, then something attacked them from behind. Whatever it was, he was strong. Tossed Laci into a tree, and clubbed Hunter hard enough to crack the boy's skull."

I hadn't seen anything to suggest superhuman strength in either of the two figures who had killed the first wendigo.

"What the hell is wrong with these kids?" Jeff continued. "There's no excuse for letting yourself get caught unaware, I don't care how horny you are."

"Did Laci notice any insects by the body? They would have been metal."

"Not that she mentioned, but I'll check when she wakes up." He sighed. "How are you and Lena doing? Neither one of you looked to be in great shape this evening."

"I think whoever killed those wendigos tried to take out Lena's tree. We dealt with it, but she's pretty wiped."

"Any idea who or what we're looking for?" There was a hunger to his words, an eagerness that made me nervous.

"We're working on a few things," I said carefully.

"Bad enough to kill those white-furred cannibals in our territory, but now they've killed one of our pack. That makes it personal. You Porters can do whatever you'd like, so long as you stay the hell out of our way."

Vigilante werewolves. Just what we needed. "Jeff, this guy tore up two wendigos, tossed a pair of werewolves around like dolls, and has magic I've never seen before." Not to mention the devourers. "This is a bad idea."

"He jumped a pair of dumb kids who weren't expecting trouble. We've hunted these woods for generations. We'll find the bastards."

"Or they'll find you." I had no idea how many insects Victor had made. I imagined metal hives hidden in the trees, a cloud of magical bugs descending upon the werewolves.

"Let 'em."

"You don't even know what you're hunting."

"What in God's name am I supposed to tell Hunter's family, Isaac? Not only are we burying one of our own, now you want us to lock the doors and sit around with our thumbs up our asses, hoping nobody else gets killed while we wait for you Porters to do your thing? All your magic has done so far is show us a shitty snuff film and knock you on your ass."

I hated werewolf-style negotiation. "First of all, bite me," I said. "Second, this is *my* investigation. One of your pack is dead, and that gives you the right to be involved, but you work with me. Be here tomorrow at nine A.M. We're driving down to Ohio to investigate a lead."

"What lead?" Jeff snarled.

"Do we have a deal?" When he hesitated, I added, "If these things are half as dangerous as I think they are, you do *not* want them coming after Tamarack. I'm going to find whoever did this, Jeff. Either be here tomorrow morning, or else stay the hell out of my way."

When Jeff finally spoke again, he sounded almost cheerful. "Nine o'clock, you said?"

"See you tomorrow."

As long as I was worked up, I went ahead and called Deb to arrange a deal with the vampires. By the time I got off the phone, it was almost two in the morning. I shut down the laptop and bundled it and the books into a plastic garbage bag for protection, crawled into the sleeping bag, and settled against the base of the oak.

Lena retained some awareness of what happened outside her tree, though I wasn't sure how much. But she would know I was here, and that was enough.

I awoke with a stiff neck, sore back, and Lena looking down at me with a crooked smile. She showed no sign of pain or weariness from yesterday. Lucky dryad.

"I need a shower and a change of clothes," she announced, grabbing my hand and hauling me to my feet. "And so do you."

The shower took a bit longer than usual, but it was certainly rejuvenating. By the time we emerged and dressed, I felt almost human again. I filled her in on the call from Jeff, then checked my messages to make sure everything was set for today.

In exchange for helping us talk to Victor, the vampires wanted either a Shipstone—a battery from Heinlein's work that would power their underground lighting needs for a century—or an official apology from Gutenberg for the incident in Detroit. A message from Nicola Pallas confirmed that the Shipstone was the more feasible choice, and authorized me to take care of it when we finished in Ohio.

My biggest concern was that the vampires would try to turn the Shipstone into some kind of weapon, but if they were foolish enough to try, they would most likely just blow themselves up. I had stressed that fact repeatedly to Deb on the phone. Even if they succeeded, Gutenberg's automatons should be able to deal with any magic-fueled weapon.

Both Jeff and Nidhi arrived as I was restocking my books. In addition to my book bag, I had retrieved a brown leather duster from the hall closet. I had lost my old jacket during the troubles earlier this year, but in at least one respect, the new one was even better. This one was fireproof.

"How's Jeneta doing this morning?" I asked as I shoved books into the various pockets sewn into the lining, trying to plan out the tools and toys I might need.

"Frightened and trying not to let it show. She spent the first hour curled up on the couch, teasing Akha with her braids."

"Sounds like she was in good company." If anyone could help Jeneta to relax, it was Nidhi's cat. Akha was, in Lena's words, a total attention-slut. She would curl up in your lap and purr until she drooled.

"Will she be safe at that camp?"

"Safer than she'd be with us. Her e-reader was destroyed, and as long as she doesn't do any more magic, there's nothing to attract attention." I tucked my microrecorder into a front pocket to make sure we could review everything we learned. It wouldn't be a bad idea to bring along a few potential weapons that would work against the undead, just in case. "She has Nicola's number as well as mine."

Nidhi watched me prepare. "Jeneta was exhausted, but she looked better than you do."

"Sleeping outside isn't as much fun as it used to be." I double-checked the safety on the shock-gun, switched it to setting four, and slid it into an outside pocket. I also grabbed books that would allow us to avoid attention and persuade any bystanders to cooperate. The final pocket got a box of Red Hots for Smudge.

Nidhi stepped away to greet Lena, leaving me with Jeff. An old-style Bowie knife was strapped to his belt, and he had holstered a revolver on his opposite hip. I doubted either was legal. Werewolves tended not to worry overmuch about things like laws or permits.

"Nidhi filled me in on those metal bugs," he said bluntly. "She also tells me we're going to talk to the ghost of the guy who made them."

"That doesn't mean one of us is behind this."

"Maybe. Maybe not. Either way, it was your man who put the weapon in their hands."

I transferred Smudge into his traveling cage, a thin rectangular box with steel mesh walls, which I clipped to a loop on the outside of my jacket. "If someone kills you, takes your knife, and stabs the first person they see, who's responsible?"

Jeff tightened a fist, deliberately cracking several knuckles. "A man chooses to carry a weapon, he'd damn well better be strong enough to stop anyone from taking it away from him."

That was when the curtain I had hung over the back door flew aside, and a rush of air passed between Jeff and myself. Jeff staggered back, and a young man in a black trench coat seemed to materialize out of nothingness, perched on the edge of the kitchen counter like a gargoyle with a predilection for goth fashion. He held Jeff's gun in one hand, the Bowie knife in the other.

Jeff's upper lip curled back, and he snarled, an incongruously deep-throated sound for a man his apparent age. Lena pulled both of her bokken and started forward.

"You must be Moon," I said hastily, trying to defuse things before they wrecked my place and each other.

"Sorry, man. I heard you two talking, and I couldn't resist." Moon twirled the knife and grinned, black-lined lips pulling back to reveal perfect teeth.

"He's the other part of my arrangement with the vampires," I explained. "He's Sanguinarius Meyerii. A sparkler. He'll be guarding the house while we're away."

"Moon?" Jeff's voice remained an octave lower than usual.

Moon laughed. "Weird name, I know. My parents were old-fashioned Ann Arbor hippies. You should have met my sister, Starshine."

"The weapons?" I said.

"Right." He handed the knife and gun back to Jeff, then brushed off his coat. He wore a black kilt and a heavy metal T-shirt underneath. "No hard feelings, old man?"

"This is who they sent? A child half stoned out of his mind?" Jeff sniffed derisively. "I can smell the pot on his breath."

"Only because I need ten times as much as I used to," he complained. "Do you have any idea how long it takes to prep that stuff? First I've got to brew it into blood tea just so I can metabolize it, and by then you've boiled off half its potency. Not to mention the work I had to do to find an anticoagulant that didn't taste like filtered diarrhea. And then the stuff barely gives me a buzz. I just drink it to take the edge off the day, you know?" He winked at Jeff. "You look like you could use a hit your-self, gramps."

"Not today," I said, cutting in before they could go any further. "Moon, I'm not sure how much they told you downstate, but the people we're hunting killed a werewolf last night and sent another to the hospital."

"Shit." Moon sobered at once. "Sorry, man. I didn't know."

"Just keep an eye on the place. Call me if anything happens."

Moon gave me a two-fingered salute. "Cub Scout's honor."

Having spent six years in scouting as a kid, somehow that didn't make me feel better.

I spent much of the drive asleep in the back of Nidhi's car. I awoke with my mouth dry and my shoulder damp from drool. Wind swirled through Jeff's open window, and a Hindi pop song was playing softly on the satellite radio.

I rubbed my eyes, then wiped my face on my sleeve. It was strange not being able to understand the words of the song. Normally, the telepathic fish in my head, cour-tesy of Douglas Adams' *Hitchhiker's Guide to the Gal-axy*, translated other languages automatically. But there was no mind in this case, no thoughts for the fish to latch onto. Just cold, dead electronics.

"Where are we?" I asked.

"We'll be leaving Michigan in about fifteen minutes," said Nidhi.

According to the dashboard clock, I had slept well into the afternoon. On the bright side, I had missed crossing the Mackinac Bridge. Strange how that bridge—particularly the fear of plummeting *off* of that bridge—disturbed me more than the idea of meeting up with vampires to talk to a dead man.

I checked the back window and spotted Lena following on her motorcycle. She could have joined us in the car, but had chosen to let me sprawl out and nap in the back seat. Or maybe she just wanted an excuse to ride the bike. Though the idea of taking that thing over the bridge would have given me nightmares.

Nidhi turned down the volume. "We picked up lunch for you."

Wordlessly, Jeff passed a paper sack into the back seat. Neither cold fries nor the greasy burger smelled the least bit appealing, but I managed to force them down without puking, which was a good sign. Between the food and the sleep, by the time we reached Columbus, I felt almost human.

We made our way around the edge of the city to a street with a row of brown townhouses on one side and a public park on the other. The houses looked identical to me, but Nidhi didn't hesitate. As far as I knew, she had been here only once before, when she was called down to help the Porters examine the scene of Victor's death.

A blue minivan with a dented door sat in the driveway, and a sedan with dark-tinted windows was parked across the street. We pulled in behind the sedan. I heard the growling of Lena's bike as she parked behind us. For one very tense moment, I thought the sound had come from Jeff.

I grabbed Smudge's traveling cage, slipped on my jacket, and waited for Nidhi to pop the trunk so I could fetch my book bag as well. I didn't need a fire-spider to know what was in that sedan. My gut churned with the instinctive need to flee. The smell of death and rot fouled the air as we approached.

Deb DeGeorge was first out of the car. While not a true vampire, she was no longer human, either. She was Muscavore Wallacea, a so-called child of Renfield. Like the character from Stoker's novel, she consumed the lives of smaller creatures, which made her stronger. Faster. Better. A magical six-million-dollar, bug-eating woman.

She looked like hell.

Deb had lost at least twenty pounds since the last time I saw her, accentuating the bones of her skull and face. Her skin was pale, and her short hair was noticeably thinner. Her bloodshot eyes flitted toward Smudge.

I reached into the pocket with my shock-gun. "Don't even think about it."

"I wouldn't dream of hurting Smudge!" she protested, but I could see the hunger in her eyes. She barely noticed my companions. By now, her condition would have stripped her of her own magical abilities, but if she wanted to, she could rip open Smudge's cage and snatch him away before I could move. Which was, no doubt, why red flame had begun to ripple over Smudge's body.

Deb sighed. "Hon, if the two of you are this jumpy around me, you're really not going to like Nicholas."

I retreated a step as she opened the back door of the sedan. Three more vampires emerged. Two guards gripped the arms of the third, a handcuffed figure with a heavy blanket cloaking his head and upper body.

One guard, a woman built like a snowplow, had a set of sharpened wooden stakes strapped to her thigh. Her choice of weapon meant Nicholas was one of the vampires who could be killed by wooden stakes, and in all likelihood, she wasn't. The second guard was smaller, almost classically nerdy, save for the semiautomatic rifle slung over his shoulder. His ears were slightly pointed, and the lumpy bone structure of his face made his condition obvious to anyone who knew what to look for. His tortoiseshell glasses perched on a lump at the bridge of his nose.

Deb nodded to both in turn. "Sarah and Rook have the pleasure of being Nicholas' keepers today."

Either of them could probably kill me between one heartbeat and the next, but it was Nicholas who made me want to get back in Nidhi's car and put a few hundred miles between us. Beneath the hood of his blanket, he made Deb look positively healthy. Yellow-and-purple blotches covered his white skin like bruises. His lips made me think of bloated purple leeches, and his limp brown hair hung past his eyes like greasy seaweed.

Smudge was a tiny furnace in his cage, glowing like an eight-legged coal in a barbeque. I saw Lena's grip tighten around her bokken. A low growl emerged from Jeff's throat. I don't know if he was even aware of it.

Blood oozed from cracks in Nicolas' lips as he smiled, revealing incongruously white teeth, clean and straight and perfect. I got the sense that he not only knew exactly how he was making the rest of us feel, he was enjoying it.

"This is the ghost-talker?" I asked.

"Strongest one in the Midwest," Deb confirmed. "They've got a prettier one down in Dallas, but you said you were in a hurry."

Nicholas stepped toward me, dragging his guards like a dog straining at the leash. Up close, his breath smelled of rotted meat. A silver chain was locked around his neck like a collar, and a smoldering wooden cross hung over his flannel shirt. Both guards clutched him by the arms, their fingers digging deeply enough to make a mortal man scream in pain.

I had been hoping for a nice Sanguinarius Meadus from the *Vampire Academy* novels. I had no idea what species Nicholas was. Possibly an experiment, fed and transfused with blood from other species, mutated into a tool and a weapon.

Over the centuries, vampires had deliberately worked to preserve as many subspecies as possible. Even the most monstrous and dangerous were kept around, locked away from "civilized" vampire society on the off chance their powers might one day be needed. I wondered how long it had been since Nicholas had seen the sun, or been given any kind of freedom.

"You think we should head inside before someone calls the cops?" Lena suggested.

"Nobody will call the police," said the woman with the stakes, her voice low and dreamlike. "The neighbors will pay no attention, and the family inside is sleeping."

"How long have you held them in a trance?" asked Nidhi. "Did you check to make sure they were okay?"

Sarah's face crinkled in confusion.

"They should be fine," I said softly. "I read that research paper, too. 'In the first twenty-four hours, side effects of magically induced sleep were rare. Of the observed effects, the most common was bedwetting.' Better that the family has to do an extra load of laundry than someone starts taking potshots at us for breaking and entering."

"When did you read that?" Nidhi asked.

"At dinner last week. You were making enchiladas. You had the papers on your coffee table." I gave her a halfhearted shrug. The study had been done four years ago by a pair of Porter researchers, a continuation of a project started in Hungary. "I see words, I read them."

"Then you know one person in that study ended up in a coma for a week."

"And the longer we argue about this, the longer those people stay asleep." Deb pulled a tin from her back pocket, popped the lid, and snatched a live snail from inside. She crunched it down, shell and all. When she noticed me staring, she extended the tin and grinned. "Help yourself."

I grimaced, and my stomach threatened to evict my lunch. Deb just laughed and shoved the snails back into her pocket.

She had been a friend once. I wasn't sure what we were now. Her laugh was sharper, honed by bitterness and cruelty. The last time she was at my house, she tried to kill me with a Tommy gun, but she had the decency to feel bad about it afterward.

"Do you miss it?" I asked as we walked up the driveway. "Being human?"

She sighed, knowing exactly what I wasn't asking. *Do you miss the magic?* "As long as I stay fed, I feel stronger and healthier than I ever have. Don't let the skin condition fool you. And there are plenty of other advantages." She cocked her head and gave me an appraising stare. "You might even appreciate the lifestyle."

Give up magic and start a lifelong diet that would make a Klingon puke? "I don't think so."

She smiled slightly. "Isaac, do you remember the moment you first realized you were mortal? That no matter what happened, you would never live long enough to read every book you wanted to read? That you'd die having accomplished only a fraction of your goals?"

I had been eighteen and fresh out of high school. Ray Walker had taken me to New York to meet with a Porter who worked for one of the big publishers. It was the first time I truly understood just how many books a single publisher put out every year.

I had known intellectually that nobody could ever hope to read or learn everything, but that was the moment I did the math and started to understand how many books there were in the world, and how many more were being written every day. For every book I explored, there were literally hundreds I would never have the chance to know. Likewise, for each bit of magic I mastered, an infinite number of possibilities went unexplored.

"What would you give for an extra century?" Deb asked, giving me a knowing look. "Time to read and learn twice as much as you could in this life?"

Trade my magic for greater knowledge. "Is that how they convinced you to let them turn you?"

"Let's just say their form of persuasion was more aggressive than mine." She chuckled bitterly and climbed the concrete steps to the front door. A wrought-iron railing bordered the small porch, and a sunflower-decorated sign welcomed us to the Sanchez home. Deb tried the doorknob, which was locked. She didn't appear to exert any effort, but the doorframe suddenly splintered inward. "There are other benefits, too."

The house smelled like dog fur and old Play-Doh. I stepped cautiously onto the brown plush carpet of a cramped family room. A thirty-something Hispanic man was asleep on the couch. A three-legged black Lab sprawled on the floor in front of him. On the TV, two New York cops interrogated a drug addict. A birdcage hung by the window. Inside, a blue-and-white parakeet lay with his head in his seed dish.

It was creepy.

Nicholas doffed his blanket and strode through the room, pulling the rest of us in his wake. He moved so smoothly he appeared to float over the floor. He stopped abruptly, reaching out to touch a patch of wall on the arched entryway that connected the family room to the kitchen. "Victor Harrison," he murmured, as if to himself. "He was afraid."

I bit back an unexpected surge of anger. Victor had been afraid because a gang of vampires had broken into his home to kill him. Fresh paint and new carpeting hid the signs of violence, but they couldn't erase what had happened here. I wondered how much the Sanchez family knew about the former owner. "Can you talk to him?"

"Given time," Nicholas said lazily.

On another day, I would have been fascinated to study a ghost-talker's magic up close. Some of the bitterest feuds among Porter researchers revolved around the matter of ghosts. There was no question that, in certain cases, *something* lingered on after death ... but was it truly the spirit of the departed?

One school of thought argued that ghosts were nothing but memories given form by survivors. Living humans created ghosts through the mourning process, much as readers provided the belief libriomancers used for our magic. That theory had been mostly debunked, as there were documented cases of ghosts providing information the survivors shouldn't have known.

Others believed that people with magical powers of their own could leave behind an "impression" of themselves, a kind of magical shadow. Unfortunately, the research had never found any statistically significant correlation between reports of ghosts and magical ability.

And then there was the theory that so-called mediums actually used a form of temporal projection, mentally reaching backward through time to read the minds of the deceased before they died. Given what I had seen and done yesterday in the woods, this line of thought held possibilities.

"How much time?" I asked.

Nicholas waved a hand. His skin reminded me of mildew-damaged paper.

Jeff's upper lip curled back in distaste. "This place smells like blood, bleach, dog piss, and too many damn people."

"Do any of those people smell like the man from the woods?" Nidhi asked. "If Victor left something behind, anyone from this family might have found it."

"I can't say for sure in this form." From the front pocket of his jeans, Jeff tugged out a worn leather pouch. He picked at the knotted cord, then peeled back the pouch to reveal an object wrapped in black velvet. "Hold this."

It was heavy and oblong, solid as stone beneath the wrap. I started to peek beneath the layers.

"Not yet, dammit." Jeff finished unbuttoning his shirt and tossed it onto the floor. He kicked off his shoes, then unbuckled his belt. "The youngsters think it's cool to keep their clothes on for the change, to burst through the seams like they do in the movies. The shredded shirt and jeans look is always in style, but then they figure out that not only are their parents going to make them pay for a new wardrobe, but shapeshifting in your clothes *hurts*. You ever tried to rip a pair of jeans with your bare hands? I've seen kids howling in pain, stuck between forms and desperately chewing at their own crotch, trying to tear out a stuck zipper."

Age-spotted skin and tufts of white hair couldn't conceal the lean strength in his chest and arms. And legs, for that matter. He kicked his shoes and jeans aside and dropped to all fours. Blue boxer shorts followed next.

"You brought me a werewolf strip show?" Deb smirked. "But I didn't get you anything."

"Now, if you wouldn't mind," said Jeff.

I tugged the wrappings loose. Silver light shone from between the layers. I slid the rest free to reveal a long, gleaming crystal attached to a loop of black leather. "Jeff, is this what I think it is?"

"Yah." Black fur poked through Jeff's skin. The sound of popping bones and tearing muscle made me wince. His next words were low and gravelly. "Kristen Britain, I think."

"*Green Rider*, or one of the sequels. Dammit, Jeff, do you know how much trouble you could get in for this?" I was holding a moonstone. A muna'riel, to be precise. Britain's Eletians, essentially an elven race, collected the light of the silver moon in these stones. The purity of the muna'riel made it an exceptional lantern, and the light tended to be off-putting to evil, which might explain why Nicholas was scowling at me. "I thought these things only worked for Eletians. Though I suppose if you pulled it from a scene in which it was already lit, you might be able to lock it into that state . . ."

"Don't ask me. I never read the book."

I could barely understand his words anymore. I didn't ask him which libriomancer had reached into Britain's books to create the stone, nor what Jeff had paid for it. The Porters kept a close eye on black-market magic, but they couldn't catch everything.

Jeff snatched the crystal from me and looped it over his head. His fingers were curled and knotted. He was panting hard. Pointed teeth dug into his lip. He grabbed his hand and bent the fingers back with a grunt of pain. The knuckles cracked so loudly I thought he had broken his bones, and he gasped. He did the same to the other hand. His fingers finally shrank into furred, clawed toes.

"Damned arthritis." Whatever else he might have said was lost as he finished his transformation into a lean, black-furred wolf. He lowered his gray-dusted muzzle to the floor and sniffed. His lips peeled back in a low growl.

"Oh, cool," I said.

"What is it?" asked Lena.

"I can understand him." Jeff wasn't speaking a true language, but the fish in my head could pick up the thoughts behind his vocalizations. "He doesn't think the family was involved, but whoever killed those wendigos was here. The scent is too faint for it to be someone who lived here."

Jeff padded into the kitchen. Dirty dishes and pans filled the sink. Others were stacked in a wire rack to one side. A toddler and his mother slept at a round table, a half-eaten jar of applesauce between them. The toddler lay with his head on the tray, black hair full of food. Nidhi stroked the hair back from his face and used a napkin to wipe a chunk of applesauce from the side of his nose.

"One of ours died here," Nicholas said, brushing his fingertips over the edge of the sink. He breathed deeply, like he was sniffing a fine wine. "She cried out in pain and anger."

"Anyone else find this guy creepy as hell?" Lena asked in a low voice.

Nidhi, Deb, and I raised our hands. I glanced at Nicholas' guards. With a shrug, Sarah raised her hand as well.

I had read the reports of Victor's murder. He hadn't died without a fight. His home was well-protected, and his tricks had taken several of his would-be killers with him. A long footnote on page three had proposed several explanations for the pair of fangs found in the garbage disposal, and recommended destroying the disposal altogether rather than attempting to study its magic. I swallowed and turned away. "We need to talk to him."

"Patience, Isaac." Nicholas closed his eyes and inhaled. His smile grew. "The instinct to survive is so strong. Stronger than love. Stronger than fear. Threaten a man's life, and you push him to truly *live*."

"That's why you agreed to do this, isn't it?" Nidhi asked. "To remember what life feels like. To touch what you lost."

The skin at the corners of his eyes crinkled, and for a moment his smile flickered. The amusement snapped back into place an instant later, along with a dismissive sneer. "You expect me to mourn my lost humanity? To weep for the forgotten days when I scurried about as one of you, an insect scavenging in the dirt?"

Deb cleared her throat. "Dr. Shah, please don't play mind games with the sociopathic ghost-talker."

"Victor fought well," Nicholas said. "But he soon realized there were too many for him to defeat. That understanding broke his will. It marked the beginning of his death."

"We didn't bring you here to give you a peep show into Victor's last moments," I said tightly.

"No, you brought me because you need my help." Nicholas turned. "There are too many dead. I have to find the moment the life left his body. Only then will he speak to me." He scowled and crossed through the family room, then climbed the steps to the second floor. A narrow hallway separated two bedrooms on the left from the stairs and bathroom on the right. The right side of Nicholas' face twitched as he looked about, his eyes tightening as if he could see through the walls. A moment later, he relaxed. "Ah, yes. Victor retreated to his workshop."

Nicholas stepped down the hall and opened a door into a pink-painted bedroom. A rainbow-colored ceiling fan spun lazily overhead.

"Watch your step," said Lena.

A young girl had stripped the blankets and pillows from her bed, turning them into a makeshift fort. She lay sleeping, a yellow pony clutched in one hand. From the array of toys spread through the room, it looked like the Jedi and the My Little Ponies had been fighting an army of Barbies and LEGO figures.

"Victor kills two more vampires here," said Nicholas. "Metal creatures bore through the heart of the first, reducing him to ash, but Victor is injured. The life and will drain from his body with every step. Another vampire follows him into this room." Nicholas stepped to the side, as if clearing a path for the phantom assailant. "Victor snaps his fingers, and the overhead light flickers. The vampire's skin begins to sizzle."

"Ultraviolet bulbs," I guessed. They would have burned many species of vampire as effectively as sunlight. "Tell me about the metal creatures. How was Victor controlling them? Where did they come from, and how many were there?"

Nicholas ignored me. "Another enters through the window. His skin sparkles in the light. He smashes Victor into the wall. Pain and confusion flood Victor's senses. He is angry. Frightened. He isn't ready for death. There's so much yet to do."

"That sounds like Victor," Nidhi said quietly.

Nicholas whirled. *"Be silent!"*

Nidhi jumped. Both guards moved in, and Jeff's hackles rose, but I didn't think Nicholas was talking to us. His attention was elsewhere, and he sounded genuinely angry.

"What is it?" I asked.

"Death attracts death. The ghosts are pulled to this place. They clamor like children."

I looked to Deb, hoping she would know whether this was normal behavior or a sign that our ghost-talker was about to snap. She spread her hands and shrugged.

"Victor's thoughts tunnel inward." Nicholas' words grew louder. "Why him? Why now? He doesn't want to die alone."

"Enough ghouling." Deb swatted him on the back of the head like he was a misbehaving puppy. "Can you talk to the dead guy or not?"

"Yes," Nicholas said grudgingly.

"Ask him about the insects," I said.

Nicholas mumbled to himself, repeating the questions in another tongue. An old form of French, if I wasn't mistaken. "He reverse-engineered one of Gutenberg's automatons."

Deb was the first to recover her voice. "He did *what?*"

"It's all about miniaturization and user interface these days," Nicholas said. The intonation was Victor's. It was spooky. "Microscopic spells laser-etched onto the inner workings, telepathic interface, and as much memory and storage as I could give them."

"Why?" I asked.

"To search out lost and forgotten magic. I sent six prototype scouts into the world. One was eaten by a bass. Another was struck by a locomotive. Three survived to report back, sharing their findings with the queen, and through her, with me."

"A bass?" I thought back to the damage they had done to Lena's tree. "That shouldn't have stopped these things."

"I could have ordered it to work free, but that would have hurt the fish."

It was such a Victor thing to say, I couldn't help but smile. "What about the sixth?"

"Lost overseas." He shuddered, then stared blankly at the empty air where Victor had died.

"Tell us about the queen," I said.

Nicholas relayed the question. "A cicada, three inches long, with carbon fiber wings and a titanium exoskeleton. A redundant twin-chip brain. The eyes were tiny black pearls. She was magnificent, Isaac. I wish I'd been able to show her off. You would have loved her."

"The queen controls the other insects?" I asked.

"The song of the cicada can reach 120 decibels. My queen's commands are silent to our ears, but her children can hear her even from the far side of the world."

"What did you tell her as you were dying?" asked Nidhi.

Nicholas stepped back and seemed to come back to himself. "Victor cupped her in his hands." He brought his own hands together, mimicking Victor's final seconds. "Past and present flooded together as the barriers of memory crumbled. In his mind, he was a child once more. He was in pain, but didn't remember where it had come from. He knew only that he wanted comfort. Like a child, he called out."

"He wanted family," Nidhi whispered, her words clipped. Her hands tightened into fists.

"Yes," said Nicholas. "Victor sent the queen to fetch his father."

Chapter 7

Frank Dearing died in late autumn, after the trees had shed their leaves, but before the snow arrived to freeze the earth.

I was asleep in my oak when he died. The shock felt as though lightning had split my tree, blackening the exposed heartwood. I ran to the house as quickly as I could, but even before I reached the bedroom, I knew he was gone.

He looked little like the man I loved. His eyes were open, and his lips were pale and dry. He had been sleeping in red long johns, which smelled of urine. His upper body was bare, and the skin on his chest was unnaturally pale.

I scooped him into my arms. His limbs hung limp. Even his skin sagged loosely, emphasizing the bones beneath.

My thoughts were clouded as if I had been drinking, though I had spent much of the night in my oak, and time in my tree usually cleansed alcohol and its effects from my body. I didn't know what to do. I had no other friends, nor had I ever wanted or needed any. Frank was my world.

I acted on instinct, carrying him from the house. I wove

carefully through the trees, making sure not a single branch snagged my lover's hair or scratched his skin. I hated the coolness of his body against me. My tears dripped onto his chest.

When I reached my oak, my first impulse was to bring him into the tree with me and never emerge, but that felt wrong. Disrespectful and wasteful.

I knew human burial customs, but I couldn't let Frank be locked away in a box, buried forever in the earth while the ex-wife who had turned her back on him waited impatiently to scavenge through his belongings.

I rested him gently at the base of my tree and drew a blanket of leaves over his body. Only then did I retreat into my tree, where I could feel his weight pressing down on my roots.

This was proper. This was love and respect for the dead.

I reached deeper into the wood of my oak. The roots curled inward, digging through the cold, hard dirt to peel open the earth. Other roots eased Frank into the newly dug hole, curling around him like a blanket and sliding him closer to the taproot.

Frank and I had been together for so many years. I couldn't lose him. I wouldn't. His body would sustain my tree, becoming part of me and giving me the strength to survive his loss.

I MIGHT HAVE BEEN the only one in the room who understood Nidhi's curses, the Gujarati words she spat so quickly I could barely keep up.

"I don't understand," I said. "Victor's insects went to find his father. How do we get from that to killing wendigos and attacking Lena's tree?"

Nidhi watched the sleeping girl, her face unreadable. "Does your family know about your abilities, Isaac?"

I shook my head. "My brother walked in on me once while I was practicing pulling coins from *Treasure Island*, but I don't think he saw anything."

Deb's lips pursed like she had eaten something sour. "My family doesn't, but the Porters cost me a fiancé about fifteen years back."

"I didn't know that," I said.

"You don't know everything about me, hon."

"Victor's father is a monster." Nidhi turned to face us. "August Harrison beat his wife for years. That lasted until Victor was eleven years old. Two days after August broke his wife's nose, Victor was watching through the window as his father mowed the lawn. He enchanted the family car, which smashed through the garage door and tore across the yard. August tried to get away, but he wasn't fast enough. The car broke his femur. He spent more than a month in traction."

I gave a low, soft whistle. Victor had always seemed so pleasant and easygoing, with half his attention permanently lost in his work. "And that's the guy he wanted when he was dying?"

"Victor's mother died eight years ago," said Nidhi. "He had no siblings, no spouse. August Harrison was the only family he had left. And their relationship was ... complex."

Jeff snarled. "Doesn't sound complex to me. Rip the bastard's throat out and be done with it." I relayed his comment for the others.

"When August finally returned from the hospital, he acted like he had changed," Nidhi continued. "He apologized to his wife and son, and promised to make things better. Two days later, he took Victor out to dinner, bought him several new toys, and asked Victor to teach him magic."

"Power and control," Lena said softly.

"Exactly," said Nidhi. "August used violence to control his family, but that was only one tactic of many. He threatened Victor's mother to control his son, and threatened the son to control the mother. He kept tight rein over the finances and their social connections, making them dependent upon him for everything. Magic would have been one more weapon in his arsenal. And Victor was a child. He loved his father. For that reason, and because he thought it would appease August's temper, Victor tried to do as his father had asked."

"An eleven-year-old trying to teach a grown man magic?" That couldn't have ended well. Magical ability almost always manifested during childhood or adolescence. If August had the slightest potential for magic, it would have shown up long before then. Victor had been untrained. He wouldn't have known how he had controlled the car, let alone how to impart that understanding to others.

"He couldn't do it," Nidhi said. "Every failure enraged August further. He accused Victor of lying, of deliberately keeping his secrets to himself. He never again laid a finger on his wife, but he beat Victor three more times. The third time, Victor fought back."

"How?"

Her lips twitched. "Do you remember Teddy Ruxpin?"

"Sure. My grandparents got me one when I was a kid. Stupid thing gave me nightmares." I stopped when I realized where she was going with this. "Victor attacked his father with a talking teddy bear? All it did was move its eyes and mouth while it played cassette tapes."

"Not when Victor was done with it," Nidhi said. "That

teddy bear climbed onto the mantel, leaped out, and garroted August with a length of mint dental floss. They left him unconscious on the floor."

"Why would Victor reach out to *him*?" Lena shook her head in disbelief.

"Death is rarely rational," Nicholas said absently. He appeared far more interested in the dead than the living.

I couldn't hold Victor's dying mistake against him. I just hoped we would be able to fix that mistake before August Harrison did any further damage. "Why didn't the Porters wipe August's memories?"

"In the beginning, they didn't realize how much he had seen," said Nidhi. "Victor refused to talk about the abuse. His parents told the Porters they thought Victor had been playing in the car, and the whole thing was an unfortunate accident. As far as we knew, neither of them suspected anything magical. We didn't learn the truth until months later, when Victor told us how his father had cowed the family into silence. The Porters visited August Harrison and did their best to erase his knowledge."

"That obviously didn't work," I said bitterly.

"It did for a time." Nidhi sighed. "Victor was never as careful with magic as he should have been. Over the years, August must have seen enough to piece the truth back together."

My parents and I hadn't always gotten along, but I couldn't imagine growing up as Victor had. I knew he had done time as a field agent, but I had never been able to imagine him facing off against monsters or magic-wielders gone bad. Now I understood. Monsters wouldn't scare a man who had grown up with one.

"If August has no magic, how does he control the insects?" asked Lena.

"Nicholas—Victor—said something about a tele-pathic interface." August couldn't have built the insects, any more than he could have pulled my shock-gun from its book. But once I made that gun, anyone could point and shoot. Likewise, if the queen was telepathic, August didn't need magic. "We know he has the queen. Who was the libriomancer with him?"

"August Harrison had no friends among the Porters," Nidhi said. "The few people who knew of him felt nothing but contempt."

"What happens if the queen dies?" asked Deb. "Do the rest of the bugs drop dead, or do they freak out and go after anything that moves?" When nobody answered, she punched Nicholas on the shoulder. "That was your cue to ask the dead guy."

Nicholas scowled, but turned back toward the place where Victor had died. "Victor isn't certain what will happen if the queen is killed. Her loss would stop them from breeding or evolving, but—"

"Breeding?" Three of us spoke at once.

"Victor used a fractal matrix for the core spells, allow-ing the queen's magic to be passed on." His eyes crinkled with amusement. "The insects aren't the true danger. Victor says you should be more concerned about the knowledge they could hold. They were designed to inter-face with his personal computer network, to better share their findings."

I sat down on the undersized pink desk chair and stared at the wall where Victor's backup server had once sat. He had disguised the machine as a potted cactus. I remembered the first time I sensed the power coming from Victor's system, and his mischievous smile as he watched me try to figure out what I was looking at.

Jeff cocked his head and let out a sharp grunt, somewhere between a bark and a growl. Of us all, he was the only one who wouldn't understand the implications.

I had no idea what a fractal matrix was, but that was the least of our problems. "Victor Harrison designed most of the security for the Porter network." Anyone else who tried to hack our database would be lucky to survive in their natural shape, but if Victor had programmed his pets to avoid such traps, and if they had access to his system and software . . .

"August Harrison could have everything," Nidhi whispered. "Personnel records. Histories."

"Research reports." *My reports.* "Oh, God."

"What's wrong?" Lena asked.

I swallowed to keep from throwing up. In my mind, I was back in the woods, standing over the broken body of the murdered wendigo. My throat felt like it had turned to stone.

Lena touched my arm. "Isaac?"

"He wanted their skins," I whispered. "That's why August had to butcher them while they were alive. Wendigos revert to human form when they die, and he needed the monster. He wanted to take their power. Their strength."

"How do you know?" asked Lena.

"Because I wrote the paper explaining how to do it."

They were all staring at me. "Explain," Jeff snarled.

Eight years ago, I had never met a nonhuman. Ray had told me stories of vampires and werewolves, but they weren't *real*. Not yet. "This was when I first started training with Ray Walker down in East Lansing. We were talking about the nature of magical creatures."

I had come dangerously close to failing out of my first semester at MSU. I hadn't cared about my introductory courses. Why waste my time in a lecture hall when I could be studying magic? My textbooks sat unopened while I tore through magical theory and history. I skipped labwork in order to practice using my own powers.

"Libriomancy is an extrinsic magic. I use books to pull magic into myself before I can manipulate that magic. Werewolves and vampires use intrinsic magic. Your bodies use that energy automatically. You can't control the process any more than I can consciously manufacture white blood cells. We've known for centuries that intrinsic and extrinsic magic couldn't exist in the same person. It's why Deb lost her libriomancy when she changed."

"Get to the point," Deb said.

"Back in the 1920s, a group of Porters were searching for a way to use intrinsic magic without losing their other abilities. They ... they started by investigating werewolves."

Jeff's lips pulled back, and his hackles were up again.

"Werewolves show up in folktales throughout the world," I said. "Armenian stories talk of God punishing women by wrapping them in cursed wolf pelts. The women are human during the day, but monsters at night, murdering and feasting on their loved ones. Other cultures tell of skin-walkers, humans who take on the power of wolves and other beasts by donning their fur. The Úlfhednar of Norway dressed in wolfskins and were said to be all but unstoppable. Countless fairy tales talk of enchanted belts that transform the unsuspecting into monsters."

I was stalling, presenting background information instead of jumping to the heart of my confession. Nidhi knew it, too. I could tell from the crease between her eyebrows.

"They experimented to see if werewolf skins retained their magic, and if that intrinsic magic from ... from freshly harvested samples ... could be transferred to human beings."

Jeff lunged at me, but Lena moved just as fast. She kicked him in the side, and his jaws clacked shut, missing me by inches. Jeff's claws scraped the floor, but before he could recover, Lena was kneeling on his neck. She clutched her bokken in both hands, holding it like a quarterstaff, and ready to strike with either end.

"Their work wasn't sanctioned," I said. "When Gutenberg found out, he put an end to it." The researchers had been transferred to other regions. A slap on the wrist, considering what they had done.

"What did *you* do?" Jeff growled.

"Their experiments failed. The skins didn't preserve the magic long enough to be useful." When I read their papers eight years ago, I hadn't thought about werewolves. I had been too busy thinking about the possibilities. What if infusing people with magic could be as easy as applying a nicotine patch?

"You thought wendigo skins might work better," Lena said.

"Their results suggested a process of rapid magical and biological decay," I said miserably. "I thought the cold might slow or even stop that process."

Jeff had stopped struggling, but his ears were flat against his head.

"The Porters have ... samples ... from various species," I said. "I requisitioned—Ray helped me to order a patch of wendigo hide. About two square inches, packed in dry ice. We used rats from the pet store, shaving their fur and applying a tiny square. Two didn't respond at all, but the third showed increased strength and hostility. The changes lasted for several days."

"How do you collect these *samples*?" Jeff snarled.

"When a werewolf goes feral, the pack hunts him or her down. Other magical creatures aren't as self-regulating, so the Porters have to get involved." I stared through the window. "The bodies are brought back for study and disposal."

"You said wendigos revert to human form when they die," Lena said.

"I know." I couldn't look at her. "I suspect they put the wendigo into some kind of stasis. It wouldn't have felt anything."

It had all been so logical eight years ago. Only a handful of intrinsically magical creatures were sentient. Most were closer to animals. The more we could learn, the better we'd be able to manage them, even protect them when necessary.

How much of our work had August Harrison been able to access? He must have found Victor's notes, and he had obviously discovered my research papers. Had he been searching specifically for ways to gain power, or had he stumbled onto my reports by accident?

"Did you or anyone else proceed to human trials with wendigo skins?" Nidhi asked. Both her words and her expression were professionally neutral.

"Not that I know of." The vampires appeared non-plussed by my revelations, but then, I wasn't telling them anything they didn't know. Deb might not have been familiar with every one of my projects, but she knew the Porters' research practices, just as she knew our history was stained by those who occasionally traded ethics for results. No doubt she had shared everything with her new masters.

"Beat yourself up later," Lena snapped. "Jeff, I'm going to let you up now. I'd thank you to not rip out my lover's throat. Whatever those Porters did, they died years ago. Should I kill you because some other were-wolf murdered innocent people a hundred years ago?"

She eased back, and Jeff clambered to his feet. His fur hadn't flattened back out, but he didn't try to kill me.

Lena turned to Nicholas. "Ask Victor if there's another way to stop his creations. A self-destruct phrase, a backup queen, anything."

Nicholas chuckled as he relayed Lena's question. "Destroy the queen, and her death *might* spread through her children."

Which would be perfect, if we had the queen. "Is there a way to duplicate her song?"

"Not by you. Victor took great care to make sure his creations could not be 'hacked.'" Nicholas frowned at that last word, making me wonder how long he had been locked away from the world. "He believed that if anything were to happen to his queen, he would simply make another."

"Can he tell us how?" I asked.

A sudden flare of heat seared my thigh. Banners of flame rippled from Smudge's back as he darted to and fro in his cage. Lena caught my eyes and gestured to the door. I checked the hallway while Lena moved toward the bedroom window.

The window cracked as if struck by a stone, and Lena jumped back.

"Ah," said Nicholas. "The ghosts have found us at last, and they've brought Victor's children home."

I yanked out my shock-gun. "What ghosts?"

Two metal wasps were attacking the window, while another trio clung to the screen. I crossed the room, held the barrel of my gun six inches from the glass, and pulled the trigger.

I liked to tell myself I had chosen the shock-gun to

practice with because it was a practical, multi-purpose weapon. At its highest setting, it could take down a zombified elephant, and at its lowest it would knock a human unconscious with no long-term damage. Nor would it draw undue attention, being designed to mimic an ordinary twenty-first-century handgun.

Those were all good and valid reasons, but the truth was, I picked this one because I got to shoot evil with lightning bolts.

The discharge etched a jagged line across my vision, and the smell of ozone filled the room. The sound was nowhere near as loud as natural thunder, but it was enough to make my ears ring. The blast shattered the window, leaving blobs of melted glass around the edges of the frame. A single insect glowed orange in the molten glass. I peered outside and spotted two men on the patio below. No, not men.

I jerked back as more wasps flew toward us. I fired again, but this time what emerged was little more than a spark of static electricity. "Oh, come on," I shouted. This gun was supposed to have enough ammo for more than a hundred shots.

The insects buzzed through the window and converged on Nicholas. He ripped two away even as more began to burrow into his chest. He crushed one between his fingers and tried to dig out the next, but he wasn't fast enough.

He spasmed as if he was the one who had been hit by lightning. His eyes bulged, and then his features eased into a smile. "Exquisite," he whispered. He took a single step and exploded into dust.

One of the wasps flew up from the ground, trailing dust like tiny contrails. Deb's hand shot out, trapping the insect between thumb and forefinger. She had it halfway to her mouth before she stopped and seemed to realize what she was doing. She caught me staring and shrugged. "Instincts."

"Yeah."

She made a face, popped the bug into her mouth, and chomped. Blood dribbled from her lip, but she kept chewing, and soon spat out bits of broken metal.

Lena stomped the other two, grinding them into the carpet with a vicious twist of her heel. Behind her, Nidhi was carefully lifting the girl in her arms.

The vamp with the glasses, Rook, scaled the wall like a spider, rifle in one hand as he peeked out the upper corner of the window. "I'm heading for the roof to get a better look—"

He squawked in surprise as he lost his grip and fell, landing hard on a LEGO castle and a green pony.

At the same time, the girl Nidhi was holding squirmed and mumbled, "Don't wanna get up."

"Focus, Sarah," Deb snapped. "Keep them under."

The vampire stared at the girl. "I'm trying," she said. "It's not working."

Lena grabbed Nidhi, dragged her and the girl into the hall, and shoved them in the closet. "Stay there," Lena said, shutting the door.

I heard the girl screaming, "No! Stranger! Let go of me!" as Nidhi tried to calm her.

Rook remained behind to watch the window while the rest of us made our way downstairs. Deb and Sarah simply vaulted over the railing, landing silently on the carpet below. "We've got more out front," Sarah called.

In the family room, the three-legged Lab had woken up and started barking. From the kitchen, a woman—presumably the mother—called, "Estrella?"

The baby was crying, too, and I saw the father stirring.

I reduced the setting on my shock-gun. Maybe it just needed time to recharge? I hoped I wouldn't have to use it on the family. Or their dog.

The father jumped to his feet, then froze. He raised his hands and stepped back, round eyes locked on my gun. "Estrella!"

"Daddy!"

"Estrella is safe." I kept the shock-gun pointed at the floor as I hurried down the steps.

"Who are you people?" he demanded in Spanish. "What did you do to my daughter?" The three-legged black Lab was doing his best to add to the chaos, barking and jumping and trying to bite Smudge, which put him in the same intellectual league as Nidhi's cat.

Jeff stepped past me and snarled. The Lab immediately backed away, tail tucked so far between his legs that when he started peeing on the floor, he managed to soak his tail in the process.

"Was that really necessary?" I asked. To the father, I said, "Está a salvo. She's safe."

He paled. "Please don't hurt them."

Something slammed through the front door hard enough to send splinters of wood flying into the house. Sarah and Lena caught whatever it was by the arms and hurled it right back out, but a second attacker raced through on all fours and knocked Sarah to the ground. A group of metal insects flew at Lena's face, driving her back.

"Con permiso, Señor Sanchez." I shoved the father toward the stairs, ducked behind the couch, and swore. Every once in a while, I really hated being right.

The man standing over Sarah was naked from the waist up. A fine layer of white fur covered his skin, and an Ace bandage was wrapped around his upper arm. His lips were blue, and his fingers were blackened from frostbite. Sarah had jabbed one of her stakes into his thighs, but it wasn't slowing him down.

This time when I pulled the trigger, the shock-gun did exactly what it was supposed to. Electricity cracked through the air, enough to put an ordinary human out for a good twenty-four hours. The partially transformed wendigo roared in pain, then jumped away before I could fire again. I had blackened the fur on his chest and pissed him off, but that was all.

From the staircase, Mister Sanchez whispered, "Who are you people?"

Before I could come up with an even halfway convincing lie, Deb emerged from the kitchen cradling the baby in one arm and dragging the woman by the wrist. "Isaac, would you mind?"

The mother had a paring knife, and was stabbing it into Deb's back. I caught her arm, holding her long enough for Deb to grab the knife and snap the blade with one hand. After that demonstration, they allowed Deb to lead them upstairs.

"What's happening?" the woman demanded, her voice weak. "My daughter—"

"Nidhi, move them all into the bathroom and lock the damn door," Deb shouted. When she returned, she was clutching her shoulder. Her blood flowed more slowly than it would have in a human, but those cuts had to hurt. "Sarah, whoever's out there, put them down *now*!"

"You think I haven't been trying?" Sarah shot back.

My phone buzzed, startling me and setting Smudge off like a tiny hydrogen bomb. The screen said "Unknown Caller."

The insects fell back to the doorway. Sarah and Lena kept an eye on the door while Deb, Jeff, and I watched the front window. Keeping my gun ready, I brought the phone to my ear. Harrison had hacked my computer and the Porter network. Why wouldn't he have my cell phone number, too? "Hello, August."

"You want to tell me what the hell you're doing in my son's house?"

Through the window, I could see a muscular, blocky-looking man with a cell phone to his ear, standing in front of a silver SUV. He was clean-shaven with close-cut graying hair. His silhouette matched Victor's, from the squat build to the flat ears.

He wore an unbuttoned black plaid shirt over what looked like old-fashioned Japanese scale armor, except that the metal scales were alive and moving. Loose khaki pants and brown leather shoes completed the look. If not for the insects, he could have been someone's crotchety old grandfather.

I couldn't make out the queen amidst the rest of the insects clinging to his body, but she had to be there. I lowered my gun and turned the chamber to setting five. One shot should be enough to take him down. The man was essentially a walking conductor.

"How did you know we were here?" I asked. If my guess was right, neither I nor the vampires were going to like his answer.

"Your friend Moon," he said, confirming my gut feeling. "He overheard you talking, and we persuaded him to share. If we'd gotten to your house a little faster, we would have caught you before you left and saved everyone time."

I studied his companions, trying to figure out how they had overpowered a sparkler. Sanguinarius Meyerii weren't invulnerable, but they were awfully close.

Three more wendigos stood around Harrison. Their features were too distorted to guess what they had originally looked like. Flattened noses sat atop protruding jaws. Their lips were chapped and bloody, stretched between human and animal. They blinked too much, a side effect I remembered from my research. In rats, the fluids of the eyes had never fully adapted to the change.

Behind them stood a man and a woman who appeared fully human. Each one held an oversized book in their hands. Both were Asian, and looked to be roughly my age, or perhaps a little younger. The woman had a single lock of green-dyed hair framing the left side of her face. The man wore an awful sweater with a piano keyboard design, which was utterly insane for this time of year, but made sense if you had been stuck in a car with a wendigo for ten hours.

"Who are your friends, August?" I didn't recognize either one, but that meant little. I was familiar with most of the Porters from the Midwest, but Harrison could have recruited help from overseas. But if they were truly libriomancers, why bring only a single book into battle?

"Why don't you and Lena come out and I'll introduce you? This doesn't have to get bloody. The rest of you are welcome to leave."

"What's he waiting for?" Deb's voice was strained. She sat on the bottom step; her head drooped over her knees. The knife must have done more damage than I thought. I was strangely relieved. The fact that Deb hadn't broken the woman's neck, despite pain and provocation, meant my friend hadn't been completely lost to the monster.

"I'm not sure." I watched Harrison, trying to read his face. Speaking into the phone again, I said, "A minute ago, you used one of your son's bionic fruit flies to kill one of our companions. Now we're supposed to just trust you?"

"He was dead long before I got here, and you know it." Harrison stepped into the middle of the street. "I know all about you, Isaac. I know you've got a vampire upstairs watching us, and two more with you and Lena. I know you've stuffed the family into the hall closet. And I know that right now you're trying to figure out some clever plan to stop me." His voice dropped. "You're not as smart as you think. Now, you and Lena are going to come with us, unarmed, or my metal friends will kill every family on this street."

"That's a bit dark, even for you. Rationalizing the killing of wendigos is bad enough, but these are human beings. You're an asshole. You're not a murderer." I covered the phone. "Lena, get Nidhi down here."

"There's an elderly couple two houses down," Harrison said. "They were playing cards together when your pet vampire knocked them out. How many people will you make me kill before you take this seriously? Do you think the sensation of steel pincers digging through skin and bone will wake them from their trance?"

Interesting. The Sanchez family was awake, but if Harrison was telling the truth, Sarah's power over the rest of the street hadn't broken. Assuming it was Harrison's ersatz libriomancers who had broken Sarah's hold, that suggested a limit to their range. Or it might mean they had selective control over the magic they countered, and like us, they preferred not to be interrupted.

Lena returned, keeping Nidhi behind her. Assuming Lena had filled her in, I got straight to the point. "Will he do it?"

"I don't know," said Nidhi. "I knew the man only through his son."

"Why does he want the two of us?" Lena asked.

She spread her hands in a silent shrug.

Harrison's voice buzzed through the phone. "Go ahead and shoot, Isaac."

"What?" He must have spotted the gun through one of his insects. I switched the phone to speaker so everyone could hear.

"I assume that's what you're discussing?" said Harrison. "Whether or not you can take me down before I command my insects to attack? Be my guest. This might be the fastest way for you to learn what you're facing."

Nobody bothered pointing out that it was a trick. Some things were too obvious for words. On the other hand, he had seen me holding what looked like an ordinary revolver. Maybe he assumed his metal insects would be strong enough to stop a bullet.

I stood up and walked slowly toward the door, trying to project confidence. Harrison didn't move. I raised the shock-gun with both hands. He smiled and spread his arms.

With a shrug, I pulled the trigger.

One downside to shooting lightning bolts was that everything happened far too quickly to see. I wasn't terribly surprised to see Harrison still standing. He wasn't smiling, though. It looked like he had jumped back a good three feet, which gave me some satisfaction.

I blinked, trying to see the afterimage to reconstruct why the shock-gun had failed. It looked like the bolt had stopped a short distance in front of Harrison. I frowned and tried again.

"Look at the ones with the books," Nidhi said.

I took a third shot, this time keeping my attention on the woman with the green hair. Before, she and her friend had just been standing there, but now they were chanting. I couldn't make out what they were saying, but their eyes were closed.

If they were libriomancers, they could—in theory—

open up the magic of their own books, then use them to absorb my attack. Any shots striking their books would be dissolved back into magic. But they would have had to move in front of Harrison to intercept my incoming fire, and they would have needed to make sure they held their books in exactly the right spot.

"Are you satisfied, Isaac?" Harrison asked. "I've been more than patient."

Deb crawled across the family room floor until she reached the pile of clothes Jeff had discarded when he changed. "Harrison's friends can mess with people's magic. How nice." She dug out Jeff's pistol and pulled herself up onto the couch.

The crack of gunfire was even louder than my shock-gun, and the metallic scent of gunpowder joined the ozone smell. August Harrison scampered around behind the SUV, but Deb hadn't been aiming for him. She fired again, and this time Rook joined in from upstairs, sending the libriomancers fleeing for cover.

"What the hell, Deb?" Three wendigos charged toward the house. Rook dropped one, and I sent a lightning bolt into the next. It crackled over the frost and fur, then arced to his friend.

Wasps flew through the hole in the door to swarm over Deb, concentrating on her hands. She shrieked and flung the pistol away, then did her best to crush the bugs drilling into her skin. From the commotion upstairs, they were going after Rook as well.

"Congratulations, Isaac," Harrison shouted. I could barely hear him over the ringing in my ears. "You've just killed two innocent people."

I shouted into the phone. "Wait! You win! We're coming out. Everybody stop shooting!" I glanced at Lena, who nodded.

"Get your bugs off of the vampires," I said.

The wasps stilled, then retreated to the door. "Leave your books and other weapons," he said. "That goes for the dryad, too."

I slid my arms from my sleeves and set the jacket carefully on the floor. Smudge's cage followed, and then the shock-gun.

Lena tossed her bokken onto the floor beside my things. She took my hand in hers and pulled my head down as if to give me a quick kiss. "What now?"

I glanced down at my phone and began to tap out a text message. "Now we take this bastard down."

Chapter 8

I slept for five days before they found me. At first, I thought the pressure on my roots was a dream, but the pain of the metal ax biting into my roots shocked me awake. I curled my injured root close and flexed the rest, toppling my attacker onto the ground. As my awareness moved closer to the surface, I began to make out their words.

"Ha! Pay up." A man's voice.

"Okay, you were right," said a second man. "The tree's magic."

"What do you think, Mike?" asked the first. "Wizard of Oz?"

"Nah. The fighting trees were more willowy. The branches bent down like vines to wrap around the scarecrow, remember. This is oak. Narnia, maybe?"

"I don't recall C. S. Lewis' trees killing random farmers and burying their bodies."

They thought I had murdered Frank. I started to withdraw again, retreating deeper into the heart of the wood.

It didn't matter what they believed. Frank was gone. Let them cut down my tree.

"If you ask me, we should be looking into the ex," said Mike. "Maybe she never got over losing Frank. 'If I can't have him, no one can,' and all that. She sounded crazy enough to do it."

"I'm more interested in that girl, Lena. The one Frank was shacking up with. Marion said Lena tried to kill her once. Wouldn't surprise me if she killed him, too. If she was a witch, it would explain the magic we picked up."

"A witch who used her power to ruin Frank Dearing's marriage and trick him into letting her work his farm for no pay, year after year?"

"What about Dungeons and Dragons? Don't they have some kind of spell or scroll we could use to figure out what this thing is? The old man locked the main rulebooks, but there's a new supplement out. It might not have been cataloged yet."

As the pain from the ax eased, so did my fear. I could hear the fondness beneath the men's banter. Their presence made me yearn for companionship. My isolation was a physical pain constricting my very core, worse than any ax. In isolation, I had been content to sleep, but now that others had arrived, the loneliness was suffocating. Before I realized what I was doing, I stretched myself from my tree and stepped lightly onto the dirt.

A young man pulled a gold-bladed sword from a scabbard at his side while the other raised a tiny gray-and-black pistol. A nylon backpack sat open on the ground a short distance away. It seemed to be stuffed with books. The ax rested against the base of a tree.

"Lena Greenwood?" asked Mike, keeping his sword ready.

"*I didn't kill Frank,*" *I said.*

"*You did something,*" *said the man with the gun.* "*Whatever magic you used, the Porters felt it all the way over in Chicago.*"

Mike lowered his sword, but I noticed how his friend stepped to one side, keeping a clear line of fire. "*We aren't here to hurt you. We've talked to your neighbors. We know how Frank treated you. If you were acting in self-defense—*"

"*No!*" *Why wouldn't they believe me?* "*I loved him.*"

They looked at one another. "*How long did you live with Frank?*" *asked Mike.*

The question confused me. "*I've always been with Frank.*"

"*John, why don't you give Doctor Shah a call?*" *Mike sheathed his weapon and smiled. While John unclipped a cell phone from his belt, Mike extended a hand.* "*Would you mind coming with us to talk to a friend?*"

I didn't have the willpower to refuse.

"*Don't worry,*" *John said as he dialed.* "*Nidhi's nice. You'll like her.*"

AUGUST HARRISON'S FRIENDS WEREN'T the only ones who could counter magic. I peeked down at the phone as I typed out the message. *Found killer. Hostages. Need distraction and automaton.*

My phone tried to correct the last word to "airmen." I fixed it and hit Send, then brought the phone to my face. "We're coming out. Call the wasps back."

I waited for the insects to retreat from the door. An answering text arrived a few seconds later. *Understood.*

I stepped onto the porch. "The wendigos, too."

"In time." Harrison sounded every ounce the gentleman now that he believed he was in control. He stood behind the SUV's hood, watching me. "Your friends will be free to go as soon as you've joined us."

An aborted squeak made me whirl. Deb froze, a guilty expression on her face, then slowly wiped her mouth on her sleeve. She was moving better, and her knife wounds had stopped bleeding. She swallowed, grimaced, and offered me a halfhearted shrug.

I looked past her to the empty birdcage. "You didn't."

"Hey, if that woman hadn't stabbed me when all I was trying to do was help, maybe—"

"What is *wrong* with you?" I yelled.

"Nothing, anymore."

I was tempted to shoot her myself. "When this is over, you're buying this family another bird."

My phone buzzed with another text message. I glanced at the screen. I didn't have time to deal with Deb. With a disgusted glare, I turned back to Harrison. "Sorry about that. We're coming out." A low double-beep signaled another incoming call as I descended the steps. When my foot touched the bottom step, I pretended to stumble. I caught the rail with one hand. With my other, I tapped the phone, bringing Nicola Pallas into a three-way call with August Harrison.

Even with the phone away from my ear, the opening bars of Pallas' song felt like she had plugged an electrical cable directly into my eardrums. I flung the phone into the grass and clung to the rail with both hands while I waited for the world to stop spinning.

As unpleasant as that tinny melody was for me, how much worse must it have been for August Harrison, who had his phone clamped to his ear. Pallas' bardic magic dropped him with the first notes.

"Go," I yelled.

Jeff bounded out the door, knocking me off my feet. Deb and Sarah followed close behind, and I saw Rook flying from the window, swooping into the street like an enormous geeky raven.

Lena hauled me inside, then grabbed her weapons. I did the same, scooping up books and my shock-gun, and clipping Smudge's cage to my jacket. Outside, the two libriomancers were doing their thing, presumably trying to suppress the magic coming from Harrison's cell phone. But even if they succeeded, the damage was done. He wouldn't be waking up for a while, and that meant he couldn't command his swarm.

"Isaac, there were more around back," Lena shouted as she followed the others outside. "Make sure they don't cut through the house."

Flames danced through the bars of Smudge's cage. I heard claws scrabbling overhead. "Watch the roof!"

Lena jumped down to the sidewalk as the first wendigo landed on the porch. She spun, one wooden sword raised high, the other low for stabbing. The wendigo ripped the iron railing from the concrete and hurled it at her. She lunged to the side, using both swords to bat the railing out of the way.

"Dumbass," I muttered, and shot him in the back. I opened the first of my books to a dog-eared page and skimmed the text. As a second attacker bounded around the corner of the house, I finished my spell and flung the book at his chest like a Frisbee. The cover flapped open as it flew, and the dust jacket tore away to flutter to the ground.

The cover art showed a single bee beneath the title: *African Honey Bees in North America.*

The bees emerged en masse and angry. They wouldn't have been a threat to a true wendigo with its thick armor of ice and fur, but this wasn't a full wendigo. He—no wait, this one was female—scrambled backward, swatting furiously.

Sarah's scream echoed down the street. I turned to see her falling backward, her extremities dissolving into dust. I couldn't tell what the two wendigos had done to her, but by the time she hit the road, only a skeleton remained. That crumbled away within seconds.

A third libriomancer had joined the other two, and I counted a total of seven wendigos in an all-out brawl with Deb, Jeff, and Rook in the middle of the road.

Lena sprinted toward them, and the green-haired girl raised her book like a shield. Lena veered toward her, one sword slashing at the book.

The sword snapped like a rotted stick. Lena flung the hilt at the girl's face, then dropped low to kick her feet out from beneath her. Before she could follow up, a wendigo leaped onto the top of the SUV and pounced.

I took another shot with my shock-gun, but as before, the lightning failed to reach its target. It looked like they had ended my spell with the killer bees, too.

I ran toward my phone and dialed Pallas' number again. "It's Isaac. We could really use that automaton right now."

"I'm aware of the disturbance. I'm waiting for approval from Gutenberg." She sounded utterly unfazed. I was pretty sure Pallas was incapable of being fazed. "I thought your plan was to question Victor's ghost."

"August Harrison had his own plan. The ghost-talker is dead, as is one of his escorts. Harrison has his own little army of mutant wendigos, not to mention three wannabe libriomancers doing tricks I've never seen before."

"This shouldn't take long. In the meantime, in case you're killed, what have you learned so far?"

"That's cold, Nicola." But I couldn't argue with her logic. Outside, another wendigo hurled Deb through the air. She crunched into a tree and didn't get up. I fired again, with no more effect than before. "August got his hands on Victor's magic bugs and used them to hack our network. He's building himself a little army of wendigos. No idea how he's controlling them."

"We have a team in Switzerland working to lock him out of our computer network."

I was only half listening. Each time I pulled the trigger, the point where my shot dissolved moved closer. Whatever barrier they were using, it was creeping toward me. The only effect the lightning had was to interfere with my phone's reception. "Gotta go, Nicola. If they kill me, just send a ghost-talker to get the rest of my report."

I tossed the phone aside, gripped the gun with both hands, and kept shooting. I picked other targets, trying to assess the size of the barrier, but however they were doing this, it was enough to shield a spread of at least ninety degrees.

A flicker of light in the front yard announced the arrival of our reinforcement. The automaton was eight feet tall, armored in small, magically linked blocks of metal. Only the extremities revealed the dark wood Gutenberg had used to craft the body centuries ago. A blank wooden face turned, eyes like oversized black pearls taking in everyone's positions.

Each automaton housed a human spirit, a mind that gave them some freedom to think and act within the boundaries of their magical programming. Every line of text stamped into their wooden bodies was a spell, allowing them to access power far beyond any libriomancer.

I hated the damned things, but at this particular moment, I was ready to jump up and cheer.

Three wendigos peeled away from the fight and charged the automaton. It strode to meet them, arms outstretched. Flame and yellow smoke billowed forth from its hands.

"Pluit ignem et sulphur de caelo et omnes perdidit," I whispered. *It rained fire and brimstone from heaven and destroyed them all.* It was a verse from the Gutenberg Bible, the text of which Gutenberg had somehow transferred to his automatons. The stench of sulfur spread through the air, making me grimace.

As the rest of the wendigos turned to face the new threat, Lena used the respite to grab Deb and haul her back from the carnage. Jeff tried to get at Harrison, but gunfire drove him away. Rook was fleeing down the street at inhuman speeds, proving him to be the smartest of us all.

Another wendigo jumped onto the automaton's back, wrapped its arms around the neck, and tried to wrench the wooden head free.

The automaton reached behind, the shoulder swiveling well beyond what any human joint could manage, and seized the attacker by the arm. With no visible effort, it flung the wendigo into the SUV. Metal crumpled from the impact, and the wendigo didn't get back up.

The green-haired libriomancer shouted, "Concentrate on the golem!" She and her two companions ran forward with their books.

The automaton stopped moving.

"How the shit did they do that?" Deb asked weakly.

"I don't know, but they look preoccupied." I raised my gun, sighted through the doorway at the closest of the libriomancers, and pulled the trigger. He must have seen my movement, because he whirled and raised his book. He took a jolt, but not enough to put him down.

The automaton shuddered, then stumbled forward. Green shouted another order. Wooden fingers ripped a slab of blacktop from the road and hurled it at the closest book-wielder. He tried to dodge, but he wasn't fast enough. The missile caught his shoulder, spinning him in a full circle and sending the book flying to the side of the road.

Another burst of flame poured forth, but this time it failed to reach its target. Instead, the fire curved toward the house.

"Oh, crap." I dove into the family room. Lena hurled Deb after me, then rolled out of the way as flame poured through the door. Jeff got a little singed, but the fire wasn't as bad as I feared. Whatever they were doing to turn the automaton's magic against us must have weakened its power.

I snatched up my satchel and pulled out an urban fantasy called *Heart of Stone*. The pages showed the faintest dusting of char, like someone had rubbed a pencil lead over the inner edges. I had used this book too often in my research, but I needed to understand what was going on out there. I yanked a pair of mirrored sunglasses from the story and slipped them on.

The enchanted lenses darkened my vision and painted a grid of glowing magical energy over the scene on the street. I could see the patches of wendigo skin, burning a sickly brown color that spread through the bodies of Harrison's pet monsters. White light cocooned the automaton, the strands of Gutenberg's magic encasing it in a dense web of power.

None of this was particularly unusual, though I rarely had to sort out so much magic all at once. But where I would normally have seen libriomantic magic pouring from the three books, there was only emptiness, like holes in the surrounding magic. Given what had happened to my spell back in the woods, I wasn't entirely surprised that those holes formed the outlines of three people standing before the automaton.

Another blast of fire poured forth, and two of the figures moved in unison, stepping into the automaton's magic and diverting it once again. The third joined in as the injured man retrieved his book from the street.

This wasn't libriomancy. The books were . . . what, exactly? Lamps for magic-eating genies? Charms to allow the ones who carried them to magically project themselves? Were the books simply bodies for a kind of creature we'd never before encountered or cataloged? Or were these the ghosts Nicholas had talked about, the ones who had distracted him from his conversation with Victor?

Two of the wendigos were dragging August Harrison toward a black pickup down the street. I aimed through the broken window and tried to stop them, but they got Harrison around the far side of the truck before I could fire. I adjusted the setting and sent a bolt of lightning into the truck, and was rewarded with the sight of one wendigo leaping back.

Unfortunately, my attack drew the attention of one of the three ghosts, or whatever they were. "Incoming!"

My warning did little good. Nobody else could see the figure that flew through the doorway, hesitated, then dove *through* Deb's body. Deb's magic dimmed, and she stumbled backward. The ghost continued to swirl around her, feeding on her power. And I had no idea how to make it stop.

Maybe another target would help. I jumped up and sent a volley of electricity toward the battle. One of the two remaining ghosts intercepted the shots, and from the corner of my eye, I saw Deb fall as her attacker turned to me.

I flung the gun out the window. It followed the weapon, and when it finished, not a trace of magic remained in my shock-gun.

A full-sized van, dark blue with tinted windows, screeched to a halt in the middle of the street. The remnants of Harrison's team crammed inside as the ghosts continued to hold back the automaton. The ghosts vanished a moment later as both the van and the pickup truck sped away.

I ran out the door and waved my arms at the automaton. "Stop them, you overgrown pile of Lincoln Logs! Get August Harrison!"

It stepped after the van, then stopped as if confused. The damn thing reminded me of Nidhi's idiot cat, whom I had once observed chasing a fly across the kitchen, only to stop halfway and look around as if she had completely forgotten why she was in such a hurry.

"Go!" I yelled.

The automaton jolted back to life and began to run. It disappeared in mid-step, reappearing at the intersection in a flash of light. The truck screeched to a halt, but once again the automaton failed to finish the job. It stood dumbly as the van turned left and the truck sped off to the right. It snapped out of its trance again seconds later and resumed its pursuit.

"Not good." I sagged against the wall and turned to look at the damage we had done. Broken glass littered the house. The door was destroyed. The road outside was even worse, from cars that had been ripped apart to the cratered blacktop and smoking yard beyond. Sirens were approaching in the distance. I fetched my phone and hit redial.

"Nicola? It's Isaac again. I think we're going to need some help cleaning this one up."

Deb was in lousy shape, but she appeared to have recovered from whatever it was the ghost had done to her. She limped down the driveway to meet the approaching police cars.

The cars stopped a short distance from the house. Deb waited with arms spread as uniformed officers exited their cars with guns drawn. They crouched behind the front of the cars, where the engine blocks would provide cover against incoming fire.

I couldn't blame them. Between the damage we had done and the sight of Deb DeGeorge standing there bruised and bloody, her skin making her look partially mummified, I wouldn't have gone near her either.

I could see the moment Deb touched their minds. She might not have been as powerful as Sarah, but she was strong enough to lure her prey into dropping their guard. The police officers lowered their weapons, and by the time they reached Deb, they moved with a slow, relaxed pace that made me think they were sleepwalking. Deb had gotten stronger since the last time I saw her.

As soon as they were fully distracted, I ran outside to retrieve my shock-gun. It was dead, as I had expected, but that could be fixed. You had to be careful, but it actually took less energy to use a book to re-form an existing magical item than to create it from scratch.

When I entered the house again, the crackle of bone and popping joints filled the room. Jeff had managed to tug off the moonstone necklace. It was glowing beneath the couch where he must have kicked it to block the light. When he finished wrenching himself back to human form, he collapsed into an old recliner and started pulling on his underwear and pants.

I grabbed my jacket from the floor, pulled *Time Kings* from one of my pockets to fix my gun, then froze. Mister Sanchez was staring at us from the hallway. The black Lab cowered behind his legs.

I watched as he gathered his courage. His hands were shaking, but he straightened and stepped closer. "What are you?"

Nidhi spun. "I asked you to stay in the bathroom, Laszio."

He stared at the broken window and door, the blood-stained carpet, and the ruins of the yard and street outside. "This is about the man who used to live here? The one who was murdered."

"Yes," said Nidhi.

He gave a small nod, looking simultaneously grateful and frightened by her honesty.

"We'll find a way to cover the damages," I said softly. If the Porters wouldn't take care of this, then I would, and to hell with the rules. There were plenty of books I could use to produce everything from gold to gemstones.

His attention flitted about, stopping briefly with Jeff, then moving to Lena and her broken sword, and finally to me. His gaze dipped to Smudge. "Your spider. Is it on fire?"

I looked down. "A little bit, yeah."

"Laszio, look at me." Nidhi moved to impose herself between him and the rest of us. "We came here because of Victor Harrison, but this fight wasn't about him. It was about us. You and your family will be safe once we're gone."

He managed a nervous smile. "No offense intended,

Doctor Shah, but if that is the case, I hope you'll leave quickly."

"We will," Nidhi promised.

And once we were gone, Nicola would send someone to alter the family's memories, just as easily as a Hollywood writer reworked a script. Just as Deb was manipulating the minds of the police outside, burying the truth beneath layers of magical falsehoods.

"He's a fire-spider. His name is Smudge." I think the words surprised me as much as anyone else. Nidhi gave me a sharp look, but didn't argue when I lifted Smudge's cage to eye level. With my other hand, I grabbed the Red Hots. "I created him when I was in high school. He's saved my life several times."

I brought a candy to the edge of the cage and waited for Smudge to snatch it up.

Laszio took a half-step closer, the fear in his eyes joined by a glimmer of curiosity. "He eats junk food?"

"Every chance he gets," I said. "He loves chocolate, but that can get messy. He tends to melt it, and you end up with stains all over the carpet."

Laszio looked down at the bloody, blackened carpet. "Yes. We wouldn't want that."

He sounded so serious, and I laughed before I could stop myself. He joined in a moment later, though I think it was more a release of fear and exhaustion than humor.

"The fire," he said. "It doesn't hurt him?"

"It's how he protects himself. How he protects me and helps me to stop people like the ones who attacked your home."

"I don't understand." Laszio kept watching as Smudge devoured his treat.

"I know," said Nidhi. "Neither did I, the first time I saw something like this. You're handling it far better than I did."

I doubted that, but I didn't say anything. Instead, I returned Smudge's cage to my hip and opened *Time Kings*. Laszio flinched when I lifted the gun. He looked back to the hall, and I knew he was thinking about his wife and children.

"It's all right." I shoved the gun back into the pages, letting the words and images of the readers transform the weapon from an empty relic back into a fully charged shock-gun. "This is what we do."

"Ay dios mio," he whispered. Both Nidhi and Lena were watching him very closely now, ready to intervene if he lost it. "Those creatures outside. What did they want?"

"You should see to your family," Nidhi interrupted. "Reassure them. We will be gone very soon, and I promise we'll make sure you're safe."

I took that as my cue. "Lena and Jeff, could you come with me? We need to inspect every house on this street to make sure Harrison's swarm left with him."

I pocketed the shock-gun. Deb appeared to have things under control outside. One of the police cars was already pulling away, its sirens dark.

"Why did you tell him about Smudge?" Lena asked as we exited the house.

"Because it didn't matter." I was surprised at the anger boiling up inside me. "Because we're going to rip every memory of today from his head. Not to protect them, but to protect *us*."

They wouldn't remember what had happened, but we couldn't completely erase the trauma. Even after we stole their memories, they would be exhausted and jumpy for a long time.

Lena stopped at the end of the driveway to pick up the broken mailbox. She twisted the post free and turned it in her hands, shaping it into a serviceable club. Then she looked back at the house. She stood there for so long I thought something was wrong. Had she spotted one of Harrison's bugs? But when I touched her shoulder, she merely turned to kiss my cheek. "I think you're wrong," she said softly. "I think it did matter."

None of the neighbors had emerged to see what was happening. I took that to mean they hadn't yet woken from Sarah's magic slumber. Smudge didn't turn into a fireball when we entered the first house, which was another encouraging sign.

"Do you think the automaton will be able to stop them?" Lena asked.

I thought about August Harrison and his swarm, the half-breed wendigos, and the ghosts that had devoured our magic. "No."

Chapter 9

Report Number: NS-US5-194
Submitted by: Nidhi Shah, MD, PhD
Location: Mason, Michigan
Subject Name: Lena Greenwood

Description: Ms. Greenwood is a physically healthy
Caucasian female, approximately five foot six
inches. She appears to be in her late thirties to early
forties. She is overweight, but not obese. Her skin
lacks any visible blemishes or wrinkles. Based on
her account of the work she performed on Frank
Dearing's farm, she is significantly stronger than she
appears.

Magical Assessment: The two field agents, John
Senn and Michael Angell, concur that Lena is a
dryad of some sort, though her appearance and
abilities differ significantly from the descriptions of
known dryads in the Porter database. Lena has

demonstrated the ability to manipulate her tree's roots to fight back after being struck by an ax. She showed no sensitivity to cold, despite the low temperatures.

Angell and Senn were able to unearth Frank Dearing's remains after Lena had been removed from the scene. While multiple eyewitnesses claim that Mr. Dearing was alive one week ago, his body had decomposed to little more than a skeleton. Angell used magic to verify that this was indeed Frank Dearing. It would appear that Lena's tree somehow consumed him.

Lena's love for Frank Dearing comes across as genuine. I'm uncertain whether the tree acted independently, or if Lena simply doesn't recognize what she had done to Mr. Dearing.

While Lena shows little awareness of the passage of time and even less understanding of the world around her, both her recollections and the information we gathered from Marion Dearing suggest Lena was living with Frank for at least forty years, which would make her a minimum of sixty years old. If so, she has aged extremely well.

Psychological Assessment: *Lena Greenwood is in many ways a child, isolated from the world, and knowing little beyond her life with Frank Dearing. Her eagerness for attention and affection make me suspect she may have been badly deprived of both while growing up, though she hasn't yet shared any information about her childhood.*

She spoke freely of her relationship, describing the details of her sexual activities with Dearing as casually as she recounted the last breakfast she prepared for him. I've observed no sign of duplicity. On the contrary, she has been eager to share with me, though she remains wary of other Porters. I would estimate her I.Q. to be significantly below average, perhaps to the point of mild disability, though I'll need to run a number of tests to confirm.

She talked about the temptation to remain in her tree and "go deeper." Given her grief and obvious fear of life without Frank Dearing, I believe Lena to be a very real suicide risk. I am requesting temporary reassignment to help her acclimate to the larger world.

Threat Risk: *I disagree with the report prepared by field agent Angell. I do not believe Lena Greenwood poses a threat to the Porters or to humanity. While she has demonstrated a willingness to use her abilities to protect herself, I believe her essential nature is that of peace.*

WE FOUND HARRISON'S INSECTS in the five houses closest to the Sanchez family. The insects weren't asleep, exactly, and they reacted when we approached, but they were sluggish, refusing to stray very far from their chosen hostages. Lena clubbed most of the insects into scrap. I caught two more with a hammer I picked up from the garage of the second house.

We got back to find Nidhi hauling the spare tire out of the trunk of her car. The rear tire had been blown apart in the fighting. The driver's side window was broken as well. Nidhi gave me a *look*, but didn't say anything.

On the bright side, having a Renfield around made it a lot easier to change a tire. Who needed a jack when Deb could lift the car with her bare hands? Lena helped with the tire while I swept out the pebbles of glass the best I could.

Deb stepped back, brushed her hands on her pants, and folded her arms. "The head bloodsuckers in Detroit aren't going to be happy about losing Nicholas and Sarah."

"I'm not thrilled either." I didn't remind her that Harrison had killed Moon as well. Or maybe she remembered, and the vampires simply didn't mind losing that particular sparkler.

I grabbed Heinlein's *Friday* from my jacket. The vampires had taken care of their side of the bargain, after all. The Shipstone battery I created was no larger than my wallet. It could light the entire vampire city, deep in the underground salt mines, but it might not be enough to make up for the death of three of their number. "Be careful."

"Don't worry about me, hon. Anyone asks, I'm putting all the blame on you." Deb shoved the Shipstone into her pants pocket. "Watch your back. And give me a call if you change your mind about wanting a few extra years of reading and study."

We waited for the first of the Porters' clean-up crew to arrive. A pair of fresh-faced field agents nodded a greeting, then set about erasing our mess. One strode into the Sanchez house as if he owned it, while the other used some kind of purple crystal to search for fragments of magic, like the expended pellets from my shock-gun.

Once we were back on the road, I examined a handful of fragmented insect parts: wings and shells, mostly, along with a few gears, a bit of wire that might have been an antenna, and a pair of oversized grasshopper legs. I squinted through my enchanted sunglasses, but the scraps were magically dead.

We knew where the bugs had come from, but where had Harrison found his accomplices? How had he persuaded them to help him butcher wendigos? More importantly, what did they all want? Harrison was motivated by power, but what did he hope to do with his magically boosted brute squad?

And why come after me? If he had gotten into Victor's system, he could have tracked down any Porter he wanted, but I hadn't heard of any other break-ins. Harrison had come to the U.P. and hacked my computer. I looked out the rear window toward Lena, thinking of my private notes. There were things I had learned about her that I refused to share even with the Porters.

If August Harrison had found those files, it would take time to decrypt them, but if he was even half as smart as his son had been, he would get there eventually. Whether or not he could do anything with that information was another question. He had no direct magical ability. I had no idea what else his would-be libriomancers could do.

I called Nicola Pallas. "The serenade worked beautifully, thank you. Please tell me the automaton has Harrison and his friends."

"Not yet."

"Dammit."

Jeff turned in his seat. "What's taking so long? I thought those things were supposed to be unstoppable."

"Not exactly," Nidhi said mildly. "Isaac destroyed four earlier this year."

Jeff cocked his head and stared at me like I had just turned into a were-rabbit. Admittedly, this was a tremendous improvement over wanting to tear me limb from limb. "Well, shave my ass and call me a poodle. How the hell did you manage that?"

"You have to know how they think." Which August might also know, depending on what he had gotten out of my computer. This just got better and better. To Nicola, I said, "Why doesn't it materialize in front of their truck, punch out the engine, and be done with it?"

"As far as we've been able to determine, the automaton is having trouble *seeing* them."

Perfect. "I need to talk to Gutenberg. The people August had with him were using magic I'd never seen or read about before."

"Hold on."

I'll say this much about Nicola: she was efficient. It couldn't have been more than five seconds before my phone beeped.

"What have you learned?" asked Johannes Gutenberg. It was his customary greeting. Never "Hello, Isaac," or "Great job cleaning up that will-o'-the-wisp situation at the strip club last month, Isaac." All he cared about was whatever new knowledge I had uncovered, whether it was the innermost secrets of a forgotten branch of Egyptian magic or the extra ingredient Loretta Trembath used for her spicy Cudighi.

I had never been able to describe Gutenberg's accent. I would have expected his words to be colored by his upbringing, but I heard no trace of Germanic when he spoke. Instead, his voice was simply ... precise. Every word, every syllable was carefully chosen and articulated.

It made sense when I thought about it. How many languages had he learned and relearned over his lifetime?

"August Harrison has help," I said. "Three people, all young and Asian in appearance. They used books to absorb or dissipate magic. I think the books held some kind of ghost that diluted or consumed whatever we threw at them."

"Describe these ghosts," Gutenberg said sharply.

I did the best I could, beginning with Nicholas' complaints about other ghosts. Nidhi and Jeff chipped in additional details. "Who the hell are these people? You said you sent me the full, uncensored history of the Porters for— For my research project. There was nothing about this style of magic."

"Tell me about the books."

I closed my eyes. "They were hardcovers. Larger than most modern books. Quartos, maybe, bound in red cloth or leather. They looked like something you'd keep in the rare books section of a library." But such uncommon or one-of-a-kind editions shouldn't work for libriomancy. Books had to be mass-produced to build up the cumulative belief and power you needed for magic. "I didn't see any embossing on the cover. The pages looked yellowed."

"Did you see what language the books were written in?"

Was I imagining the urgency in his words? "I didn't get close enough."

"It's not libriomancy," Gutenberg said quietly.

I waited for him to explain. Eventually, I started to realize I could be waiting a very long time. "Then what is it?"

"I'm not sure."

I didn't buy it. He might not know for certain, but he wouldn't be this pensive if he didn't have suspicions. "So guess, dammit."

The silence that followed gave me time to realize I

was barking orders at the founder of the Porters, a man with five hundred years of magical experience who could probably fry me through this phone without a second thought. I saw Nidhi's hands tense on the wheel, and even Jeff gave me a small shake of his head.

"I won't know anything for certain until you bring me back their books."

I forced myself to count to ten, in Latin, before responding. I should have gone to at least thirty. "You remember I'm a researcher now, not a field agent, right?"

"You are whatever I order you to be, Isaac Vainio. The Porters are not your personal social club. We are a guild, bound to a purpose, and I am master of that guild. I've given you a great deal of leeway, due to your contributions and potential. But there are limits to my patience."

"Yes, sir." The words slipped out automatically in response to his unspoken threat. "But can't the automaton bring back whatever you need?"

"Normally, yes." His anger shifted into frustration. "However, as near as I can determine, my automaton is stuck. I'll send you the location."

"Stuck?"

"Locked up. Paralyzed. Bluescreened. Frozen."

"How?"

"Presumably your friends with their book-ghosts have found a way to throw a wrench into my magic."

"Are you serious?" The words slipped out before I could stop them. "If these people can overpower your spells, what exactly do you expect me to do?"

"Improvise. As you did before."

Take control of the automaton. I shook my head. "Lena and I both could have died last time."

"Then find a better tactic. Our enemies have shown themselves to be exceptionally good at avoiding detection. We may not have another opportunity. If you strike now, while their efforts are concentrated on containing and depowering the automaton, you may not need such extreme measures."

"All right." I took a deep breath. "Any other advice?"

"Yes, in fact. If I'm not mistaken, Mister Harrison has awakened. He's sending his creatures after you. Use them to weaken him before you attack."

"How the hell do I do that?"

Nobody I knew could pack as much weariness into a single sigh as Johannes Gutenberg. "*Think*, Isaac. How does August Harrison control so many creatures?"

"Through the queen. Victor built a telepathic interface."

Silence.

"Feedback," I said, feeling like an exceptionally slow student struggling to keep up. "That's why he didn't come after us last night when we destroyed the insects in Lena's tree. He felt it. If we kill enough of his pets, we can take him out right now."

My phone went dead. A second later, the screen lit up with a new text message: *Automaton is approximately 10 miles north of your location, at the intersection of Wilcox Rd. and Allegan St.*

"What did he ask you to do?" Nidhi asked tightly.

"Stop Harrison." I handed the phone up to Jeff, who nodded and typed the location into Nidhi's GPS. "He also warned me we're about to have company."

I dug through my satchel, looking for a book I wasn't entirely sure I could use. But if this worked, I should be able to knock August Harrison on his ass.

The roof of the car began to ring like it was raining gravel. A beetle hit the windshield hard enough to chip the glass. It clung there, boring deeper into the tiny crater.

Nidhi flipped on the windshield wipers. The beetle

held tight, and the wiper blade slid over it with a thumping sound. She switched on the washer fluid next. That was enough to dislodge the beetle, but more bugs were rattling down on us.

"Speed up," I yelled. The faster we went, the harder it should be for the insects to hold on. I tried to ignore the clatter of bugs, concentrating instead on the pages of a good old-fashioned dungeon crawl. Gutenberg locked most role-playing manuals, but there were plenty of tie-in novels out there.

The page I had bookmarked described an enormous warrior cowering in the back of a cave as a creature that looked like a super-sized cross between an armadillo and a cockroach waddled closer.

I couldn't blame the fighter for his fear. When I was a kid, my paladin had lost a +3 bastard sword and a full suit of enchanted plate mail to this particular monster, leaving me all but defenseless against the goblin ambush in the next tunnel.

I immersed myself in the scene, imagining the mage's laughter as he watched the burly fighter shout in fear. Even the normally stoic cleric chuckled before raising his wooden cudgel to strike. The creature dodged the first attack. With surprising speed, it scrambled between them, oblivious to anything save the glorious feast of steel laid out before it. Twin antennae whipped out to strike the warrior's breastplate.

Instantly, the steel armor lost its sheen. The priest knocked the monster away, but it was too late. A dark stain of pitted rust spread across the armor, and bits of brown metal fell to the floor.

I seized that moment in my mind and reached through the book, grasping one of the antennae in my hand. It felt like a dry, armor-plated snake.

The beast wouldn't fit through the pages, and even if it did, I had no idea how to control it. Nor was I certain I could rip an antenna off and use it effectively. But if I could channel its power—

What looked like a bumblebee built from scrap metal and a broken sparkplug punched through the windshield and flew toward my face. Without thinking, I yanked my hand from the book to swat it away.

The bee bounced against the door and dropped onto the seat. The wings buzzed, but the sound had changed. The pitch grew higher, like a tiny electrical motor burning itself out. Brown fog spread in a tiny cloud as the remnants of the wings rusted away. The body corroded next. A leg broke free. The bee collapsed onto its side, remaining legs curled inward, until nothing remained but an orange-brown smear of rust.

"That's a new trick," Jeff commented, staring at my hand. "Did you mean to do that?"

"Not exactly, no." Leathery brown plates gloved my hand, stopping at the wrist. I curled my fingers, feeling the plates grind together like stones. There was very little sensation. I tugged at the wrist where armor met flesh, hoping I could peel it free, but this was my skin now.

I didn't know what I had done, if it was permanent, or what it would do to me in the long run, and I had no doubt I would begin freaking the hell out very soon, but for the moment, there were bugs to kill.

A wasp burrowed through the hole the bumblebee had left and landed in Jeff's hair. I plucked it away with my thumb and forefinger. It tried to sting me with an inch-long needle that looked thick enough to penetrate bone, but the tip rusted away as soon as it hit my hand.

I used my left hand to unbuckle my seat belt, then rolled down the window. I pulled the upper part of my body out until I could see the roof. I squinted against the wind and stretched out very carefully to flick away a cockroach. A ladybug crept toward me, and I reached over—

A passing truck honked. I jumped, and my hand slammed down on the ladybug. I yanked it back, but it was too late. The bug rusted away, as did an oversized handprint in the roof of Nidhi's car.

"What did you do?" yelled Nidhi.

"Nothing!" I twisted around, trying to reach the ones on the rear windshield. The magic of this particular monster affected all metals, regardless of whether they were ferrous or not. But as long as I didn't hit hard enough to crack the glass, the windshield should be fine.

Lena was pulling closer. I waved her back, then pointed to the insects. The last thing I wanted was to knock them off Nidhi's car and onto Lena or her motorcycle.

Lena pointed right back, not at me, but at the tires.

"Oh, crap." I ducked back into the car and grabbed my seat belt, only to have the buckle crumble like thin Styrofoam in my hand. "Nidhi, we're about to lose the tires."

I slid into the middle seat, trying to work the belt left-handed. I bumped Smudge's cage in the process, and the thin bars melted away. I got the buckle clicked into place and scooped Smudge into my hand. The armor protected me from his nervous flames.

Nidhi had slowed down to about forty when the first tire blew out. Other cars honked and swerved around us as she fought for control. Her arms and hands tightened as the second tire followed the first, and the car lurched hard to the right. The front wheels hit dirt, and then we were spinning around, and centrifugal force pinned me to my seat.

By the time we jolted to a stop, we were in a ditch staring up at oncoming traffic. I set Smudge down and fumbled with the buckle. The airbags had gone off, body-slamming Jeff and Nidhi into their seats. They were both alive, and I didn't see blood. As for me, I had a twinge in my neck that would no doubt evolve into something much worse, but I was pretty sure nothing was broken.

I opened the door and stumbled out of the car. Most of the swarm was flying away like silver sparks in the sun. I swatted the few that remained, hoping August Harrison felt every one.

Lena pulled off the road a short distance ahead. She jumped from the bike and sprinted toward us, bokken in hand. "Is everyone all right? Isaac, your hand—"

"Yah, that didn't go quite the way I had hoped." I walked around the car to check the damage. Both tires were shredded. We had driven on the rims for those last forty feet or so. This thing wasn't going anywhere without major work.

"Whatever hand sanitizer you've been using, I'm staying the hell away from it," said Jeff as he climbed out.

"Is it permanent?" Lena asked.

"I'm not even sure what I did." I suspected it was similar to the way people could reach into books and infect themselves with various strains of vampirism. They weren't being bitten by literal vampires; they were simply remaking their bodies through magic.

What worried me was the fact that such magic was intrinsic, robbing the person of their ability to use extrinsic magic. If this was permanent, or worse yet, if it began to spread . . . "I'll be fine. I just need something to wrap around my hand so I don't keep breaking everything I touch."

Nidhi popped the trunk and pulled out an old blanket. Lena ran her index finger over the length of her bokken, restoring the wood's edge, then handed the weapon to Nidhi. With a nod of thanks, Nidhi began cutting.

"I saw the things that took out the tires, and they were bigger," said Lena. "More like birds than insects. I couldn't tell if they got away, or if they were destroyed when you spun out."

"Nicholas—Victor—said something about the insects breeding and evolving."

Another car slowed, but Lena waved them on. We circled the car, searching from top to bottom for any stragglers, but the insects were gone.

"Next time, we're taking your car," Nidhi said.

I started to answer, but my phone buzzed in my pocket. I set Smudge on my shoulder and reached for it, then caught myself. The case was mostly plastic and glass, but there was enough metal trim that a single touch could turn the thing into a useless brick.

"Allow me." Lena grinned and slipped a hand into my pocket. For several seconds, I forgot about August Harrison, mutant wendigos, and my messed-up hand. She planted a quick kiss on my neck that sent goose bumps down my spine, then pulled out the phone.

I blinked and concentrated on the message from Gutenberg. The automaton was dying, which meant we were running out of time. "Harrison is close by. If Lena and I ride together, we can still catch him."

Nidhi's face was expressionless. She tossed the wadded-up length of blanket to me and climbed back into the car without a word to get the GPS. Nidhi had told me she was struggling to adjust to our new relationship, but this was the first time I had seen that struggle.

"I'm sorry," Lena said quietly, watching Nidhi. "That was stupid. I was worried about you. I saw you fighting off those insects, and then you were moving around in the back seat and the car was out of control. You scared me. You both did."

I grabbed the end of the blanket and began wrapping the rest around my fist. "So go tell her."

Lena studied my eyes, like she was searching to see if I meant it.

"Your girlfriend was just in an accident, and the first thing she saw was you hugging and getting friendly with me."

She stared at me, then smiled. "I chose better than I realized."

"I'll meet you at your bike."

Intellectually, I had more-or-less come to terms with our relationship weeks ago. But this was the first time I had been able to walk away from the two of them without feeling those barbs of jealousy and insecurity. I didn't turn around to watch Lena's good-bye—I wasn't certain how stable this newfound peace was—but it was a start.

Chapter 10

Winter whispers his song.
    Strips her branches,
    Abandons her naked before the heavens
    As souls slumber beneath,
    And dirt becomes stone.

Spring celebrates the tandava,
    And the newborn feels only the
    Heartbeat of the dance,
    Sings only her love
    Of an undiscovered verdant world.

Under a moonless night,
    She remembers the cold.
    Her song warms the earth,
    And her dance begins anew,
    Celebrating the return.

But none shall ever sing so purely
    As the newborn spring.

Forever after, her dance is tempered
By foreknowledge of winter's return.

I LEFT SMUDGE BEHIND with Jeff and Nidhi. Without his cage, I didn't trust him on the back of a motorcycle. I waited while Lena strapped her spare helmet over my head, then climbed onto the back of the bike. I tucked the bottom of my jacket between us to keep it from getting caught in the wheels.

"Hold tight," she said, and then we were darting onto the road.

I felt her laughter as she wove through traffic. On another day, I might have shared it. Lena had the irrepressible ability to not only find joy in life, but to express it without fear or self-consciousness. She loved without fear. It was one of the things that made me crazy about her.

But even as I clung to her waist, feeling her body pressed against mine, breathing in the woodsy smell of her hair, I couldn't stop thinking about August Harrison. About how casually he had threatened to murder innocent people. About the anger I had seen when he murdered that wendigo in Tamarack. About his willingness to transform human beings into monsters, using techniques *I* had developed.

Where had he found his would-be wendigos? Were these allies who had volunteered to be transformed, or were they more victims? They had dragged the unconscious bodies away, leaving nobody who could answer those questions.

The magic in Harrison's two pelts wouldn't last forever. The rat had reverted to normal after three days, though that had been a smaller sample of skin, one which had been preserved for years before use. We didn't know how long the magic of a fresh skin might endure.

I kept an eye out for insects, but either Harrison hadn't noticed Lena's bike, or else I had stung him too badly when I swatted his last batch.

Another possibility taunted me. Maybe this was what Harrison wanted. He had tried to get the two of us to surrender back in Columbus, and here we were, speeding down the highway to find him. Victor had been a genius. I couldn't afford to underestimate his father.

The GPS led us to a small Baptist church. Scorch marks covered the parking lot. Streaks of black rubber showed where someone had swerved around a car parked by the main entrance. The van was here, having smashed into a basketball hoop on the far side of the lot. Tire tracks on the grass suggested the truck had kept going into the field behind the church, where a row of pine trees stood like a living fence.

Lena parked her bike on the side of the road. I tugged my helmet off with one hand and clipped it to her bike. As we approached, I heard shouts from the field.

"Oh, shit." Lena took off running toward the front door. A body lay slumped against the brick wall, half hidden by the bushes alongside the walk. Lena pushed the bushes aside, and from the way the urgency drained from her movements, I knew we were too late.

Sharp claws had opened the woman's throat and shoulder. Her eyes were wide. Blood dribbled from the wounds, soaking into the gravel. Whoever she was, she didn't look like she could have presented a threat. Thick glasses, a close-permed frizz of brown hair, and a round face gave her a vaguely jovial appearance, even in death. She had died clutching her purse to her chest. I knelt and opened her purse.

"What are you doing?" Lena whispered.

"I'm not sure." I just wanted to know her name. This murder struck harder than the others. Maybe the still-warm body just felt more *real* than vampires who turned to dust or ash, or the wendigos who had been hacked apart until they were nothing but meat. Or maybe it was my own human prejudices, the idea that a human death meant more than the others. After all, wasn't I the one who had experimented with old wendigo hide like it was nothing more than a toy?

I pulled out a leather wallet. The driver's license identified her as Christina Quinney, age fifty-three. Killed by monsters because she was in the way. I returned the wallet and closed her eyes. As I stood, I ripped the blanket away from my hand and stretched the armored fingers, then donned my enchanted sunglasses. "Come on."

Lena tested the edges of her bokken, then nodded. I debated preparing an additional weapon or two of my own, but I didn't want to push it. Not yet. Smarter to wait until I knew exactly what would be most effective at ending August Harrison.

We made our way around the back of the church, keeping close to the wall. The pickup had driven through a small flower garden, overturning a bench and smashing a birdbath before coming to a stop by the trees. A starburst of blackened grass and the smell of sulfur showed where the automaton had taken another shot at the truck. Through my glasses, the charred grass shimmered as if someone had spilled gold glitter: the remnants of the automaton's magic.

The battle had moved to the edge of the woods, where three people stood around the automaton. Insects lay dead and scattered, like flickering embers. Harrison and his wendigos formed a second ring, but only those inner three were actually fighting. Each held a book, and with the sunglasses, I could see three ghosts circling the automaton, draining the life from its body.

What the hell were they? I had seen possession before, where fictional characters crept into the mind of a careless libriomancer. If I kept pushing things, I'd see it a lot closer. But that was a known and somewhat understood magical phenomenon. Like possession, these beings appeared to come from books, but they behaved like the *absence* of magic.

"How long do you think we have before the police show up?" Lena asked.

"They won't. Not until this is over. Automatons can become invisible when necessary, but they also divert the attention of anyone who doesn't know what they are. Call it an apathy field, for lack of a better term." The automaton stumbled. A patch of metal fell away from its wooden body, and three of the spells woven into its shell went dark. "Anything magic I throw their way, they can intercept."

Lena stepped away, returning a short time later with several chunks of broken blacktop. "So we hit them hobbit style. Nothing magical about a flying rock."

"I don't know what's sexier," I said. "Watching you prepare to take on bad guys, or the fact that you're making *Lord of the Rings* references as you do it." I pulled out a copy of *The Marvelous Land of Oz*. "If we hit them from two directions, we should be able to draw off their attack enough for the automaton to start smacking heads."

The automaton staggered, and the others closed in. More of its armor dropped into the grass. Two more insects flew in and burrowed into the exposed wood.

I set the Oz book aside and grabbed Plato's *The Re-*

public. Reading was tricky with only one working hand, but I soon held the Ring of Gyges. I had done an honors paper as an undergraduate, arguing the similarity between Plato's tale and Tolkien's One Ring. I shoved *The Republic* back into my pocket and started in on *The Marvelous Land of Oz*.

"Dare I ask what you're planning to do with a ring and an old pepperbox?" Lena asked when I was done.

I beamed. "It's a surprise. Give me two minutes to get ready."

I slipped the ring onto my finger and vanished. In theory, true invisibility should have left me blind. Vision relied on the interaction between light and the cells at the back of the eye, but thanks to the ring, the light passed through me as if I wasn't here.

Fortunately, libriomancy obeyed belief over physics, and few modern-day readers thought about invisibility on a cellular level. I ran back to Christina Quinney and took a lipstick from her purse, then hurried toward the garden. Once there, I dropped behind the overturned bench.

The seat and back were slabs of polished black granite. The engraving along the back read, *In memory of Annette Butler*. Had the truck hit this thing head-on, it probably would have broken both the bench and the truck, but it looked like they had struck it at an angle.

"I'm sorry about this, Annette." I uncapped the lipstick and drew two red eyes and a large mouth. I wasn't much of an artist, especially since the lipstick had turned invisible when I picked it up, but it left visible, waxy lines on the granite. I added a pair of angry eyebrows as well, along with uneven ears to either side.

I put the lipstick away and pulled out the pepperbox. Creating the powder of life from *The Marvelous Land of*

Oz had been the easy part. The challenge was getting through the ritual to use it. I opened the box and sprinkled the powder over the bench, then raised my left pinky and said, "Weaugh." Next was the right thumb. "Teaugh." Finally, I raised both arms and waved them like a dancer doing jazz hands. "Peaugh."

L. Frank Baum wrote some weird magic. I just hoped I had pronounced it correctly.

Through my glasses, the powder looked like white sparks melting into the metal and granite. The whole contraption gave a shiver. Lipstick eyes blinked, and the ears perked up.

"Hello there," I said. "I need you to do me a favor . . ."

A wendigo was the first one to spot the bench bounding toward them. With a snarl, it broke away from the circle to meet this new threat.

The bench didn't even slow down. It charged with a straight-on waddle, as if it wanted nothing more than for that wendigo to plop down and enjoy a nice, comfy seat. Instead, the wendigo grabbed the bench and lifted one end into the air.

It was an impressive display of strength, one which did the wendigo no good whatsoever as the seat and back clapped together like enormous granite jaws. The wendigo let out a high-pitched yowl of pain.

Lena used the distraction to sprint toward the trees. Two of the wendigos spotted her, but a chunk of brick downed one before it could react. A lucky shot with my shock-gun took care of the second. I was a lousy shot with my left hand, but the nice thing about the shock-gun was that even grazing the target was enough to drop it.

Harrison whirled, but thanks to the Ring of Gyges on my hand, he stared right through me.

He recovered quickly, ordering the wendigos back. A

ghost flew from the automaton and swooped through the bench, weakening my spell.

My gun spat lightning at the three mages, but it fizzled into nothingness without reaching them. With everyone worrying about me and the bench, Lena was able to race out from between the trees, slip an arm around a wendigo's throat, and haul it backward.

The wendigo's choked cry was enough to attract attention. Two more wendigos bounded after Lena. I almost felt bad for them. Attacking Lena among the trees was a particularly bad idea.

I moved to the corner of the church and braced my arm against the bricks, sighting in on August Harrison, but one of the ghosts swooped into my line of fire. It could see me, even if Harrison couldn't.

In the field, the bench staggered as another ghost continued to siphon its magic. Cartoonish eyes drooped, and its movements turned sluggish. But when another wendigo approached, the bench valiantly reared up and kicked it in the chest.

The ghost in front of me closed in. I pointed over its shoulder, uncertain whether it would see or understand the gesture. "Too late," I said, grinning.

With two of the three ghosts focused on us while Harrison and the wendigos chased after Lena, the remaining book-mage was left alone to try to contain the automaton. It wasn't enough. Wooden hands creaked, and a blast of hellfire shot outward. The woman with the green hair tried to jump out of the way, but the flames caught her in the side. She spun away, protecting her book even as she screamed in pain.

She tried to run, but the automaton struck a wendigo hard enough to knock its body into her. They both went down, and her book flew into the grass. The ghost in front of me peeled away, streaking back toward the automaton.

I didn't stop to think. I simply ran. I held my shock-gun ready, but my attention was on that book. The wendigo who had been hit was very dead, but Green was groaning and trying to pull herself free from beneath the body. She was reaching for her book.

I got there first. The book disappeared when I snatched it up with my armored hand. The woman screamed again, fury overpowering pain as she struggled to follow.

I retreated to the church to study my prize. It became visible again as soon as I set it down. White silk cords bound wooden boards covered in red cloth. I opened the cover, then pulled my hand back. "Rice paper," I whispered.

Strong and smooth, the paper held the ink far better than most modern paper. The columns of brown Chinese characters were as clear and sharp as the day they had been drawn. The pages were folded and pasted together, like a long scroll flattened accordion-style and bound into a single book. There were illustrations, but no color.

Based on what I had seen, this book was more than seven hundred years old. Give or take a century. That made it significantly older than Gutenberg himself. Of course, I was no expert, and I couldn't know anything for certain without further research.

I turned carefully to the front pages and frowned. The first few pages were printed, either woodblock or movable type. But the inner pages appeared to have been written by hand.

I moved the book out of sight behind me and returned my attention to the fighting. Only two of the ghosts remained, and all but three wendigos were unconscious or too injured to make a difference. Harrison was red-faced, his angry shouts growing shrill with panic. My animated bench was limping and the automaton was in bad shape, but we were winning. Harrison launched another small swarm at the automaton, only to have their magic sucked away before they reached their target. Harrison cried out again, this time in pain. I grinned and started shooting, and he dove for cover behind the truck.

"Guan Feng?"

The voice belonged to a woman, and it had come from the book. I had heard whispers from books before, but this was different. It didn't feel like misplaced snippets of dialogue sneaking into my thoughts. Whoever had spoken sounded more aware, more *here.*

At the tree line, roots broke through the earth to twine around a wendigo's ankles. I aimed at the two remaining book-mages and pulled the trigger.

The book behind me screamed. The words were in another tongue—one of the Chinese languages, I thought . . . possibly Mandarin—but I understood them perfectly as they tore through my skull.

"Begone, Porter!"

In order for my magic to translate her words, those words had to be spoken by a living mind. This was no character brought to pseudolife to fight for August Harrison. Not only was this a real person, she knew what I was. And she was terrified.

"Bi Wei!" The woman with the green hair dragged herself free and began hobbling toward us. Harrison shouted an order, but she ignored him. I heard the book calling out to her, to Guan Feng, pleading for help.

I raised my shock-gun. I had endless questions, but we could sort things out as soon as everyone stopped trying to kill me.

The book screamed a second time. Magic poured forth, and I watched the gun dissolve in my hand.

The fact that I could see my hand meant the Ring of Gyges was fading as well. I scooted backward, but Guan Feng had spotted me. The book continued to scream, and a shadow darkened my vision. The sunglasses fell apart and dropped to the ground, leaving me blind to the magic swirling around and through me.

I couldn't see what she was doing, but I could feel it. The armor on my right hand broke away like oversized scabs. I supposed I should have been grateful for that small blessing, but it didn't stop.

As the ghost tore through me, my mind flashed back to the attack in Detroit. The devourer had seized me from the inside out, claws unraveling my memories and my thoughts. I had come so close to drowning in its hunger and rage. It had been an incoherent, instinctive attack. The devourer had no understanding or awareness of what I was, or of anything save the need to destroy me. This was different. Instead of incoherent fury, I sensed both fear and determination. Her attack was similar, but more controlled.

She was also stronger. These books, and whoever or whatever was acting through them, had been holding back.

I felt her attention splinter. She lashed out to slap the bench, which broke in two and stopped moving. Another strike knocked the automaton to the ground. She had plunged us all into a whirlpool of naked power. Even Guan Feng looked afraid as she limped toward us.

Where had they come from, and why would they follow a man like Harrison? Their power dwarfed whatever magic he had managed to steal from the Porters.

"Lena, get out of here!" I crawled away from the

book and used the wall to push myself upright. A wendigo was bounding toward me on all fours. "Tell them we've been chasing Saruman."

I hoped she would understand. Saruman was a dangerous villain in *Lord of the Rings*, but he hadn't been the true threat. If whoever or whatever was trapped in these books got loose, they would make Gutenberg look like an amateur stage magician fumbling his way through cheap card tricks.

Several hundred pounds of wendigo slammed into me like a wrecking ball. My head bounced against the ground, and I rolled several times before coming to rest. As my vision gradually came back into focus, I found myself looking up at a snarling, frostbitten face that retained just enough humanity to be truly monstrous.

"I think you and I both know Lena's not going to leave you alone." August Harrison strode toward us, one thumb hooked through his belt loop. Metal creatures crawled over his chest and shoulders, like piglets fighting for their mother's teat. Many were larger than the insects we had seen before, more like those Madagascar hissing cockroaches some people kept as pets. I searched for the queen, the cicada Nicholas had described, but couldn't find it.

Harrison pulled an old paperback from his back pocket and fanned through the pages. I swore when I spotted the cover art. A yellow-and-red border framed an image of two scantily clad warrior women fighting over a well-muscled man chained to an oak tree. Harrison had tracked down a copy of *Nymphs of Neptune*.

"You write well, Isaac. Such detailed reports. I can't begin to tell you how helpful you've been to my little army." He tugged a rusted metal millipede off of his shirt and held it out for me to see. "I might not have Victor's gifts, but I know my way around a machine shop. If he had shared these secrets with me, let me help him build sturdier, stronger creatures, he might have survived that attack."

I heard genuine regret, even grief in his words as he stared past me. Despite everything he had done, Victor had been a part of his life for years. What must it have been like when the cicada arrived? If it was telepathic, did that mean it had shared Victor's final, agonized moments with August Harrison?

Harrison brought the millipede closer, and any sympathy I had disappeared. Pointed iron legs clicked together. A series of overlapping brackets formed the segmented shell. Instead of antennae, a single slender blade protruded from the center of the millipede's face, like some kind of stiletto-headed unicorn bug. The millipede was long enough to circle Harrison's wrist with several inches to spare.

He dropped it onto my chest. I tried to fling it away, only to have the wendigo stomp on my arm. If I had been on pavement instead of grass, he would have shattered bone. I lay perfectly still as the millipede crawled higher and circled my neck.

Harrison turned to shout. "Miss Greenwood, I'm tired of games. I'll give you thirty seconds, and then I'm going to let one of my pets bore a hole through your lover's skull."

He was sweating beneath that coat of bugs. I could see the dampness as they moved. His face was red, and he was out of breath.

Guan Feng approached, hugging her book to her body. She scowled at me like I was the genetically engineered offspring of Adolf Hitler and Jack the Ripper.

"Perhaps she needs more encouragement." Harrison

turned to the trees again. "You've lost one oak this year. Are you strong enough to survive the death of another?"

"Going after Lena's tree didn't work out too well for you last time," I said. "How many more of your son's toys can you afford to lose?"

He waved a hand, and the millipede's grip tightened with a metallic click.

"You have no idea what you've allied yourself with, do you?" I asked. I didn't bother hiding my smirk. If he was going to kill me, the least I could do was piss him off before I died. "You're nothing but a parasite. I don't know what they need you for, but as soon as they get it—"

"August." Lena emerged from the trees carrying a long wooden spear. One of the wendigos jumped in front of Harrison to shield him, but Lena only laughed and hefted the spear over one shoulder. "You think I can't put this thing through both of you?"

The millipede raced onto my face. It was heavier than I had expected, and its legs stung like thorns. I heard a whirring sound, and pain pierced the center of my forehead.

Harrison raised his book. "Even if that were true, killing me would guarantee Isaac's death, and we both know you can't do that."

Blood dripped down the side of my head. I turned my head to keep the blood from running into my ear, which brought Guan Feng into the center of my vision. She was staring at Lena, and her eyes had filled with tears. She didn't seem to be afraid. Not of Lena, at any rate. If anything, she looked like she was afraid to trust what she was seeing, like she wanted to touch Lena to confirm that she was real. She noticed me watching, and her expression turned to stone.

Lena stabbed her spear into the earth. The millipede pulled back, obeying Harrison's unspoken command. My jaw unclenched, and I forced myself to breathe normally.

"Search her," Harrison barked at Guan Feng. "Strip her of any magic, and don't let her have any wood. Not even a toothpick."

Lena smiled and spread her arms, never taking her eyes from August Harrison. Her unwavering attention even made me nervous. "If you hurt Isaac, I will shove an acorn down your throat and force it to take root in your gut. Care to guess how tall it will grow before you finally die?"

Harrison stepped forward and backhanded her. I pushed myself up, but the wendigo gave me an almost absentminded kick in the head.

Lena never even blinked. "Is your hand okay?"

Harrison grimaced and rubbed his knuckles. "It doesn't matter. As long as I have him, you're mine. And once you've spent enough time in my company, you'll kill him yourself."

Lena's gaze dropped to me, and for the first time, her confidence cracked. As strong as she was, we both knew Harrison was right.

Chapter 11

I understand humans are unable to remember their first years of life. Their bodies and minds develop so much, and so quickly during that time. Perhaps that's why I remember so little of those early sessions with Nidhi Shah. I've read her case notes, but much of the person she describes is a stranger.

Only two thoughts etched themselves into my memory during that first meeting. The first was Nidhi's smile, beautiful and warm and reassuring. The second was my realization toward the end of the day that I was completely in love with her.

I learned so much from her. Nidhi said one way Frank controlled me was to make sure I never acquired the skills to be independent. Because it made her happy, I threw myself into study.

I mastered reading in three weeks. We began with children's stories, like Doctor Seuss and the Berenstain Bears. (I learned later that she had deliberately avoided giving me a copy of The Giving Tree.*) Once I could make it through those, she brought me a handful of comic books.*

I devoured them. Tank Girl and Wonder Woman, She-Hulk and Batman, Catwoman and Katana. I wanted to meet them. I wanted to be them. I shaped my first wooden sword from my oak tree, mimicking the exaggerated, thick-bladed weapon from Katana's appearance in an early Outsiders *comic.*

I was catching up on Black Widow one evening when I felt Nidhi watching me. I continued reading, enjoying her attention. I knew she was attracted to me. I could feel her fighting it every time we spoke, every time I hugged her or sat beside her on the couch. She had brought me into her home because I had no place to go. Now I couldn't imagine living anywhere else.

"You've changed your hair," she said.

I pulled my fingers through the black locks. I had done nothing. I hadn't even noticed the darkening color until a week ago. My skin had turned a deeper brown as well, far more than it ever had before, even when I was working day in and day out beneath the sun. "Do you like it?"

She didn't answer, but instead walked over to see what I was reading. "I loved that issue."

"Me, too."

I could have seduced her as I had done with Frank Dearing, could have taken her desire and grown it like a new-budded flower. But I refrained. Whatever happened, it was important that it be her choice. I wanted her to love me on her own terms.

She sat down, not on the couch beside me, but in the rocking chair at the end of the coffee table. "You've grown so much since you lost Frank. The Porters are asking for my evaluation. I believe you're ready to live on your own."

I jumped to my feet, heart pounding. "I'm not. I can't—"

"You don't need a counselor anymore," Nidhi said. *"You've adjusted to everything so easily. You're far stronger than any of us imagined."*

It was the way she lowered her eyelids that did it, shielding her eyes while staring at me through her lashes. A month ago she had been a stranger, and now I could read her simply by watching those long, expressive lashes. "You're right," I said. "I don't need a counselor anymore."

I saw her swallow, saw the skin of her neck and face darken slightly. "Lena, it's normal for a patient to develop feelings for her therapist . . ."

"What about the therapist's feelings for her patient?"

"I care about you. I hope you haven't misunderstood—"

"I haven't misunderstood anything." I smiled, trying to show her that it was okay. "I know what you want. I can feel it."

To her credit, she didn't try to lie. Her forehead crinkled. "You can sense emotions?"

"Only that emotion." I laughed, delighted to see her blush deepen. "I didn't say anything because I thought it would make you uncomfortable."

"It would be inappropriate," Nidhi said, *but I could feel her resolve melting.*

I leaned back in the couch, my skin tingling with the anticipation of her touch. "I certainly hope so."

She blinked once, then started to laugh. I had heard her laughter before, but never like this. Loud, joyful, and utterly unrestrained, her delight called to my own, until I was laughing with her.

She joined me on the couch and placed a hand on my thigh, and soon laughter gave way to other sounds.

A PAIR OF HARRISON'S wendigos shoved us into the back of the pickup truck. It was like being manhandled by Frosty the Snowman, only Frosty's breath probably hadn't smelled of raw hamburger, nor would his claws have drawn blood. The millipede circled my neck like a grotesque choker, the tip of the blade resting against the base of my skull.

A metal cat jumped awkwardly onto the tailgate behind us. It appeared to have been pieced together with scraps from a wrecked car. This was a cruder creation than the others I had seen. The head looked like a rotor assembly from the alternator, and the major joints were exposed wheels and belts, as if someone had simply smashed the engine into a new form. Smaller insects were crawling through its innards.

"That's disturbing." I tucked my feet in close, out of reach. "What's your name?"

The cat arched its back and made a sound like the grinding of worn-out brake pads. Its teeth were mismatched slivers of fiberglass, and the claws were black metal screws. Various rods and springs acted as tendon and muscle.

August shut the tailgate and the truck cap, locking us in. He climbed into the back seat of the pickup and slid open the rear window so he could talk to us. His smugness had returned in force, perhaps compensating for his earlier fear.

"Give me your hands, Vainio." He used a thick plastic zip tie to bind my wrists together. "The cat will look better once he's finished."

"How does it work, exactly?" I asked. "You come up with the idea, and Victor's insects bring it to life?"

"Don't be naïve. That thing's no more alive than this truck." He shouted out the door for everyone to hurry up, then turned back to me. "I spent twenty years working as an electrical engineer for the power company. Last year, we lost another line worker after a storm. Damn fool had been working overtime, and wasn't paying attention. Tell me, Isaac, why did that man have to die when something like Victor's bugs could have made the repairs faster and more safely?"

"You're saying you want to fix things? Because so far, all you seem to have used them for is killing people."

"You and I have very different definitions of people." He didn't bother to tie Lena's wrists. He simply pointed to the cat, then to the millipede around my neck. "We'll be watching."

Guan Feng climbed into the seat opposite Harrison. One of the wendigos took the front passenger seat, which would have been amusing to watch from a safer distance. First he caught his fur in the door, and then he fumbled with the seat belt for a good minute before giving up. I felt a little sorry for him.

Another of the book-mages drove, which surprised me. Harrison didn't strike me as the kind of guy to let someone else take the wheel. Maybe the battle had taken more out of him than I thought.

"I was able to call Nidhi and tell her what was happening," Lena said.

I grinned, then nodded to show I understood. Harrison could listen in all he wanted, but I doubted he was fluent in Gujarati. I might not be able to respond in kind, but half a conversation was better than none. Better yet, this meant the translation spell in my brain was working again. Whatever Guan Feng's book had done to me, the effects were already fading.

I checked out our mobile prison, doing my best to avoid any sudden motion that might spook the cat. The truck cap was old, made of fiberglass and plastic on an aluminum frame. The tinted plastic would hide us from view, but Lena could rip this thing apart without breaking a sweat. And Harrison would kill me the instant she tried.

She sighed and leaned against me. Between the sounds from outside and the changing speed, I was able to tell when we reached the highway. The sunlight filtering through the window meant we were heading roughly north. Back to Michigan, then.

I watched the insects crawling in and out of the metal cat like shiny maggots on a corpse as I tried to fit the missing pieces into place. The magic in Guan Feng's book was strong enough to stop any libriomancer. Why hadn't *they* killed Lena's tree? Why had they held back at Victor's house? I doubted all of us together would have been a match for what I had just seen and felt. Or maybe the question was what had been holding them back?

I looked through the window at Guan Feng. It was only after I had taken her book that everything went to hell. She wasn't a libriomancer, but what if she was the book's keeper? Though the relationship was deeper than that. The voice I heard had been terrified for Guan Feng. And terrified of me.

"I won't let him turn me against you," Lena said quietly.

"I know." We both knew what Harrison would turn her into. Just as we knew she would choose to die before she let him take that choice away. "You should have run."

"I *couldn't*." She didn't try to hide her frustration. "Isaac, where did these people come from?"

Harrison slid open the window. "Speak English, or shut the hell up."

She put a hand on the aluminum frame, blocking him from shutting the window. "Don't the bugs creep you out?"

"They're tools. Solid and reliable." He plucked a silver dot the size of a ladybug from his sleeve and watched it crawl over his fingers. "Victor was always better with machines than he was with people. Caused him no end of grief in school. I tried to help, to teach him to stand up for himself, but his mother insisted on coddling him."

I fought the urge to reach through the window and throttle him, but Lena simply nodded. Her quiet anger from moments before had vanished, and she listened raptly to Harrison's every word. "You wanted him to be strong."

"That's right." He glanced at me. "I didn't want my son to grow up to be the kind of man who let his girl-friend fight his battles for him."

Lena cut me off before I could respond. "He didn't. He was outnumbered, but he killed several vampires and injured more."

"It wasn't enough, though, was it?"

"I guess not."

I stared. He couldn't possibly be buying into Lena's submissive act ... or maybe he could. This was a man who had treated both his wife and son as mere possessions. Why wouldn't he look at Lena in the same way? He might see Lena's passiveness not as a front, but as her right and natural state. Especially if he had read *Nymphs of Neptune*.

And Lena knew it.

"Isaac killed the man who was responsible for Victor's death," Lena said softly.

"I know. I read about what happened." Harrison turned away.

"Who are your friends?"

"They call themselves Bi Sheng de du zhe."

Normally, I would have heard the words in English as well as Mandarin, but that only worked if the speaker knew what his words meant. Fortunately, Guan Feng turned and repeated the phrase, correcting Harrison's pronunciation without bothering to disguise her annoyance. "*Bì Shēng de dú zhě.*"

I stared at Guan Feng, wondering if I had heard correctly. *The students of Bi Sheng.* The actual meaning blurred the line between "students" and "readers."

Bi Sheng had begun experimenting with movable type during China's Song Dynasty, centuries before Gutenberg invented his press. But Bi Sheng's porcelain letters had been too fragile for large-scale printing.

"I don't understand." I ignored Harrison and spoke directly to Guan Feng. "Bi Sheng's press couldn't produce books in large enough numbers for magic."

She glared. "The Porters' flaw has always been arrogance."

"That's not—okay, yeah, you're probably right." I started to say more, but the millipede's legs pinched my neck.

Harrison dragged the backs of his fingers down over the metal shells covering his chest, making an irregular clinking sound. "I could force that millipede to crawl into your mouth," he said lightly. "To clamp its legs into your tongue and dig its sting into the back of your throat."

"How did you find them?" Lena asked. "The Porters don't even know they exist."

I thought back to Gutenberg's reaction when I described our attackers. One Porter had known, or at least suspected.

"Victor built his pets to seek out magic." Harrison clearly enjoyed being in a position of power, doling out knowledge like an animal trainer tossing scraps to a performing monkey. "Feng and her fellow caretakers have hidden for centuries, but they couldn't hide from me."

"Hidden from what?" Lena asked.

"From us." I braced myself, but Harrison let my guess pass without punishment. He even smiled, like his pet had mastered a new trick.

"Would you like to learn the *true* history of libriomancy, Isaac?"

I knew he was taunting me, but dammit, he had also discovered a branch of magic I had never heard of. If Victor's bugs were as good as I suspected, he had probably gotten into areas of our network I had never seen, too. I tried not to let too much of my annoyance show. "Sure, I love a good story."

"I suppose Gutenberg told you *he* invented libriomancy?" Harrison rested his elbow through the window.

"You've got a better theory?"

It was Guan Feng who answered. "Bi Sheng and his students were exploring the magical potential of books centuries before Gutenberg. Gutenberg discovered our art and stole what secrets he could. He spent years trying to duplicate Bi Sheng's magic."

"He never—" I stopped myself. Who was I to say what was or wasn't true? More than a decade of Gutenberg's early life was a mystery. Not even Porter historians knew what he had been up to during the 1420s, though there were plenty of theories.

"Gutenberg was afraid of competition," Guan Feng continued. "Afraid to let anyone else have power. So he created his automatons and sent them to wipe us out."

Gutenberg's invention had spawned upheavals that

spread throughout the world. The printing press had spread chaos on every level imaginable: political, religious, and even magical. In a single generation, he upended a magical balance of power that had existed for millennia. While Gutenberg and his growing guild of libriomancers lacked the raw might of the old sorcerers, they made up for it in numbers.

According to the histories I had read, other practitioners had been jealous of Gutenberg, afraid of the following he was amassing. They sought to destroy him, and he created his automatons out of self-defense. Gutenberg had eventually used the automatons to help establish the Porters. Together, they united the world's magic-users and laid out the laws to put an end to such conflicts.

I knew those histories were incomplete. They made no reference to the other mission of those original twelve Porters. Even then, Gutenberg had been aware of the devourers, and his Porters had worked to keep them from entering our world.

What else had Gutenberg omitted? History was written by the survivors and reshaped by those with power. Few people had ever gained as much power as Johannes Gutenberg. He portrayed himself as a man forced to make ugly choices for a greater purpose. But he had enslaved the souls of his enemies to create the automatons and enforce peace. He manipulated the minds of his own Porters to keep them from abusing their power.

If he had seen the students of Bi Sheng as a threat, he would have acted without hesitation.

"Gutenberg is a tyrant," Harrison said. "His army has manipulated this world from the shadows for centuries."

"If we ruled the world, I guarantee you they never would have canceled *Firefly*," I countered.

He sighed. "Make your jokes while you can. Thanks to you, Gutenberg's army will soon fall."

I was no longer listening. I stared at the book in Guan Feng's lap as I made the connection. I forgot about Harrison, the metal millipede around my neck, everything except that ancient text and what it represented. "When I grabbed that book, you shouted a name. Bi Wei."

Guan Feng's eyes widened, and she tightened her grip on the book as if I would somehow snap through my bonds, rip it from her grasp, and plunge my hand into the pages to seize its magic.

"Holy shit," I breathed. "That's where they went, isn't it? When Gutenberg's automatons attacked, they preserved themselves in their books."

Automatons worked similarly, trapping ghosts . . . souls . . . whatever you wanted to call them. A single phrase etched in metal bound the mind to the wooden body. But I had entered an automaton and touched the mind trapped inside. There had been precious little left of her humanity.

The books were different. I had guessed Guan Feng's book to be several hundred years older than Gutenberg. "The books had to have been prepared long before the attack. Passed down and guarded for emergencies, like magical escape pods. They fled into those books, and you've protected them ever since."

"Gutenberg wanted to destroy us," Guan Feng said. "He failed."

How long could you survive like that before the madness took you? Before despair turned to hunger, to resentment and hatred toward everything you had lost. Until all that remained was the need to devour whatever you touched.

"You couldn't save all of the books, could you?" I

asked. Her silence was answer enough. I turned to Harrison. Despite the summer heat, I suddenly felt cold. "You said you found them. Are you sure?"

He frowned. "What are you talking about?"

I thought back to what Jeneta had said about the insects, about the devourers who had attacked her thoughts. The queen was telepathic, and telepathy went in two directions. "How do you know they didn't find you?"

"You know what's worse than going over the Mackinac Bridge in my little convertible?" I spoke softly, with as little movement of the neck or mouth as possible. Harrison hadn't been pleased about losing control of our earlier conversation, and he had expressed his annoyance by perforating the skin beneath my jawbone.

"Going over the bridge in the back of a pickup?" Lena guessed.

I closed my eyes as we moved onto the metal grating in the center lanes, where wind rushed up from below and the only thing keeping us from plunging into the Great Lakes was a stretch of glorified screens.

I understood the engineering well enough to recognize that we were perfectly safe. Unfortunately, intellect had a hard time making itself heard over my gut, which was currently insisting we were all about to plunge to our deaths.

She twined her fingers with mine. "Captured by a murderer with a metal worm around your neck, and you're worried about heights."

"Did you know the middle of this bridge can sway more than thirty feet in high winds?" In truth, I was almost grateful for the distraction. I had spent the past hours thinking about Guan Feng's book and the devourers, trying to understand our true enemy. There were too many gaps, too much I didn't know.

The first pages of her book were block printed. In theory, if enough copies of the text had been made, that could create the magical resonance you needed for libriomancy. But the rest of the book had been copied by hand.

Was this an unfinished work? If the original wood blocks had been lost, someone might have tried to finish it manually, but not even the most careful scribe could have achieved the perfection of the printing press.

Ask yourself the real question, coward. If the students of Bi Sheng fled into their books, and some of them were lost to madness, does that mean the Porters created the devourers?

The timeline didn't fit. Gutenberg had shared documented encounters with the devourers from centuries before his time, meaning they had come into existence before Gutenberg was ever born. I supposed those documents could have been faked, but why?

The voice I heard at the church—Bi Wei's voice—hadn't been a devourer. She was frightened and angry, not crazed. Her power had sapped our magic. She hadn't destroyed us.

I banged my head against the side of the truck, then twisted to watch Guan Feng, who had been reading for at least two hours. Was that how she communicated with Bi Wei? Her eyes scanned slowly up and down the text, completely focused.

"Libriomancy only works if thousands of people have read the same book," I said quietly.

Lena shifted her weight, resting her head on my shoulder. "So I've heard."

"What happens if one person reads the same book thousands of times?"

"I imagine they'd get extremely bored."

"Depends on the book. Remind me to give you a copy of *Good Omens* when we get home."

Back in the sixties, a libriomancer named Ghalib al-Mun'im had collaborated with the Bibliothèque nationale de France to develop a list of the most commonly reread titles, books that were checked out again and again by the same patrons. The Porters had learned to estimate the strength of a book's potential magic based on the number of readers. Al-Mun'im wanted to build on their work to measure the impact of rereading.

According to his findings, those frequently reread books were less powerful than books read an equal number of times by unique individuals. I remembered his math being rather fuzzy in several spots, but he had suggested that if the Porters wanted to increase the power of books, encouraging more people to read a wider variety would be roughly five times as effective as pushing them to reread their favorites.

But what if you didn't have a large pool of potential readers? What if you had only a few copies of the books in question and couldn't risk printing more, for fear that your enemies would find out?

How many times had that book been read and reread through the centuries? How many times had it been repaired to survive, or did Bi Wei somehow strengthen the physical book?

I squinted out the window, trying to guess where we were going. I was almost certain we had taken 28 after the bridge. We stopped for gas a short time later, but the sign outside told me nothing beyond the cost of cigarettes and unleaded gas.

The sun was setting when we finally left the highway. I had started to drift to sleep. The change of speed jolted me from a Wonderland-style nightmare in which I fled through an endless library, my footsteps echoing on the marble floor, trying to escape from invisible pursuers. I was relieved to be free of my dream, up until I remembered where I really was.

We drove into a hilly, wooded area. I felt the road turn to gravel, and the truck's jostling made the millipede around my neck twitch and dig in tighter.

"Let Harrison feel like he's in control," Lena whispered in Gujarati.

"He pretty much is."

She swung a leg over my lap to straddle me. She kissed my ear, then brought my bound hands toward her. She pressed my fingers against a hard lump beneath the skin of her forearm, like a dislocated bone. Before I could ask what it was, she tensed her arm, and a sliver of wood poked through the skin to jab my fingers. "Take it," she whispered.

I took the tip of wood and pulled. Lena gasped, but with her body blocking the mechanical cat's view, Harrison would hopefully take that as a sound of passion rather than pain. I slid a thin wooden stiletto about eight inches long from her skin.

"How?" I asked.

"Flesh. Blood. Wood. They're all a part of my body." She kissed me again. "August Harrison is as arrogant as any Porter, and it's going to cost him dearly."

Harrison pounded a fist on the window. "I said knock it off with that foreign talk."

Lena winked at me, then helped me to tuck the knife into my sock. I can only imagine what Harrison thought we were doing.

The truck stopped, and a man I hadn't seen before unlocked the back. Lena exited first, then offered me a hand as I climbed down from the tailgate. I leaned against the truck and tried to rub the stiffness from my thighs. I smelled water, though I couldn't see the lake. The cold, fresh air tasted like home.

We were in a parking lot edged with wooden posts. Seven small brown cabins were spread out before us, identical in shape and size. Maple and spruce trees shaded most of the lot.

A pair of metal rats perched like gargoyles atop an old freezer humming outside the closest cabin. The freezer's curved lines and heavy steel handle, along with the orange rust along the bottom, suggested the thing was probably as old as I was. Such freezers could store enough venison to feed a small family for months. Or preserve the hides of murdered wendigos.

"More friends of yours?" I asked, nodding toward the other cars.

"The followers of Bi Sheng bought this place two months ago," announced Harrison. The cat bounded down and waddled along behind him like a bad-tempered and extremely pointy duckling.

A path beyond the cabins led down to what appeared to be sand dunes. The U.P. was full of these small lakeside hotels and campsites. The building marked as the office had a "Closed" sign, and the windows were dark. But people were emerging from the other cabins. I spotted two more carrying the oversized books. Others held rifles pointed in my direction. I got the impression that they knew exactly who and what I was, and that any one of them would be happy for an excuse to pull the trigger.

"Is this the dryad?" asked one of the men.

"I told you I'd bring her, didn't I?" Harrison snapped.

"You also told us the libriomancer was no threat, that you'd have them both long before they discovered you and your stolen magic."

Harrison sniffed and turned to address the group as a whole. "I brought the dryad. Let's get on with it."

"Where are the others?" someone else asked in Mandarin.

"They're safe," Guan Feng answered in the same language. "The van was destroyed. They're making their way back. The Porter and his friends were stronger than Harrison anticipated." She checked Harrison, as if making sure he wasn't paying attention. "They were able to report back to Gutenberg. He sent one of his automatons."

The man with the rifle swore. "How much do they know?"

"I don't know. I was too busy saving this bèn dàn." She gestured toward Harrison.

I bit my lip to keep from smirking as I made a mental note of that one. If I survived, I could teach Deb how to call someone a dumbass in Mandarin.

"All right, you've busted your asses to catch us," I said. "What happens next?"

Guan Feng looked down at her book. When she spoke, her words were soft and reverent. "Now the dryad will help us to restore the Bì Shēng de dú zhě."

Chapter 12

Eight months into our relationship, I returned home to find Nidhi sitting on the couch, her hands folded over a book in her lap.

When I sat down, she stiffened like she was fighting the urge to pull away. "I'm sorry I was late." I had been volunteering with the local food bank, encouraging the fruitfulness of their gardens. I thought I had told her we were picking and packing today, but maybe I'd forgotten. "Nidhi, what's wrong?"

"It's not you. Not anything you've done." She shifted to face me, putting more distance between us in the process. It felt like she had physically struck me. "The Porters have encountered a handful of dryads over the centuries, but the things you can do don't match their accounts. I've been reading about dryads ever since we found you."

She set the book on the coffee table and slid it toward me. It was an old library book, the spine heavily creased. She had tucked an origami butterfly into the pages to mark her place.

"Nymphs of Neptune?" The hairs on my neck and arms rose when I touched the book, like I had entered a haunted graveyard. I had to force myself to read the opening pages.

The words made me ill. I could get through brief passages, but the longer, descriptive sections left me dizzy and confused. I struggled to focus as the words blurred and doubled, and when I looked up, it felt like the house was tumbling around me. I squeezed my eyes shut, waiting for the effects to pass. *"What is this?"*

"The Porters who found you believed your tree was magical, created through libriomancy. I think they might have been right."

I closed the book and read the back cover. The summary text didn't hit me as hard as the story had, at least not physically. "You think I'm a character from this book? A slave?" I whispered.

"A fantasy." She answered so quietly I barely heard.

I wanted to destroy the book, to rip it apart and burn the pieces. Instead, I carefully set it back down and tried to absorb what I had read. If I was one of these nymphs— and both my reaction to the story and the description of the nymphs' powers suggested I was—then Nidhi hadn't been helping me. She had been *molding* me, transforming me into her perfect lover. I dug my fingers into the cushions, feeling the rage expand in my chest, a scream demanding release.

I had never experienced anger like this when I was with Frank Dearing. He had wanted an obedient, compliant companion, and so he had denied me my anger. He couldn't have known. He hadn't noticed or cared that I was . . . incomplete. What else had he taken?

And what had Nidhi kept from me?

"Why?" Humans asked the same questions. Why am I

here? What's my purpose? But my question could be an-swered. James Wright had deliberately written these nymphs into his book, describing every curve in meticu-lous detail.

I was here to fulfill the needs and desires of my lovers.

"We think someone pulled an acorn or sapling from the book," Nidhi said. "I doubt they even realized what they had done. If it was a fluke, an untrained accident, they probably scared themselves and ran away, leaving you to grow in this world."

That's why I had been alone when I awoke.

"I'm so sorry, Lena." This angered her, too. I could see it in the tightness of her body.

I refused to cry. "What will you do now that you know what I am?"

"I'm not sure. Nobody has the right to . . . to control another person like this."

"But I'm not really a person, am I?" My hair, my skin, my favorite flavor of ice cream, everything about me was a reflection of her. I was a fantasy. I had more in common with the airbrushed centerfold of a men's magazine than I did with a real human being.

I stormed away to our bedroom and slammed the door. I could hear Nidhi crying, and part of me longed to com-fort her. Instead, I clung to the anger, nurturing it like a sapling. What if she sent me away? My next lover could be someone like Frank. I might never experience this kind of hurt and anger again.

When Nidhi joined me, hours later, I was sitting amidst a circle of her comic books. Ridiculously clothed women stared up at me from the pages, bodies contorted into bone-bending poses that better displayed their exagger-ated curves.

"If you leave me, what then?" I reached out to turn the

page of a recent issue of Catwoman. *In one panel, the breasts straining to burst from her leather bodysuit were larger than her head, and her waist was thinner than her neck.* "Who will I be passed to next, and what will I become?"

Nidhi didn't answer. She didn't have to. My anger was nothing but a reflection of her own conflict, meaning she hated this just as much as I did. And dammit all to hell if that didn't make me love her more.

She sat down beside me, kissed my hair, and whispered, "Huun tane prem karuu chuun."

"I love you, too," *I said automatically. Whatever I was, those feelings were real to me.* "When I was born, I looked for the other dryads of my grove. For my sisters." *I picked up a* Red Sonja *comic.* "I've finally found them."

THE OTHERS FELL IN behind us as we walked deeper into the woods. I counted eleven wendigos and twenty-three humans, not including August Harrison. Far too many to fight, even if Harrison hadn't swiped my books.

How many ghosts walked with us? At least ten of my captors carried books. I thought of Bi Wei's magic ripping through me. She had been alone, trapped within her book. What might they do together if they were freed?

"Who were they?" Lena asked, pointing toward the wendigos.

"Some are volunteers," said Harrison. "The students of Bi Sheng assign one reader to each book. The readers' magic is too weak for the Porters to notice or care about, but they're trained to use that magic to maintain the life of their books. Often, their friends and family are recruited to serve as protectors. I just made those protectors stronger."

He brought us to a small, circular clearing. Fresh stumps marked where other trees had been cut down to create space around the oak in the center. How long had they been preparing for this?

"You remind me of my son." Harrison pulled my ratty old copy of *Star Wars* from his back pocket. He must have grabbed it from my jacket. "Always certain you're smarter than everyone else, that only you have the answers."

He ripped the book in half, then flung it into a puddle. Insects flowed down his leg to chew the pages into pulp.

I had owned that book for seventeen years. I couldn't remember how many times I had read it; I had stopped counting after forty-three.

"Easy," Lena whispered. She slipped an arm through mine to stop me from doing anything stupid.

I nodded slightly. This was what he wanted. To prove his power over me. There was no other reason to destroy my books. Even if I managed to get my hands on one, his millipede would stab its blade through my spine before I read a single sentence.

As my initial anger passed, I noticed something interesting: I wasn't the only one glaring at Harrison. Several of his companions were frowning, including Guan Feng. One man turned away in disgust.

"Bi Wei is waiting." Guan Feng walked toward the tree, turning her back on Harrison, so she missed the way his jaw tightened at being upstaged. She crouched at the base of the tree and carefully set her book into a depression among the roots.

"What exactly are you expecting me to do?" asked Lena.

Harrison straightened, visibly regaining his composure. "Two months ago, Isaac lost his physical body. He entered an automaton, transforming himself from flesh and blood to magic, just as the survivors of Gutenberg's attack did so many years ago. And then you accomplished something none of the students of Bi Sheng have been able to do, though they've tried for more than five hundred years. You pulled him back. You recreated his body." He waved at the tree. "Feng will guide Bi Wei's ghost into the tree. You will make her human again."

Lena approached the tree. Four rifles snapped up to point at her, and the wendigos snarled. The millipede tightened around my throat. Lena simply shook her head. "I saved the life of my *lover*, and it almost killed me. What makes you think I can restore a stranger from a book I've never read?"

"The magic is the same," Guan Feng said. "You recreate your human body each time you emerge from your tree. The tree holds the pattern of your human form, just as this book does for Bi Wei."

She was paraphrasing my own reports about Lena. Harrison must have shared my private files with them all. "What do you get out of this?" I asked him.

"That's none of your concern," he snapped.

"Maybe I'll offer your friends a better deal," Lena said lightly. "Isaac and I will do everything in our power to restore Bi Wei, and in return, they'll stay out of the way while I kick your ass."

"After so many centuries, do you think they're going to trust a Porter and his slave?" Harrison asked. "They need me. I can give them the location of every Porter archive and network server. I can provide personnel files on the Regional Masters, or the psychological assessments suggesting who in Gutenberg's organization could most easily be turned against him."

"None of which will bring back their dead," Lena pointed out. "If they want me to try to help them—"

"This isn't a negotiation." A portion of his magical hive poured off of his body and flew onto mine. Metal feet poked through my clothes, and tiny barbs tugged my skin. "The only question is how much pain you'll put your lover through before you cooperate."

Lena stepped toward Harrison, and suddenly a hundred metal stingers were stabbing my body.

I've read a lot of books where people get tortured. Conan the Cimmerian was unbreakable, enduring whatever his captors inflicted through sheer, testosterone-fueled barbarian rage. The Jedi from *Star Wars* could separate their minds from their bodies, surviving torture through mental discipline. In Feist's *Riftwar* books, torture led the character of Pug to a magical breakthrough, making him more powerful than ever.

What few of those books ever bothered to truly explain was how much torture *hurts!* I tried and failed to keep from screaming. My muscles were rigid. I tried to physically pull the bugs away, tearing cloth and skin, only to have their hinged legs reverse and dig into the meat of my fingers. I clenched my fists, but that only drove their stingers deeper.

I tried to stand, though there was nowhere I could run to escape. Even as I pushed myself upright, they crawled into my shoe and stung the bottom of my foot, making me stumble. Others crawled up my pants legs to attack the skin behind my knees.

I had no books, nor could I have concentrated long enough to use them if I did. I could hardly breathe, let alone read. The knife Lena had given me wouldn't do anything against these bugs. I did manage to scoop a rock from the dirt and hurl it at August Harrison's head between spasms. I missed, but the gesture made me feel a tiny bit better.

My muscles began to give out, and I curled into a ball, covering my face with my hands and praying they wouldn't crawl into my ears or . . . into anything else. As the assault dragged on for what felt like hours, I thought about the wendigo outside of Tamarack. He had fallen into the same agonized position right before he died.

"Enough," said Harrison.

The insects stopped moving, but it still felt like the barbed slivers of metal were thrusting obscenely into my skin, an echo of pain that refused to end. I gasped and blinked tears from my eyes. Lena was walking toward the tree, escorted by two wendigos. Her fingers sank into the tree. The roots curled around the book.

Guan Feng started forward, but an older woman caught her by the shoulder. Neither spoke, but the subtext was easy enough to read. Guan Feng was terrified. She brought her hands together, fingertips touching her chin, as if in prayer or meditation. She paced slowly, each step careful and deliberate, but it didn't ease the tension in her body. She never took her eyes from her book.

Lena reached deeper, stepping into a parody of an embrace with the tree.

This was my fault. I looked at Harrison, at the hybrid wendigos he had created with frozen chunks of skin, and fought to keep from throwing up. Whoever Lena helped them create, whatever Bi Wei and the others did once they were restored to this world, I was the one who had given them the key.

I started to push myself to my hands and knees, but a series of warning stings killed that idea. Instead, I curled tighter and slipped the wooden knife from my sock, transferring it to my sleeve.

As Lena stepped into the tree, a handful of insects rose from Harrison's body and flew toward her. They landed on her back, and then she was gone, taking the insects with her.

Guan Feng whirled. "What did you do?"

"You know what she is," Harrison shot back. "What she could do to us from within that tree. I'm protecting us all."

Green leaves sprinkled down. A branch as thick as my arm fell to the earth, barely missing Guan Feng. The wendigos backed away, but she remained at the base of the tree, crouched protectively over her book.

"What's happening?" asked the woman who had stopped Guan Feng.

"All magic has a cost," I said before Harrison could answer. I remembered how much it had taken for Lena to pull me back from the automaton, and I was someone she had known and loved. How much harder would it be to restore a stranger, one who had been gone for so many years? "You can't create life from nothing. That life comes from the tree."

And from Lena herself.

The roots shifted, and the book sank deeper into the earth.

"Bi Wei!" Guan Feng grabbed the book, but it slid inexorably downward.

"How long does this take?" Harrison asked. "You, drag Isaac over here. Perhaps when her roots taste his blood, she'll try to speed things up."

A wendigo yanked me upright. Cold, foul breath puffed against the back of my head as she hurled me forward. My foot caught in the roots, and I fell hard on my side. Dozens of metal legs pierced my skin, driven deeper by the impact.

I looked like a victim from a bad horror movie. My

shirt was red with blood, and my skin was swelling, making my movements stiff. Individually, the stings I had suffered were relatively minor, but there were so many. One bee sting was an annoyance, assuming you weren't allergic. A thousand could kill a full-grown man.

I had landed less than a foot from Guan Feng. My fingers tightened on the knife beneath my sleeve. I was close enough to stab her before anyone reacted, but what good would it do?

Looking up at her, I wasn't sure I could have done it. She had released the book, and now twisted her fingers into her shirt. Her lower lip was trembling. She reminded me of a frightened child.

"They'll be all right." I placed my hand on the base of the tree. "She knows we're here."

The look Guan Feng gave me suggested she would happily take over for Harrison's insects and finish skinning me herself, but after a moment, she reached out and touched the roots closest to the book.

"We're waiting," Harrison said.

"Bèn dàn, indeed," I muttered.

A flash of emotion—amusement, maybe—passed over Guan Feng's features. It vanished as quickly as it had appeared.

Lena's hand pushed out through the bark, knocking chunks of dry, dead wood onto the two of us. Her arm muscles strained as if she were trying to scale a cliff. I reached up to take her hand, but the insects stabbed my wrist and elbow, killing that plan.

Slowly, Lena emerged from the tree. Normally, the bark would have re-formed behind her, but not this time. Branches broke away with every movement, and the entire tree creaked, drawing nervous whispers from around us. Neither Guan Feng nor I budged.

Lena gasped for air and stopped, one leg and arm still trapped within the wood. Her eyes narrowed when she saw me. "Get those damned things off of him."

My head sagged. "I love you, beautiful."

"I know."

"You have Bi Wei?" asked Harrison.

Lena wrenched her other arm free. A slender bronze-skinned hand clasped hers.

Metal wings vibrated against my wounds, and then they were gone, returning to their master.

Lena braced her other hand against the tree and pulled, like she was hauling Bi Wei out of a pit. The woman she dragged forth was naked, roughly Lena's height, but emaciated. Her skin hugged her ribs and hipbones. Atrophied legs collapsed, and she clung to Lena's arm to keep from falling.

"Xiǎo Bi." Tears spilled down Guan Feng's cheeks.

Another woman stepped forward holding a heavy robe of deep maroon silk, trimmed in gold. Before she could reach them, Lena's fingers sank back into the tree and pried loose a two-foot length of pale wood, which shifted into a long, curved dagger. She curled her arm around Bi Wei's throat, placing the tip of her newly created weapon under her chin.

Guan Feng screamed. "Stop! Wei has done nothing to you!"

Harrison simply smiled. "You have no power here, dryad. My pets will strip the skin from your lover's body, a millimeter at a time."

Lena matched his smile. "You think you know me because you read an old book? That's cute." She shifted her stance, and a wooden tendril punched out of the dirt and circled his ankle.

He snarled and grabbed the root with his hands, try-

ing to rip it loose. Bad idea. More roots moved like serpents, twining around his wrists. I could see smaller
tendrils stabbing into his skin, poetic justice for what he
had done to me.

"I've read Isaac's reports," he snarled. "Bi Wei is an
innocent woman. You won't kill her. But you know I
won't hesitate to end him."

"You know what Isaac wrote about me. You don't
know *me*." Lena's words grew softer. "Isaac Vainio is one
of the smartest people I've ever met, but he makes mistakes. A surprising number, actually."

"Thanks a lot." To Harrison, I said, "What do you
think Lena will be doing to you while your bugs kill me?
I've watched this woman go toe-to-toe with an automaton and win. And believe me, you've pissed her off far
more than that automaton ever did."

Behind Harrison, the cat crouched, metal tail lashing
through the dirt. I wasn't the only one to call out a warning. Guan Feng and one of her friends shouted at Harrison to stop, but the cat was too quick. It bounded toward
Lena and leaped for her face.

Lena's toes curled into the roots as her left hand shot
out to catch the cat by the throat. Lena grimaced, but
kept her knife to Bi Wei's throat while the cat dug steel
claws into her wrist and tried to rake her arm. Lena
stepped to the side, dragging her prisoner along with her,
then swung the cat in an arc, smashing it against the oak
tree like she was beating dirt from a rug.

She tossed the remains of the metal cat at Harrison's
feet. It looked like someone had run over a garbage disposal. Broken legs twitched, and with every movement,
small gears and scraps of metal popped free. "Don't do
that again."

Harrison snarled, and the insects on his body began

to buzz. Two wendigos started toward Lena. She spun, keeping Bi Wei between herself and the closer of the wendigos. I lunged forward and stabbed my knife into the other's thigh. It wouldn't have worked on a full wendigo, but this one's armor was weak. The blade slid through the cracks in the ice, into the flesh beneath. It backhanded me to the ground, then howled and clutched its leg, where the knife appeared to have taken root.

A cloud of insects rose from Harrison's body, but as one, their bodies locked up and they fell into the dirt. The roots twined around Harrison's limbs stopped moving. Lena's forehead furrowed, but the roots no longer responded to her will.

Four students of Bi Sheng stood with their books open, whispering to whatever presences lived within those pages. Had I been able to see their magic, I knew I would have seen four ghosts suppressing both Harrison's magic and Lena's.

Harrison tore the roots from his limbs and started toward Lena. Bloody welts marked his forearms, and his pants were shredded.

Guan Feng jumped to stand between him and Lena. "Everyone stand back."

Lena's knife never wavered. They might be able to stop her from reshaping the wood, but I doubted they could prevent her from stabbing the blade through flesh.

My hands shook as I ripped the lifeless millipede from my throat, prying one segment free at a time. Blood made the metal slippery, and the damn thing had dug in pretty good, but I finally got it free. I flung it onto the ground, and Lena smashed it with her heel.

Lena kept her attention on Harrison. Bi Wei was breathing so fast I thought she might hyperventilate or pass out. She had one hand on Lena's arm, but lacked the strength to pull the knife away from her neck. Her head moved in frightened twitches, like a rabbit trapped by wolves.

"Do you remember your name?" I asked. She stared blankly. I mentally kicked myself. Torture had apparently messed with my faculties. Of course she wouldn't recognize twenty-first century English, and my knowledge of Mandarin was limited to a few simple phrases from a trip six years ago. "Ni jao . . . shen ma ming zao. No, wait. Ming zi?" Dammit, where were my books? I needed a universal translator.

"Isaac Vainio?"

The hairs on my arm stood straight up when she spoke my name. There was no recognition in her eyes, but for an instant, contempt edged her voice. Not only did something within her know me, it hated me. What the hell had Lena brought back? I reached out and touched her arm, and a dozen weapons jerked toward me.

I pulled away. That one touch had confirmed my hunch. The power flowing beneath Bi Wei's skin was like the pages of a magically active book.

She spoke again, but I understood nothing. Whatever her friends had done, it had suppressed my ability to understand other tongues. Guan Feng answered in the same language.

If they had blacked out my magic, what had they done to Lena? "Are you all right?"

"It's not pleasant," she said tightly, "but I'll survive."

"What now, Porter?" asked one of the men in accented English. "Will you kill her and finish what Gutenberg began?"

"No." Kill her? I wanted to *talk* to her. Lena had just restored a woman centuries old, one who had vanished into magic and somehow survived. I had a thousand questions. How had she held on to who she was? Had she been aware of the passage of time, able to observe the world? I wanted to ask about her magic, the students of Bi Sheng, her conflict with Gutenberg. I would have been utterly content to spend the next year learning from her.

Lena snorted.

"What?"

In a low voice, she said, "You've just been tortured, you're surrounded by people who wouldn't hesitate to kill you, and to top it off, you're standing in front of a naked woman. If I'm not mistaken, all you can think about is the history lessons you could learn."

I flushed, then gestured to the woman with the robe. She stepped forward, her every movement as slow and careful as a surgeon's. Lena kept her knife in place while Bi Wei slipped her arms through the sleeves and hugged the robe shut.

"Isaac isn't the only one who will pay for your choices today." Harrison had regained some of his composure, but his face and neck were red with barely restrained rage. "Doctor Nidhi Shah lives at 189 Depot Street, yes? Apartment C, according to the Porters' records."

Lena went utterly still. "Sooner or later, one of the people you've crossed is going to catch up with you. You should pray very hard that it's not me."

The woman who had carried Bi Wei's robe hissed in frustration. "*Enough*, all of you!"

Harrison whirled. "Have you forgotten what the Porters did to your ancestors, Crystal?"

Crystal stood like a statue. "Never."

I would have been thrilled to see this kind of split within Harrison's ranks under other circumstances, pretty much any circumstance that didn't have Lena and me in the middle of that conflict.

Despite what Lena had said, I doubted she would kill Bi Wei. Lena was exceptionally protective of those she saw as victims, and Bi Wei had nothing to do with our current situation.

"Toss me the keys to the truck," I said. Every second we stood here was another chance for the situation to explode. "I want my books back, too."

A man tossed a set of keys on a Rubik's Cube keychain into the dirt in front of me. "Your belongings are in the back seat."

"Tell Bi Wei to cooperate, and we'll let her go," said Lena.

Guan Feng did so. At least, I assume she did. I hated being unable to understand what people were saying. August Harrison simply stared as if imagining the many inventive ways he could kill me.

Lena moved toward the trail, the knife never wavering. The circle parted to let her pass.

"Wait." I shoved the keys into my pocket, then dug in the dirt at the base of the tree. The roots were dry and crumbled like cork. Lena had killed this tree in the process of restoring Bi Wei. One strong wind, and it would come toppling down. I just hoped it would wait until Lena and I were out of reach.

I brushed the dirt away from Bi Wei's book. Roots passed through the cover and pages like giant worms. I grabbed the broken millipede from the ground and used the blade to saw through the roots, trying to cut the book loose without ripping or damaging anything.

"Please don't," Guan Feng called. Despite everything, the anguish in her words made me hesitate.

"I'm sorry." I severed the last of the roots, jammed the millipede into the dirt, and pulled the book free. If she hadn't hated me before, she certainly did now. But I needed time to study and better understand what we were dealing with.

Bi Wei was remarkably calm as we retreated to the parking lot, especially for someone who had been reborn only minutes before. Though who knew what she and Lena had shared during that process? If it had been anything like Lena's restoration of me, Bi Wei would have had a nice little mind meld. She would know Lena was unlikely to harm her unless absolutely necessary.

When we reached the lot, I carefully set the book into the back seat of the truck. Harrison and the others stopped at the end of the trail. Pretty much every gun was pointed my way, and I was certain their magic was prepped to take us down if we gave them the slightest opening.

I pointed to an older woman with a black handgun. "Do me a favor and shoot out the tires on the rest of these cars. It's nothing personal, but I really don't want you all following us."

It took a frustratingly long time, and we had to wait for her to reload twice, but eventually she put a bullet through the last tire. I opened the truck's tailgate and kept an eye on Harrison and the rest while Lena and Bi Wei climbed into the back.

"You promised you'd let her go," Guan Feng said.

"And we will, just as soon as we get a mile down the road. Assuming nobody and nothing tries to follow us." I climbed into the truck, started the engine, and opened the window to the back. "Ready?"

"Don't drive too fast," Lena said. "Potholes and knives don't mix."

I toyed with the idea of trying to take Bi Wei with us. It wouldn't be the most honorable move, but she was dangerous. She might have the shape of a woman who disappeared five hundred years ago, but she carried something else inside. She had become the embodiment of everything I had learned to fear these past months. Of everything Gutenberg had feared since the founding of the Porters.

But she was also a refugee from a magical war that had been erased from our history. She hadn't asked for any of this. She hadn't known what she would bring back. More practically, I didn't have a clue how we'd be able to hold her. Lena couldn't keep a knife to her throat forever, and Bi Wei's magic could flatten any spell of mine.

We pulled away at a leisurely pace. I split my attention between the road and the mirrors, watching for any of Harrison's metal pets.

After five minutes, I stopped long enough for Lena and Bi Wei to get out. Lena walked Bi Wei to a birch tree at the side of the road. She twined the branches and roots around Bi Wei's wrists and feet, and molded a wooden blindfold as well. Another branch held the knife to Bi Wei's throat.

I slammed the gas pedal to the floor the instant Lena was inside. The rear tires spun out, raising a cloud of dirt as we tore down the road. I didn't know what Bi Wei could do, but I didn't expect Lena's precautions to hold her for long.

I watched the rearview mirror, but nobody appeared to be following us. Not yet. But they would. And next time, they would have all of Bi Wei's power to back them up.

Chapter 13

I pushed open the door of the Dearborn Martial Arts Academy. A bell jingled overhead, the sound a gentle contrast to the sharp yells of the people within.

The floor was pale, waxed wood. Strips of cypress segmented the white walls. Black-and-white photos of Japanese men with swords hung by the front window. Red-and-gold banners decorated the far wall, along with the flags of Japan and the United States.

The students were moving back and forth in pairs, swinging bamboo swords at one another. They wore metal masks and heavy padding to protect their necks, shoulders, and chests.

A man in a loose black uniform stepped away from the two women he had been helping and approached me, his smile warm and welcoming. "Can I help you?"

I dug a crumpled coupon from my pocket and showed it to him like it was a permission slip. "I'd like to learn to fight. Your advertisement said I could get a free lesson."

He barely glanced at the coupon. "Why?"

A thousand answers danced through my thoughts. Because it would make me more attractive to Nidhi. Because according to Nymphs of Neptune, *fighting was part of who I was. Because physical exertion made me feel good, whether it was working in the garden or making love to my partner. Because I could, and because there were so many people who couldn't.* My forehead wrinkled as I sorted my reactions, searching for the words.

"There's no wrong answer," he said. "But if you or someone else is in trouble, we should talk about that right now."

"Someone's always in trouble," I said without thinking.

He studied me, then chuckled. "That's true enough. Were you hoping to study kendo?" He gestured behind him. "We also offer classes in aikido and women's self-defense."

I nodded eagerly. "Yes, please. All of them. I have money."

I cringed inside. It was money Nidhi had given me. I didn't want to keep taking money from her. Not for this. I would have to look into finding work.

He continued to frown, and I braced myself for rejection. Instead, he took the coupon and said, "Remove your shoes and socks, and place them beneath one of the chairs by the wall."

While I hurried to obey, he turned and barked, "Ryan!"

A lanky boy with blond hair backed away from his partner, bowed, and ran toward us. He bowed again. "Yes, sensei."

"Take our new student . . ." He paused.

"Lena."

"Please take Lena through the basics of etiquette and stance."

"Stance?" I asked.

"Everything begins with stance. Power, balance, movement. All the strength in the world is little use without stance. Once you learn to take root, you'll be able to apply your full power to every strike."

I curled my toes, feeling the dry strength of the wooden floor, and smiled. "I can do that."

I T TOOK ME TEN minutes to make my way from the back roads to Highway 28. I called Nicola Pallas the moment I figured out exactly where we were. I gave her a mostly complete account of what we had learned, including the location of Harrison's camp. "I don't know how much magical whoopass you have on call, but I recommend sending all of it."

I was unsurprised when Pallas called back a short time later to tell me the camp was abandoned. Harrison and his followers had known their cover was blown the second I escaped. They hadn't been able to take their vehicles, and they had left the majority of their supplies in their cabins, which I took as a consolation prize. The inconvenience didn't make up for what they had done to Lena and me, but it was a start.

Lena called Nidhi next, and put her on speaker. The second Nidhi answered, Lena said, "You've got to stay away from the apartment. Harrison knows where you live. You can't go back there."

"But Akha—"

"The cat will be fine. She'll scamper off and cower behind the couch like she does every time someone knocks on your door. Or the TV switches on. Or she decides the curtains are evil monsters trying to eat her soul."

"Where are you and Jeff now?" I asked.

"Lower Michigan. About twenty miles south of Flint."

They were hours away, which meant they were probably safer than the two of us. I concentrated on driving while Lena filled Nidhi in on the students of Bi Sheng. I was having a hard time staying focused. My adrenaline rush had worn off, and the abuses Harrison had inflicted were catching up with me.

Highway 28 hugged the shoreline of Lake Superior, with stretches of dunes on both sides. I pulled off the road and parked our stolen truck behind a station wagon. Down by the water, a family was splashing in the water.

"Hold on, Nidhi," said Lena. "What's wrong?"

"Shock." I fumbled through my books until I found *Roc and a Hard Place* by Piers Anthony. I flipped to the dog-eared page where the heroine found a healing spring, and reached into the pages. The book resisted at first, but whatever the students of Bi Sheng had done to suppress my magic was wearing off. Once I touched the spring's magic, I tilted the corner of the book to my lips. Water spilled over the yellowed paper, and a thousand stinging cuts gradually cooled. I passed the book to Lena. I still looked like a butcher's shop had thrown up on me, but the redness and swelling had faded, and I could move without pain.

While Lena drank, I told Nidhi about Bi Wei. "I don't know what she was before. If Bi Sheng's followers had been this powerful when the Porters attacked, they would have crushed Gutenberg and his automatons." I thought back to what I had seen, watching in my mind as Lena entered the tree. "Several of Harrison's bugs snuck in with Lena. I never saw them come out. I'm guessing they infected Bi Wei with whatever devourer magic they were carrying."

"You think the devourers are what make her so powerful?"

"I'm not sure." I thought back to what I had sensed. "Her magic wasn't like the devourer that attacked me in Detroit. I know this sounds crazy, but she felt like a book. When I read a book, it becomes a doorway to magic. In her case, the book is a part of her, and the doorway is always open."

"Have you reported this yet?" Nidhi asked.

"I wanted to talk to you first." Nidhi was no longer my therapist, but she was damn good at helping me sort out my own conflicts. "Bi Wei scares the hell out of me, but none of this was her fault. When Gutenberg finds out, he'll do whatever it takes to destroy these people. Harrison can go light a match and stand behind a flatulent dragon for all I care, but what about Bi Wei and the rest?"

"We don't know exactly what happened," Nidhi pointed out. "We don't know if their version of events is any more or less reliable than Gutenberg's."

"Yes, we do." Lena closed the book and returned it to me, so I could end its spell. "Wei and I were together in that tree. I saw her. She knows time has passed, but doesn't remember the passage itself, beyond fragmented dreams and nightmares. She's terrified of Isaac and the Porters, and I can't blame her. I saw her last memories."

"I'm not going to like this, am I?" I asked.

"Wei was running, along with her fellow students. Three automatons were destroying their temple, ripping the walls down and collapsing the building on top of them. She fled to an underground library where a man was waiting for her. Her brother, I think. She didn't want to leave him, but there was no time. They hadn't expected Gutenberg to strike so soon. Her brother stood with her as she read." Tears dripped down Lena's cheeks.

"His last words to her were a promise to hide her book so she would be safe. He knew he would never escape the temple."

How many had died to keep those books from Gutenberg, and to get them into the hands of people who could protect them? "Could Bi Wei communicate with the others in their books?"

"She was alone," Lena said flatly. "She remembers that much. Her readers were her only link to the world. Nothing else existed. The first time she knew anyone else had survived was when we were in the tree together. I felt her grief for how few remained."

I picked up the book I had taken. That I had stolen. Broken roots appeared to impale the cover and the pages within. "I think the devourers were like Bi Wei. People who somehow fled into magic, but lost themselves in the process."

"How did Bi Wei survive?" asked Nidhi.

"Because she had people to help her."

Lena took the book and carefully tugged the thickest of the roots free. It left no hole, nothing but a smear of dirt on the cover.

"You're not responsible for Gutenberg's actions," Nidhi said. "Whatever happened five hundred years ago, our focus has to be the present. Harrison has Bi Wei. What will they do next?"

"If they fled the camp, it means they don't feel strong enough to face the Porters yet," I said. "He's not stupid. Eventually he'll come after Lena again, but first he'll want to assess Bi Wei's power and build up his army."

"Wendigos are supposed to be wild, foul-tempered creatures. How is he controlling them?"

"Probably the same way he controlled me." I tugged at my shirt to unstick the blood from my skin. "He's the alpha male." Transforming innocent people into monsters was only the first step. They also needed to be taught their place.

"Harrison didn't force the students of Bi Sheng to help him," Nidhi said. "They've been willing partners. As for Bi Wei, whatever she once was, she's been corrupted."

"We don't know that," said Lena. "She might be able to control whatever is inside her."

"She might, yes," said Nidhi. "Or she might not. But even if she retains control, her last memories were of death and war. What makes you think she'll stop fighting that war now?"

Neither Lena nor I had an answer for that.

"Where are you going next?" Nidhi asked.

"Home." I started the engine and pulled back onto the road. "I need more books, and we have to do something to protect Lena's tree."

"You can't exactly relocate her oak," Nidhi said.

I could, but it would be tricky. Maybe a shrink ray to make it portable? If I zapped Lena's tree, would it have any effect on her human body? Probably not. The tree had grown taller and thicker in the past two months, with no corresponding change in Lena's height or weight.

I hesitated, then said, "Nidhi, you know Gutenberg's mind better than I do."

"As much as anyone can understand that man's mind. There hasn't exactly been a lot of research on immortal wizards."

"Bi Sheng was working with movable type long before Gutenberg was born. He and his followers developed their own form of book magic. Do you think Gutenberg could have stolen those ideas? Then tried to wipe out Bi Sheng's students to make sure no one found out?"

Nidhi didn't answer right away, and when she did speak, her words were slow and careful. "I don't know. He's not the same man he was. How much have you changed in your lifetime, Isaac? Your beliefs, your values, your knowledge, they all evolve with time and experience. Gutenberg has been evolving for five centuries." She paused, then added, "Besides, you don't really want to know what I think. You've already come to your own conclusion. You just want me to talk you out of it."

I had forgotten how annoying Nidhi could be when she was right.

"Thanks. We'll check in again soon." I hung up and tried to concentrate on the road.

Invention always built on the shoulders of those who came before. Would Gutenberg have been able to develop his machine if he had never seen a wine press, or if others hadn't developed wood-block printing and engraving plates? If not for the metallurgists, the coin-stampers, and more? Not to mention the foundations of magic, work and research going back thousands of years.

But the Porters' records had no information about Bi Sheng. Gutenberg had obviously known of them, which meant he had deliberately omitted that information from our archives.

A year ago, I would have taken on faith that Gutenberg had a good reason for his actions. Maybe Bi Sheng had discovered magic strong enough to turn all of humanity into sentient custard, or summon Cthulhu to devour Australia. Maybe Gutenberg was trying to make sure nobody ever recreated and used those spells.

Or maybe he was simply hiding evidence of his own crimes.

Bi Wei and Guan Feng had seen the Porters as monsters. I was starting to fear they might be right.

My house appeared to be undisturbed. I waited while Lena circled around to the backyard. A minute later, the lights came on inside the house. She opened the front door to wave me in.

"I half expected to find the house burned to the ground," I said.

"Are you complaining?" Lena shot back.

"It makes me nervous. Harrison knows where we live. How hard would it be to send a few bugs to short out the fuse box? What are they up to that he didn't have time for a little petty revenge?" I shook my head. "The man was pissed. Sooner or later, he's going to want payback."

"He's not the only one," said Lena.

I hurried to the office to grab my laptop and the July issue of the *New York Library Bulletin*. A paper clip on page forty-six marked an article I had originally wanted to use to try to decipher the Voynich manuscript, a fifteenth century tome currently housed at Yale.

I stuffed the magazine into my bag and hurried to the living room. Lena stood at the back door, looking at her oak. "I hate moving," she said quietly.

"I could rig up a force field to protect the garden."

"And any one of the students of Bi Sheng could use their books to rip it down. Anything you do to protect my tree, they can counter."

"So you find another oak," I said.

"They sniffed me out once. What's to stop them from doing it again?"

I had circled through the same arguments in my head as we drove. I hadn't yet found an answer. How did you fight people who could both sense and consume magic? Maybe shrinking her tree really was the best option. But then she'd be unable to enter it. Like libriomancy with books, Lena's tree needed to be large enough to physically hold her.

She left the house, heading toward the garden. I started to follow, but she stopped in mid-step.

"I'd prefer to be alone for this," she said without turning around.

Her answer surprised me. Lena was pretty much the opposite of shy. "Let me know when you're ready."

While I waited, I tossed my ruined outfit in the garbage and grabbed an old pair of jeans and a blue T-shirt Deb had sent me as a present back when I started working at the Copper River Library. Not that I could wear a shirt that said "Librarians: Kicking Ignorance in the Balls for Over 4000 Years" on the job.

I returned to the kitchen and sat down at the table with the *New York Library Bulletin*. It had been ages since I tried to use a magazine for libriomancy. In theory, magazines worked precisely the same as books, but there were several complicating factors. Magazine circulation had been declining for years, resulting in fewer readers and less cumulative belief for us to tap into. The fact that more people tended to skim articles or skip some altogether didn't help either. Then there was the impermanence of the format. How many magazines ended up in the recycling bin within a month? The power attached to magazines faded far more quickly than with books.

These days, print publications had to compete with the Internet, and the NYLB hadn't had a huge readership to begin with. I wouldn't have been surprised to see it go fully digital within the next few years.

I wondered if Jeneta Aboderin's magic would work with Web sites. If she could use e-books, why not online content? That opened up a tremendous number of possibilities, some more disturbing than others. She could flood the entire planet with kittens and porn, not to mention certain categories of fanfiction ...

I read the article again, concentrating on the paragraphs that described research into smart glasses that could scan and translate text as you read. My fingers moved over the glossy print, trying to reach beyond.

Nonfiction was a different beast than fiction, but the emotions were the same. I touched eagerness and excitement, imagination and possibility. I pressed until my fingernails whitened, and then I was through. My fingers closed around thick-framed glasses, which I pulled carefully from the pages. I swore as my palm snagged on a staple. Yet another downside of magazine-based libriomancy.

"Those are ... not stylish," Lena said from the doorway. In her hands, she held a single branch from her oak, roughly four feet long. It looked like she had filled a small plastic bag with damp soil and tied it around one end of the branch. Leaves on the opposite end rustled gently as she shifted on her feet.

"Are you all right?" I asked.

"I feel broken." She managed a pale smile. "What's up with the geek specs?"

Black earbuds dangled from the hinges. The single-piece lens was dark glass, and might have looked awesome if not for the bulky gray frames and the red-ringed camera that stuck out from the nosepiece like a high-tech zit. "These are going to help me read Bi Wei's story."

We drove to Tori's Pub, one of the oldest businesses in town. People said the first miner came to Copper River on a Tuesday, and by that Thursday, Tori's bar was fully stocked and ready to go.

The smell of peanuts, pizza, and stale beer poured over us as I opened the door. Old logs paneled the walls, giving the place a woodsy cabin feel. Framed newspaper articles from the local paper hung on the wall closest to the bar, along with color photos of high school football teams going back to my parents' time. Sheets of acrylic plastic covered the tables, preserving graffiti carved into the wood more than a hundred years ago.

A handful of people called out greetings. I waved and forced a smile, then hurried to snag a small booth where we would be able to keep an eye on anyone coming in.

I brought out Bi Wei's book while Lena ordered a late dinner of pizza, chocolate ice cream, and a Long Island Iced Tea. "And Isaac will have a pasty. With extra rutabaga."

"I'm not hungry," I protested.

"I don't care." Her eyes dared me to argue.

I surrendered as gracefully as I could. After doublechecking the instructions in the *New York Library Bulletin*, I donned the glasses and pressed a small button on the right side of the frame. A cheerful ding rang through the earbuds.

"Translation on," said a pleasant but stiff female voice. I opened the book and studied the vertical characters on the first page. My vision flickered, and the image froze for a quarter second. A second picture appeared over the first. The new layer was semi-transparent, but easy enough to read. *The [UNTRANSLATABLE] of Bi Wei.*

"Sweet!" I turned the page and waited while the glasses translated the text.

"How do they work?" asked Lena.

"Optical character recognition networked to the world's largest translation engine. At least, that's the theory. The translation database doesn't exist in the real world yet. So far, the company's prototypes only do very basic word- and phrase-level translations, and their software is limited to English, Spanish, and French. But by the end of the decade, they're hoping to create and market a set of glasses that will translate any language pretty much instantly. That's what I used for the spell."

I tapped the hinges of the glasses and read aloud. " 'The palace lady takes no delight in idleness, but devotes her mind to the latest verse. For poetry can be a substitute for the flowers of oblivion.' Remind me to have Jeneta look through this thing."

I flipped ahead to the handwritten portion of the book and continued reading.

At thirteen I raised my gaze from the moss-covered paths to the angler with his brush and ink. As the slivered moon smiled down, he gathered me to his net of words. My grandfather's tears shone from Heaven, and his pride opened the waters of the world.

The glasses converted everything into a simplistic computerized font, but I could also see the characters Bi Wei had brushed onto the page, the precision and the artistry with which she wrote.

"The angler could be Bi Sheng," said Lena.

"Or another of his followers or descendants. Bi Sheng died centuries before Gutenberg's time. Bi Wei wouldn't have known him." Or maybe we were reading too much into it, and Bi Wei just liked fishing a lot. Poetry wasn't my strong suit. "She really did it. She wrote herself into the book."

How many weeks had she spent preparing? How desperate must they have been to believe such precautions were necessary?

Words alone couldn't create a complete mind. No author could. The amount of text it would take to capture a fraction of the complexities and memories of a human being would make Jordan's *Wheel of Time* series look like a child's board book. That was part of the reason intelligent characters went mad when they interacted with the real world. There simply wasn't enough to them.

I thought about Smudge, remembering the damage he had done when I first created him. He was smart for a spider, but not intelligent or sentient enough to lose his mind. Not completely. Even so, he had been terrified, and nearly burned down my high school library before I managed to calm him enough to get him out of there. I had taken him to one of the old mine sites by Tamarack and let him scurry about in an empty cave for hours until he finally began to trust me.

From that standpoint, what Bi Wei had done should have been impossible. But maybe you didn't have to perfectly transcribe the entirety of someone's experiences. Nobody remembered every second of their life, right? I had a near-eidetic memory, but I couldn't have said what shirt I wore two months ago, or what presents I got on my third birthday, or what color our first dog's eyes had been.

Was it the total of all of our experiences that defined us, or was it the key moments and choices that truly mattered? How much of who I was today stemmed from the day I discovered magic? From my first kiss with Jenny Abrams in seventh grade? From the road trip I took out west after high school, and seeing mountains for the first time?

If I could capture those moments in text and somehow imbue them with magic as Bi Wei had done, would that be enough, not to create a new me, but to anchor myself to this world after my body was gone?

Bi Wei had preserved herself for centuries. How long could such magic last? How far into the future could you travel? Assuming someone was waiting to pull me back out, I could watch the evolution of mankind. I could see rocket cars, colonies in space, everything I ever dreamed of and so much more that I couldn't possibly imagine.

"You know it's a one-way trip, right?" Lena asked.

"Since when can dryads read minds?" I said grumpily. Mostly because she was right. I would lose my family and friends. I would almost certainly lose Lena as well. But the chance to glimpse the future, to see what we would learn and discover and become . . . I would pay an awful lot for that chance.

I set up my laptop, waited for our waiter to finish putting down our food, then logged into the Porter database. Magical Internet access: one more gift from Victor Harrison.

I began with the poem from the first page of Bi Wei's book. The vagaries of translation complicated things, but by plugging different phrases into the search engine, I eventually identified it as a snippet from *New Songs from a Jade Terrace*, a collection of Chinese poetry published almost fifteen hundred years ago by Xú Líng. I e-mailed a copy of the text to myself to study later.

I had less luck finding information on Bi Sheng. The earliest reference to his work was a book written by Shěn Kuò, decades after Bi Sheng's death. I did manage to dig up some basic biographical information. Bi Sheng was a commoner, born in 990 AD during the Song Dynasty. He died in 1051, only a few years after developing the first known system of movable type. I sent myself a copy of *Dream Pool Essays*, Shěn Kuò's book, and kept reading.

"Did you know there was a crater on the moon named after this guy?" I had spent many nights examining the lunar landscape, but Bi Sheng's crater was on the dark side. Much like the man himself, who seemed to be little more than a historical shadow. Johannes Gutenberg's life had been endlessly detailed and distorted with a combination of historical records and random speculation, not to mention deliberate inaccuracies spread by the man himself, like his alleged burial site, which just happened to have been destroyed during the Napoleonic War. Bi Sheng, on the other hand, appeared to have been all but forgotten. For all I knew, it could have been Gutenberg himself who had erased Bi Sheng from the history books.

I shut the laptop and forced myself to eat a few bites, though my stomach grumbled in protest. Next, I turned my attention to Bi Wei's book. I skimmed one page after another, searching for anything that would tell us more about how she had grown so powerful and what the limits of her power might be. I found nothing but a brief prayer that she would never have to use the book's magic. I yanked off the glasses and rubbed my eyes. "This isn't working."

"You need sleep." Lena licked the last of the ice cream from her spoon. "Magical healing fixed the cuts to your body, but your mind is exhausted."

"I need better information." I traced my fingers over the carefully brushed characters. Five centuries of readers had imbued these pages with magic, preserving Bi Wei's life and experiences.

"The last time I saw that look, I ended up driving you

to Chicago so Nicola Pallas could try to put your mind back in one piece."

"This book anchored Bi Wei for all those years," I said. "That connection wouldn't just disappear when you restored her body, any more than your connection to your tree does. Which means I might be able to use the book to touch her thoughts."

She was shaking her head before I finished talking. "Wei is terrified of you, and of Porters in general. If she catches you breaking into her thoughts and memories—"

"I'm not planning to go as deep as I did in Detroit. I don't want to seize control of her body or climb into her mind. I just want to listen in."

She sat back and folded her arms, her silence saying better than words what she thought of this plan.

"I promise I'll be careful."

"Tomorrow," she said. "You're *not* trying this until you've slept."

"But the longer we wait—"

Her hand came down on the book, and I felt a stirring of magic from the wooden table as it responded to her anger.

"Right. Tomorrow it is."

Chapter 14

I held the cat carrier in one hand while an aging Siamese cat yowled in protest. Melinda Hill was strapping her one-year-old son into the car seat in the old minivan, while Hailey, the volunteer from the Dearborn domestic violence shelter, stuffed a hastily packed bag of clothes, diapers, and formula into the back. Hailey and I had arrived ten minutes before, and Melinda hadn't stopped shaking that entire time, but she didn't let that stop her. She clicked the last buckle into place and stepped back.

By contrast, Hailey was completely calm. Her every movement was careful and deliberate. She took the cat carrier from me and set it into the back seat beside the boy.

Melinda jumped every time someone drove up the street. Thankfully, midmorning traffic had been relatively light. I heard another car approaching and offered her a reassuring smile.

Melinda stiffened, and then every muscle in her body seemed to turn to mud. I turned to see a red Jeep speeding *down the block. Only a madman would do forty down a residential street. A madman or a pissed-off husband. He wasn't slowing down, and I reached for Hailey, preparing to fling her onto the grass if the driver tried to ram us. He slammed on the brakes at the last minute, tires screeching against the pavement.*

"Shit." Hailey stepped in front of me. This was only the third time I had helped to escort a client. I was technically still a trainee and Hailey's responsibility. "Get in the van with Melinda, lock the doors, and call 911."

Melinda was whispering, "I'm sorry," over and over. Her eyes were dry. It frightened me how quickly and thoroughly she had faded when her husband appeared, becoming a ghost of who she was.

I helped her into the van, then retrieved the oak cane I had tucked beneath the seat. "You're going to be all right."

I couldn't tell if she heard me or not. By now, Hailey had pulled out a handheld radio and was holding it like a beacon. "Mister Hill, the PPO says you're not allowed to be within one hundred yards of your wife. This conversation is being recorded. I know you're angry, but please get back in your car and contact Mrs. Hill's lawyer to resolve this."

Christopher Hill didn't look like an evil man, nor was he particularly imposing. He was in his mid-twenties, dressed in a bland gray shirt and paisley tie. It was his shoes that caught my eye, black and polished like glass. Perfectly clean, just as the house had been.

This wasn't how I had imagined the man who had broken three of his wife's ribs and cracked her left eye socket.

He didn't say a word, probably hoping that would prevent the recording from being used against him. He strode toward Hailey and reached for the radio. I stepped between them.

"Dammit, Lena," said Hailey. "I told you—"

"I'm all right." I rested both hands on the cane. "Mister Hill, you need to leave."

His mouth opened, and then his eyes twitched toward the radio. With a grimace, he reached out to shove me aside.

I bent my knees, rooting myself to the pavement, and smiled. He pushed harder.

Hailey's composure was slipping. "Mister Hill, you're committing an act of battery against Lena Greenwood. You need to return to your car."

He scowled and tried again to shove past us. I moved with him, keeping my body interposed.

"This is my house," he hissed in a low voice. "That's my son. My wife."

My smile grew. "Not for much longer, I think."

His first punch was, frankly, disappointing. I don't think he expected much from a heavyset Indian girl leaning on a cane. I shifted my stance and swung the cane with both hands to intercept his blow. Wood cracked against the bone of his forearm.

"Son of a bitch!" He jumped back, clutching his arm.

"Lena, don't," Hailey warned.

I was doing exactly what I had been trained not to do. We were supposed to deescalate conflict whenever possible, and to get away and call the police if we were in danger. But those rules had been written for human volunteers.

He rushed me again, and I struck his knee, dropping him to the road. I switched to a one-handed grip on the cane and reached down to twist my fingers into his shirt. I had never felt so strong, so powerful. I flung him onto the grass. He scrambled to his feet, but I rapped him on the side of the head with the end of the cane.

"Stop it!"

The shout had come from Melinda. She was crying. Hailey was holding her back, but she twisted free as I watched. She ran past me, interposing herself between me and her husband just as I had done seconds before when I tried to protect her.

I lowered the cane. "I don't understand. He—"

"Get in the van, Lena." Hailey's face was red. She clipped the radio back to her belt. "Shut up and get in the goddamned van."

I looked past her to Christopher Hill, silently daring him to get up. He groaned and sagged into the grass. Then I turned my attention to Melinda, who stood over her husband, ready to fight off anyone who tried to hurt him.

I hadn't understood until then. Christopher Hill had bound his wife to him. He had twisted who she was, making himself the core of her being. She couldn't leave him. Not without first freeing herself from his power.

She was like me.

Without another word, I retreated into the van.

BOTH MY PLACE AND Nidhi's were on Harrison's hit list. After a brief debate, I drove to the library instead. It was as secure a location as any to spend the night, and if Harrison did come after us, I'd have plenty of books on hand.

I parked around back, out of sight from the street. I checked through the windows, then unlocked the back door. The alarm system beeped at me until I punched in the six-digit code to deactivate it.

Lena walked through the darkened library, bokken in one hand, the branch from her oak in the other. I set my books down, then returned to the car to fetch an old blanket from the trunk. I re-armed the alarm as soon as I was back inside. It wouldn't do much against a pack of wendigos or whatever constructs Harrison sent after us next, but maybe it would give us a few seconds' warning.

She set the branch in a corner. "Do you have anything to drink here? I get dehydrated when I'm away from my tree."

"There's water in the break room, and we might have some juice boxes left from the picnic last week."

By the time Lena returned, I had cleared floor space in the children's section and dragged three battered beanbag chairs together to serve as pillows. The lights from the street filtered through the windows to silhouette the curves of her body. She stood there, sipping juice through a too-small straw and watching me.

"I never used to understand what you loved about libraries." She crumpled the box and tossed it in the trash. She disappeared between the shelves, and I heard her fingers passing over the plastic dust jacket protectors. When she emerged again, she leaned against the shelves, clasped her hands over her head, and stretched, the movement slow and luxurious. Cats throughout the world could have taken lessons.

I settled into the beanbags. "And now?"

"The doors are locked, everything's powered down for the night. This place should feel empty, but it doesn't. That's what you found here, isn't it?" She spun on one foot like a ballerina. "Libraries kept you from being alone."

"I wasn't—"

"Don't." I could hear her smiling. "Books were your friends growing up. Your companions, your teachers."

"I had friends." I tried not to sound too defensive.

"How many of those friends understood you as well

as the books did?" she teased. "Every book opened your mind, showed you the infinite paths that lay before you. Each one connected you to another soul."

"When did you get so poetic?"

"Tell me I'm wrong." She stepped closer. "I dare you."

"You're not wrong." I breathed in the familiar smells of the library. Paper and ink, cloth-bound books and binding glue, magazines and old newspapers. A faint scent of coffee. Even steam cleaning had failed to completely remove that stain after Jenn accidentally knocked her travel mug off of the desk. Then there was the underlying smell of the hundreds of people who passed through the library every month.

"Thank you for sharing this with me, Isaac." She leaned down, and her lips brushed mine. Then, with a mischievous smile, she straightened and backed away until the soft light from the exit sign painted her a deep red.

Moving with exquisite slowness, she peeled off her shirt and tossed it onto a nearby table. She pulled off her shoes and socks next, then slid her jeans down over her hips and kicked them aside.

The lines of her body flowed so beautifully, one curve leading to the next. My eyes traced her neck and shoulders, then moved inward to the swell of her breasts, straining slightly against the confines of her bra. From there to her stomach, where softness concealed the steel beneath, and down to the muscular curves of her hips and thighs.

She stood there a moment longer, then picked up her bokken and grinned. "All right, now that I'm comfortable, why don't you go ahead and get some sleep while I keep guard?"

I groaned and thumped my head into the beanbag. "The alarm is on. I think we're safe."

"Are you sure? I wouldn't want to take any chances." She twirled her bokken, then settled into a low stance, weapon ready.

"If you're trying to get comfortable, why not go all the way?" I said. "Or are you afraid to fight evil naked?"

"When you're built like me, a good-fitting sports bra is non-optional for battling wendigos and other nasties." She tilted her head, and her tone turned serious. "What is it? What's that look for?"

"You." I couldn't stop staring. She shifted her weight and rested the sword on her shoulder, simultaneously strong and sexy and dangerous and so damned beautiful it hurt. I imagined my fingers stroking the outer curve of her leg, then tracing up the softer skin of her inner thigh. Her toes curled, as if even the feel of the old carpet beneath her bare feet was a source of pleasure.

She laughed. "That's all you have to say? Are you just going to lie there and stare at me all night?"

"Works for me."

"Mm. But then you wouldn't get any sleep," she teased.

"I'm willing to accept the consequences of my choice."

"Are you, now?" she whispered. Placing her hands on her hips, she surveyed me and made a disapproving *tsk* sound. "My dear Isaac, I do believe you're overdressed."

By the time I tugged off my T-shirt, Lena had set her bokken on the floor and joined me in the beanbags. She brushed her fingernails down my chest and stomach, then lower.

I slid a hand through her hair. The other cupped her breast, my thumb teasing her nipple through the spandex. Her hips pressed into me as I slipped my fingers beneath the elastic and slowly pulled off her bra.

"What is it about libraries?" she whispered, her breath

tickling my ear. She took the lobe gently in her teeth. "You used to work at the MSU library. Did you have many students sneaking into the stacks to study biology?"

"A few. I think it was the excitement. The fear of getting caught."

"I can understand that." She grinned and rolled on top of me, and I pulled her mouth to mine. Lena might be a dryad, but tonight my hunger matched hers. We rolled across the floor until we bumped into a shelf.

She broke away, laughing. Before I could draw her back, she jumped to her feet and stripped off her underwear. Then she walked toward the front of the library. At first, I was content to simply watch, but she wasn't stopping.

I followed her into the front room. "What are you doing?"

"Do you ever get tired of hiding, Isaac?" She stood three feet from the main window, hands on her hips, looking out at the street. Gods, she was gorgeous.

I hurried and grabbed her hand, trying to pull her back to the relative seclusion of the children's section. Instead, she spun around and kissed me. Her fingers clamped my head like iron, and her tongue danced with mine. One of her hands undid the button of my jeans, then tugged the zipper down.

Headlights played through the library, and I swore. This time, she let me pull her down, out of view. We didn't move until the car had passed.

Lena covered her mouth with one hand, but it wasn't enough to hide her laughter. Laughter which proved to be highly contagious. The fear and pain and dread of the past two days gradually poured out as we collapsed on the carpet. I could feel her body shaking beside mine. I rolled on top of her and kissed her neck, right beneath the jawbone.

Slowly, her laughter changed to moans of pleasure. "I love you, Isaac Vainio."

"I love you, too."

"Good." She broke away and grinned. "Because there's something I've wanted to do since the first time I came to Copper River, and it involves you, me, and that circulation desk."

Lena and I had been together since the start of summer, but we had never truly slept together.

We had done plenty of *not*-sleeping together, but when it was time to retire for the night, she always returned to her tree. On the nights she spent with Nidhi, I'd hear the growl of her motorcycle around midnight as she returned home, not to my house, but to the oak tree out back.

Tonight was different. We lay naked on the blanket, nested among the beanbags. Her thigh rested atop mine, and her body pressed against my chest. The warmth of her skin was a comfortable contrast to the cool air.

Despite my exhaustion, both magical and physical, it took me a long time to drift off to sleep. Once I did, my dreams jerked me awake throughout the night. The third time, I rolled over to find myself alone.

Lena had moved to the corner of the room, where she lay curled around the branch from her oak. Her fingertips disappeared into the wood. "It's four in the morning," she murmured. "Go back to sleep."

It was good advice, and I tried to follow it, but my body was abuzz like I had mainlined an entire pot of coffee. After tossing fitfully for another fifteen minutes, I gave up and pulled on my pants. I walked to the break room and grabbed a granola bar from the cabinet. I had no appetite, but forced it down anyway. I picked up Bi Wei's book on the way back, along with a portable reading light from my bag.

The light was designed to clip directly to a book, but I didn't want to risk damaging the cover. I settled for clipping it to my jeans pocket.

As I opened the book, I found myself missing Smudge, who would have been trying valiantly to blister my skin and warn me away. But we needed information, and I couldn't think of another way to get it.

I switched on my glasses and skimmed from one section to the next, trying to decide where to start. A description of Bi Wei's first encounter with magic caught my attention, and I flipped to the beginning of the story. It was her great-grandaunt who introduced her to Bi Sheng's teachings. They had spent most of the day hiking to the top of a rocky hill outside of their village. Bi Wei could have made the walk in half the time had she been alone, but she was happy to match her great-grandaunt's pace, and wouldn't have dreamed of complaining.

They talked of trivial things along the way, but Bi Wei knew this was no ordinary outing. She longed to ask what awaited them and why her parents had been so somber the night before, but she suppressed her curiosity.

The clouds blazed that evening. A glowworm clung like a beacon to a stalk of grass, bobbing in the warm breeze. Great-Grandaunt unrolled a reed mat on the grass. Atop the mat, she opened an atlas of star charts. Times and seasons were written into the margins, while pictures of familiar stars spread across the rest of the page.

"Find them," she said.

I looked skyward. Clouds and splintered sunlight hid the night sky from view. The stars wouldn't be visible for some time yet. "How?"

"Read with me." She turned the page, and we read a description of the northern stars. The author had written both of the stars' usefulness in navigation and of their beauty, for shouldn't the most useful things be also pleasing to behold?

As we read, it was as though the starlight he had looked upon—and I somehow knew both that he had watched the stars as he wrote, and that the writer was a man—it was as if that same light brightened within me. Shock tore my manners asunder, and I cried out.

Great-Grandaunt was not angry. Instead, she smiled and turned back to the star map. "Find them," she repeated.

This time, when I looked to the clouds, I could see the stars burning beyond. "The Celestial Spear." Despite the sunlight, I saw the constellation more clearly than ever I had before. I felt as though I could touch them, gather them to my breast like jewels. "How?"

"Through the [UNTRANSLATABLE] of your ancestor, Bi Sheng. This book was printed a hundred years ago. It and its sisters were shared and read by those with spiritual and magical strength. As each of Bi Sheng's [UNTRANSLATABLE. SUGGESTIONS:DESCENDANTS, APPRENTICES] read the book, the words grew stronger. We read each book again and again, refilling the cup of its magic."

Just as Guan Feng had done for Bi Wei. How many times had someone read this book over the years to sustain her? Thousands? How many hours did the students of Bi Sheng spend with these texts, fighting to keep their ancestors alive?

I laughed with delight, an outburst that would have earned disapproval from others, but Great-Grandaunt understood. This book had brought the night to life. I saw not just pinpoints of light, but the Emperor of Heaven, the Celestial Kitchen, the First Great One . . . I saw what they represented, the meaning we had painted on the sky throughout the ages.

"Why me?" I asked, not daring to hope that there might be more.

"Because you see beyond the words. They open your eyes to the world, and you give them power, just as Bi Sheng did. Just as I did. And it is time you learn to use those gifts."

It was a connection I had felt with few others: the excitement of libriomancy, of magic. None but another libriomancer could understand the wonder and amazement of that discovery, the thrill of our first forays into magic. With Bi Wei, I relived that delight through the prism of her life. If anything, her joy had been even stronger than my own.

In that moment, I touched her mind.

Joy vanished, replaced by pain and confusion. Everything about this place and time was strange. The only constant was the violence and war that had followed her. She had fled the Porters centuries before, and had awakened to find herself threatened by them once again.

Or had she awakened at all? Was this the madness that had claimed the Lost Ones? Power clawed like a beast trapped within her chest, fighting to tear free. Even as she struggled to contain the beast, it slithered through her fingers, seducing her with the promise of magic. It had been so simple to use that power to grasp the words of those around her, the angry orders of the one called August Harrison, the broken-but-familiar words of the Bì Shēng de dú zhě.

Her own descendants practically worshipped her. Whereas August Harrison treated her with derision, as if she were nothing but a Miáo slave. Guan Feng often cursed him under her breath, but she obeyed his wishes out of gratitude and respect. He had been the one to restore Bi Wei.

He was the one who could bring back Wei's friends.

Feng held her hand as they walked alongside a palisade of sharpened poles that led to a square watchtower. The ground was hard-packed earth, bordered by old wood and stone buildings. Fireflies crawled over the walls—no, not fireflies. Those were Harrison's insects. Bi Wei was seeing the magic in each one.

Wherever they were, Harrison was taking no risks. He had ordered everyone along this time: twenty-four of the twisted monsters he called wendigos, sixteen readers, and another twenty guardians, not counting Bi Wei and Guan Feng. Roughly half of the humans carried firearms. The handheld cannons were as frightening and disorienting as the metal cars they had stolen to get to this place, traveling at unimaginable speeds.

"The north wall," said Harrison.

Bi Wei didn't move.

"What is it?" asked Feng.

She looked around, searching. "We're being watched."

I slammed the book shut.

"What happened?" Lena asked, fully awake and alert.

"It worked." I studied Lena more closely. Her eyes were red and shadowed, her hair a disheveled mess. "Are you all right?"

"I essentially tried to switch from sleeping on a king-sized bed to a little throw pillow." She managed a pale smile. "I'm fine. This isn't the first night I've spent away from my oak. What did you learn?"

"Not as much as I wanted. I think Bi Wei might have seen me. She's disoriented, but determined to save the rest of her people. There are at least sixteen more of these books, and a bunch of people she called guardians. They must have had a second camp or base somewhere."

"Did you see where they were? How close are they to finding us?"

"Harrison isn't after us. They're looking for something else. Something magical, I think." I stared at the book, reconstructing what I had seen. That palisade was familiar. "Oh, shit."

I grabbed my phone and called Nicola Pallas. The instant she answered, I said, "Harrison's going after the archive at Fort Michilimackinac."

"How long would it take you to get there?" Pallas asked calmly.

"Too long. He's there now, and he knows where the archive is."

To Pallas' credit, she didn't ask me how I knew. "Do you know what he wants?"

"Let me pull up the catalog." I hurried toward the front desk and powered up the computer. I could connect to the Porter network and see what books and other toys were stored at the old fort. Hopefully something would jump out— "Wait. Nicola, did the Porters transfer everything from MSU to Michilimackinac?"

"Everything save a handful of books and artifacts that were destroyed when the building collapsed."

I remembered the Michigan State University library, both as a student and as a field agent investigating the attack that crushed the entire building. I had cataloged some of the locked books the Porters used to store in the library's secret subbasement. Of all the titles we had kept there, one would hold particular interest for August Harrison. "He's going after *Nymphs of Neptune*."

Lena had been discovered in lower Michigan. Until Lena, the Porters had thought it impossible to pull intelligent beings from books. You could infect humans from our world with vampirism and other afflictions. You could even yank something like Pixel the cat out of Heinlein. But a fully sentient mind? Impossible. Until it happened. Until an acorn from that book grew into a dryad's oak, giving birth to Lena Greenwood.

Nidhi was the one who had discovered Lena's origins in a secondhand copy of *Nymphs of Neptune*. Gutenberg had locked that book the very next day. I didn't know how he did it, though I had heard whispers of an invisible inscription, a spell that spread out to affect every copy of a book. The locked book with Gutenberg's enchantment had been moved to our archive in East Lansing for safekeeping.

"I can't send another automaton," Pallas said. "Gutenberg is still trying to repair the last one. Do you think Harrison has the ability to unlock books?"

I didn't know how strong Bi Wei had become, but Harrison wouldn't try to steal that book unless he thought he could use it, and that meant ripping open Gutenberg's spell. "Probably. What about using an automaton to teleport someone else in?"

"The archive is magically shielded, remember?"

"How could I forget?" The Porters had chosen Michilimackinac because of its latent magical wards, spells placed more than three hundred years ago by French traders. Gutenberg had worked with Jane Oshogay, a historian and retired libriomancer who had moved here from Minnesota, to strengthen and build upon those wards. Wards I had foolishly volunteered to help test.

It had taken a day and a half for our healers to reverse the various curses, and another two weeks for my hair to finally start growing back.

"I'll see what else I can do," said Pallas. "And remember, I need your report on the Columbus incident." She hung up without saying good-bye, which wasn't unusual for her.

"He wants his own dryad," Lena said tightly.

"It's worse than that." One dryad would allow him to restore the other students of Bi Sheng, but it would take time, and Harrison didn't strike me as a patient man. "Why stop at one? He's going to create an entire legion of dryad slaves."

Chapter 15

My mistake cost me my position with the shelter, though a number of the other volunteers privately thanked me for living out their fantasy, and several stayed in touch for a while. And then Hailey called two months later to tell me Christopher Hill had shot Melinda four times before putting the gun beneath his own chin and pulling the trigger. She said she thought it was better if I heard the news from a friend.

Nidhi found me curled at the base of my tree, crying. I recognized her by her footfalls on my roots. "I should have killed him."

She knew without asking what had happened. Maybe she had already heard the details from a colleague, or on the radio. "You can't save everyone, Lena."

"I could have saved her." I dug my fingers into the earth, seeking the strength of my tree. I wouldn't give up what Nidhi and I had for anything, but for the first time, I found myself missing the simplicity of my life with Frank.

"You tried to give her a choice."

"She made the wrong one."

She sat down beside me and hooked her arm through mine. "So you should have taken that choice away from her?"

"What about her son's choice?" I asked. "His parents are both dead. I wanted—"

"I know what you wanted," Nidhi said softly. "You think I haven't imagined similar things? Protecting the helpless, saving those who have been hurt."

"You do something better. You help them to protect themselves."

"Sometimes." She rested against my shoulder.

"What would have happened if I hadn't been there?" Perhaps his showing up to confront her would have hardened Melinda's resolve to leave. Hailey had been trained for this. She could have helped Melinda to make the right choice. Instead, by attacking Melinda's husband, I had driven her back to him.

"You didn't kill that woman, Lena. He made the choice to pull the trigger, not you. Don't you dare take that responsibility away from him." We sat in silence as the sun drifted lower. "I spoke with the Regional Master of the Porters this morning about the possibility of you becoming a field agent."

She raised a hand before I could give words to the burst of hope in my chest. "Pallas said no. Gutenberg doesn't allow nonhumans in the Porters."

"Can you blame him?" I sank back against the tree.

"Yes," she said evenly. "But there may be another option. So far, my only magical clients have been human, all classified as low-risk. Field agents mostly, with the occasional researcher. But there are others who need help. Displaced nonhumans. Recently turned vampires, werewolves, and others, trying to come to terms with their new existence. Peo-

ple considered too unstable and dangerous for a mundane
psychiatrist to help."

"What are you saying?"

"I've asked that my client list be expanded to level two
and three patients," Nidhi said. "If they approve my request,
it would mean more travel, and I'd need someone along for
my protection. That person doesn't have to be a Porter."

I swallowed, torn between hope and fear as I realized
what she was offering. "What if I screw up again?" I whispered. "If I lost you—"

"I trust you," she whispered.

THE BOOK I NEEDED wasn't on the shelf. I ran
back to the computer and pulled up our circulation database, drumming my fingers on the desk
as I waited for the program to open.

"Even if he can unlock the book, he can't create a
fully formed dryad." Uncertainty turned Lena's words
into a question, a plea for confirmation. "It took time for
my tree to grow. Years, probably."

"Your tree grew naturally. Harrison isn't going to
wait." I waved impatiently at the science fiction and fantasy section of the library. "Belgarath, from David Eddings' *Belgariad*. Irene in Piers Anthony's *Xanth* books.
The water of life from L. Jagi Lamplighter's *Prospero
Regained*. The magic of those books could grow an acorn
into a fully grown oak within hours, and Bi Wei knows
enough of libriomancy to make it happen."

"What about the other books at the archive?" Lena
asked. "If she can unlock one, why not others? There are
weapons in those books that could wipe out all of Michigan."

"Xiǎo Bi wouldn't do that," I said. "She wants to restore her friends, but she won't give those books to a madman."

"Xiǎo Bi?" Lena's brows rose.

"Bi Wei." I had used the familiar term instinctively. It was hard to think of someone as a stranger after touching their memories and sharing one of the happiest moments of their existence. "She doesn't want to fight a war."

Lena's fist cracked the desk. "Do you think August Harrison cares what she wants?" she shouted.

Shock robbed me of words.

"She's going to give Harrison an army of dryads. You can't—" Her voice broke. "You don't know what they're capable of. What I'm capable of."

"I've read your book," I said, trying to reassure her. Where was Nidhi when I needed her? "I've seen what you can do. You're amazing, but you're not omnipotent, and you're not a monster."

"You haven't seen everything." She moistened her lips and moved her hands over the front of her body.

Between one breath and the next, I forgot all about August Harrison or *Nymphs of Neptune*. Blood pounded hot through my body, as if she had stripped away all traces of civilization, leaving only raw, primitive lust. I wanted to tear her clothes away, to take her right here. My chair clattered backward. I took her by the arms and pressed her against the shelves, hard enough that several books fell around us.

I didn't care. My pelvis ground against hers as I yanked her shirt roughly over her head and flung it aside. I thrust my hand down the front of her pants, and she writhed with pleasure.

"Stop." She pushed me away and held me at arm's

length. I tried to twist free, but her grip was unbreakable. Slowly, my arousal faded to more human levels, though my jeans still felt painfully constrictive. From the tightness of her nipples and the quickness of her breath, Lena was having similar struggles. "All right," she gasped. "Maybe that wasn't the best demonstration."

I swallowed and backed away. "What did you do to me?"

"I'm sorry." She turned away. "I told you once that I could feel lust in others. I never told you I could manipulate that lust."

"Chapter four," I whispered. The fourth chapter of *Nymphs of Neptune* put protagonist John Rule in the middle of a territorial conflict between a river nymph and a dryad. It was yet another layer of the author's wish fulfillment fantasy, with both nymphs battling first over their borders, then over Rule himself, each stoking his desire until he was little more than an animal. He wound up bedding them both, naturally. "Before you and I got together . . ." I trailed off, uncertain how to finish the question.

"Never," Lena said firmly. "Not since before I met Nidhi. Sometimes I have to work to stop myself, but I wouldn't do that to you, or to her."

A part of me was angry at the loss of control. Another part wanted desperately for her to do it again.

"Imagine what I could make you do. What I could make men do. Many women as well." She folded her arms over her breasts. "I used to seduce Frank when I wanted him. Or when I wanted to punish his wife."

I bit the inside of my lip. The pain helped me to focus.

"I fought her once," Lena continued. "She couldn't take it anymore, so she attacked me. I broke her hand."

"You were protecting yourself," I said.

"Marion was never a real threat. I hurt her because I

wanted to. Because I enjoyed it. I liked fighting for Frank. I liked the power I had over her, and the sound of her crying." She bent to retrieve her shirt. "The dryads Harrison creates will be worse."

I nodded and returned to the computer. "Then let's find a way to stop him."

According to our system, Robin McKinley's *Beauty* was on the reserved shelf. Thankfully, the person who had placed a hold on the book hadn't yet been by to pick it up.

The Copper River Library might not have *Nymphs of Neptune*, but the Beast's magical library in *Beauty* held a copy of every book ever written. As I reached into the story, I found myself wondering at the implications of such a library. Did the Beast sit around reading fairy-tale retellings? What would he make of modern erotic fiction like *50 Shades of Grey*? Had he discovered his own book, and what kind of magical paradox might I create if I used this book to create a new copy of *Beauty*?

This wasn't the time for experiments, dammit. I focused on the book I needed, and pulled *Nymphs of Neptune* through the pages.

"Can you lock it?" Lena asked.

"I don't know how." I opened the book and swore. Both times I had read *Nymphs of Neptune*, it had felt empty: a void whose life was locked away by Gutenberg's magic. As I skimmed the opening pages now, I could feel the book's magic waiting just beneath the page. I ran my fingers over the rough, yellowed paper. "They've got it."

"If we call Gutenberg—"

"Do it, but I'm not sure it will work. Bi Wei might be too strong."

Those words broke something within Lena. She tried

not to let it show, but her entire bearing changed. She closed her eyes, and the energy and alertness that always reminded me of a pacing cat drained from her body. When she spoke, her words were listless. "Can you stop them from using it?"

"Maybe."

While she dialed the phone, I reached into the pages and allowed the icy air of Neptune to flow into the library. If there were a way to fine-tune the flow of this book's magic, I might never need to pay for air conditioning again.

"Nobody's answering," she whispered. "What are you doing?"

"Breaking one of the cardinal rules of libriomancy," I said. "I'm going to deliberately char the everliving hell out of this book."

I reached deeper until my fingers touched frigid snow.

Lena dialed another number. "Exactly how dangerous is this plan?"

"Calling it a 'plan' might be a bit of an overstatement."

She turned away, and I heard her filling someone in on what was happening. Hopefully Gutenberg could fix this, but I couldn't afford to concentrate on that conversation.

John Rule had been transported from Earth to the underground world of Neptune. According to the author's ridiculous pseudoscience, the ice of the frozen surface somehow focused the rays of the sun like a giant magnifying lens, providing light and just enough warmth to the inhabitants below.

I pulled that environment into our world, channeling the book until my breath began to fog and frost crept across the floor.

I heard the characters calling to me. Whispering seductively, giggling as they invited me back to lavish bedchambers furnished in the thick furs of ferocious alien beasts. I heard their grunts and cries as they fought each other for the entertainment of their Neptunian lords. Just as Lena had fought Frank Dearing's wife.

This was the book that had birthed Lena Greenwood. One of the strongest women I knew, and she had been written as a sexual plaything. I wanted to bring the author back from the grave purely so Lena, Nidhi, and I could take turns punching him in the face. And yet, without his trash, Lena would have never been a part of my life.

"He's trying, but Bi Wei is holding the book open somehow." Lena covered the phone. "Isaac, your arm."

I glanced down. The skin of my wrist and forearm had taken on a faint bluish tinge, and I couldn't feel anything from the elbow down. I wrenched my hand free of the book. Pain hit a moment later as blood flow returned to my numb fingers. I clamped my jaw to keep from shouting.

Cold continued to flow from the book. "I probably should have done this out back," I said through clenched teeth.

The voices were growing louder. John Rule shouted defiantly at the Prince of Harku'unn, the northernmost kingdom of Neptune. I tightened my fist, feeling the weight of his stone-bladed sword, and his need to act. I would strike down the tyrant who would torture and enslave the free people of Harku'unn, including the exiled nymph who had saved my life.

"Isaac!"

One of the prince's dryads stepped closer, her barbarian weapon held in a defensive position. I raised my own sword.

"Oh, hell." The dryad parried my thrust and stepped inside my guard. Her other hand caught my chin and lifted, twisting my spine and forcing me off balance. She kicked my front leg out from under me before I could recover.

I landed hard enough to knock the air from my lungs. My sword fell, and my shield fluttered to the ground.

I blinked. I was reasonably certain shields weren't supposed to flutter.

"Concentrate on my voice," said the dryad. "You're Isaac Vainio. You're in Copper River, Michigan, and we don't have time for this!"

Snow gusted through the cave. A stone sword with a blade like chipped blue glass lay beside me. I rubbed my face and tried to focus.

"Don't move." She left me shivering on the floor, but returned seconds later, ripping open a cellophane package. "Eat this."

Strong fingers shoved something spongy and chocolate into my mouth. I chewed without thinking. "You raided my Tastykake supply?"

"Tastes and smells are powerful triggers. They can help to anchor you in the real world." Lena crammed another bite past my lips. "You once told me how your parents used to bring them back from trips out East, remember?"

I stared at the book on the floor beside me. The pages were blackened, charred by the amount of magic pouring through. No sane libriomancer would use a book so badly damaged, not if they wanted to hold on to that sanity. Like Gutenberg's lock, that damage would flow through other copies of the book, and only time would heal it.

I placed both hands over the book and wrenched my

spell closed, then took the second cupcake from Lena, trying to keep from trembling. Color had begun to return to my skin, but I could also see the faint overlay of char, like a layer of ash just beneath the surface. I had done this to myself once before at Mackinac Island, after channeling a Martian death ray through my own flesh to fight off a group of undead horses.

I had a peculiar life.

To my surprise, the cupcakes helped. The voices pressing into my head were still there, but no longer threatened to drown me. I scraped the last bit of chocolate frosting from the wrapper with my finger. "I'm sorry," I said as I realized what I had done. "Did I hurt you?"

A single elevated eyebrow and an amused smile was all the answer that question needed.

The taste of chocolate didn't block out the faint scent of methane and ammonia. Cleaning this mess would take hours. Jenn was going to kill me. Not to mention the damage the moisture would do to the books. I needed to get to the basement and bring up the portable dehumidifiers.

As my mind continued to clear, I noticed Lena was shivering. Charring her book shouldn't have hurt her. Unlike my time-viewing spell back in Tamarack, Lena was a fully formed magical creation. Her connection with her book had ended the moment someone pulled her acorn from the pages. "What's wrong?"

"The smell." She scooped a handful of snow from the floor and stared at it, entranced. "I remember this, even though I know it's not real. I've never touched snow like this before, but my body recognizes it, and suddenly everything else seems wrong. You, the library, even these clothes."

I jumped to my feet, grabbed her elbow, and dragged

her back to the children's section. Lena stumbled drunkenly along. I snatched her branch and pressed it into her hands. She gripped it like a lifeline.

"Stay with me, Lena." I punched in the alarm code and propped open the back door, then pulled her into the fresh air.

She stood like a statue, holding the branch from her tree and staring into the distance. Eventually, she reached over with one hand and tugged me to her. She kissed me fiercely at first, and then I felt her body begin to relax. She broke away and rested her head on my shoulder.

"Thank you," she whispered.

"I'm sorry," I said at the same time.

"What for?"

I tucked her hair back over her ear, then traced the edge of her ear down to the curve of her neck. "I'm an idiot. I should have known better."

Nidhi would have caught my mistake. She would have made certain Lena was safely out of range before I opened up a portal to the fictional world that had birthed her. I could think of no better way to induce a schizophrenic break than blurring the lines of Lena's two realities.

"Did it work?" she asked.

"I think so." It was five in the morning. I had held that book open for more than a half hour. I smiled wearily. "August Harrison is going to be *pissed*."

The mess inside made me sympathize with the Sorcerer's Apprentice. If I had the slightest idea how to enchant the mops and brooms to clean up the library, I'd be tempted too.

I ended up using a push broom to sweep most of the snow out the front door, then brought the dehumidifiers up. After an hour, the smell had dispersed enough for Lena to come back inside with no apparent ill effects.

By the time Jenn arrived, I had propped open the doors for airflow, returned the beanbags to their proper place, and wiped down the circulation desk. Jenn stopped in the doorway, sniffed the air, looked from me to the dehumidifiers, and sighed. "I don't want to know, do I?"

"A friend called me around four in the morning. Said he saw a couple of kids snooping around in here. They had gotten the chemistry books out, and as far as I can tell, I think they were trying to make their own little drug lab."

Jennifer Latona had about twenty years on me. I fought to keep a neutral expression as she gave me a *you-expect-me-to-believe-that* look that was eerily reminiscent of my mother. "How did they break in?"

"The alarm was armed, so if I had to guess, I'd say they came in during the day, snuck into the basement, and hid out until everyone left."

"Did you catch them?"

"They must have ducked out of sight when we pulled up. Lena and I started cleaning up the mess, and they took off through the back door."

She set her briefcase on the desk and rubbed her temples. "You cleaned up the evidence? Did it ever occur to you to call the police? Or to call *me*?"

"I can honestly say it didn't." I gave her an apologetic shrug. "I was just trying to save the books. Can you imagine the damage if this stuff seeped under the shelves? We did the best we could, but we need to get steam vacs in here if we want to avoid a major mold problem. Not to mention the bugs."

"I'm supposed to have a children's story group in here at eight-thirty." She popped open her suitcase, grabbed a pair of old socks, and waved them under my nose. "I brought sock puppets! I can't have kids sitting around in a library that smells like a chem lab."

I peeked outside. "The sky looks pretty clear. Why not do puppets in the park?"

"I never had this kind of trouble when I was working down in Lansing." Before I could answer, she raised a hand and said, "Just get someone in here to do the carpets."

I gave her a quick salute, then sat down to call Cody Terzaghi about renting his steam cleaners. Nicola called back on my own phone as I was wrapping things up with Cody.

"Harrison got the book," she said without greeting or preamble. "Jane Oshogay is dead."

I slumped lower in the chair. "How?"

"Jane was first on the scene, and arrived as Harrison and the others were leaving. Her orders were to wait, but you know libriomancers and their books. From the look of things, she put up a good fight."

"Damn." I hesitated. After reading Bi Wei's book and touching her mind, some part of me had hoped she would object to Harrison's rampage, that she would stop him from hurting anyone else. "I, um, kind of charred *Nymphs of Neptune* last night. I don't think they'll be able to use it, but we should make a note in the catalog."

"Good. I need you to stay where you are. Once we're done cleaning up at the fort, we'll join you at the library."

"We?"

"Gutenberg, myself, and every other Porter within traveling distance. It's time to put an end to this."

"Past time." Relief hit first, followed closely by fear.

Gutenberg had tried to destroy the students of Bi Sheng once before. I had no reason to believe he wouldn't attempt the same thing. But Bi Wei might be a match even for Gutenberg. Regardless of who won, the collateral damage would be ugly.

Copper River was about to become ground zero in a magical war the likes of which the world hadn't seen in more than five hundred years.

Chapter 16

Even deep within the slumber of my oak, Nidhi's scream cut through me like the freshly sharpened blade of an ax.

I leaped from my tree, one of six oaks planted in a row on the northern side of Nidhi's small yard. My feet hadn't even touched the grass when a man slammed into me like a rhino. We crashed together into the tree.

"Not smart." I spat blood, twisted a branch from the tree, and clubbed my attacker in the side of the head.

In my hands, the branch grew into a short spear. Whatever he was—I suspected a vampire, given his strength and speed—he didn't seem surprised. My toes gripped the roots for balance as I stepped toward him. My next strike knocked him into the yard.

He had destroyed my garden, uprooting every plant, from the grapevines to the tomatoes. My roses were torn to mulch. One way or another, this bastard was going down.

He came at me again, and the roots wrinkled like inchworms. His speed worked against him now. The roots looped up to catch his ankle and hardened like steel. The end result was a vampire face-first at my feet, screaming in pain as he tried to free his dislocated ankle.

I jammed my spear through his shoulder to pin him in place. "How many?"

He hissed and reached for my wrist, so I twisted hard.

"Three more," he cried. "Inside the house."

I didn't want to kill him. Most vampires had no more choice or control over what they became than I did. Their condition rarely involved truly informed consent. I let the spear take root, which should have been enough to keep him from causing further trouble. But he was stronger than I realized. He snarled and reached behind him, crushing the wood with one hand. He pushed himself up off of the broken spear, and his ankle popped into place with a sound like cracking stone.

I kicked him in the chest, then pulled the broken spear free. When he came at me again, I sidestepped and swung two-handed, forming an edge even as the wood hummed through the air. The newly made blade cut cleanly through his neck. I was inside the house before he had finished dissolving into ash.

I ran through the living room and vaulted the couch. Two figures were dragging Nidhi toward the front door.

I ran one through and used my weapon as a lever to fling him back. The second threw Nidhi against the wall and flew at me. Literally. She seized my neck and slammed me into the brick fireplace.

I dug my fingers into her hands. I might not be human, but I still needed oxygen, and my brain liked its blood flow. I managed to break her left thumb, but that only pissed her off.

And then I heard the chainsaw snarl to life in the backyard. Metal teeth bit into my oak, and I screamed. The saw felt like it was cutting through my bones, and while the oak was strong, every second chewed through bark and wood. I tried to strengthen the tree, but I needed to free myself first.

Instead of fighting the vampire's hold, I jabbed my fingers at her eyes. Either the eyes were vulnerable, or she hadn't been dead long enough to outgrow her human reflexes. She flinched back, one hand coming up to protect her face.

I punched her in the throat, grabbed her hair, and flung her over me and into the fireplace. If we had kept it burning, we could have had a proper fairy-tale ending. I settled for grabbing an iron poker and running her through.

I staggered to my feet. Ash stung my eyes, but I spotted Nidhi on the floor. She was still breathing. I started toward her, but the vampire was back on her feet, the poker protruding from her chest.

I felt the moment the oak's strength failed, when the weight of the tree overwhelmed the wood that remained. Fibers snapped and popped, and the world swayed around me. The vampire punched me in the side, cracking two ribs, but I barely felt it. My senses were imprisoned by the slow fall of my tree.

"Run," said Nidhi.

The oak slammed into the earth hard enough to shake the house. I screamed from pain and grief, forgetting vampires, forgetting even Nidhi as a part of me died.

Then I was ducking and falling back by reflex as the vampire attacked. I made it to the backyard, where her partner came at me with the chainsaw. Had I been stronger, I would have wrested it from his grip and cut him down, just as he had done to me. But the oak was my strength, and it lay on the ground, branches smashed through the fence. Leaves and broken sticks littered the yard.

I jumped onto the trunk and ran through the branches.

*My oak protected me one last time as the life leaked from
the wood. The branches let me pass while snatching my
pursuers like barbed wire.*

Seconds later, I was alone.

JEFF AND NIDHI GOT to the library around nine
in the morning. Jeff stopped in the doorway, wrinkled his nose, and announced, "I'll be out by the car,
where it doesn't smell like I've fallen into a chemical toilet."

Lena got up to greet Nidhi, leaving me to pore over a
chart I had begun working on more than a month ago.
They kept their reunion low-key. The library was mostly
empty, save for Alex at the main desk, and Dustin La-
Joie, who was checking out a stack of *Curious George*
books for his two-year-old daughter.

Lena had created a second bokken from a tree down
the street, and had reshaped them both into a spiral cane.
It thumped against the floor as she and Nidhi walked
over to join me at the public computer terminal.

"Do you have Smudge?" I asked.

Nidhi checked to make sure Alex wasn't watching,
then pulled a translucent yellow hamster ball from her
purse.

"You put him in plastic?" I opened the lid, and Smudge
darted up my arm. His feet dug into my sleeve as he
crouched protectively on my shoulder. Jennifer would
have yelled at me had she been here, but Alex thought
the spider was, in his words, "freakishly awesome."

"It's the first thing I could find at the pet store," Nidhi
said. "If Harrison came after us, melted plastic was going
to be the least of our worries."

"Hey, buddy." I pulled a jellybean from my candy pocket and handed it to him. Lena made puppy-dog eyes, so I tossed one to her as well.

"What's this?" asked Nidhi.

"A chart of all recorded encounters with the devourers." I traced the curve of the two-axis graph. The horizontal was labeled *Year*, while the vertical tracked the decreasing interval between incidents. "Gutenberg first touched these things in 1488, though he believes there are references going back at least a thousand years. For the next few centuries, there were only four recorded times when they reached through to touch our world."

I pointed to different points along the graph. 1523. 1601. 1699. 1743. As I moved closer to the present, the frequency began to increase. Several were flagged and linked to names in red, beginning with Géza Csáth in 1919 and running through François Robin in 2008.

"Who were they?" asked Nidhi.

"Writers. Specifically, writers who committed suicide. When Gutenberg examined their published writing, he found traces of devourer magic. He believes they may have had minor magical abilities, enough to call to the devourers through their work. He locked them all as a precaution." H. P. Lovecraft was noted in yellow with a question mark. He hadn't killed himself, but having read his work, the man hadn't been entirely right in the head, either.

A click of the mouse added a vertical dotted line. "This is the point where the interval is projected to become zero, and for all practical purposes, the devourers fully enter our world."

A point both Gutenberg and I had estimated to be within the next ten years, tops.

I pointed to the start of the sixteenth century. "Correlation doesn't prove cause, but the increase began right around the time Gutenberg founded the Porters. I thought it might be something we were doing. Libriomancy meant far more people could perform magic. Maybe that was weakening the barriers between magic and the real world. Or maybe magic simply called to them. They might see magic as anything from a challenge to a mating call for all we knew. But the timing also coincides with Gutenberg's assault on the students of Bi Sheng."

I had spent the past hour scribbling notes on colored flyers from last year's library sale. I spread them over the table and pointed to the lime-green one. "Normally, when a libriomancer returns an object to a book, it dissolves into undifferentiated magical energy. If you tried to put Smudge back in his book—well, he'd just set it on fire. But if you found a way, he'd be gone. You could create another Smudge, but it wouldn't know us. It wouldn't have his memories or experiences."

Because it helped me to think more clearly, I had sketched out the equations for converting magic into real-world matter and energy, and vice versa. We had never been able to fully work out the formulas, but we could do a rough approximation for certain basic feats of magic.

Because I was overtired, I had then illustrated the equations with a doodle of Smudge looking unhappy and setting things on fire.

"Bi Wei endured because of her connection to her book, a book which was read countless times through the centuries." Those readings would have become ritualized, almost religious in nature. A prayer connecting Bi Wei and her readers. "There was no physical dissolution. Nobody cut off her head and stuffed her brain into the book. Instead, the book became the backbone for an unbroken chain of belief linking Bi Wei's last moments in the temple to the oak tree where Lena brought her back."

I pointed to another flyer. "What happens when that chain breaks?"

"You get a devourer?" Nidhi guessed.

"But if they lost that magical template of belief *and* they have no physical bodies or anchors in the real world, they should have dissolved into nothingness." I had illustrated the devourers as a series of swirls that looked like badly drawn tumbleweeds. "So what keeps the devourers alive?"

Nidhi pointed to the computer. "Could they be using the authors and libriomancers they possessed? Traveling from one mind to another?"

"There are too many gaps," I said excitedly. "Only one incident in the sixteenth century? What happened to them for the next seventy-eight years?"

"You think they have another anchor," said Lena.

I snatched another set of equations. "It's only a theory. I don't know if it's more books or another kind of magical artifact, or something else we've never considered, but the simplest explanation is that something or someone is preserving them, just like the students of Bi Sheng did for Bi Wei."

Shouts from outside made me jump. Smudge spun to face the front of the library, but he wasn't burning. Lena snatched her cane and headed for the door.

I opted for the window. Outside, Jeff was holding the arms of a woman with bright green hair. "It's all right," I assured Alex.

"How exactly is this all right?" asked Nidhi. "If she knows where we are, we should either be fighting or running."

"I'm not sure." But Smudge wasn't worried, and when I listened to Guan Feng arguing with Jeff, I didn't hear a threat. Only fear and desperation. "Lena, would you please ask Jeff to bring her inside?"

Guan Feng sat down between us. Her foot tapped nervously against the floor. Jeff had taken the seat behind her, while Lena sat with me, not-so-subtly surrounding her.

All that remained was to get Alex to stop staring. I thought at first that he had noticed one of us doing something magical, but it wasn't us he was watching. His interests were more natural than supernatural.

He gathered his courage and walked around the desk. When he saw me looking, he veered away and pretended to reshelf a book. One casual step at a time, he made his way toward Guan Feng. "Hey, are you okay? You look pretty shaken up." The rest of us were effectively invisible. "I could get you a pop from the break room if you'd like, or maybe some tea?"

"Feng's an English major at NMU," I said. "She's looking for summer work, and stopped by to ask about the library."

Alex lit up. "You'd love working here. Do you need me to show you around?"

"She has a boyfriend," I added.

Alex blushed so hard I couldn't help but feel bad for him. "Oh. I mean, that's all right. It's still a great place to work." He retreated far more hastily than he had approached, and busied himself sorting through the returned books.

"How did you find us?" I asked Guan Feng.

She gave the answer I had expected. "Bi Wei."

"Does Harrison know?"

She shook her head, and her eyes turned glassy. I wasn't happy about how easily she had tracked us down, but Smudge remained calm. If this was a trap, or if she had brought one of Harrison's bugs, even unknowingly, he'd have set something on fire by now.

"What happened?" Nidhi asked gently.

"He put one of those things around her neck while she slept." She had an accent, but spoke with the confidence of long practice. "Like he did with you. But it wasn't enough. He built three metal snakes, only a few inches long. The millipede held its blade to her neck while they burrowed into the skin of her chest. He says they're coiled around the aorta."

"Why?" I whispered.

It was Lena who answered. "To control her."

Tears spilled down Guan Feng's cheeks. "For six years, ever since my father died, I've been her reader. I was only thirteen years old, one of the youngest to be given such an honor. To become a reader, let alone a reader for a direct descendant of Bi Sheng ... It was my responsibility to sustain and protect her. And if we could find a way, to restore her." She raised her chin. "I would rather see my ancestors sleep another five hundred years than let Harrison chain them as he did Bi Wei."

"He sent his insects into the tree when I brought Wei back," said Lena. "Why did he need more?"

"He lost his connection to them, and believes they were destroyed," Guan Feng said furiously. "He doesn't understand the truth. They became a part of her, a tumor spreading through her spirit."

I leaned closer. "Does Bi Wei know?"

"Yes. She recognized the touch of the sǐ guǐ jūn duì, the Ghost Army."

"Wait, you know what they are?" For two months I had pored over old manuscripts and reports, trying to piece together fragments of information and rumors going back five centuries. Meanwhile, Guan Feng knew our enemy by name.

"Some are students of Bi Sheng who lost their way. Their books were destroyed, or their readers neglected their duties. Others . . . we don't know. The ghosts existed before Bi Sheng's time. Throughout the years, there have been attempts to control them and the power they command."

She turned to the computer and attacked the keyboard with two fingers. A short time later, she opened up a translated Tang Dynasty poem by Dù Hàorán titled "Waiting for my Teacher to Return From the Land of Midday Dreams." She scooted to the side so I could read.

"'Dark clouds grow thin, and the song shall summon the dead to war.'" The poem described a sorcerer named Yuan Jiao and her battle against a man who had drowned in the river of magic. The man's ghost had returned, far more powerful than before. He sought to drag others down. Yuan Jiao set forth into the Land of Midday Dreams, where she battled the ghost for seven days. But the more she fought, the stronger he became.

I thought about my hallucinations earlier this morning, how I had attacked Lena without recognizing her. Midday Dreams, indeed. I had come close to losing myself in Detroit, drowning in my own magic. That was when the devourer had struck.

"What will happen to Bi Wei?" I asked.

"She spent five hundred years adrift in the river of magic. That river flows through her now. It gives her tremendous power, but the first time she loses control, the ghosts will pull her down." She stomped one foot on the floor. "August Harrison dismissed the dangers as 'ignorant fears born of Oriental folklore and superstition.' He and his dryad will turn our ancestors into vessels for the Army of Ghosts."

Lena went rigid. "His dryad?"

"Wei pulled a single acorn from the book before Isaac destroyed it." Guan Feng's mouth tugged into a grim smile. "August was furious when Wei told him what you had done. He started swearing and talking about what he planned to do to punish you. But he had the acorn, and Bi Wei helped it to grow. The dryad was born hours after the attack on your archive, near St. Ignace. He named her Deifilia."

Deifilia, meaning daughter of God. How egotistical could Harrison get?

Nidhi took Lena's hand. "Do the others know what Harrison and the Army of Ghosts have done to Bi Wei?"

"They know, but they don't believe. Some agree with Harrison." Her nose wrinkled and her lips tightened, as if the words soured her mouth. "The Army of Ghosts is little more than a legend, but Gutenberg and the Porters are real. We remember what the Porters did to our ancestors. Every time we read their books, we relive their fear as they watched Gutenberg's ambition grow. They see Bi Wei's power. She lived for years as a woman, but spent five centuries as a creature of magic. Her rebirth blended both lives. The others believe Harrison has given us the chance to not only restore our ancestors, but to fight back against the Porters."

"What does August get in return?" Nidhi asked.

"His son. He believes Victor can be restored as Bi Wei was."

From the way Nidhi stared, she obviously hadn't expected that answer any more than I had.

Jeff was the first to speak. "How's he expect to pull that off? Victor didn't have one of those old books."

"He hacked our network." I spoke slowly, giving myself a chance to piece together what I knew. "He has Victor's notes and reports. Magic was Victor's life."

"Would that be enough to bring him back?" asked Lena.

"Not by any magic we understand," said Guan Feng. "The books must be printed and bound using the same materials, the same techniques. The individual's words are encased by Bi Sheng's magic. Computer files would not work. We've explained this to him, but he refuses to accept that his son is gone." She looked at the floor. "And . . . we allowed him to hold on to that hope."

"If he thinks there's a chance, he'll keep helping you," Nidhi said.

"Yes."

"I don't get it," I said. "August and Victor hated each other."

"The dynamics of abuse are complicated and ugly." Nidhi paced behind us. "August Harrison did unforgivable things to his wife and son, but there were moments of kindness as well. He taught Victor how to work with machines, how to build and repair circuit boards. Victor described moments of pride, even warmth and love. I imagine those were the moments Victor clung to when he sent the cicada to his father. But by the time August arrived, he was too late to save his son. He might see that as his ultimate failure as a father."

What would happen when he realized he couldn't restore his son, that Bi Sheng's magic couldn't affect a collection of computer files any more than I could reach into . . .

"What?" asked Jeff.

I was already making a phone call. I browbeat the boy who answered into running out to make sure Jeneta was okay. If August Harrison had read my work, he knew Jeneta was his best option at turning electronic files into magic. I twitched impatiently until the boy confirmed Jeneta was out canoeing with the rest of the girls from her cabin.

"Great," I said. "Tell her—" Dammit, her e-reader was destroyed, and I hadn't had time to get her a new one. But she could work magic with her phone, too. "Tell her that poems can protect you from nightmares, and to make sure she has some ready."

"You want me to give her a message about poetry?"

"It's a librarian thing. She'll understand." I hung up and called Nicola Pallas next. "We need a Porter at Camp Aazhawigiizhigokwe. August might be going after Jeneta next."

Pallas rarely wasted time on idle chitchat or pointless questions. "I can have a field agent there in twenty minutes. I believe Myron Worster is closest."

"Thank you. If anything happens, have Myron get her out of there. Don't try to fight." I covered the mouthpiece and asked Guan Feng, "Are they still in St. Ignace?"

"We left the fort as soon as you destroyed the dryad's book. I snuck away after we stopped for the night. I don't know where Harrison meant to take Deifilia."

I relayed that to Pallas, and promised to fill her in on the rest when she and Gutenberg arrived.

Guan Feng was twisting her hands into her pants. "I'll tell you anything you want, but please give me back Bi Wei's book. She struggles to hold on. Let me help her."

"We will." I rummaged through my own books. "Has Harrison been creating more wendigos?"

"Yes. He took two people from the fort yesterday, and talked of collecting others."

"He killed a Porter," I said. "He knows Gutenberg will be coming in force." I donned my jacket and pulled another shock-gun from *Time Kings*. I shouldn't have been doing magic so soon after ripping holes in *Nymphs of Neptune*, but sometimes the universe didn't wait around for you to rest up. I knew the gun would take a wendigo down or cook one of his metal bugs. I was more worried about how to counter Bi Wei's power.

The smell of burning dust rose from my shoulder. Smudge was watching the door, and waves of orange rippled over his thorax, dangerously close to my hair.

Nidhi saw it too. "Feng, is there any way you could have been followed?"

Comprehension and fear widened Guan Feng's eyes, and she jumped to her feet. "I was careful. I didn't tell anyone where I was going. I swear on my father's grave."

"He probably forced Bi Wei to tell him where you were." I shoved the gun into my pocket, pulled on my jacket, and grabbed the rest of my books. "It's all right. He would have found us anyway. I'm a little surprised the destruction of *Nymphs of Neptune* didn't attract his swarm, but it sounds like he was busy practicing horticulture."

Lena untwisted her cane into two sharpened swords and strode toward the door.

"How many?"

"Only one. But you might want to make sure you've got a change of underwear before you see this thing."

Alex came around the desk to intercept me. "Isaac, tell your girlfriend she can't bring weapons into *holy-shit-your-spider's-on-fire!*"

I clapped him on the shoulder. "Alex, this would be a very good time for you to go on break. Somewhere else."

Jeff had joined Lena by the door. Neither one of them moved. Not a good sign.

The scream of tearing metal filled the street, followed by silence. I shoved past Alex toward the back and hurried to see what we were up against.

"All right," I whispered. "I admit it. I'm impressed."

I had been expecting to see Harrison, Bi Wei, and the dryad at a minimum, along with his insects. Possibly wendigos as well, depending on whether or not he was ready to announce his presence to the world.

I hadn't expected a six-legged dragon made of old mining and construction equipment.

The thing was roughly the size of a bus. The yellow legs looked like they had come from mismatched backhoes. The mouth was a pair of toothed bulldozer blades. Heavy steel wings folded over the body to form an additional layer of armor.

The tail was perhaps the most terrifying. Imagine Paul Bunyan's chainsaw. Disengage the chain and make it prehensile, then start whipping it through the streets of Copper River. As I watched, it peeled the roof from a parked car and gouged brick from the building beyond.

"Go on break," whispered Alex. "Right."

"I promise I'll explain later." Not that it would matter. If this thing didn't kill us all, the Porters would be by to erase Alex's memories, along with everyone else in town. So far, people were keeping off the street, but I saw faces pressed against windows, and at least two phones filming the carnage.

A gun went off from across the road, but the dragon didn't appear to notice. Standing in the doorway of the barbershop, Lizzie Pascoe raised her hunting rifle to her shoulder and squeezed off another shot.

The dragon was more interested in the library. Thick

steel cables flexed and tightened within its body as it charged.

The entire building shook, and a good chunk of the front wall crumbled away. I yanked out my shock-gun, switched it to maximum, and sent lightning crackling into the dragon's mouth. The attack left a glowing orange patch of metal the size of a dinner plate, but the dragon didn't even slow down. The tail swiped through the wall, destroying windows, books, and the Back-to-School book display I had spent two hours putting together. Books and debris battered us all, and the shock-gun fell from my hand.

Lena hauled me toward the back of the library. Once there, I snatched *The Complete Short Stories of H. G. Wells* from my jacket and turned to "The New Accelerator." I had been meaning to try this story for a while.

I struggled to focus on the words as enormous jaws ripped away part of the roof like it was made of cardboard. I kept remembering the ruins of the MSU library, reduced to a heap of crumbled brick and twisted metal. I was *not* going to let Harrison's latest pet do that to my library. I reached into the story and pulled out a small, green phial of thick liquid.

"If Bi Wei and the others are here, they'll be able to counter any magic you use," Guan Feng warned.

"Sure," I said. "If they're fast enough."

I transferred Smudge to the drinking fountain where he'd be less likely to set anything alight, then downed the potion and closed my eyes while I waited for the magic to take effect.

The sounds of battle slowed, then died completely. I opened my eyes again and strode carefully past my seemingly motionless companions, releasing the phial over the trash can on my way out. It hovered in the air, its downward motion invisible to my hyperaccelerated eye.

Beneath the anger and, if I were honest, the overwhelming terror, a part of me was looking forward to this. It was the same part that cheered for every David-and-Goliath tale of underdogs triumphing over impossible odds and unbeatable foes.

It was time to slay a dragon.

Chapter 17

Plato once said that human beings were created with two heads, four arms, and four legs, until Zeus split them in half. Ever since, humans have spent their lives searching for their other half, the one person who could complete them.

What a narrow-minded, messed-up, asinine system.

Do the math. There are more than seven billion people on this planet. Say you do a lot of traveling, and manage to meet a million of those people in your lifetime. That gives you a mere 1 in 7000 chance of finding "the one."

Maybe that's why they created me. To be their other half, the answer to the myth. Easier than scouring the planet for an impossible dream. Easier, too, than learning to set aside the dream and embrace a human being who is as flawed and imperfect as you.

Humans are so obsessed with true love, the perfect relationship. They imagine that one elusive person who fits their quirks and foibles and desires like a puzzle piece. And of course, when a potential mate falls short of that *perfection, they reject them. They were too old, too young, too silly, too serious, too fat, too thin. They liked the wrong TV shows. They hated chocolate. They voted for the other guy. They didn't put the toilet seat down.*

They invent a million excuses for rejection, a million ways to find others unattractive. Their skill at seeing ugliness in others is matched only by their ability to see it in the mirror, to punish themselves for every imagined flaw. No matter who I've become, I never understood that facet of humanity.

I remember when Isaac introduced me to Doctor Who. *In one episode, the Doctor met a man who said he wasn't important. The Doctor replied, "I've never met anyone who wasn't important before."*

I've never met anyone who wasn't beautiful. People have simply forgotten how to see.

Frank Dearing was a selfish, petty, controlling bastard, but when he was working in the field, the hard muscles of his body shining with sweat as he coaxed life from the dirt . . . the man was an asshole, but he was a hot *asshole.*

Nidhi Shah was softer. She dressed to minimize the physical. Age and stress had mapped faint lines onto her face. And she was gorgeous. Even before you stripped off her clothes and kissed your way down her neck . . .

Then there was Isaac Vainio, a skinny geek of a man who lugged his pet spider around everywhere he went. But he had such passion, such raw joy and excitement. That passion transformed him into something sexier than any rock star.

The more we narrow the definition of beauty, the more beauty we shut out of our lives.

IT WAS AS IF I had put the entire universe on pause. Time hadn't stopped; I had simply sped myself up by a factor of a hundred thousand or so. If all went well, I'd have taken care of the dragon before the phial had fallen more than an inch.

I wanted to run, but even my cautious, steady pace warmed my skin and clothes, courtesy of friction and compression of the air. Relatively speaking, I was a meteorite streaking through the atmosphere, and it would be all too easy to burn myself to a crisp.

"Why doesn't the Flash ever have to worry about this?" I sank slowly to the floor to retrieve my shockgun. Weapon in hand, I began climbing over the crumbled remains of our front wall.

Something stung the side of my face. I thought at first that Harrison's insects had found a way to get at me, but when I looked, I saw a triangle of broken glass hovering in the air. Other shards sparkled like ice, frozen in time and sharp enough to do all kinds of damage if I wasn't more careful.

I grabbed a broken section of shelving and moved it to and fro like a broom, pushing the glass shards out of the way. Even a relatively slow impact shattered the shards into smaller fragments. I was tempted to try to calculate the amount of kinetic energy in each swing, but Wells' magic formula had a limited duration. I could play with the math later.

Once I had cleared a path, I ducked outside and made my way down the steps onto the sidewalk. An overturned Chevy Cavalier had smashed into the front wall. I couldn't see whether there was anyone inside. The dragon's tail was curved back like a bullwhip, ready to rip through the library a second time.

"My name is Isaac Vainio," I said. "You smashed my library. Prepare to die."

Everything went better with *Princess Bride* references. I aimed at the base of the tail and squeezed the trigger.

There was an interminable wait while the ionized pellet crawled toward the dragon. It took what felt like five seconds just to travel the six feet between me and my target. I watched, fascinated, as the pellet deformed and broke apart.

I braced the gun with both hands, waiting for the lightning and rethinking my plan. In real time, the lightning followed within a fraction of a second, meaning the barrel of the gun was still aligned with the path laid out by the tracer pellet.

What happened if the gun moved? Would the lightning make a new path? My arms were starting to tire.

Five seconds to travel six feet. The gun was supposed to have an effective range of almost a mile. Call it six thousand feet for easy math, and assume the speed of light to be more or less instantaneous, which meant the lightning couldn't start until the pellet had time to travel the full mile. In real time, it all happened too quickly for human senses to follow. At my relative speed, I'd be waiting more than an hour.

Screw it. I let go, and the gun began to accelerate downward at 9.8 meters per second squared. It should fire long before it had descended the first inch.

I returned to the library and removed a hardcover of John Scalzi's *Old Man's War* from the shelves. Reading without utterly destroying the book was harder than I had expected. After accidentally tearing the binding and four separate pages, I was ready to toss the book aside and attack the dragon bare-handed.

Instead, I released the book and used both hands to slowly and carefully search for the chapter I needed.

The all-in-one superweapons from Scalzi's novel were much too large to fit through the book. Even if I could create them, I wouldn't be able to fire the CDF standard-issue MP-35 Infantry Rifle without some extra hardware in my brain.

The projectiles, on the other hand, I could create. Specifically, projectiles that had just left the gun.

The MP-35 had six modes. The only question was whether to use the rockets or the grenades . . .

I was dragging Lizzie Pascoe back into the barbershop when the shock-gun discharged a bolt of lightning into the dragon's tail. I set Lizzie down behind the counter, away from the windows. I did the same with her husband and their single customer. I checked the post office across the street next. One by one, I dragged everyone into the back, laying them out like firewood. The antiques store was a lost cause, full of ceramics and glass. I ended up hauling the occupants over to the barbershop instead.

The shock-gun shouldn't have gone off yet. Either my math was off, or the time-dilating effect of Wells' story was beginning to wear off. By the time I finished getting everyone behind cover, I was confident my math was correct. I couldn't hear the thunder from my gun, but I could feel it, like a subsonic massage to my skeletal system.

I grabbed my gun out of the air and double-checked to make sure the street was empty. As I hurried back to the library, I could see the three small projectiles inching their way into the beast's open maw.

My exposed skin felt like I was rubbing it with sandpaper. When I got inside, I brought Lena, Nidhi, Jeff, and Feng to the break room. After one last trip to grab Smudge, I hunkered down with them to wait.

By the time the explosion went off, the spell had pretty much ended. I heard glass shatter, and the shock wave shook the entire building.

"How did we get—Isaac, what did you *do*?" Nidhi shouted. I could barely hear her over the echoes of the explosion, and her voice was far deeper than normal, presumably due to a kind of temporal Doppler effect.

I crept out of the break room. The explosion had taken out every remaining window in the library. Books and papers were everywhere, and shrapnel had torn through the walls.

Outside, the dragon's head lay in three pieces on the ground. The tail had snapped free, and spasmed like the death throes of a decapitated snake. The rest of the body simply stood there. "Maybe I only needed two grenades."

We knew the destruction of Harrison's insects pained him. I hoped that pain scaled with mass, and that I had just handed him the mother of all migraines.

I retrieved Smudge, who scrambled up to my shoulder and clung there, but he wasn't—quite—hot enough to burn me, which I took as a good sign. Lena was already checking on Alex out back.

I sagged against the wall. The worst part was knowing every building on the block had been hit by the same shock wave. I had wrecked buildings and businesses that had stood here for more than a hundred years.

I couldn't possibly come up with a story to bury this. Copper River was a small, tightly knit town. If gossip was a competitive sport, we'd have been sending teams to the Olympics and bringing back gold. There must have been at least fifty witnesses to what just happened, not to mention the dead metal dragon blocking the road. "I am so screwed."

"You'd be surprised how much humanity will ignore when it falls outside of their beliefs."

The calm words were an electrical shock through my spine. I straightened like a cadet coming to attention before an officer. Johannes Gutenberg stood by the crumpled book return bin, an oversized red book tucked beneath his arm.

"You couldn't have gotten here five minutes sooner?" I asked.

For all his power, Gutenberg was a physically unimposing man. Short and slender, he looked to be in his mid-thirties. A thick black beard and mustache couldn't conceal the narrowness of his face, especially the nose. A fringe of hair poked out from beneath a black small-brim fedora. He wore a brown vest and scarf over a white shirt, with matching white pants.

"We arrived ten minutes ago, in fact. Time enough to take care of the dragon's keeper before he could counter your magic." He bent over to pick up the H. G. Wells collection. "Temporal acceleration. That would explain your windburned complexion."

"We?" asked Jeff.

"I have eleven field agents setting up a perimeter around the library. Two others will be going door-to-door. Jeneta Aboderin is safe, by the way. Myron Worster is keeping an eye on her." Outside, the lightning-flash of automatons announced the arrival of more reinforcements.

Reinforcements who would be working their magic on my neighbors, editing the memories of people I called friends. Lizzie Pascoe had tried to help against an enemy she couldn't have understood. She had stepped forward despite her fear. In return, I had blown out every window in her shop, and now her very thoughts would be violated and rewritten.

"You certainly seem to have gotten Mister Harrison's attention." Gutenberg rapped a knuckle against the book he carried. "Fascinating spellcraft. Far more stable than I would have guessed, to last for so many years with so little corruption. The fellow imprisoned in these pages was able to contain our magic long enough for his master to escape. Fortunately, I believe I can eliminate that threat."

He plucked a gold fountain pen from his breast pocket and opened the book.

"What are you doing?" Guan Feng shoved past me. "Stop!"

Gutenberg tilted his head, the nib of the pen hovering over the rice paper. "You must be one of the Bì Shēng de dú zhě." His expression didn't change, but the air inside the library seemed to drop twenty degrees. "You neglected to mention a prisoner in your phone call to Nicola, Isaac."

"She came to ask for our help," I said. "Harrison was able to create his own dryad. He's going to use her to restore the rest of Bi Sheng's students from their books, and to enslave them."

"His friends have done an excellent job of hiding him. But all magic has limits." He touched pen to paper and began to write.

Guan Feng lunged for the book, but Lena caught her in a bear hug and held her back. I stepped closer, trying to see what Gutenberg was doing. The pen left no visible mark on the paper, but I could feel the book reacting to the words.

I shouldn't have been able to feel it at all. I was too raw and exposed from the past few days. "You're hurting him."

"Indeed," he said without looking up. "It will be over soon enough."

Smudge crawled around to the back of my head, tickling my neck. I half expected him to set my hair alight, but he was unnaturally cool to the touch. Whoever was bound to that book, he was lashing out, trying to counter Gutenberg's magic. Invisible fingers curled through my body, searching for purchase. Gutenberg merely clucked his tongue and continued to write.

"Please." Guan Feng's face was wet. She had stopped struggling against Lena. "He'll die."

"He died five hundred years ago," Gutenberg said. "This was a collection of memories, nothing more."

"You're locking the book." More than anything, I felt disoriented. Off balance, as if I was falling in every direction. Desperation built like steam—desperation that belonged not to me, but to the man bound to that book. I heard a whisper in my head, but I didn't understand the words. And then the struggle simply stopped, replaced by resignation and a sense of acceptance.

A second later, there was nothing.

"Very good." Gutenberg capped his pen and returned it to his pocket.

I reached over to touch the book. Magically, it was cold and dead. "He's gone."

Guan Feng wiped her face, the movement violent. "His name was Lan Qihao. He was a poet. He was seventeen years old the day your automatons attacked. His parents were farmers. He lost his sister at the age of twelve, during a flood."

She stared at the book, her eyes unfocussed. "He was

in love with another student, a girl of nineteen, from Ho-pei. She was from a riverboat family. They spoke of running away together, but neither would dishonor their studies. When shelved, their books were always placed next to each other."

"A touching story," Gutenberg said. He drew a thin paperback from within his vest and turned in a slow circle.

"What's that?" I asked.

"I want to be certain Harrison hasn't left any of his pets behind to eavesdrop." He clapped the book shut. "Isaac, I'm told you had acquired one of these books when you and Lena escaped from August Harrison."

With his attention on me, he didn't see the sudden panic on Guan Feng's face, nor the desperate pleading in her eyes.

"It was stolen during the fight," said Nidhi. "While the dragon distracted Isaac and Lena, a second creature entered the library. A metal dog or wolf. It snatched the book and tried to attack Guan Feng. Lena was able to fend it off."

I had never been a good liar, but Nidhi was amazing. Perhaps a second and a half of real time had passed while I battled the dragon and moved people to safety. There was no way Lena had fought anything during that time. Yet as I listened to Nidhi, I almost believed her.

"I see." Gutenberg somehow managed to shove the oversized book into the back pocket of his trousers. Another trick I would love to learn one of these days.

"Harrison and Bi Sheng's students aren't the only threat." I told him about the Army of Ghosts. "They've infested Harrison's insects, and they did the same to Bi Wei when Lena restored her. We've got to assume everyone he and his dryad restores will be similarly infected."

Gutenberg frowned. "Victor didn't create his insects to house such things. Every documented encounter has involved human beings."

"He did make them telepathic, though," I said. "When we spoke to Victor's ghost, he said at least one insect had gone missing overseas. It was supposed to be seeking out magic."

"We'll have to see about finding that lost insect," said Gutenberg. "In the meantime, our priority is August Harrison. The Ghost Army is using him. They helped him learn how to build monsters for his protection, and how to restore the students of Bi Sheng, all as a way to provide vessels for their own return."

"Harrison knows where I live," I said. "Nidhi, too."

"We have both places under observation. For now though, we'll remain here."

"Here?" I stared. "But he's already attacked the library once. If they return—"

"Stop thinking so defensively, Isaac. Small and damaged though it may be, this library is our strongest fortress."

"Small?" I bristled, but held my tongue before I could say things I would regret. On a per capita basis, the Copper River Library had more books than just about any other library in the country. I watched in silence as he browsed the broken shelves, selecting a book seemingly at random. He fanned the pages, and Guan Feng dropped to the floor unconscious. Nidhi crouched to touch the girl's neck.

"She's alive," Gutenberg said, pulling out his gold pen once more. As he moved toward Guan Feng, understanding twisted my stomach.

All libriomancers knew Gutenberg could lock books, sealing away the most dangerous magic. Only a few of us knew he could do the same to people, suppressing any magic they might possess. He had even been known to wipe people's memories of magic, and to erase them from the memories of others. Gutenberg argued that it was the most humane way to deal with magical criminals, and he wasn't entirely wrong. You couldn't exactly send them off to a mundane prison, which meant the only other alternative would be to kill them.

To most of us, death would be preferable. "She doesn't have any magic."

"Are you certain?" asked Gutenberg.

"What she does have is a connection to Bi Wei," I continued. "A connection we don't understand. Bi Wei appeared sane when we escaped. For all we know, Guan Feng is the one helping her to hold on to that sanity, and to resist the influence of the Ghost Army. Do you know what severing that bond might do?"

He pursed his lips. "When did you learn such caution, Isaac?"

"About the fourth time I nearly eradicated myself from existence." I watched his pen as if it were a loaded gun. "Why did you try to wipe out the students of Bi Sheng?"

Gutenberg slid the pen back into his pocket. "Do you think I was the first to attempt to build an organization like Die Zwelf Portenære? There were many guilds and circles of magic-users throughout the world. Some were only too happy to join with me. Others viewed the Porters as a group of impertinent upstarts with no respect for the laws of magic who threatened the proper order."

"It sounds like you threatened more than 'the proper order.'" My throat was dry. Provoking Gutenberg was near the top of my list of stupid ideas, just below throwing snowballs at a wendigo.

"The Archbishop Adolph von Nassau was the first to

challenge me. He sent his soldiers to burn my press when he learned what I could do. Two of my apprentices died in the blaze. I would have been killed as well if not for the protection I gained from the grail. This was no ordinary fire, Isaac. The flames were alive, sent by magic. After five hundred years, I can still see the smoke pouring forth, like the black breath of hell itself." He shrank inward. "I pulled Peter from the fire, but I was unable to save him."

He brushed his sleeves, visibly regaining his composure. "That was the first of many such attacks. We were at war. My discovery meant the mastery of magic was no longer limited to a handful of individuals. Hundreds, even thousands now had the potential to use such power, and to challenge those who once thought themselves untouchable." He pursed his lips in amusement. "The great conquistador Juan Ponce de Leon took particular offense at my presumption, at least in the beginning."

"*Your* discovery?" I pressed.

He inclined his head in acknowledgment. "Bi Sheng crafted a primitive form of book magic. I took libriomancy to its full potential."

"Bi Sheng's 'primitive' magic preserved his followers for five hundred years," Lena pointed out.

He waved her comment off with a sharp gesture. "The original twelve Porters were under constant assault. Some campaigns were waged through rumor and gossip, seeking to destroy our reputations in both the magical and the mundane worlds. Other practitioners arrived to challenge us directly. The only way to prove the legitimacy of my art was to accept and defeat all such challenges."

"Bi Wei never challenged you," I said quietly. "She knew nothing of Porters or European libriomancy. Her ancestor's magic showed her the stars, and you sent your automatons to kill her."

"Did she tell you about the hēi shēng?"

The words translated to "dark afflictions." I shook my head.

"They were similar to Victor's insects in some respects. The hēi shēng are small creatures of folded paper, made from the pages of books penned by Bi Sheng's students. They stowed away on Portuguese trading vessels and eventually made their way to Germany. They came during the night, cutting flesh so cleanly their victims never even stirred. The wounds resisted magical healing. I watched five of my students suffer for weeks, their wounds turning septic." He unbuttoned his vest and the top of his shirt, then pulled back the collar to display a thin purple scar over his shoulder. "Even I never fully healed."

"Earlier this year, a former Porter enslaved and destroyed vampires. Should the rest of the vampires retaliate against all Porters, like you did with Bi Sheng's followers?"

"It's easy to stand in judgment," Gutenberg said softly, "from the luxury of the magical peace and security I provided. And perhaps you're right. Ponce de Leon thought as you did, and it's true I've made mistakes. But while you stand there self-righteously condemning my choices and actions from five hundred years ago, August Harrison and his followers prepare for war. I suggest you reconsider your priorities, Isaac."

He righted a table and began gathering books. I waited without speaking until he vanished into the history section, then hurried to grab my things from behind the desk. I pulled Bi Wei's book out of my bag and shoved it into a file drawer, behind a bulging folder of old library card applications.

By the time Gutenberg returned with more books, I was standing at the front of the library looking through the ragged opening at the Porters talking to Lizzie Pascoe. As I watched, she smiled and invited them into the barbershop.

"Whatever remains of Bi Wei's mind now shares a body with the devil itself." Gutenberg sighed, and for a moment, I saw not the most powerful libriomancer in the world, but an old man, exhausted from burdens he had carried for centuries. "This isn't a war between Porters and Bi Sheng's descendants, Isaac. Do you think the Ghost Army will stop with the Porters? You've felt their hunger. They will devour *everything*." He pointed outside to the broken dragon. "And they will begin with Copper River."

Chapter 18

Every religion I've studied has laws or commandments against killing.

Historically, humanity has shown tremendous creativity in finding every possible loophole, rationalization, and justification to ignore those commandments.

Animals kill for food, and to protect their territory, which suggests killing can be a normal, natural part of life. But humans are civilized. They've supposedly moved beyond mere instinct. Yes, animals kill. They also eat their young, but if you suggest a human mother do the same, people tend to react poorly. Animals will happily interbreed with their siblings as well, but that's frowned upon among humans. (Though some of them do it anyway, and many others fantasize about it.) The behavior of animals does not provide moral justification for human beings to do the same.

Is killing ever a moral choice? What if the personal decision to avoid inflicting harm leads to a greater evil? Countless writers have penned tales of traveling back in *time to kill Hitler. Would such a murder be right if it prevented millions of other deaths?*

Isn't doing nothing while a vampire attacks my loved one a greater crime than destroying the vampire? Both choices lead to death. One choice stops a killer.

In The Fellowship of the Ring, *Gandalf praised the pity of Bilbo Baggins in sparing Gollum, despite Gollum's evil nature. As it turned out, that choice saved all of Middle Earth in the end. But then, it's easy to present simple answers to ethical questions when you're the one shaping the story. What of those times when Gandalf rode his moral high horse into battle, helping to kill countless orcs and goblins?*

Gollum was a victim of the ring, corrupted and twisted. The vampire is diseased, driven by maddening thirst and inhuman urges. And I . . . given a cruel enough lover, I could become a creature much worse than any of them. Can I judge and kill others for acts I have the same potential to commit?

I've killed before. To defend myself and those I love. Was that the right choice, or simply the easy one?

The day Kawaljeet Sarna began teaching me Indian stick fighting, he began with a simple lesson: Prevent, Practice, Protect.

Prevent conflict when you can. Avoid the enemy. Diffuse their anger. Take their mental balance, and search for peaceful resolution.

Practice confrontation. Learn to deescalate the conflict, to dampen the flames instead of adding fuel. Seek peace, even in battle.

Protect yourself and those unable to defend themselves. When possible, protect your opponent as well.

Protect your physical self, but also your mental and emotional selves.

If any of the words I've written here have the power to shape who I am, let it be these. If I'm unable to hold to these rules, if I become a monster like those I've fought, then I ask only that others not hesitate to end me.

THE FIRST PORTER TO join us in the library was Antonia Warwick, who greeted us each in turn. She whistled softly as she surveyed the damage. "I've heard of giving an old building a facelift, but I'm pretty sure this isn't what they meant."

Like Nicola Pallas, Toni was one of the handful of Porters who wasn't a libriomancer. She performed sympathetic magic, manipulating small objects to create larger effects. I had once seen her summon a nasty ice storm with nothing but an old Snoopy Snow Cone maker. She lived in Winnipeg, but her talents were always in demand, meaning she traveled more than most field agents.

She was in her early forties, with faint wrinkles by the eyes and a crooked nose. Dreadlocks hung just past her shoulders. She wore a black tank top, exposing well-muscled arms. Around her waist was what appeared to be the result of a one-night stand between a handyman's leather tool belt and Batman's utility belt. Gleaming silver studs decorated the black leather belt, which was weighed down by an array of pouches and tools of every shape and size. Additional straps rose over her shoulders for support.

She had a mug of pop as big as her head, and sucked absently at the straw as she studied me more closely. "What the hell have you been doing to yourself, Vainio?"

"The usual."

"That would explain it." She climbed onto the desk and studied the broken ceiling beams. "Lena, you're good with wood, right? How about you get up here and let's see if we can keep this place from caving in any more."

Normally, I would have been fascinated by the way they worked together. Lena strengthened one of the cracked beams, giving it life enough to grow and heal. Toni spread that strength to the rest. The ceiling groaned, and we backed away as plaster and insulation snowed down, but by the time they finished, the exposed beams were visibly stronger.

I watched the entire process, but my thoughts were elsewhere. "How much worse is this going to get?"

"That depends on how swiftly we can find and stop August Harrison," said Gutenberg.

I had lost control of the situation the instant Gutenberg arrived. Not that I ever really *had* control. Harrison and his wendigos I could have dealt with, but the students of Bi Sheng and an Army of Ghosts? I needed help.

I just wished I knew what the cost of that help would be. How much of Copper River would be left when this was over?

One by one, the rest of the Porters gathered in my library. Most I had met, at least in passing. All were field agents, with the exception of Nicola Pallas and Gutenberg himself. The amount of active magic in the air tickled my skin. I dug my nails into my palms to keep from scratching.

Every libriomancer carried his or her own arsenal of books. Some wore backpacks or messenger bags. Whitney Spotts had fashioned what looked like a makeshift skirt of books, each one clipped to a thick leather belt by a light chain. John Wenger's books simply followed him through the door in a self-propelled red wagon. I had no idea how it had navigated the broken steps.

Then there were the weapons. I saw two different Excaliburs, a monofilament whip, some sort of electrified jumpsuit (in neon pink), a steampunk-style short rifle, and a pair of six-shooters that could have come straight from Billy the Kid's holsters. Toni was one of the few who appeared unarmed, but in her hands, just about anything was a potential weapon.

"Is the town contained?" Pallas asked.

Maryelizabeth, a libriomancer from New York who worked for one of the major publishing houses, tugged a small black gas mask from her face. "Diluted spray of Lethe-water took care of most of the bystanders."

"Electronics are covered," said John, waving a trade paperback. "Broad-field magnetic blaster. Anyone who tried to record this on their phones will have a very bad day. A few shots probably leaked onto the Internet, but we can track those down and discredit them later."

"I intercepted the cops," said Whitney. "They're back at the police department, writing the whole thing up as a nasty traffic accident."

One by one Pallas took their reports. In less than a half hour, the Porters had swept through the streets of Copper River and erased most of the evidence of our battle with the dragon. Even the dragon itself was no longer recognizable, having been carved into scrap. I didn't know how the Porters meant to pass off the huge pile of metal in the road as a traffic accident, but I had no doubt they would find a way.

"Good." Pallas was rocking back and forth, snapping her fingers to a rhythm nobody else could hear. She was even less comfortable with noise and crowds than I was, and music was one of the ways she coped. I wondered if it would work for Jeff DeYoung, who was looking from one person to the next, trying to watch everyone at once. He knew and liked me, but he was a werewolf, and part of his brain instinctively classified the Porters as potential predators.

Given what I had learned, I couldn't entirely disagree with that assessment.

Pallas turned to Gutenberg. "We have between 90 and 95 percent containment. We can finish cleaning up later. Dream-manipulation should help take care of any lingering memories."

Without preamble, Gutenberg set the last of his books atop the pile and said, "As some of you know, when Victor Harrison died earlier this year, we were unable to control the scene before the police arrived. As a result, August Harrison was able to gain access to his son's work, including a swarm of mechanical insects. He used those insects to break into the Porter network, as well as to access Isaac Vainio's private research notes. He also discovered a cult called the Bì Shēng de dú zhě, the students of Bi Sheng.

"Harrison then tracked and killed a pair of wendigos near Tamarack, Michigan. Using the magic preserved in their skins, he attempted to create monsters of his own, soldiers who would be stronger and deadlier."

"How many?" asked Whitney.

"At least twenty-four," I said. "They're not true wendigos, but they have most of the strength and temper. Depending on the amount of skin he used, the transformation might not be permanent."

"The wendigos are the least of our concerns. Harrison has also created his own dryad." Gutenberg extended his arm toward Lena like a museum curator showing off an exhibit. "Unlike Ms. Greenwood, this dryad is new and untrained. However, she possesses the same strengths and weaknesses."

"What weaknesses?"

I didn't see who asked the question, but I cringed as Gutenberg began detailing how the loss of Lena's tree could cripple her, how her skin would resist normal weapons, but not magical ones. She stood like a statue, her eyes fixed on the wall as Gutenberg verbally dissected her. I took her hand, offering what comfort I could. Nidhi squeezed her other hand.

"Why go to the trouble of breaking into our archives and making a dryad if he already had wendigos?" That was Whitney again.

Gutenberg nodded at me. I grimaced and stepped into the center of the ring of libriomancers. "Five hundred years ago, some of the students of Bi Sheng were able to preserve their thoughts and memories in books. Their descendants have spent centuries protecting those books, and searching for a way to restore them. When Harrison hacked into my private notes, he found the answer. Not only does Lena recreate her physical body each time she leaves her tree, but earlier this year, we discovered she can do the same for another person."

Everyone began talking at once. New comments and questions poured forth, one atop the next.

"That's a hell of a magical kluge."

"Can you change the body you create? Make it younger or thinner?"

"Or better looking? Especially for Bobby over there."

"Bite me. What about cloning? If you had access to the mind, how many copies could you make?"

"Have you examined the body at the genetic level? Are they affected at all by their dryadic birth?"

"Do they have belly buttons?"

Lena turned to me and mouthed the word "libriomancers" while rolling her eyes. I gave her a sympathetic smile.

Gutenberg clapped his hands once. "August Harrison forced Ms. Greenwood to restore a woman named Bi Wei. In her time, Bi Wei would have been a rudimentary libriomancer of limited ability, but time in her book gave her a more direct connection to magic. She was a part of magic, able to manipulate it without books or other tools. While she appears to have retained this power, the greater danger is what else Lena brought forth. Bi Wei had been touched by what the followers of Bi Sheng call sǐ guǐ jūn duì. The Ghost Army."

Maryelizabeth snorted. "Wendigos, insects, dead libriomancers . . . how many armies does this dude need?"

"Harrison doesn't know about the Ghost Army," I said. "They're using him, not the other way around."

"Why haven't we heard any of this before?" asked John. The handle of his book wagon wagged back and forth like a scolding finger.

"Because libriomancers are utterly incapable of letting sleeping dragons lie," Gutenberg said calmly. "The Ghost Army slumbered for centuries. I was aware of *something* that occasionally reached through to corrupt and consume whoever it touched, but such contacts were rare. I feared that too much poking and prodding would rouse it, so research into the Ghost Army has been restricted and carefully monitored."

"Carefully?" Lena asked. "You assigned Isaac to study this thing."

"Only when we realized it had begun to stir," Gutenberg said sternly. "Isaac survived an encounter with these ghosts, an accomplishment limited to only a handful of Porters throughout the years."

He raised his hands, forestalling further questions. "Isaac was attacked when he channeled more magic than he could control. These ghosts strike when our barriers are weakest. They are awake, and they are watching. Use precision over power. Do not overextend yourselves."

"How do we find them?" asked Whitney.

"Originally, I intended to use Ms. Warwick." Gutenberg waved Toni forward.

"Worst assignment in years." Toni grimaced. "If I can touch the corpses of the wendigos Harrison butchered, I'm pretty sure I can find him, or at least his pets."

"And what do you intend to do about the war you'll be starting with every werewolf in Michigan?" Jeff asked, his words a full octave lower than normal.

Toni looked from Gutenberg to Jeff. She was a good field agent, but occasionally neglected the research side of things. She clearly had no idea how close she was to starting a brawl in the middle of my library.

"Werewolves were originally scavengers," I said. "They dug up graves to feed on corpses. They've spent centuries trying to distance themselves from that piece of their past, to the point where they'll circle a half mile out of their way simply to avoid the smell of road kill. It's almost a religious taboo. The wendigos are buried in a werewolf cemetery. Messing with their burial sites is a good way to get yourself torn apart."

"But wendigos aren't werewolves," Toni protested.

"Which is why Jeff hasn't tried to kill anyone yet," Nidhi said.

Toni folded her arms and turned to Gutenberg. "You never mentioned that." She sounded like a pissed-off parent.

Gutenberg studied Jeff, giving everyone just enough time to imagine how such a confrontation would play out.

"Fortunately, we have a simpler option." He took an old pulp novel by A. E. van Vogt from the closest stack of books. "Even unconscious, Guan Feng's memories should guide us."

"She doesn't know where Harrison was going," I protested.

"She said she didn't know. Even if she told you the truth, the brain retains much more information than it can consciously process or remember." He skimmed the book and strode toward Guan Feng. As he bent over, golden tendrils flickered from his scalp, like an afterimage that faded when you tried to look at it directly.

I hadn't read *Slan* since I was in middle school, so the details of the story and its rules for mind reading were vague. Gutenberg would be able to read Feng's thoughts, but I didn't think the process would hurt her.

"Feng flew to the U.S. six weeks ago," Gutenberg said slowly. "The students of Bi Sheng are spread throughout the world. We face fewer than half of their total number." He grabbed his gold pen and appeared to scribble a series of notes in the air. Magical note-taking so he would remember the locations of the rest?

"In the beginning, Harrison's hope was infectious," he continued. "He saw himself as a savior, and when he showed them a selection of documents he had taken from our computers, they saw salvation. As the weeks passed, he spent more and more time alone. When not locked in his cabin, he sent his insects to spy on Lena, watching through their eyes.

"Two weeks ago, Harrison left the camp. When he returned, he was quite drunk. He said the time for planning was past. In order to overpower Lena, he needed soldiers. If they wouldn't help him to capture a wendigo, he would do it alone."

"Two weeks?" Nidhi asked sharply. "Was this the twentieth?"

Gutenberg nodded.

"What happened July twentieth?" Lena asked.

"That was Victor Harrison's birthday."

"They tracked and killed the first wendigo the following morning," Gutenberg said. "The body you investigated in Tamarack was the second murder."

"Where did they go after they attacked Michilimackinac?" Toni's impatience was palpable.

He raised a hand and stared at Guan Feng, as if he could dig out the truth with his eyes alone. "The tree he prepared for Lena didn't survive the restoration of Bi Wei. He needed a stronger oak for his new dryad, as well as additional soldiers to defend her."

"Between Bi Wei and Deifilia, they could grow a new oak anywhere," said Lena.

"But it was to be hidden. Protected." Gutenberg blinked. "Harrison asked Deifilia whether her oak could survive underground."

Without the sun . . . but how difficult would it be to conjure sunlight? Jeff carried the moon's rays around in a rock. Bi Wei could provide whatever Deifilia's tree needed. "They're at the mine."

Gutenberg nodded, the transparent tendrils on his scalp making him look like Medusa. "Isaac is correct."

That would explain where the dragon had come from, and the mine employed more than enough healthy, strong people to build Harrison's wendigo army.

"Find them."

I turned to Lena. "Find what?"

"I didn't say anything."

"Nidhi?"

Nidhi's brow creased. "What did you hear, Isaac?"

The room grew silent. My neck and cheeks warmed as I realized everyone had stopped to look at me. "I'm not sure."

"Find Huǒ Niǎo."

Slowly, I stepped toward the edge of the library to look out at the sky. Despite the rising sun, stars burned clearly in the sky, stars which were completely wrong for this time of year. I searched until I spotted the constellation known as the Phoenix. "Oh, damn."

Not too long ago, I would have tried to cover up what was happening. I would have blamed my confusion on the ringing in my ears from the explosion. But if I was seeing nonexistent stars, I was far too vulnerable. That didn't make my next words any easier. "I need to stay behind."

I tried to tell myself I wasn't betraying Lena, Jeff . . . all of Copper River, really. If I was hearing voices, then the next spell I cast could be enough to let the Army of Ghosts into my head. Trying to help could get everyone killed.

"Are you armed?" asked Pallas.

I showed her the shock-gun.

"Isaac."

I clenched my fists and focused on my surroundings.

"Lena will remain here as well," Gutenberg said.

"No, she won't," Lena shot back. "Nobody knows what Deifilia can do better than me."

"Nor do we know what will happen if the two of you face one another." He sounded deceptively calm. He reached out, fingers coming together as if he were snatching an invisible thread. As he did so, printed type seemed to crawl over his tan skin, the characters burrowing into his body too quickly for me to read.

Lena's knees gave out.

Nidhi jumped to catch her. "What did you do?"

"Lena is book-born." Gutenberg released his hold, and the color slowly returned to Lena's face. "If I can take her power, what do you think Bi Wei might do? What if she does worse? She could rewrite Lena, transform her into an enemy."

"Can you do that?" I asked sharply. "Rewrite her?"

Gutenberg's mouth tightened ever so slightly. "I cannot, no. But while Bi Sheng's magic is similar to ours, we do not know all his secrets. Lena stays here."

He neither raised his voice nor changed his expression, but everyone in the library recognized the discussion was over. Almost everyone.

"She's my responsibility," Lena pressed.

"In what way?" asked Gutenberg. "Did you create her? Did you write the book from which she sprang? Was it your stolen research that allowed our enemies to discover what she could do? Did your defenses fail to protect our archive? In what way are you responsible, Lena Greenwood?"

"Because she's family."

"That's one more reason you will not be accompanying us." He raised his voice. "I will lead a team to the mine. Nicola will command the others in Copper River."

"We're splitting our forces?" asked John.

Toni snorted. "You think they're just waiting around for us to visit? They know Guan Feng has been spilling her guts to the Porters, they know Isaac blew their toy dragon all to shit, and they know he has reinforcements."

"Indeed," said Gutenberg. "They will attack Copper River for all those reasons, and to attempt to keep us from finding the mine. The longer they hold us off, the more of Bi Sheng's students they can restore, and the stronger their power grows."

Toni Warwick pulled a small roll of purple duct tape from her belt. She used utility scissors to snip the end from one of her dreadlocks, and sprinkled a few strands of hair onto the sticky side of a square of tape. She slapped the tape onto John Wenger's shoulder. "This should let me track you, and give us limited communications. Please don't scream into the duct tape."

One by one, she did the same for the rest of the Porters. I was the last to receive my duct tape communicator, which she pressed onto my shirt with a whispered, "Sorry, man. For what it's worth, I'm jealous as hell that you got to fight the dragon."

Gutenberg wasted no more time in assigning a small group to protect Copper River, then led the rest out of the library. A single automaton waited like a statue in the middle of the road.

Pallas was snapping her fingers again. "Isaac, I could use your help deciding where to position people. You know the town better than anyone here."

"Some of us were living in these parts before Isaac's parents were born," Jeff muttered.

I trudged toward the ruins of the entryway and dug out one of the brochures that described all the exciting things to do in Copper River, Michigan. It was a relatively short brochure. However, it included a decent enough map on the back.

I pointed to various locations that would give us— that would give *them*—a better vantage point against incoming forces. "The water tower. The clock tower at City Hall. The mine's north of here, so I'd suggest putting people at the railroad bridge here. It has a good view of the river."

In twos and threes, the Porters set out with their books and weapons. Toni and Nicola were the last to go, leaving me, Lena, Nidhi, and Jeff alone with the unconscious body of Guan Feng.

"I don't care what anyone says," Jeff announced once they were gone. "That man is a douchebag."

"Isaac, please."

I made my way around the front desk and retrieved Bi Wei's book from the drawer. The whispers in my head grew louder when I touched the cover.

"What are you doing?" Nidhi asked warily.

"I can hear her." I sat on the floor and flipped through the pages.

"Isn't that a good reason to *not* read the book?" Jeff asked.

Even without donning my translation glasses, I could almost understand the words. "I'm not going to try magic. I promise. I just . . . I don't think this is possession. She's asking me for help."

Lena leaned over my shoulder. "Do you trust her?"

"I'm not sure." I could barely hear her, as if she were shouting from a great distance. I made out August Harrison's name, and something about ghosts, but we needed a stronger connection. I sagged back in the chair. "The Porters tried to kill her five hundred years ago. Now we—I—gave Harrison the tools to bring her back, and to let the Army of Ghosts into her mind. She's fighting for her sanity. She's a victim. Our victim."

"Or she's trying to get her hooks into your head so she can find out what the Porters are up to," Jeff said.

"I don't think so." I pulled the glasses from my jacket, unfolded the earpieces, and slipped them on. Text flickered to life. I started to read, then hesitated. "But if I start spewing pea soup or anything, I'd appreciate it if you got me the hell away from this book."

I chose a page at random and began reading about Bi

Wei's first attempt at magic, the continuation of a project her great-grandaunt had begun years before her birth. They had hoped to create a book in which writing on one of the blank pages would cause the same message to appear on other copies. The goal was to find a replacement for the signal beacons on the Great Wall.

Using blocks of movable type painstakingly carved from wood, they created identical books using a technique known as butterfly binding. Printed pages were folded in the middle and stitched together, leaving the reverse sides blank. The text included everything from poetry to military strategy, with one thing in common: thematically, every piece emphasized the importance of communication.

Imagining Bi Wei poring over her copy of the book, reading and rereading as she attempted to imbue its pages with magic, made me feel ashamed. My own early magic had been entirely selfish, limited to pulling toys and trinkets from one book after another.

How open had the practice of magic been in China during the Ming Dynasty? Had the Emperor been aware of Bi Sheng's students? What of the common people?

"Isaac."

I jumped. "Xiǎo Bi?"

"Where is Guan Feng? Is she—"

"She's alive. Gutenberg put her to sleep."

Her words seemed to come from the book itself. *"You heard me."* I sensed the quiet laughter she wouldn't let reach her lips. *"It worked."*

I found myself smiling in return. I had theorized that something like this might be possible, but the last time I had tried, a ghost had attempted to eat my soul. "Are you thinking in English or Mandarin?"

"Mandarin, which is how I hear your words. You hear English?"

"That's right." I wanted to warn her to get as far from the mine as possible. Instead, I simply asked, "Wei, what's happening?"

"August Harrison collapsed a short time ago, and hasn't awakened."

"That was probably my doing," I said smugly. Blowing up the dragon had hit him harder than I could have hoped.

"Then you may have destroyed us all. Deifilia has bound him in ropes of living oak. She brought two of my fellow refugees from their books, and she now commands Harrison's metal creatures."

"Deifilia's in charge of the magic bugs?" I blinked and looked to Nidhi, trying to split my focus between the book and the real world. "That doesn't make sense."

Nidhi was shaking her head. "August Harrison would never surrender his power to Deifilia, nor would he want a lover who desired his power. It shouldn't be possible for her to take control of his weapons. She can't act against his wishes."

She brought her fingers to cover her mouth. From the shock in her eyes, she had made the same leap I had. There was at least one way for a dryad to grow beyond the desires of her mate.

"She has another lover," Lena whispered.

"She's existed for less than twenty-four hours." It had taken days for Lena to begin to bond with me, for my desires to come into conflict with Nidhi's.

That conflict was the key. The tension between our desires gave Lena a degree of freedom. Every time she argued with one of us, whether it was about the ethics of killing in self-defense or whether Douglas Adams should have stopped his trilogy after the fourth book, she lit up inside. It was hard to stay angry with someone who took such obvious joy in being able to disagree.

"I would love to see Harrison's face when he finds out." My moment of schadenfreude passed quickly. How could this have happened? Given Harrison's possessiveness, Deifilia wouldn't have sought another lover on her own. At least not deliberately . . . "Lena, your personality began to change even before we—"

"I prefer 'evolved,'" Lena said. "But you're right. Sex isn't the key. Frank Dearing owned me long after his body lost its potency."

"Wei, when Harrison collapsed, did Deifilia take a large insect from his body? A cicada?"

"She wanted to protect him, and to keep anyone from taking control of his weapons."

The cicada which was telepathically connected to the Army of Ghosts. Lena had created a degree of freedom for herself by taking another lover. Deifilia had found an entire army. An army that wanted only two things: to live, and to destroy.

Nidhi summed it up with surprising succinctness. "Oh, shit."

Chapter 19

The automaton was centuries old, charred and cracked from the unimaginable heat of Isaac's battle. Fingers of carved walnut hung limp, hinged with pegs fitted so precisely they were invisible. The body and limbs were oak, taken from a tree that had stood for more than a hundred years before falling to the bite of the ax.

The jaw creaked open, shedding chips of black-and-gray carbon. "You'd be risking your life," said Isaac Vainio.

He didn't understand. How could he? He was human. Had been human, rather. Before he pulled his dying flesh into the body of a wood-and-metal monster, a golem built by one of the most powerful magicians in history, all to stop a madman.

I could feel the life slipping from the wood, like water leached away by too much sunlight. The automaton was dying, and Isaac with it. Had it been a tree, the leaves would be brown, and the branches would have snapped in the slightest wind.

Gutenberg had known. He understood my nature far

better than Isaac. Better than Nidhi. Perhaps even better than me. I loved Isaac Vainio. Loved him as much as Nidhi, though in different ways and for different reasons. I couldn't let him go.

My fingers tightened around the burnt limb. With my other hand, I pulled myself up to touch the carved, featureless face.

"What are you doing?" he asked.

"I'm not sure."

I reached for the memory of oak, and the feel of Isaac's arms around my body, my mouth on his. He had tasted like coffee with not enough cream, just as I had doubtless tasted of waffles and strawberries, but neither one of us had been willing to break off that first frantic kiss.

My fingers sank into the automaton, and I felt my own life fighting to inhabit the dead wood. Cells long-since dried and broken struggled to heal, and then to grow as I forced myself deeper into the broken body of my lover.

And then we were one. The libriomancer and the dryad, joined in a way I had never known, not with Nidhi, nor with Frank.

Nidhi's love had given me strength and power. Now Isaac's love gave me the strength to use that power in a way I had never imagined.

If you ask Isaac when we first made love, he'll say it was two days later, in the damp grass of his backyard. Which isn't as romantic as you'd think, given the mosquito population here in the U.P. They didn't bother me, but he kept squirming and slapping until I laughed and rolled us over, climbing on top of him and driving all other distractions from his mind.

But what we did beneath the cloudy sky that night was merely the completion of what we began in that dying wooden body.

"CALL GUTENBERG," I said. "Tell him what he's facing."

"What *is* he facing?" asked Nidhi.

"Hell if I know." The Ghost Army wouldn't care about restoring Victor Harrison, which meant Jeneta should be safe. They cared only about their own return. "Bi Wei, when Deifilia restored your two companions, what did she do to their books and their readers?"

Her grief surged through me, confirming my guess. *"How did you know?"*

"We're very clever. She destroyed them, didn't she?"

"Chu Zao was the first to be brought back. No sooner had Deifilia drawn him forth than she used the insects to destroy the book. His reader was taken away to become another wendigo. What remained of Chu Zao . . . his body lives, but my friend is gone. I tried to stop Deifilia, and her insects almost killed me. By the time I awoke, she had done the same to another of us."

"They've tried to possess Porters through the years, but even when it worked, they were trapped in a damaged body with an even more damaged mind. They tried to take you, but you fought back."

"It appears I owe you thanks," Bi Wei said. *"Deifilia would have torn my own book to pulp if you hadn't taken it, and I would be dead."*

"Wei, are the other books the same as your own? The same appearance, the same format and title?"

"The Yang/Soul/Story, yes."

There was no equivalent English word, but I saw in her thoughts the untranslatable characters from the cover of her own book. *The Yang/Soul/Story of Bi Wei,* safeguarding her spiritual soul. "I have an idea, but I'll need names."

She saw what I had in mind, and gratitude flooded through our shared connection. In that instant, I knew the names of her fellow students as well as she did.

Raw fury followed a moment later, so sudden I cried out. Lena yanked me away, and Nidhi slammed the book shut. A part of me cringed to see such an old book handled so roughly, but it worked. My connection to Bi Wei weakened, though I could feel her horror and guilt as she realized what had happened.

The Army of Ghosts was still inside her. I hadn't sensed them through our connection, but they had been listening from the shadows of her mind. "I need McKinley's *Beauty*, and we're about to have visitors."

"No more magic," Nidhi insisted. Lena moved to stand beside her, their shoulders touching. Jeff simply looked puzzled.

"Deifilia restored two more of the students of Bi Sheng. And then she destroyed their books. It ripped their minds and souls apart, leaving the bodies as vessels for the Army of Ghosts. She's going to do the same to the rest."

"The ghosts—the devourers—were deranged," said Lena. "How is Deifilia controlling them?"

That made me pause. "I have no idea."

"Call another libriomancer," Nidhi insisted. "Let them do the spell."

"They don't know the books we need." I could see the titles in my mind, but I lacked the words to explain them, even to a fellow libriomancer.

I touched the duct tape square on my shirt. "Toni, how much of this did you hear?"

"Enough." Strange to feel her voice buzzing against my chest. "Gutenberg's team is at the mine, but it will take time to work their way through the tunnels. The ghosts are already weakening their magic. Isaac, we've got incoming, and they're playing dirty."

"What's going on?"

"Most of them are flying high and fast. Aimee says they took some of 'em out at the bridge, but the damn things didn't even slow down. Looks like they're heading your way."

"Understood." Where was the book? I had returned it to the reserves shelf, which had fallen when the dragon attacked.

"I'm going up to intercept them. Let's see these fuckers try to ignore me."

"Be careful." There, beneath an overturned filing cabinet. The spine was ripped, and the pages were beginning to tear free. This needed professional repair. I couldn't do anything but press the pages carefully back into place and hope for the best. As I finished gathering my things, fire bathed Smudge's body. He crouched low, watching the sky. "I think we're out of time."

Jeff ripped a leg off of a table. "Get out of here. I'll watch over Guan Feng and give you as much time as I can."

Three metal falcons streaked into the library. Lena stepped past me, and her bokken whipped through the air to rip the wing off the first. Two more went after Jeff.

True falcons shouldn't have been able to hover and dart about like hummingbirds. Within seconds, Jeff's hands were bleeding where they had cut him with their knifelike beaks. Screams in the distance meant the rest of Deifilia's forces were closing in fast.

I pulled out my shock-gun, dropped to one knee, and braced my arm against the shelves. My first shot missed, but my second sent a falcon into a tailspin. Jeff smashed it, then took out the third falcon on the backswing.

"Go," said Jeff. "I'm gonna call in a few friends, see if we can't teach you Porters how to fight."

"Thank you." I handed Nidhi my keys. These things would shred her rental car like tinfoil. "Please tell me you know how to drive a stick."

Oily black smoke streaked the windshield over Smudge. He was keeping an eye—all eight of them, actually—on the metal mob chasing us down the road. He would have melted right through the dashboard by now if not for the trivet secured to the plastic.

We drove with the top down so Lena could protect us from aerial assaults. She sat in my lap, one knee in the seat. In her left hand, she swung her bokken at anything that came within range. With her right, she fired lightning bolts into the sky.

I did my best to ignore the thunderclaps going off two feet from my head and read. I couldn't save the two books Deifilia had already destroyed, but if I could concentrate, I might be able to create backups of the rest.

From the moment I touched the pages, I felt the characters trying to reach into my head. The conflict of the title character Honour, who preferred to be called Beauty. Her brother-in-law's fearful warnings about the woods. Her father's shame as Beauty chose to give herself to the Beast to save his life. The one thing the characters shared was the need to escape, whether it was the hardship of their new lives in Blue Hill, the father's guilt, or the Beast's castle. And my mind would provide them that escape if I wasn't careful.

I didn't have time for careful. I grabbed another book and turned it diagonally, trying to pull it free without destroying both books in the process. *Beauty* was a hardcover, but the books I needed were larger, and if the binding completely failed, the book would fall apart in my hands. I slid the book out and tucked it behind the seat.

"Where are we going?" Nidhi asked.

"Water tower," I said. "Toni's team ought to be able to help us out, and the tower's built on a hill, so it should be more defensible."

Lena shifted her weight and smashed a beetle that had landed on the trunk.

"Watch it," I protested.

Nidhi yanked the wheel, swerving around an overturned truck. A wendigo was clawing at the truck's door, and I heard screams from inside. Nidhi slowed long enough for Lena to shoot both the wendigo and the truck. Hopefully the rubber tires had insulated the driver.

"Hold on." Nidhi lurched over the curb and into a parking lot. We wove between cars, barely missing the cart corral in front of the grocery store.

"Where did you learn to drive?" Lena demanded as we zoomed around the back of the store and down the grassy hill beyond.

"Isaac's always bragging about what this car can do," she said tightly. "I wanted to see if he was exaggerating."

I could feel the Triumph's traction spells kicking in, fighting to cling to the wet grass and mud. Even as the magic won out and we climbed onto the road, the book distorted my perceptions, turning black steel into exhausted horses, their coats streaked with sweaty froth.

"Isaac?" Lena fired at another falcon, set her bokken down, and squeezed my shoulder. "Stay with us."

There were too many books to create. The longer I held *Beauty* open, the stronger the voices grew. If the ghosts got hold of me now, I doubted I'd be able to resist them. I needed to end this.

I spread the book on my lap. Given the battering it had taken, the hardest part was overcoming my own revulsion at what I was about to do. I gripped half the pages in each hand, prayed for forgiveness from whoever might be listening, and finished cracking the book's spine. I tugged the covers until the endpaper began to tear free, then plunged my hand back into the Beast's library.

My vandalism allowed me to stretch the pages an extra three quarters of an inch. It wasn't much, but it was enough to speed the process along. The crack of thunder faded. Nothing mattered but the next book.

"Isaac . . ." Lena grabbed my hand, then pointed up the road as we crossed the railroad tracks and saw the war waging in front of us.

"Oh, my God."

The water tower had fallen onto the road. It looked like a giant jellyfish, the body partially crushed under its own weight, the metal tentacles bent and stiff. One of the legs had smashed a minivan, nearly cutting it in half. The water had flooded the parking lot of the restaurant on the opposite side of the road, pushing two cars into the front wall.

Toni Warwick stood uphill on the broken concrete foundation of the water tower. She appeared to be holding off a small swarm of bugs with a drinking straw and a yo-yo. A team of libriomancers flanked her, fighting a small herd of rusty metal beasts. Lawrence Hume held a bulky rifle of a design I didn't recognize, while Whitney lay on the ground flinging pennies at their attackers. Even from here, I could see that her leg was broken.

One of her coins bounced off the head of a wolf, who slipped and rolled into the path of a charging moose.

"Unlucky pennies," I guessed. The moose trampled the wolf, which didn't get back up. "Nice."

Nidhi pulled off the road and killed the engine. I scooped Smudge onto my shoulder, grabbed the books, and snatched the keys from the ignition. I hurried to the back and popped the trunk. The Triumph had better protective spells than any of us. I shoved the books inside and slammed the trunk.

Lena handed me the shock-gun. "How many were you able to get?"

"Ten, including Bi Wei's." *Beauty* had fallen apart when I tried to pull out the eleventh book. It wasn't enough.

I counted five fallen beasts, but others were circling the three Porters, trying to get up the hill to surround them. In addition to the wolf and the moose, there were several deer, two dogs, what looked like a fox, and a handful of rats. Sparkles on the ground showed where Toni had taken out many of the bugs.

I stopped to shoot at a metal snake which was trying to circle around to flank them. My third shot took it down, but attracted the attention of its friends, and the metal mob that had pursued us from the library was closing in fast.

"I hope you have a plan, Vainio!" Toni shouted.

Lawrence used the confusion caused by our arrival to fire at another wolf. The metal body began to hum like a tuning fork, the sound rising in pitch until my eardrums threatened to rupture. Then the wolf simply blew apart. Shrapnel dented a deer, but it regained its balance and kept coming.

"I need a hand. 'Eat me.' End of chapter one." I yanked *Alice's Adventures in Wonderland* from my jacket and flung it toward Whitney. I gave Nidhi a boost up the hill and started to follow, but the moose had recovered from its collision with the wolf and was charging toward me.

"Mine." Lena sprinted past, swords raised. Just before she collided with the moose, she jumped to the right and stabbed one of her swords into the joint where the front leg met the torso. The move took her off balance, but she turned her fall into a roll and bounced to her feet, gripping her remaining weapon in both hands and knocking a rusty dog aside.

The moose staggered. Sprigs of green sprouted from the shaft of the sword. It was the same trick she had used with the toothpick and the metal beetle back in my office. Her bokken grew through the moose, entangling and paralyzing the inner workings before it could reach me.

"Incoming," Whitney yelled, pointing toward the swarm of birds and bugs flying up the road. She turned her attention to my book, reached inside, and yanked out a small glass box.

I scrambled up the hill to snatch it from her hand. Inside was a small cake. Currants spelled out the words "EAT ME." I collapsed on the dirt, opened the box, and set both it and Smudge on the ground. "Time for lunch, buddy."

A swarm of rats had cut Lena off from the rest of us. I readied my gun, but before I could aim, Lawrence shouted, "Watch the trees!"

A pair of wendigos bounded toward us. I rolled and hit one in the leg. Lawrence shot the other, causing the ice that armored its skin to shatter. I didn't know what kind of weapon he was using or where he had gotten it, but next chance I got, I was definitely looking that sucker up in the Porter database.

On the road, Lena jumped onto the back of the dying moose and smashed a rat off of her leg. Another sank metal teeth through her shoe. She cried out, then kicked off the shoe and rat both. More rats climbed up the moose. I grabbed another book, hoping Whitney or Lawrence could control the rust magic better than I had.

I didn't get the chance to find out. With crumbs of magic cake stuck to his mandibles, Smudge charged into the fray.

I had cared for that spider since high school, and he had saved my life more than once. He was more than a partner. He was family. And despite all we had been through, the primitive, reptilian part of my brain wanted only to get as far as I could from the flaming spider I had magically enlarged to the size of a station wagon.

Apparently magic rats felt the same way. They jumped off of the moose and backed away.

They weren't fast enough. Smudge snatched the first one up without breaking stride. His mandibles punched through the metal body like an old-fashioned can opener, and then he was moving toward the next.

Exhaustion and triumph made me giddy. I pumped my fist in the air and whooped like a hockey fan at the bar during playoffs. Smudge grabbed a possum-looking creature and bit into it. Two rats tried to climb his leg, but his flames deepened from red to purple, and they fell back.

There was little question that Smudge remembered what these things had done to him back at the house. Nor was there any doubt in my mind that he was enjoying his payback.

I began firing into the second wave, trying to slow their approach. Once Smudge cleared most of the smaller creatures away from Lena, he charged toward the swarm Toni had been holding off. As he neared, fire rolled off his body and legs. Glowing bugs fell like rain.

Toni shouted and dropped to the ground. She slapped frantically at her dreadlocks, swearing up a storm. Smudge's enthusiasm had burned through her yo-yo string as well.

"Easy, buddy!" I shouted. "She's on our side!"

With everything I had seen today, the sight of a giant flaming spider slinking sheepishly back to the road barely warranted a second glance. Whatever guilt he felt didn't last long. He skittered toward the railroad tracks and reared up on his back four legs to snatch an oversized batlike thing from the air. The rest of us took up positions around Nidhi.

"Whitney, get your Pratchett ready." Toni jammed her straw through her belt and pulled out a portable fan, roughly the size of a small digital camera. "The rest of you, cover us."

Lawrence and I shot at anything shiny that got too close, while Whitney switched books and started reading. Lena moved toward the trees to intercept another wendigo.

Whitney hobbled over to join Toni. Her face was white with pain, but she made it. She clutched Toni's shoulder for support, then opened another book with her free hand. "Isaac, get your spider out of there."

I switched my gun to my left hand and grabbed a laser pointer from another pocket. I had to shine the dot directly over Smudge's face to get his attention, but once I did, he was all over it. I played the laser over a metal coyote, which Smudge happily trampled as he pursued the elusive green dot uphill.

"Man, you have the weirdest pet," Toni said. The plastic blades of her fan whirred to life. "Brace yourselves!"

It was as if she had uncorked a portable hurricane. The wind blew insects and birds back, and even the larger creatures had to dig their claws into the pavement to hold on.

We were out of the wind's direct path, but the negative pressure yanked my coat like a cape, the weight of my books threatening to drag me away. I pocketed my gun and grabbed the broken concrete foundation of the water tower. Lena stabbed her bokken into the ground and clutched it with one hand. Her other was locked around Nidhi's wrist.

"How are we supposed to shoot these things if we can't even stand?" I yelled.

"It's a two-part plan. That was part one." Toni and Whitney stood together in the eye of the storm, seemingly untouched. Whitney maneuvered her open book like a tray full of fine china, raising it above and slightly in front of the fan. Then she tilted the book forward.

Liquid spilled from the pages and sprayed forth like mist. Toni and Whitney turned together, moving to and fro like firefighters attacking a blaze.

"Welcome to part two," Whitney crowed.

Whatever the stuff was, it hit the metal creatures like a blowtorch to an igloo. By the time Toni switched off the fan, the moose had fallen backward in a frothing, bubbling mass. The crumpled water tower had begun to dissolve as well. The pools of water in the parking lot bubbled and steamed like a Halloween cauldron.

Whitney closed her book, clipped it back onto her belt, and collapsed to the ground.

"What book was that, exactly?" Lawrence asked.

Whitney managed a grin. "*Mort*, by Terry Pratchett. That was pure scumble. One of the most potent drinks in all of Discworld. You should try it. That shit makes the best tequila taste like distilled water. Now shut up and let me do something with this leg."

If she had tasted the stuff and survived, then presumably it wouldn't do to flesh what it had done to metal. I made my way down to the road, gun ready in case any stragglers had survived. "If you messed up my car with that crap, I . . . oh, no."

I sprinted across the road. On the far side of the water tower, partly hidden by the wreckage, was the flattened remnant of an old SUV. The metal continued to dissolve, courtesy of Whitney's aerosolized scumble. Though the shattered windshield obscured the details, I recognized Loretta Trembath in the driver's seat. She was a regular at the library, always coming in to e-mail her grandchildren.

I reached instinctively for a book from one of my front pockets, but it was too late for magic to make any difference. From the look of things, Mrs. Trembath had died instantly.

I made my way to the restaurant next. It had begun its life as a residential home back in the early 1900s. From a distance, it seemed to have escaped more or less unscathed. Not so the people inside.

The doorframe was splintered inward. Blood mixed with the water pooled on the floor. Metal claws had gouged deep lines in the walls.

I spotted three bodies in the dining area. I knew them all. Andy Marana fixed computers for the mine and sold racy pinup-style oil paintings on the side. I had gone to high school with Peg Niemi's little sister. Joe Malki had just started up a landscaping business this summer.

"I'm sorry, Isaac," Lena said quietly.

I moved toward the kitchen. "Is anyone there?"

The restaurant was silent. I found Steve Guckenberg

in the back, along with a metal beast that looked like a housecat with six-inch blades for fur. I switched the shock-gun to setting six and melted a hole through the damned thing.

How many more bodies lay broken and dead throughout Copper River? No magic, at least none the Porters knew of, could truly restore the dead. The few recorded attempts to do so had ended badly. "August Harrison came here because of me."

"This isn't your fault," Lena snapped. "If not you, then he would have gone after some other Porter. It would have happened anyway."

"It happened *here*." I knew this place, these people. Peg walked her hyperactive border collie past the library every morning, rain or shine. I always thought the crazy thing was going to yank her arm out of the socket. Joe had mowed my parents' lawn after I went downstate for college.

I walked outside, stopping at the remains of the metal moose. It lay on its side, broken and pinned by the wooden sword that continued to grow through its body. Roots dug into broken concrete, and bright green leaves had begun to uncurl from new-formed branches.

The smallest bolt was thicker than my thumb. The cables inside were too big to flex. They might as well have been steel rods.

"More mining equipment?" Lena guessed.

I nodded. "The rear legs look like rock drills." Normally, the drills could punch deep holes into solid rock, but they had been magically warped to fit the shape of the moose. A few kicks from those could easily have brought down the water tower.

Toni was walking down to join us. She held a slightly charred wooden yo-yo in one hand, and was replacing the string. A corroded beetle was stuck to one side of the yo-yo. That must have been how she had held off the rest of the bugs, by whipping this one in a whirling pattern and imparting the same motion to its friends. "The moose charged the tower before we could stop it. Lawrence barely had time to jump free."

Sweat sparkled on her forehead, and she was on the verge of hyperventilating. "No more magic," I said, tugging the yo-yo from her hand. "You need a break."

"We all do." She coiled one of her dreadlocks around her hand and closed her eyes. "The other teams around town report that they're in a little better shape. We've got three injured and one dead. Damn." She blinked and stared at me. "Apparently a trio of shotgun-wielding werewolves in a pickup truck just ran down a wendigo. Your doing?"

"Jeff's," I said gratefully.

"Nice."

"Remind them that the wendigos are victims," Lena said. "Harrison did this against their will."

"Will do." Toni tucked her chin into her shoulder, relaying the reminder through her own hair. "Nicola, what's happening with Bookmaster G?"

While Toni communed with Nicola, I turned to Lena and Nidhi. "How many ghosts do you think there are? How many broken minds trying to dig and claw their way back into the world?"

"Too many," said Lena. "Thus the word 'Army.'"

"They've found the tree," Toni said before I could respond. Her next words turned relief to dread. "The mine was abandoned. There were a few ambushes and some partially constructed metal nasties, but no wendigos, no resurrected cultists, and no dryad."

"They knew we were coming." I could use Bi Wei's

book to find them again, but not without Deifilia and the Ghost Army being aware.

Could she have gone after Jeneta after all? I grabbed my phone to call the camp, but before I could dial, Lena's fingers clamped around my wrist.

"I know where they went," she whispered, her face pale.

"How—" Understanding sank its fist into my gut. "Your tree."

"She's inside me. I can *hear* her."

Nidhi took Lena's elbow, and we lowered her carefully to the ground.

"What's going on?" Toni asked.

Lena could barely stand. I had a shock-gun, a giant spider, and a collection of books that would probably cost me my sanity if I tried to use them at this point. There was no way we could take on Deifilia by ourselves, let alone the ghost wizards she had resurrected.

Gutenberg might have a chance if they struck fast enough, hitting Deifilia with everything they had.

"What about the graft from your tree?"

She glanced at Toni, then switched to Gujarati. "If I hadn't taken that graft, I'd be comatose right now. You don't understand. She's inside me. I *can't* separate myself."

Meaning if Gutenberg dropped a magical nuke on Deifilia, it would kill Lena as well.

Lena grimaced. "She's offering a trade. The books . . ."

I nodded to show I understood. The books for Lena's life. I took out my car keys. "Toni, I need you to hide something for me."

"Oh, hell, Isaac. What are you planning?"

I peeled the square of tape from my shirt. To Nidhi, I said, "If you don't hear from us in thirty minutes, tell them."

Nidhi nodded. Together, we helped Lena to her feet. Her body was trembling. She rested against me and whispered, "My oak is just the start. If you don't give her those books, she'll destroy Copper River and everyone in it."

Chapter 20

I often wonder what became of my first oak, whether it yet survives in the woods outside of Mason, or if it succumbed to old age or one of the winter ice storms. Or those woods might have been bulldozed years ago, paved and transformed into another subdivision with spindly maples and anorexic pines in place of the majestic trees that once grew there.

I've never had any desire to revisit that part of my past. It feels morbid, like visiting your own grave.

I know my fallen oak at Nidhi's house was taken by a lumber company, but I never learned what they did with it. Perhaps it was mulched for wood chips to spread beneath playground equipment or to landscape someone's yard. I prefer to believe it was dissected into usable timber, that my tree went on to become something beautiful. Bookshelves, perhaps. A comfortable chair. A bedframe.

In C. S. Lewis' book The Magician's Nephew, Digory planted the core of a magical apple from Narnia, and the seeds grew into a wondrous tree. When the tree blew down *in a storm years later, he had its wood fashioned into a wardrobe, the same wardrobe that transported four children to a magical world a generation later.*

What power might my trees possess once I leave them behind? What magic could one pull from shelves made of my oak? Where might a door built of my former body lead?

None of my acorns ever gave birth to another dryad. I don't know why. It was an acorn from my own book that created me. Most of the time, I consider this sterility a blessing. The last thing I wanted was to bring forth an entire race of slaves. Fortunately, by the time I was aware enough to worry about such a possibility, it had become clear that my own seeds could produce nothing but ordinary saplings.

But what about my human body? Could this flesh become pregnant? I never had with Frank, and with Nidhi, it hadn't been an issue. But if my lover wanted a child, and my body responded to his desires . . .

What would a human/dryad baby become? Strong and powerful? Beautiful and pliant?

Would she be free?

I often wonder.

QUESTIONS AND HALF-FORMED PLANS clamored in my head like a basket of hyperactive puppies. How had Deifilia and her followers escaped the mine without Gutenberg noticing? How many more of Bi Sheng's students had she created, and were they protected by the books I had made? How had they entered Copper River unseen?

There were countless weapons we could use. I could fly in and drop a fairy bio-bomb from *Artemis Fowl*. Or let Gutenberg unlock the D&D handbook, and see how

Deifilia liked playing catch with a sphere of annihilation. Assuming they didn't simply absorb the magic of our attack and dissolve our weapons into nothingness.

"Lawrence, Whitney, what books do you have?" I hadn't stocked up for a direct assault on Deifilia.

"Isaac . . ." Toni began.

"Thirty minutes," I promised. "One way or another, you'll know."

It was an older fairy-tale-style romance that offered what I thought was my best chance at walking away from a confrontation with Deifilia. When I told Lawrence what I wanted, he looked past me to Toni, as if asking for permission.

"You're sure about this?" Toni asked.

"Not in the slightest. But people are dying." I waited for Lawrence to reach into the book. "Tell Pallas to evacuate the town."

Toni folded her arms. "She'll want to know why."

"I know. Tell her I'm doing something stupid again." I returned to the car and waited while Lena and Nidhi said their good-byes.

"What about megaspider over there?" Whitney asked.

Smudge scurried toward us. Whitney, Lawrence, and Toni jumped back as he placed his front legs on the bumper, as if he wanted nothing more than to climb up onto the Triumph and become the world's first road-surfing spider.

"I don't think so, partner," I said. "Would one of you mind pulling the White Rabbit's fan out of Wonderland and shrinking him back down to his travel-size?"

Once Smudge was back to normal and sitting—rather sullenly, if you asked me—on the dashboard, Nidhi and Lena ended their kiss. Nidhi stepped back.

"Isaac . . ."

"I know." I glanced at Lena, who was slumped in the seat, her eyes closed. She held the branch from her tree across her chest. "I'll keep her safe."

Before, I had been too intent on staying ahead of our pursuers to truly see the damage Deifilia's creatures had done. Driving back through town, I noticed everything. The playground behind the tennis court looked like a tornado had touched down. Whatever had come through here had ripped chain-link fence like cobwebs.

Sirens wailed from every direction. Twice we had to backtrack because police cars blocked the roads. Dogs were howling from their yards. Others sprinted through the streets in a panic. We passed a pair of EMTs assisting a man covered in blood. A half mile farther on, the mining museum was on fire. I slowed the car.

"I know what you're thinking," said Lena. "You're in no shape to help."

"I've got two books in this car that could give me enough elemental control to—"

"They've got a fully equipped fire engine. Let them do their job. If you overdo it, you're likely to make things worse."

I tightened my fingers on the wheel and kept driving.

"What's in that vial Lawrence made for you?"

I started to answer, then hit the brakes as a wendigo staggered out of McDonald's. Its stomach bulged like an overstuffed sack. Before I could grab my shock-gun, a blue Harley-Davidson sped at the wendigo from the opposite direction. The driver appeared human, but the woman in the sidecar was in the hybrid form some weres could take, all muscle and fur and teeth, but still humanoid. She jumped out of the sidecar and tackled the wendigo while the driver pulled onto the sidewalk and grabbed an aluminum bat.

"Don't kill it," I shouted.

"Easy for you to say."

It was anything but easy. The wendigo had fed recently. I suppose it could have stuffed itself on Big Macs and fries, but I doubted it.

"The vial?" Lena asked again as I turned into the drive-through to get past the fight. Wendigos were slower when sated, and the werewolves appeared to have things under control.

"The Porter database catalogs it as Love Potion 163-F. It's fast-acting, works on contact, and lasts for up to ten years."

She pushed herself up in her seat. When she spoke, she didn't bother to disguise her anger. "One dryad isn't enough for you?"

"You know I don't want Deifilia for myself. I want to stop her. If we fight her head-on, she'll crush us. But if I can create more of a conflict inside her, split her loyalty long enough for Bi Wei and the others to act, we might have a chance. We might even be able to save her."

"Save her?" Lena repeated softly. "With the magical equivalent of a date rape drug?"

"I wouldn't—"

"I know. That doesn't make it right."

I couldn't argue. I had racked my brain for another way to stop Deifilia and resolve this mess. But even if I could have risked using my own magic, it never would have worked. Lena and I would have to fight through wendigos and metal beasts while the students of Bi Sheng countered my every spell.

"163-F has an antidote. If we can capture her alive, we can reverse its effects. I'm open to other suggestions, but people are dying, Lena."

"I know," she said again.

"The trick is getting it to her. She's going to make sure we leave any potential weapons behind. No books, no swords, and nothing magical. But she's new to our world, and there are things she might not recognize as weapons. One of those old prank calculators that's actually a squirt gun, or maybe—"

"You think your love will be enough to overpower the Ghost Army's wishes?"

"I only have to distract her, to create enough of a conflict for us to act."

She took the test tube from my hand and carefully locked it away in the glove box. "I'll do it."

"You'll do what?"

"The same thing I did to you in the library," she whispered.

"How is that better than my so-called magic date rape drug?"

"It's not." She straightened. "But Deifilia is family. A sister. She's my responsibility. If anyone does this to her, it will be me. Not a human."

"And what if she turns that power back on you?"

Lena managed a smile. "One way or another, you'll have your distraction."

I hadn't liked my original plan. I liked this one even less. It was one thing for me to try to enchant Deifilia, and to risk whatever backlash might come if my plan failed. It was my research that had started all of this, after all. But if Lena failed, she would take the brunt of Deifilia's punishment.

I turned onto my street, and a metal eagle swooped down to land on the top of the windshield, talons grating against the crystal. I slammed the brakes, stalling out the engine. Smudge lit up like a flare.

"That's why you didn't get to stay supersized," I said

as I waited for my heart to recover. "You'd have set the whole car on fire." I nodded to the eagle. "We're alone."

The eagle spread rust-edged wings and gave an ear-stabbing shriek. Tiny, layered scales of sheet metal served as feathers. The edges were irregularly cut.

"I have the books." I restarted the engine and edged the car forward. The eagle didn't appear to object, though it watched me closely with eyes made of iron pellets. I was more fixated on the damage Deifilia had done.

I lived on the edge of Copper River, in a moderately wooded area. Deifilia had turned the trees against my neighbors. Using oak and maple as giant clubs, she had smashed rooftops and fences, flattened cars, and ripped through power lines. My house was the only one undisturbed. Deifilia had put the trees behind my house to another use.

I couldn't decide whether to call it a grove or a fortress. Oak trees had sprung up in a rough circle throughout the backyard. Branches wove together to create a fence of living wood. The trees were a good forty feet higher than any others, and the smallest was three feet in diameter.

Wendigos watched us from the upper branches. Metal glinted among the bark and leaves. I saw no sign of Deifilia or her human followers. Presumably they were inside the grove.

"That's impressive," I said. "Terrifying, but impressive. Of course, now all the neighbors are going to want one."

We stopped in the driveway and climbed slowly from the car. The moment Lena's foot touched the grass, she froze. "It's all one tree. Isaac, this is my oak, and Deifilia is inside of it."

On another day, I would have come up with something better to say than, "Wow." Not only had Deifilia created a grove of cloned oak trees, she had done it in less than an hour.

"Be careful," said Lena. "Anywhere the roots or branches touch, she can strike. The roots will encircle and break your legs, or drag you into the ground until you suffocate. Or maybe they'll just sprout spikes and impale you."

"Making Deifilia into Sleeping Beauty and the enchanted hedge all in one. Perfect."

A slender figure stepped out from between the trees, the branches bending aside to let her pass. Bi Wei gave no outward sign that she knew me, though we both knew Deifilia was aware of our earlier contact. "Leave the car and any weapons. Including your books."

I stripped off my jacket, tucked my pistol into an inner pocket, and set it inside the car. Lena did the same with her bokken, but she kept the graft from her tree. She rested one end on the ground and leaned on it like a crutch. At this point, the branch was probably the only thing keeping her upright.

Bi Wei studied us both. A pair of metal grasshoppers nested in her hair. They could have been decorative, save for the way they rubbed their forelegs together as they watched us. Harrison's millipede circled her throat. "You carry spells," she said, stepping closer. Her fingers touched my temple. "Here. And another, deeper within."

I tapped my head. "I have a fish in my brain. *Hitchhiker's Guide to the Galaxy*. It translates languages for me. Slimy and a bit gross putting it in, but it works well."

For an instant, I saw amusement in her eyes, and something more: a libriomancer's delight at discovering a new trick. But the emotions didn't reach her voice. "What of the other spell?"

I had left the potion in the glove box, and I wasn't

carrying any other magic. Everything was locked in the car, my books, my jacket, even— "Smudge. I created him, and it's my magic that helps to sustain him. He's staying with the car."

Bi Wei tilted her head, listening to sounds I couldn't hear. "You've brought our books?"

If I said yes, they could kill us and rip the car apart to find them. They'd be pissed to discover the books weren't there, but that would be little comfort, what with me being dead and all. "First I need to talk to Deifilia. She needs to leave Lena and Copper River in peace."

She bowed slightly, then beckoned for us to follow.

"I like her," Lena said. "She's cute for her age."

Each step we took whittled away at my confidence, and I hadn't been terribly confident to begin with. Partly it was a matter of scale. From the street, the trees looked enormous. Here in their shade, with the roots turning the ground to hard lumps and coils of wood, it was like crossing into another world, a world in which Deifilia was creator and goddess. The trees muffled the sounds from outside. The canopy turned the sky green. Leaves swirled through the air, a gentle and deceptively peaceful effect.

Wendigos climbed lower, preparing to pounce. I tensed, but Bi Wei never slowed. These wendigos were fully transformed. The students of Bi Sheng must have found a way to complete the process. Flakes of ice drifted from their bodies like snow as they moved about.

The branches parted, and Bi Wei escorted us inside.

Nothing remained of Lena's garden. Her oak stood in the center of a swamp of tree roots and fallen leaves, without a single flower or blade of grass to be seen. Lena's central tree was unchanged, but dwarfed by the surrounding oaks.

A man and a woman stood in front of the central oak.

I could feel the magic wafting from them, like heat rolling from an open furnace. Both wore loose silk tunics, but the embroidery didn't appear to be Chinese. The necks were cut in a low V, revealing white undershirts. The man wore blue leather boots that rose just past the ankle. I'd have to check my books, but the fashion looked European. Not the wardrobe I would have expected from Bi Sheng's followers.

Neither one showed any hint of sanity. They didn't move at all. I didn't think they were even breathing, and if they blinked, it was too quick for me to see. Their eyes were wide, their mouths parted as if to speak, though they never did.

"Their books were destroyed?" I guessed.

Bi Wei said nothing, but her back tightened.

The others Deifilia had restored were trapped within the roots, bound so tightly they could move only a finger here, a toe there. She hadn't bothered to provide clothing, though little flesh could be seen through the gaps. I counted four more.

August Harrison was here as well, and he was awake. He sat, shirtless, at the base of Lena's oak. A single root circled his neck. Judging from the bruises around his arms, he had been bound more tightly until recently.

Had I been a more petty man, I might have gloated. This was the man who had broken into my house, stolen my research, and used it to attack my town and the woman I loved.

On second thought, I had time for a little pettiness. "You see what happens when we steal other people's magic toys and try to use them without knowing what we're doing?"

He watched in silence as Lena and I stepped carefully over the outer edges of the roots. I stepped carefully, at any rate. Lena was barefoot, and strode as easily as a cat. Being here seemed to have restored some of her strength, though she still leaned on her branch for support, her fingers lost in the budding leaves.

"This is your doing," Harrison said. "Victor's death at the hands of creatures the Porters hid from the rest of us. The students of Bi Sheng, victims of Gutenberg's war."

"And this is your plan to make it better, eh?" I pretended to look around. "How's that working for you?"

His face reddened, but before he could respond, the root around his neck pulsed. His fingers went to his throat, and then he settled back. He glared hatefully, not at us, but at the trunk of the oak, where Deifilia was emerging from the wood.

Harrison's dryad had auburn hair, and her skin was a lighter tan than Lena's, but she had come from the same mold. She was eerily familiar: short and plump and delightfully curved, like an assembly line doll painted by a different artist.

A sleeveless gown made of interwoven leaves clung to her skin like scales. Her legs were bare from the knees down. A wooden sword hung from her hip, though I saw nothing holding it in place. It could have been a part of that living dress. A smaller wooden knife clung to her opposite hip. Both had straight double-edged blades and heavy pommels.

She stepped toward Harrison and stroked her fingers through his hair. To Lena, she said, "You have something for me, sister?"

"I thought you loved him," I said, nodding toward Harrison.

She smiled. "He's a beautiful man. I owe him my existence."

"What do your other lovers think of him?" Lena asked.

Her loving expression never changed. "She sees a pathetic, magically worthless worm of a man."

"She?" I repeated. Jeneta had referred to a "she" when talking about the devourers in her dreams. "Does this other woman have a name?"

"You'll learn her name soon enough," she said lightly.

"How did you get out of the mine without Gutenberg seeing you?"

"You don't understand." She gestured to the two people standing like zombies. "Your Porters study magic, but they *are* magic. We flew through earth and stone as easily as air."

"Cool."

Lena's toes dug into the roots. "It must be difficult, loving someone you can never touch."

I searched for the glint of metal among the green of Deifilia's dress. The leaves clung like a second skin. The cicada had to be on her, but where?

"She's waited more than a thousand years," said Deifilia. "I can wait, too."

"You long for her, don't you?" Lena stepped closer. "You hear her whispering to you, but a ghost isn't enough. You want to feel her legs curling with yours, the sweat as your bodies tighten against each other."

Deifilia didn't answer, but I saw goose bumps on her skin.

I caught Bi Wei's attention, wishing there were a way to communicate without Deifilia overhearing. She inclined her head ever so slightly. Doubtless she could feel Lena's magic. I turned toward Deifilia's two mindless guardians, both of whom were now watching Lena.

"I know what it's like to feel alone." Lena pointed to Harrison, then to me. "They would have us kill one another, the only other person who understands what it's like. Who knows the strength and passion of the oak."

"His wishes no longer matter," Deifilia said.

"Can you imagine the things we could do together?" Lena whispered.

There was a question with more layers than I could count. Yet, on some level, I think she meant it. The longing in Lena's words wasn't sexual. Not just sexual, at least. She reminded me of myself years ago; the first time I met other Porters. The first time I truly understood that I wasn't alone.

Deifilia's answering desire was enough to flatten me. She spoke, but the drumbeat of my blood deafened me to her words. All I could see was the longing in her eyes.

Lena's hand snapped out, catching my arm and stopping me from walking toward her, from pulling those leaves away one by one.

The touch of Lena's hand both helped and made things worse. I clasped my fingers over hers, my mind careening into a new and utterly inappropriate fantasy involving my lover and the woman who would happily destroy everyone and everything I knew.

Lena bent my arm, wrenching me around behind her without ever breaking eye contact with Deifilia. With her free hand, she reached for the other dryad.

Just before Lena made contact, Deifilia realized what was happening. Her arm snapped up, striking Lena's hand away. Lena spun with the impact and whirled around like a dancer to slam the back of her fist into Deifilia's cheek.

"Oh, hell," I muttered to myself. "All right, time for plan B."

Chapter 21

I don't believe in immortality. Which is odd, considering I've met Juan Ponce de Leon and Johannes Gutenberg, both of whom are effectively ageless. Not to mention vampires who have survived unchanged for centuries.

I've killed some of those vampires. Ageless doesn't mean immortal, and there's always something capable of taking you out. Even if that something is simple entropy.

Gutenberg relies on the magic of the grail, which he created using his first mass-printed Bible. It's kept him alive for five hundred years, but that's nothing in the larger scheme of the world. Christianity is only 2000 years old. Who's to say his religion will last another millennium, and what happens to the power of the grail when all those who believe in it are gone?

Or maybe he'll go on indefinitely, until the sun falls into its death throes, cooking all life from this planet. Hopefully, humanity will have moved on by then, but even the universe will end someday. Unlike the heat-death of Earth, the universe will die in cold silence, taking even the so-called immortals with it.

Perhaps science or magic will offer a way to outlive the universe. I have a hard time proclaiming anything impossible these days. But by any reasonable standard, death is a certainty.

I blame Isaac for this train of thought, for the endless "What ifs?" I've found myself asking lately. For the nights spent dreaming in my oak, imagining not only the coming years, but the centuries.

I've survived the death of my tree. My human body appears not to age, save for cosmetic changes dictated by the unconscious desires of my lovers. I don't know what would happen if this body were killed but my tree survived. Nor do I have any interest in finding out.

(All right, fine. Maybe there's a small, nagging streak of curiosity, which I again blame entirely on Isaac.)

The point is, if I'm both careful and lucky, I could survive longer than any ordinary human being. Perhaps even longer than Gutenberg.

At the same time, I've already died more than any of them, and my deaths are potentially as limitless as the stars. Even if my body survives, my lovers pass. Each time that happens, the person I was dies with them.

METAL RODENTS SWARMED DOWN the side of the tree, and the buzz of insects grew deafening. Birds swooped from the branches, and wendigos leaped to the ground.

I spun, only to have bark shear away from the undulating roots beneath me. My foot slipped, and roots the size of my thighs pinched my ankle in place. Something popped in my knee, and pain exploded through my leg.

The problem with plan B was that it required a great deal of concentration on my part. Between the pain and the fact that the world's largest and grumpiest oak grove was trying to smother me, this was going to be difficult.

Deifilia ripped her weapons from her side. Lena raised her branch to parry. Deifilia's first overhead blow dropped her to one knee. I saw the roots of Lena's grafted branch twining around her fingers, sinking into her skin, until the weapon was a literal extension of her arm. The wood flattened, and the buds and twigs ripped away with Lena's counterattack.

Both dryads moved too quickly for me to follow. Within seconds, Deifilia was bleeding from cuts on her arm and thigh. The right side of Lena's face was bloody as well.

Lena dodged past Deifilia and scrambled up the tree like Spider-Man. Her hand and feet sank into the wood, giving her just enough traction to climb out of reach of the roots.

I didn't know much about Lena's study, but I was certain no sensei had ever taught the stance she adopted next. She turned to face Deifilia. Her left leg was stretched up over her head, anchored to the wood, while her right braced her full weight. Her leg muscles shook as she swung her sword two-handed, knocking Deifilia's sword from her hand.

Lena's training and experience gave her an edge over Deifilia, but it wasn't enough. A rat dropped onto Lena's back and sank metal teeth into the flesh between her shoulder blades. She jumped down, smashed her back against the tree, then spun to cut the arm from a wendigo sneaking up behind her. In that time, Deifilia scooped up her sword and lunged. Lena parried, but the blade sliced the skin over her ribs.

I tried to concentrate on Deifilia. Gutenberg had demonstrated how easily he could rob Lena of her power. I had seen him perform the same trick two months before, pulling Smudge's magic into himself and flinging fire against an enchanted car. Smudge hadn't liked that one bit, so I had excused him from guinea pig duty, but I had tried time and again to duplicate Gutenberg's feat. For the most part, I had failed utterly.

But I had been relatively stable those times. Given how magically raw and exposed I was now, I should be able to tap into any book-related magic I touched. The real trick would be holding on to my sanity long enough to use it.

A root shot upward, shaping itself into a spear. Deifilia dropped her dagger, snatched the spear, and thrust the point at Lena's chest. Lena twisted and stepped inward. She caught Deifilia's other wrist, blocking a sword thrust, and smashed her forehead onto Deifilia's nose.

Until now, the two empty shells who had once been students of Bi Sheng had been content to watch. Maybe Deifilia was enjoying the fight, or maybe the Army of Ghosts needed time to adjust to their human bodies. Whatever the reason, they acted now.

I saw them move toward Lena, and then my vision flickered, and there was only magic pouring forth to tear her from existence. It was like staring at an optical illusion, a landscape that suddenly resolves into the face of a man, or a goblet that becomes the silhouette of two faces. They weren't casting a spell; they *were* the spell. They reached out, flesh and magic stretching to touch Lena's arm, to unravel the cells of her body one by one.

I couldn't read the expression on Lena's face as she collapsed. Fear? Sadness? She didn't appear to be in pain, for which I was grateful.

"Wait!" I could bargain for her life, trade the books for Lena. Trade myself, if that was what Deifilia wanted.

Deifilia stepped back and watched, completely entranced by Lena's pain. She seemed not to hear me at all.

Nor did she see as Bi Wei reached skyward and pulled down the stars' fire upon the two magical ghosts.

They should have died instantly, but I could see them moving within the twin pillars of white flame, pulling Bi Wei's attack into themselves, trying to reshape her magic.

Bi Wei's eyes bulged. Blood trickled from her neck as the millipede clamped tighter, cutting off her breath and the circulation to her brain. Inside her body, tiny metal serpents seemed to be finishing the job. She would be dead in seconds, as would Lena.

I studied Deifilia, trying to see not the physical form, but the words that had brought her to life. I didn't have her book with me, but the text was seared into my memory. I focused on the final battle when the nymphs and the commoners rallied together behind John Rule to overthrow a false ruler. I knew this book, knew the snippets of text that defined her powers.

Her hand glided over the shaft of her spear. The wood thickened in response to her gentle touch.

Correction: I knew the snippets of *really bad* text that defined her powers.

Branches swung low, weaving together to form nets, ripping soldiers from their footing and dangling them in the air like freshly killed smeerp.

Her fingers sank into the crevasses of the bark, touching the hot wood beneath.

Why would the wood be hot? Neptune was a cold planet, even with— I stopped myself. Following that trail of thought would only lead to distraction and frustration.

Under ordinary circumstances, the nymphs were no

match for the Lords of Neptune, but here in her grove, the
strength of her oak pumped through her veins like fire.

I could imagine my fingers sinking into the text, but
the wood of the tree remained stubbornly solid. How
had Gutenberg done it? He hadn't touched Smudge to
take his magic. He had simply reached out and drawn it
from the air between them.

I stretched my arm toward Deifilia. The movement
sent new pain tearing through my leg.

Bi Wei collapsed. Blood dripped from her mouth and
nose. The starfire was fading, leaving behind a smell like
an arc welder. The two ghosts remained standing, but
they were in bad shape.

I wasn't strong enough. Not without my books. I could
see the words, but I couldn't touch their magic. I wasn't
Gutenberg. This was my plan, and it was going to fail,
and I was going to have to watch Lena die in front of me.

Even Gutenberg used books for magic, though he
was a lot cooler about it than I was. But he hadn't had
Smudge's book, and I doubted he had bothered to read
it before that encounter. He had never struck me as a
fan of lowbrow sword and sorcery. How did you tap into
the magic of a book you didn't have and had never
read?

But he *had* read it. During that battle two months ago
and again at the library, I had seen words inked beneath
Gutenberg's skin. And he had referred to spells written
on my being.

I needed to stop thinking of the book as separate. The
text was a part of Deifilia. Her core. Her soul.

I imagined the overlapping blocks of printed text
swirling through Deifilia's center. I had done this before.
I had glimpsed Gutenberg's spells. I had read the words
printed into the automatons. As I stared at Deifilia, I saw

the magic sparking within her. I saw it in Lena, too, though the words were blurring.

Deifilia pressed a hand to the trunk of the tree. Bark pulled free in a long, thick strip, which lengthened into a dagger.

I concentrated on the words I had seen in that moment. Gutenberg had made this look so easy, dammit. I didn't even have to cast a spell. That work had already been done. I just needed to borrow it for a minute. But without that physical connection, I couldn't—

"Idiot!" I *had* a physical connection. This was Deifilia's grove now. She had raised these trees, and she had all but taken Lena's oak for herself.

How many times had Lena explained that the tree was as much her body as her human form?

I reached into the tree, read the magic there, and pulled it into myself.

I had to close my eyes to keep from passing out. I could feel my roots sinking deep into the earth, the dry taste of the soil and the moisture trapped far below. The trees swayed with every breeze, the leaves catching the wind like tiny sails. I felt every one of the metal insects and rats and squirrels scrabbling over my bark. I felt each restricted breath of the prisoners trapped in the roots, the heat of their bodies, the feeble strain of muscle against wood.

I felt Lena struggling to rise, tasted her blood and sweat. With a movement as natural as shrugging a shoulder, I twisted the roots beneath Deifilia. She stumbled, but it wasn't enough to stop her from thrusting her dagger.

The wood was mine now. It shattered like balsa when it struck Lena's chest.

I freed the students of Bi Sheng next, but the tree

wasn't the only thing holding them prisoner. Deifilia had sent her insects into their bodies as well. They doubled over in pain as magical parasites bored through their insides.

I pinned Deifilia's leg and grew shoots of wood through her foot, trapping her in place. The ghosts were next. I opened the roots, pulling them deeper. Wood coiled round their bodies and through their flesh. Bi Wei had weakened them, and the oak—*my* oak—finished them off.

Lena snatched her fallen weapon, spun, and thrust.

The sword pierced Deifilia's chest and struck the oak behind her. I could feel the wood sending threads into the rest of the tree. The bark swelled outward to engulf the tip of the sword. Blood dripped from Deifilia's human body, and the graft dragged her toward the oak.

"The queen," I said.

Lena put her hand on Deifilia's left shoulder. Her fingers curled through the leaves, and she ripped a gleaming cicada from Deifilia's skin. She clutched the metal body in one hand, gripped the head in her other, and twisted.

The end of Victor Harrison's enchantment spread like a shock wave. Metal rained from the branches. A clockwork squirrel hit August Harrison on the back of the head. Even the insects felt like stones pounding down. I twisted to avoid a falling rat that smashed into the roots beside me.

The students of Bi Sheng were using magic to heal the damage the insects had done. I watched them reach into one another's bodies, dissolving metal into dust, sealing pierced organs and arteries. All save Bi Wei.

"Can you help her?" I asked.

I don't know if they understood me. I could hardly see them anymore through all of the magic.

Lena eased Deifilia's body back against the oak, even as the branch protruding from the other dryad's chest continued to grow. I couldn't make out what they were saying. Lena whirled around as a wendigo landed behind her, but the creature was only interested in fleeing. It smashed through the branches and disappeared.

Lena was walking over to August Harrison. She tugged at the roots holding him in place. "Isaac, it's all right. I've got him. Please let me bring him to Deifilia. She wants to say good-bye."

I tried to relax, to cede control of the oak back to Lena. I pulled my hands from the wood and clenched them against my body. It seemed to be enough. Lena tugged Harrison free and led him to his dryad lover. Lena whispered something in Harrison's ear, and he nodded. Deifilia took his hand. She was crying.

"Isaac?" Lena dropped to one knee in front of me. "Can you hear me?"

Her right eye was bruised and swollen, and a cut traced a line down her cheek and jaw. Her knuckles were cracked and bloody, and her upper sleeve was a shredded mess, as was the skin beneath. She had left sticky footprints on the roots where blood had trickled down her leg.

"Isaac, look at me."

I tried to focus, but broken lines of text floated through my vision. *"I am yours now, John Rule of Earth." She knelt on the ice, head bowed, blonde hair flowing like a golden river over the voluptuous curves of her body.*

Strong hands lowered me to the ground.

"He is lost. Soon, the Ghosts will find him."

That voice was unfamiliar. He spoke in another language, but I understood. My hands were shaking from the ice. No, the ice wasn't real. I was in the grove. Lena's grove. For a moment, I saw one of the students of Bi Sheng looking down at me.

"He knows us. Knows our books."

"None shall harm him while I live." Lena's words, or her book? I couldn't tell anymore. *"I am his, and I shall slay any who try to hurt him."*

It had to be the book. Lena would have skipped the posturing and punched the man in the throat.

"He saved your lives."

"He serves Gutenberg."

How was Lena able to understand them? Were they speaking English now? I couldn't even tell.

"If he served Gutenberg, we would all be dead now. I brought Bi Wei into this world. Bring Isaac back for me."

Bi Wei. Had they been able to save her?

"How didst thou come here?"

"I don't know." I remembered the ice giving way. I had fallen deep into the blue glacier, my ice ax ripped from my gloved hands. I remembered the shouts from my team, and then a web of golden light.

"We cannot help you, Isaac Vainio of Earth. There is no returning from this place. If you would stay, you must earn your place among the People. You must fight."

"Stay with me." One of the nymphs cradled me against her. My knee throbbed. I must have twisted it in the fall.

"What happened?" Gutenberg's voice.

Why had the warriors of Harku'unn taken me to this cave? How could I pass their trials with no food or water, no weapons of any sort? The Ghosts of Neptune circled like the vultures of Earth, waiting for their prey to die. Each time I drifted off, their talons raked my skin, and their beaks tore flesh. They wouldn't wait for me to die. They would devour me alive.

"You let them escape? Freed them from their bonds, and did *nothing*?" Gutenberg shouted.

Another presence approached through the darkness. The strongest of the spirits cupped my face in her claws and opened my mind like a tin can. Her fingers stirred my thoughts.

"Even if I wanted to help the man who betrayed the Porters, he's too far gone."

Empty syllables. The spirits pulled me deeper, and a woman laughed from the shadows.

"Two months ago, Isaac Vainio saved your life. You *will* help him, damn you." The words jolted me awake. Lena's voice, furious and determined. The magic of her tree surged to life, even as the spirits tightened their grip.

"Who are you?" I demanded.

Laughter. *"Would you like me to show you, Isaac?"*

"Look at him, Lena. His skin charred by magic, power tearing through him from within. I know of only one way to stop that power from destroying him."

I could see her now. A small woman emerging from the darkness, clad in bronze armor. She smiled at me, but her eyes were empty holes into nothingness.

"What's your name?"

The world jerked into focus, and I saw Johannes Gutenberg standing over me, a gold pen in his hand. I tried to pull away, but I could no longer feel my body. The cold had frozen my blood, turning me to a statue. I would die here, trapped beneath the surface of an alien world.

The bronze woman stretched out a hand and whispered a single word. *"Meridiana."*

And then the world shattered.

Chapter 22

Thank you, Nidhi Shah.

Thank you for compassion. For strength and intellect.

Thank you for helping and protecting those who need it. For acceptance and ambition in balance, and pleasure free of guilt.

For juice from the grapes we planted and harvested together.

For the magic of scent, of herbs and candles and food simmering for hours in the kitchen, the aroma seeping into every corner.

Thank you for the ability to stand among giants and not feel small.

Thank you, Isaac Vainio.

Thank you for wonder, and for curiosity.

For the beauty of Saturn's rings and the Northern Lights off the shore of Lake Superior, waves of green reflected in the water.

Thank you for the joy and loyalty to be found from a simple spider.

For the love of books and stories that never stop imagining what might be possible.

Most of all, thank you for your stubborn faith that there is always a solution.

There is always hope.

SLEEP WOULD HAVE BEEN a kindness. My body needed all the rest it could get, and my mind yearned to escape the real world. But even more than dreams, I wanted that brief period of awakening when dreams and denial blurred together to soften the impact of the real world. Let me blanket myself in delusion and hide from my loss for a few moments longer.

The universe had been rather short on kindness lately.

"Isaac, look at me."

Sunlight turned the leaves overhead to green glass. I squinted and shielded my eyes until they adjusted enough to focus on Nidhi Shah sitting cross-legged beside me. Lena stood behind her.

The grove was still crowded, but now it was the Porters who had gathered here, and most of them were staring at me. Pallas and Gutenberg stood at my feet. I spotted Whitney and John, but not Toni. Maryelizabeth's arm was in a sling. A woman I didn't recognize was leaning against a tree while another libriomancer regrew her leg.

"Lena—"

"I'm all right." The exhaustion in her eyes suggested otherwise, but at least she was alive.

Nidhi touched my wrist, feeling for my pulse. "What do you remember?"

I had been Nidhi's client, and I knew her therapeutic

voice. This was something else. Calm, but she wasn't trying to hide her grief.

"Enough." There was a woman in bronze, and a name, but when I tried to remember, the syllables slipped from my memory. I brought my fingers to my head, touching the skin where Gutenberg's pen had traced his spell.

Hot pinpricks scampered up my ribs. I looked down to see Smudge crouched on my chest. "Hi, buddy." I pushed myself up on my elbows and looked at Pallas. "How are things in Copper River?"

"Contained, but not controlled. We've cut off communications with the outside world while we work on damage control."

I nodded. "How many casualties?"

"We won't know for at least a day," said Gutenberg. He picked up a lifeless metal grasshopper and held it to the light. Rainbows shimmered along the edges of the iridescent wings. He touched one wing, which was sharp enough to draw blood, though the cut healed quickly. "What happened to the students of Bi Sheng?"

"I honestly don't know."

He pulled a book out of his pocket, and it was all I could do to keep from swearing. It was the same A. E. van Vogt book he had used at the library to read Guan Feng's mind. "Is Feng—"

"Gone," said Pallas. "Jeff was found unconscious in the library. He hasn't woken up yet, but I'm told he will recover."

Gutenberg tapped the cover, and golden tendrils grew from his scalp, reaching toward Lena and myself. I watched it all happen again in my mind. Deifilia battled Lena. The two ghosts attacked. Bi Wei stopped them from killing Lena, then fell.

I remembered seizing control of the tree and turning it against Deifilia. What happened after was unfamiliar.

I saw through Lena's eyes how she had locked Harrison in place, twisting the branch around his neck and trapping him with his dying dryad. Then she ran to me. She argued with the students of Bi Sheng, while to the side, another man worked over Bi Wei's body. A woman knelt to touch my face. The last of the wendigos dropped to the ground and fled.

"The two of you let them go," Gutenberg said, enunciating every word.

"They helped us to stop Deifilia and the Army of Ghosts."

"Despite the sayings people repeat unthinkingly, the enemy of my enemy may not in fact be my friend." He waved a hand, and the tendrils faded away. "You've freed an enemy we cannot see. They carry madness within them, Isaac. What happens when the first of their number loses their battle against the ghosts?"

I looked at Nidhi. "I could refer them to a good therapist."

Several of the Porters cringed. I couldn't blame them. Sassing Gutenberg wasn't a wise life choice. But he had taken my magic, and I found it hard to care what else he did to me.

"Toni Warwick was found unconscious at the edge of town," Gutenberg said. "She told us what you had given her, but she was unable to guard them from Bi Wei and her companions."

Bi Wei had survived. I wondered if he could see my relief. "Will Toni be all right?"

"Eventually." He leaned closer. His breath smelled of peppermint. "What was done once can be done again. Tell me of the books, their titles and content."

I frowned. I could see myself pulling the books from *Beauty* as we drove through Copper River, but I couldn't remember the titles. Nor could I recall the names of Bi Wei's companions. Even the content of Bi Wei's book eluded me, though I had a vague memory of poetry ... "I don't remember."

Pallas stepped forward. "Sir, it was through Isaac's relationship with Jeff DeYoung that the werewolves came to assist us. Without his help—"

"I know." Gutenberg raised a hand. "He stopped Deifilia. He captured August Harrison. He ended the attack on Copper River, and no doubt saved many lives, including some of our own. But he risked much more. Had he contacted me when he learned of Deifilia's assault on Lena's tree, we could have contained the situation."

"Bi Wei and Guan Feng trust me," I said. "I can try to reach out to them, negotiate a truce."

"You will do nothing of the sort," said Gutenberg. "This is a Porter matter."

It took me a moment to realize what he was saying. When understanding hit, I felt like he had transformed me to stone, starting from my stomach and working outward.

Nidhi put a hand on my shoulder, as if to restrain me. "Independence—impulsiveness, really—is one of the qualities shared by many of your best libriomancers."

"It's also a quality shared by most of our fatalities," Gutenberg snapped. For the first time, he sounded truly angry. "Bi Wei and her four companions have escaped, and the Army of Ghosts is awakening. Tell me, Doctor Shah, will you continue to defend him if it turns out he saved this town only to damn the entire world?"

I tugged free of Nidhi's grip and stood. "The day I joined Die Zwelf Portenære, you made me swear to protect this world, to help us expand our knowledge, and to preserve the secrecy of magic." I gestured at the oak trees towering over us. "I think that third part is pretty well screwed, but what about the rest? Bi Wei and the others knew about the Army of Ghosts, the danger you've feared for five hundred years. You *tried to murder* the only people who could have helped you fight them."

I was yelling at Johannes Gutenberg. Oh, God, I was so dead. "How much knowledge have you burned because you were afraid it *might* be used against you? How many people have you killed because you were afraid?"

I swallowed and waited for him to transform me into a cockroach and feed me to Smudge. Instead, he simply sighed.

"I was young, and the world was different. Though people remain much the same. They say you learn from your mistakes. I've learned more than anyone else in recorded history. But the mistakes of the past do not excuse the mistakes of the present. Nor do they protect us from the consequences of those mistakes."

I really didn't like the emphasis on the word *consequences*. Neither did Lena, judging by the way she edged closer and shifted her stance.

"Isaac could still help us," Pallas pointed out. "Even without magic."

Gutenberg tilted his head in acknowledgment. "You assume it was my choice to dismiss him from the Porters, but Isaac made that choice before we arrived. Didn't you?"

I straightened, determined to face this head-on. Locking my magic had been the first step, and it had saved me from madness. But Gutenberg wouldn't stop there. Having determined that my memories were of no use to the Porters, he would take them from me as well. I would be erased from the Porter archives, and from the minds of my peers. No wonder he hadn't worried about holding this conversation in public; when he was finished, no-body else would remember it.

Lena stepped in front of me and kicked at Guten-berg's hand. He dodged and stepped back. Before Lena could follow up, I grabbed her in a bear hug from be-hind.

"Are you insane?" I whispered. She could have bro-ken free with ease, but she held back, presumably to keep from hurting me.

She turned in my arms to face me. "He's going to take your memories."

"I know."

"No, you don't." Lena was crying now. "Think, Isaac. None of the Porters will even remember your name. *I* won't remember you."

I hadn't realized until now what that meant. Whatever independence or freedom she had gained from being pulled between Nidhi's desires and my own would be lost. "I'm so sorry, Lena."

The other Porters were shifting and muttering uneas-ily, all save Nicola. They didn't understand. Few among us knew the truth about how Gutenberg dealt with those he considered criminals.

Gutenberg sighed. "I don't do this to be cruel, Isaac. You acted to protect your home, using the best judgment you could. I understand that. I hope you'll understand I'm doing the same."

I kissed Lena, then pushed her toward Nidhi. I watched Gutenberg raise his pen and approach once again. If he was going to rob me of everything I loved, he could damn well look me in the eye when he did it.

The touch of the pen was like a syringe jabbing through my skin. Cold tingled over my body. Every mus-cle clenched painfully tight.

Gutenberg jumped back, and for a second, I thought I saw the shadow of Bi Wei standing between us. He flung the pen to the ground as if it were on fire.

He studied me, eyes flitting side to side as if I were an enormous newspaper. "It would appear you've made a friend."

I sagged in relief, and might have fallen if Lena hadn't caught me.

"Very well." Gutenberg retrieved his pen and tucked it back into his pocket. "Perhaps as you see the damage caused by the forces you've allowed to escape, you'll change your mind about aiding us. In the meantime, we *will* be watching you, Isaac Vainio." He turned to Pallas. "I've given the other Regional Masters a summary of what we're facing, but we'll need to gather and share as much information as possible. First, we need to make sure this site is fully neutralized, then do what we can to control the rumors."

"Why bother?" Knowing Gutenberg couldn't take my memories had made me bold. Or stupid. Probably both. "The students of Bi Sheng are free. You think they're going to worry about keeping your precious secrets?"

"What do you suggest?" Gutenberg asked, his words deceptively mild.

"I lost friends today. Their families deserve to know why. They deserve the truth."

"You don't know what the truth would do," he said softly. "I've seen how they respond to truth. I've lived through the Inquisition and the witch hunts. I've watched my loved ones burn."

"Sir," Pallas said, "whatever we do, we should act soon. I've called for healers, and can split the rest of our forces into teams."

Gutenberg nodded and stepped toward the edge of

the grove. He turned around to look at me, his expression unreadable. "Farewell, Isaac Vainio."

The Porters did their best, but they couldn't manipulate the minds of an entire town, let alone everyone who had seen or read about the story online. A photo of the dragon smashing its way into town had gone viral, and a six-second video of a wendigo at the ice cream shop kept popping up on various social media sites no matter how many times the Porters tried to take it offline.

Nor could they find and destroy the remains of every one of the hundreds of metal insects and other creatures Harrison and Deifilia had sent to attack us. They did their best to track down the wendigos, but I had no doubt we'd be seeing more "Bigfoot sightings" for months to come.

The Porters had trapped a fair number of wendigos, but they hadn't found them all. Nor were any of the people they restored to human form associated with the students of Bi Sheng. I knew Harrison had transformed some of his own people, but Bi Wei and her friends must have hunted them down, saving their own and making sure they couldn't be captured and used by the Porters.

None of which was my concern anymore.

I sat in the grass, my back against one of the outer oaks of Lena's grove, and tried to read. I had picked up Gaiman's latest, but I hadn't managed to get past the first two pages. Not because of any problem with the writing, but because when I read his words, I felt nothing.

I knew there was magic here. Given Gaiman's fanbase, I should have been able to touch this book's magic in my sleep.

I sighed and set the book aside. Maybe I would be

better off rereading an old favorite. Preferably something light. Pratchett's Discworld series would keep me busy for a while.

Lena had somehow shrunk the surrounding oaks of her grove to a more reasonable height, and was currently clearing a section of the canopy, folding the branches back to allow us a better view of the stars and a distant comet that should be visible through the telescope later tonight. I had a new eyepiece for the scope that I'd been wanting to try.

I pulled a crumpled piece of green paper from the pocket of my jeans. The front was an advertisement for a book club that had met at the library over the summer. On the back, I had done my best to recreate the lines Gutenberg had engraved into my skull.

Sileo. Latin for *I am silent*.

"Any progress?" Lena asked as she emerged from the grove.

I shook my head. "It's not a form of libriomancy I understand. If he had written a longer phrase, I might be able to find a source, but this is just a single word. It could refer to anything. I suspect the pen is as much a part of the magic as the writing. I'd give half my books to get my hands on it."

I didn't tell her about the e-mail I had received from Nicola Pallas yesterday. I hadn't told anyone, though I had reread it until I memorized every word. I was certain Nicola had broken some rule or another in sending it, which was amazing all by itself. Or maybe there were simply no rules for a situation like mine, and she had taken advantage of that omission.

The e-mail had been short and businesslike. Pallas began by reminding me that I was no longer a Porter, and that any attempt to access Porter resources or data would be ill-advised. Because of my service to the organization, she thought it only fair that I receive my final paycheck. It would be deposited into my savings account at the end of the month, and that would be the last time they contacted me.

Then, at the very end of her message, she warned me against trying to undo Gutenberg's spell, explaining that historically, almost all such attempts had ended badly.

I knew Nicola Pallas. She was far too careful in her writing to have used the word "almost" by accident. Just as importantly, she knew me well enough to know I would pounce on that word as proof that it could be done.

She had given me hope.

"I heard on the radio that a sparkler photobombed a live news broadcast down in Detroit," Lena commented.

My lips quirked. For the past two days since the attack, I had been inseparable from my computer, reading every article and blog post I could find about the attack on Copper River, Michigan. Theories ranged from the outlandish to the mundanely predictable: mass hallucinations, government experiments gone wrong, aliens, and more.

The physical repairs to the town had undermined many of the stories. I had driven past the water tower, standing tall once again. I couldn't find a single weld to show where the legs had broken. The restaurant remained closed, but the door and windows had been fixed.

It was the same throughout town, and the reporters who arrived in search of a story met with confusion and conjecture from people who remembered nothing of the past days. On the other hand, there were always people eager for attention who were happy to confirm whatever explanation the reporters wanted, so long as it gave them their fifteen minutes of fame.

The last article I read had taken the government conspiracy approach, claiming that Copper River was a test site for hallucinogenic weapons, and everyone who stayed would be dying of cancer over the next decade.

I told myself I wasn't obsessing. I was trying to read past the stories, to find out what the Porters had been up to, and whether they had been able to track down Bi Wei and the others. With no access to the Porter database and no magic of my own, this was my best chance to reconstruct their movements.

I watched Smudge climb slowly up one of the oaks, stalking a firefly. I hadn't been certain what would happen to him with my magic gone. How much did Smudge exist independently of me, and how much was his magic bound to my own? The first time I watched him toast a cricket, my relief had been overwhelming.

As had the envy that followed.

Lena slid down beside me. "What happens now?"

I pointed to the sky. "Later tonight, between Ursa Minor and Cassiopeia, we should be able to see —"

"Dork." She kissed my ear. "You know what I mean."

"I've still got the library job. I asked Jennifer to move me back to full time." No matter what else the Porters had done to me, at least they had repaired my library. I had been going there since I was three years old. I blinked hard and waited for the tightness in my throat to ease.

I could feel the depression trying to pull me down and smother me, as it had done at random times for the past two days. Nidhi was ready to start slipping Zoloft into my drinks. She would have been happier if I was talking to someone, but I couldn't exactly go to a normal therapist with my problems, and Doctor Karim wasn't allowed to meet with me anymore, since I was no longer a Porter.

I had also been volunteering around town, trying to pitch in wherever I could. I had donated blood, run an impromptu story time for kids, helped out with a charity fundraiser for the "unexplained" deaths that had taken at least twenty-one people ... anything to be useful. Anything to keep from feeling powerless.

When I walked past the cemetery and saw the freshly dug graves, nothing seemed like enough.

"I've got something I want to show you." Lena sounded uncharacteristically shy. "Nidhi, too. A project I'll need both of you to help with."

Before she could say more, Nidhi emerged from the back of the house with Jeff and Helen DeYoung in tow. I was starting to get used to having an extra houseguest in Nidhi. I knew perfectly well she was staying because she was worried about me, and wanted to make sure I wasn't suicidal. It wasn't an unreasonable fear, but after coming so close to so many different flavors of death, I had no desire at all to go there again.

"Later," Lena whispered.

Jeff and Nidhi waited while Helen navigated the deck with her crutches. She had taken on a pair of wendigos on the south part of town. I hadn't been able to pry anything out of her, beyond, "You should see the other guys, eh?"

Jeff was in slightly better shape. The first time I saw him, he had looked half-mummified in bandages from the cuts he had suffered, but the worst of his wounds had scabbed over and were beginning to heal. By the time the next full moon rolled around, he should be good as new.

Guan Feng had slept undisturbed through the attack, and most of the creatures had abandoned the library to come after me. I had gotten the rest of the story from Helen, how the students of Bi Sheng knocked Jeff unconscious with a flick of their fingers, until one of the rescue workers found him curled up and snoring in the library the next afternoon.

"We brought cedar-smoked salmon," Helen announced. She had become far friendlier when she learned I was no longer welcome among the Porters.

"And a thank you from Laci's and Hunter's families." Jeff dug a pair of knitted mittens and matching hat from the pocket of his sweatshirt and tossed them to me. "For taking care of the bastard who attacked their kids."

They were surprisingly soft, gray with a dappling of black spun through the wool. "Thank them for me."

"They'd been saving the yarn," Helen said. "Spun it themselves."

I hesitated. "What exactly am I holding here?"

Jeff chuckled. "Nothing too weird. They brushed it from Laci and Hunter the first year they went through the change. It's tradition, at least in these parts. You spin the fur into wool and use it for something special. Wear those, and any werewolf will know from the scent to treat you like family."

"Thank you," I repeated, humbled.

"Won't be long until word gets out about us," Helen said. "The Porters are trying to cover things up, but it's like trying to put the egg back into the shell. There have always been rumors about Tamarack, but now folks will start putting the pieces together. Two families have left town already. The rest are stocking up on weapons and ammunition."

"If the Porters can't stop the signal, they'll do their best to control it," Lena said.

"Has anyone in Copper River figured out what you do—what you used to do, I mean—on the side?" Helen asked.

"Not yet." Earlier today, after attending the first of what would be many funerals to come, Pete Malki had asked about the additional trees in my backyard. Several of my neighbors wanted to know how my home had survived the destruction that had taken out the rest of the street. Thus far, they'd all been willing to take my word that I was as baffled as the rest of them. "I'm sorry I can't do anything for your leg."

She waved off my concern. "I've had worse. Did I ever tell you about the time I was out hunting, and a black bear managed to creep up behind me? She was downwind, and I was recovering from a cold, so by the time I sniffed her, it was too late to run."

I settled back to listen, though I wasn't sure how much of her story to believe. I certainly didn't buy the one Jeff told next, which started with a home-brewing project and ended with Jeff punching a moose.

Nidhi brought chairs out from the house, and Jeff eventually retreated to the kitchen to heat up dinner. Lena grabbed a six-pack of beer a short time later, along with a two-liter bottle of Cherry Coke for herself.

By the time the sky grew dark, I had been thoroughly briefed on gossip about half the werewolves in Tamarack. I had shared a bit of salmon with Smudge, who apparently felt it was horribly undercooked, but otherwise approved. I thought it was delicious, and even went back for a second helping. It was the first real meal I had eaten since losing my magic.

Eventually, Helen tapped her husband on the shoulder, interrupting his tale about a rather acrobatic foursome he and Helen had participated in when they were younger. I had no idea whether or not they were embellishing or making the whole thing up. I was fairly certain the bit about the hammock was a lie, based on simple physics. Either way, it was definitely making me blush. Meanwhile, I could see Lena taking detailed mental notes.

"We need to start heading back," said Helen. "Now you call us if there's anything you need, understand?"

"Yes, ma'am," I said, climbing to my feet. "And thank you."

They both seemed to understand that I wasn't talking about the food. Each of them hugged me in turn, then did the same with Nidhi and Lena.

"Try to stay out of trouble for a while, eh?" Jeff said as he left.

"Not really part of my skill set," I called back, earning a laugh from them both.

Nidhi stood with her arms folded, studying me. Whatever she saw must have satisfied her, because she turned to go back inside.

"Wait." Lena jumped to her feet and ducked into the grove, to her oak. She crouched at the base of the tree, reached into the roots, and pulled something from the dirt.

When I saw what she carried, I backed away. "Is that what I think it is?"

"Yes and no." She extended the book to me.

I thought at first that Bi Wei had left her book behind, but I couldn't imagine her taking such a risk. When I took the cloth-bound tome, I saw that the cover text was slightly different, though I couldn't read it.

The writing inside was identical to that in Bi Wei's book, at least the beginning. I turned to the middle, where carefully formed Chinese characters were replaced by English. "This is your handwriting."

"I found it in the roots of my tree," Lena said. "They made it for me. I think it was a gift from Bi Wei. When I pulled her from her book, she must have seen more of my thoughts than I realized."

Nidhi pressed close, reading over my shoulder. I turned the page and read, "The oak is ever divided . . ."

Lena stared at the ground. "I'm not saying it's good. I never claimed to be a poet."

"It's beautiful," I said. "Jeneta would—" Only I was forbidden from talking with her.

"They used these books as an escape," Nidhi said. "A way to survive in a time of war."

"I want the same thing," Lena said. "To survive." She took the book back and held it almost reverently. "I'm not done with it yet, and I don't know if it will work, but I want to try."

Lena's nature couldn't be rewritten. Gutenberg had said so himself. Then again, Gutenberg had said a lot of things that turned out to be untrue or incomplete. If these books could sustain the students of Bi Sheng for so many years—if they could give them a foundation even now to stave off the madness of the Army of Ghosts— who was to say it couldn't do the same for Lena?

"I'll need you both to read it," Lena continued. "Each day, if you can."

"Of course, love," said Nidhi.

"Twice a day on weekends," I promised.

"Thank you." She kissed each of us, then returned the book to the safety of her tree. When she returned, her eyes were somber. "When do you think the Army of Ghosts will return?"

Not if, but when. "They're awake now, and they've planted their seeds in Bi Wei and the others. If the ghosts can't take control of them, they'll look for another way into our world."

And when they got here, they would certainly remember who had derailed their plans. Twice.

I thought of the armored woman I had seen in my

madness, and my hand went to the shock-gun in my pocket. Technically, I should have turned that in when they kicked me out of the Porters.

On the other hand, screw them.

"This isn't over, is it?" asked Nidhi.

I peered through the telescope and adjusted the knob until the stars came into sharp focus. "The world is about to discover magic. This is only the beginning."

Epilogue

JENETA DREAMED SHE WAS back in the car
with Myron Worster, a white-haired Porter in a suit
and tie, with sharp wrinkles at the corners of his
mouth. For a glorified magical babysitter, he was nice
enough, if you could get past his penchant for show
tunes and the perpetual smell of pipe tobacco.

"Are you sure we don't have time to see Isaac?" Jeneta asked. "Just to say good-bye, and to thank him."

"I'm afraid not. Pallas' orders."

She could have used magic to influence him, but it
wasn't worth the risk. He had demonstrated his magic in
her cabin at Camp Aazhawigiizhigokwe, pulling various
potions and magical ointments from the books in his
suitcase. He explained in excruciating detail how he had
spent fifty years studying the effects of different potions,
learning how to combine them for maximum potency,
from flight and invisibility to speed and strength. Given
a few minutes to mix his magical cocktails, he was all but
unbeatable.

He had spent several days watching over her, his senses and reflexes magically enhanced. As far as Jeneta knew, he hadn't slept once, nor would he until she was safely on the plane home.

Only he hadn't kept her safe. She remembered finding a dead butterfly in her cabin, the body the size and shape of a bullet, with wings of milky glass. Worster reassured her that August Harrison's insects had all died with the destruction of the queen, but he had destroyed the butterfly to be safe. He snapped the wings and broke the body in half.

Only after he left to dispose of the remains did Jeneta notice the tiny bead it had left behind, like a dull metal egg. The bead clung to her finger when she touched it.

She recalled the pinprick of legs crawling through her thoughts. They chipped at her mind, consuming her memories one by one, and the more she tried to protect herself with magic, the quicker they fed.

"Sleep, girl."

The voice in her head was her own, but she hadn't spoken. She fought the compulsion to obey, to sink deeper into dreams and nightmares. Terror helped her to kick toward the surface long enough to glimpse her surroundings.

She was on a moving sidewalk, striding through a tunnel with curved walls. Colored light rippled along the wall in time to music. At the end of the walkway, the crowd split apart, following overhead signs directing passengers to the proper terminals. This was an airport. How had she gotten here?

"The Bì Shēng de dú zhě demonstrated you could survive death in a book," said the other voice. *"Even one so small as a computer chip. Assuming you found someone who could touch its magic."*

"I know you," said Jeneta. The devourers had found her first through her nightmares, and then through the insects in Lena's tree. She had known they wouldn't stop.

The scent of cinnamon rolls attracted her attention, and she paused in front of a small shop. Her lips curved upward. She pulled out her phone and brought up Maya Angelou's "Amazing Peace." Seconds later, the customers and staff sat entranced, utterly at peace. No one even noticed as Jeneta reached around the counter, grabbed a roll, and walked off.

"Such an efficient little spellbook."

She strode toward the gate, ending her spell with a mere thought. She sat in one of the uncomfortable plastic chairs by the window and looked out at the planes rolling to and fro along the runway.

She remembered Worster escorting her into the airport. Once inside, she had used her magic to reassure him and send him on his way. After that, it was a simple enough matter to confuse the necessary people and change her flight plans.

"Is this your first trip to Beijing?" asked a man sitting two chairs over.

Jeneta fought to scream, or to beg the man for help, but like a dream, she had no control of her words or body. "Not exactly."

"You look a little young to be flying to another country by yourself."

"I'm older than I look." She licked frosting from her fingertips. *"Enough. Back to sleep with you."*

Jeneta could no more resist that command than she could stop the night from falling. Darkness consumed her, and sounds grew distant.

"Vacationing?" asked the stranger.

"Retrieving an . . . inheritance."

As Jeneta sank back into nightmare, memories of a face cast or carved from brass flowed through her mind. The features were exaggerated: an elongated nose, and full lips. An overly high brow, creased in thought. Her hair was plaited, interwoven with tiny clumps of gold, five-petaled flowers.

And beyond that mask, a legion of the dead, waiting to follow.

Bibliography

TITLES MARKED WITH AN asterisk (*) were made up for this book.

Adams, Douglas. *The Hitchhiker's Guide to the Galaxy*.

Anthony, Piers. *Roc and a Hard Place*.

Asimov, Isaac. *The Best of Isaac Asimov*.

Baum, L. Frank. *The Marvelous Land of Oz*.

Bentley, Peter J. *Why Sh*t Happens: The Science of a Really Bad Day*.

Britain, Kristin. *Green Rider*.

Carroll, Lewis. *Alice's Adventures in Wonderland*.

Colfer, Eoin. *Artemis Fowl*.

Conrad, H. Allen. *Time Kings*.*

Daly, Randy L. *African Honey Bees in North America*.

Eddings, David. *The Belgariad*.

Foglio, Phil and Kaja. *Girl Genius*.

Foster, Alan Dean and Lucas, George. *Star Wars: From the Adventures of Luke Skywalker*.

Grimm, Jacob and Wilhelm. *Household Tales*.

Heinlein, Robert. *Friday*.

Heinlein, Robert. *Stranger in a Strange Land*.

Homer. *Odysseus*.

Xú Líng. *New Songs from a Jade Terrace*.

Ikeji, Lisa. *Heart of Stone.**

James, E. L. *50 Shades of Grey*.

Lamplighter, L. Jagi. *Prospero Regained*.

Lewis, C. S. *The Magician's Nephew*.

McKinley, Robin. *Beauty*.

Mead, Richelle. *Vampire Academy*.

Oliver, Jana. *The Demon Trapper's Daughter*.

Pierce, Tamora. *Circle of Magic*.

Plato. *The Republic*.

Pratchett, Terry. *Mort*.

Pratchett, Terry and Gaiman, Neil. *Good Omens*.

Rey, H. A. *Curious George*.

Scalzi, John. *Old Man's War*.

Shěn Kuò, *Dream Pool Essays*.

Silverstein, Shel. *The Giving Tree*.

Stevenson, Robert Louis. *Treasure Island*.

Tolkien, J. R. R. *The Fellowship of the Ring*.

Van Vogt, A. E. *Slan*.

Wells, H. G. *The Complete Short Stories of H. G. Wells*.

Whitman, Walt. *Leaves of Grass*.

Wright, James. *Nymphs of Neptune.**

Coming soon from DAW,
the third novel of *Magic ex Libris*
by Jim C. Hines:

UNBOUND

Read on for a sneak preview.

WEREWOLVES VS. BIGFOOT

SUMMARY: *VIRAL VIDEO CLIP claims to show shotgun-wielding werewolves hunting Bigfoot from the back of a pickup truck.*

Status: Inconclusive.

Sample Email:

> Hey, check out this monster-on-monster cellphone video, captured by a 17-year-old girl in Copper River, Michigan.
>
> You can't see the driver, but look at the two shotgun-toting hicks in the back. And before you say it's just a couple of hairy guys in masks, wait for the 0:42 mark, when a white-furred giant streaks across the road.
>
> A good makeup artist can create a convincing werewolf, but that dude jumped at least ten meters FROM A MOVING TRUCK to tackle what looks like an albino Sasquatch. Both of them bounce back from the impact like it was nothing.
>
> Copies of the video have already been pulled from YouTube and three other sites for "copyright violation." Screen-caps are below, in case they yank this link too.

Background: Many rumors have been spread about the recent tragedy in Copper River. At least 34 people are known to have died, but initial reports of property damage appear to have been wildly exaggerated. The official cause of most deaths was listed as accidental, according to police reports. [Sources: Associated Press, Copper River Journal, CBS News]

This video first appeared on the Internet on August 5 of this year. On August 8, Reddit user BlackCapsFan12 posted a detailed analysis of the background motion to determine that the "impossible" jump was a result of camera trickery. Other users argued the video was genuine, and submitted evidence suggesting BlackCapsFan12 was a sockpuppet account.

Another theory is that the video is part of a viral marketing campaign for an upcoming movie or television show. (See also "Vampire Photobombs Live News Report.") Hollywood is certainly capable of producing a video of this quality. However, no studio has claimed responsibility, nor has anyone been able to connect the video to a specific forthcoming release.

Conclusion: While most people scoff at the idea of monsters, there is no conclusive proof that the video was faked. In addition, materials such as the George R. R. Martin Letter suggest that we must at least consider the possibility of such things being genuine. Therefore, ChainBusters.com has given this story a verdict of INCONCLUSIVE.

Related Stories:

- Iron Dragon Escapes from Copper River Mine, Attacks Local Library

- Secret Government Drug Testing Goes Horribly Wrong in Michigan's Upper Peninsula?

———◆———

I CALLED DEB DEGEORGE, who had been a good friend back in the days when she had a pulse and didn't snack on bugs. The first twenty seconds of our conversation, once I told her what I needed, were her laughing at me.

"Isaac, the first time you got involved with us, a madman bombed the shit out of our Detroit nest," she said when she recovered. "Then you got a very expensive ghost-talker killed. If I so much as mention your name, I'm likely to get myself fed to the ferals. Unless you're interested in converting—"

"No thank you," I said quickly.

"Then I'm sorry, hon. You're on your own. Good luck, and try not to get yourself killed."

I sighed and leaned my head against the window. There were books with the power to show limited glimpses of the past, but nothing that would let me contact a man who died a thousand years ago. Even if they could, the Porters were forbidden from working with me.

The students of Bi Sheng could probably help. Assuming I could find them. Given that they seemed to be successfully hiding from Gutenberg and his automatons, the odds of me tracking them down were slim.

A quick stop at the archdiocese resulted in several photocopied references to Pope Sylvester II, but nothing about Meridiana. Fortunately, Nidhi wasn't the only one with friends who owed her favors.

Evening found us driving through Tamarack, home of the majority of Upper Michigan's werewolf population.

Those who weren't living in the wild, at least. Tamarack was a broken-down, half-empty ex-mining town, and made Copper River look like the big city. Minutes later we were pulling up at the home of Jeff and Helen DeYoung.

Jeff was an old, arthritic werewolf with a take-no-shit attitude and a penchant for flamboyant dress. More importantly, after the events of a month before, he considered me a member of his pack.

Jeff and Helen were sitting together on an antique wooden porch swing when we arrived. Jeff took a swallow from a half-empty beer bottle as he watched us climb out of the truck. Both he and Helen visibly relaxed when they saw who we were.

Jeff removed his right hand from the revolver holstered to his hip. Helen slipped a knife back into a sheath beneath her sweater. With magic's veil of secrecy beginning to unravel, every sentient nonhuman was on edge. At least a quarter of Tamarack's werewolves had retreated to the woods over the past month.

Jeff greeted me with a back-cracking hug and a quick sniff of my neck. "You smell like seaweed."

"Long story." I turned to hug Helen, who finished the spinal rearrangement her husband had begun on me. "We need a favor."

"Beer first." Jeff finished hugging Lena, then scooped up Nidhi. "Favors after, eh?"

He disappeared into the century-old house, returning with three beers and a plate of what appeared to be bacon-chip cookies. Given the choice, I grabbed one of the bottles and leaned against the railing as Jeff and Helen filled us in on the latest werewolf gossip, most of which centered around who was sneaking into bed—or into the woods, or the backseat, or in one case the middle of the gas station parking lot—with whom. Werewolves treated sex like a professional sporting event, occasionally with spectators and cheerleaders.

I waited politely for as long as I could, which turned out to be approximately half a bottle. "Jeff, I need you to hook me up with some black-market magic."

The wrinkles in his forehead furrowed like plowed farmland. Helen turned dagger eyes toward her husband.

"Don't start," he said to Helen. "You know I haven't run in those circles for decades. Isaac, this is a bad idea. Even for you."

"What's that supposed to mean?" I shook my head. "Never mind. I have to talk to a ghost. A man who died a thousand years ago."

Helen set her beer on the porch. "Why?"

I was ready for this. "To find whoever took Jeneta. She was my student. My responsibility. My pack."

Jeff rolled his eyes. "You throw that damn pack thing at me every time you want something."

"Only because it works."

He flipped me off, but he was chuckling, too. "Do you have any idea what you're getting into? If these people suspect for one second that you're still with the Porters, they'll kill you. Not to mention what the Porters will do if they catch you going after underground magic."

"I did my time as a field agent," I reminded him. "I know what's out there."

"Didn't the Porters have to pull you out of the field?" Helen asked. "The Mackinac Island incident, wasn't it?"

"That's beside the point. Jeff, what did it cost you to get your moonstone?" I was referring to the magical crystal he used to control his transformations into wolf form. It had come from one of Kristen Britain's *Green Rider* novels, meaning he must have gotten it from a libriomancer.

"They asked me for a favor." He stared at the porch. "I don't want to talk about it."

"That should tell you everything you need to know," said Helen. "I've been married to this mutt for forty years, and I can count on one hand the number of times he *didn't* want to talk."

"Look, I hate to ask, but isn't this something the Porters should be doing instead of you?" Jeff continued to avoid eye contact.

I took a drink before answering, using the beer to force back the hollow ache his words triggered. The despair was stronger than before, no doubt a side effect of Euphemia's song. "Yah, it is. But they've had a month to search, and they haven't found her. They haven't stopped the Ghost Army. The woman we're hunting is named Meridiana. I can track her down, but I need more information."

"What happens when you find her?" asked Helen. "You make a citizen's arrest? Blow your bad guy whistle?"

"How far are you willing to go, Isaac Vainio?" Jeff leaned close. "What rules will you break to get what you want? What price will you pay?"

"I know the price of not stopping her. You saw what the Ghost Army did to Copper River. Not to mention that they've done their best to strip away my sanity on two separate occasions."

"Did a pretty good job from the look of it," Jeff muttered.

I let that pass. "Jeneta called them devourers. Lena and I fought one in Detroit, a construct of death and char and hunger. The two of us together could barely

stop the damned thing. We had to drop an entire building on its head, and even that only stunned it. If the rest
break through, they'll destroy everything they touch.
And Meridiana can control them."

I had seen it in Lena's grove. The ghosts were her
tools, and she had used them to seize the students of Bi
Sheng, to consume their minds and turn them against us.

"Idiot," Jeff muttered.

"No more than you were at his age," Helen said.

"Which is why he should listen to me." Jeff walked to
the corner of the porch and stared out at the empty
street. "My libriomancer contact died eight years ago.
There's a black market troll living in Niagara who deals
in architectural magic. I might be able to bargain a name
out of her. But if you mess up, these people will eat you
alive. Some of them literally. Do you understand what
I'm saying?"

I nodded.

"Go home. I'll make some calls."

"Thanks, Jeff."

He snorted. "Thank me by coming back with your
body and soul in one piece."

Once upon a time...

Cinderella, whose real name is Danielle
Whiteshore, did marry Prince Armand.
And their wedding was a dream come true.

But not long after the "happily ever after,"
Danielle is attacked by her stepsister Charlotte,
who suddenly has all sorts of magic to call upon.
And though Talia the martial arts master—
otherwise known as Sleeping Beauty—
comes to the rescue, Charlotte gets away.

That's when Danielle discovers a number of disturbing facts: Armand has been kidnapped; Danielle is
pregnant; and the Queen has her own Secret Service
that consists of Talia and Snow (White, of course).
Snow is an expert at mirror magic and heavy-duty
flirting. Can the princesses track down Armand and
rescue him from the clutches of some of
Fantasyland's most nefarious villains?

The Stepsister Scheme
by Jim C. Hines
978-0-7564-0532-8

"Do we look like we need to be rescued?"

DAW 130